ADVANCE PRAISE FOR *VOLK: A NOVEL OF RADIANT ABOMINATION*

"David Nickle's compelling *Volk* extends and expands upon his *Eutopia: A Novel of Terrible Optimism*. In elegant, engaging prose, Nickle explores the darker highways and byways of the middle decades of the last century, when science joined hands with frightening ideology. It's the latest contribution to what is emerging as one of the truly substantial bodies of weird fiction in the early twenty-first century, and further cements David Nickle's reputation as one of the leaders of his generation of writers."

—John Langan, author of *The Fisherman*

"David Nickle's sequel to his eugenicist novel *Eutopia* switches the action to 1930s Europe, but jumping to a different continent doesn't mean the gruesome horror is about to diminish. *Volk* is a worthy book with plenty of secrets to unravel."

—Silvia Moreno-Garcia, World Fantasy Award-winning editor

"David Nickle's distinctive mastery of voluptuous horror makes for a sequel every bit as enthralling and disturbing as *Eutopia*."

—Molly Tanzer, author of *Vermillion*

PRAISE FOR *EUTOPIA: A NOVEL OF TERRIBLE OPTIMISM*

"Nickle (*Monstrous Affections*) blends *Little House on the Prairie* with distillates of *Rosemary's Baby* and *The X-Files* to create a chilling survival-of-the-fittest story. . . . [His] bleak debut novel mixes utopian vision, rustic Americana, and pure creepiness."

—*Publishers Weekly*

"*Eutopia* is the kind of book I'd recommend to literary snobs who badmouth the horror genre while completely ignoring the multitudes of splendid books on the shelves. Nickle comes from a different cut of cloth than a lot of current horror authors. He's created a unique world that's a far cry from any of the current trends in horror fiction. In fact, his style seems generations removed from all the apocalyptic zombie and vampire novels on the market. Thankfully, he understands that the most important ingredients are strong characters, originality, and a compelling story. That his novel is also dark, frightening, and beautifully written is just icing on the cake."

—*All Things Horror*

"Toronto author David Nickle's debut novel, the follow-up to his brilliantly wicked collection of horror stories *Monstrous Affections*, establishes him as a worthy heir to the mantle of Stephen King. And I don't mean the King of *Under the Dome* or other recent flops, but the master of psychological suspense who ruled the '80s with classics like *Pet Sematary*."

—*The National Post*

"Nickle's debut novel *Eutopia*—an entrancing amalgam of historical thriller, dark fantasy and weird fiction—is an utterly creepy, bladder-loosening, storytelling tour de force."

—*Barnesandnoble.com*

"Try to imagine a collaboration by Mark Twain and H.P. Lovecraft, with Joe R. Lansdale providing the editorial polish. Or if that's too difficult to imagine, read the book and see for yourself."

—*The New York Review of Science Fiction*

"A dark, complicated and frequently harrowing read . . . *Eutopia* is a compelling exploration of the horror of good intentions."

—*Locus Magazine*

"[*Eutopia*] is immensely readable: a quick-paced mountain stream of a novel, cool and sharp and intense, and terrifically adept at drawing a reader in. . . . *Eutopia* accomplishes what the best horror fiction strives for: gives us characters we can care about and hope for, and then inflicts on them the kind of realistic, inescapable, logical sufferings that make us close our eyes a little at the unfairness of not the author, but the world—and all the while with something more to say for itself than the world is a very bad place."

—*Ideomancer*

"*Eutopia* is a fantastic read, a frighteningly good first novel, and a solid and worthy contender for the Prix Aurora."

—*AESCIFI.CA*

"If smart, innovative horror is nice, it still has to strike at the base of the skull. . . . Nickle knows that horror needs to strike at nerve endings and not get too cerebral; *Eutopia* does that by getting out of its own way."

—*Philadelphia City Paper*

"*Eutopia* is as frightening in its social message as it is with its religious themes, and features irresistible prose. . . . A top-notch novel all around."

—*The Horror Fiction Review*

PRAISE FOR *THE 'GEISTERS*

"Anyone who enjoys ghostly yarns or supernatural dark fiction should add this perverse, spine-tingling tome to their collection—stat!"

—*Rue Morgue*

"The language of *The 'Geisters* does an exquisite job of capturing the struggle for language in the face of horror and violence, the way that the brain can fail to interpret what the eyes are seeing. . . . It is this groping towards making sense of what the characters are seeing and experiencing that makes *The*

'Geisters succeed in its most wrenching and visceral moments, as horror or fractures in logical reality gradually take shape in the mind of the reader and the characters together. These dawning moments of horror, or spookiness, or dread, or simultaneous arousal and disgust, are what make *The 'Geisters* at once so desirable and so deeply uncomfortable. This is a book that buzzes in your ears, climbs your crawling skin with multiple barbed feet, feeling with exquisitely sensitive antennae for the next new and terrible revelation."

—*The National Post*

"Few writers do psychosexual horror as well as Toronto's David Nickle, and with *The 'Geisters* he's back with another tale of voluptuous terror and the supernatural."

—*Toronto Star*

"The book doesn't just explore the attractiveness of terror—it embodies it in a narrative that demands (excites even as it repels) your attention. It's a(nother) strong novel by one of the best, most interesting horror writers working today."

—*Bookgasm.com*

PRAISE FOR *RASPUTIN'S BASTARDS*

"This novel is supernatural eeriness at its best, with intriguing characters, no clear heroes, and a dark passion at its heart. Horror aficionados and fans of Stephen King's larger novels should appreciate this macabre look at the aftermath of the Cold War."

—*Library Journal*

"*Rasputin's Bastards* is a testament to the fact Nickle can write anything."

—*The Winnipeg Review*

"A plot so dissected is not easy to get right, but Nickle juggles it incredibly well. And it's just the right kind of style for this book."

—*Newstalk 1010*

"*Rasputin's Bastards* is a book with such a vast canvas and sweep, handled with such command and care by Nickle, that it is a must-read for anyone who wants to know what amazing things can be done with dark historical fantasy."

—Tony Burgess, author of *People Live Still in Cashtown Corners*

"To read David Nickle is to be reminded what the best storytellers can do, and to glory in unbridled imagination released on the page. David's achievements in *Rasputin's Bastards* are innumerable. He reminds me of no one so much than maestro Dan Simmons, another writer unconstrained by the limits of genre. When it comes to narrative, David dances where others plod, and dares where others play it safe. This is all to say, David Nickle takes no prisoners, and leaves a magnificent bruise as a reminder of the encounter."

—Corey Redekop, author of *Husk*

PRAISE FOR *MONSTROUS AFFECTIONS*

"[L]ike the cover, the stories inside are not what they seem. But also, like the cover, the stories inside are brilliant. . . . You'd think that you were reading a book full of what you had always expected a horror story to be, but Nickle takes a left turn and blindsides you with tales that are not of the norm, but are all the more horrific because of surprise twists, darkness and raw emotion."

—*January Magazine's Best Books of 2009*

"Bleak, stark and creepy, Stoker-winner Nickle's first collection will delight the literary horror reader . . . 13 terrifying tales of rural settings, complex and reticent characters and unexpected twists that question the fundamentals of reality. All are delivered with a certain grace, creating a sparse yet poetic tour of the horrors that exist just out of sight. . . . This ambitious collection firmly establishes Nickle as a writer to watch."

—*Publishers Weekly* (starred review)

"David Nickle writes 'em damned weird and damned good and damned dark. He is bourbon-rough, poetic and vivid. Don't miss this one."

—Cory Doctorow, author of *Little Brother*

"Rich characters and a love of unique twists top of a captivating and sometimes gruesome collection of nightmares."

—Corey Redekop, author of *Husk*

DAVID NICKLE

VOLK

A NOVEL OF RADIANT ABOMINATION

CZP
ChiZine Publications

FIRST EDITION

Distributed in Canada by
Fitzhenry & Whiteside Limited
195 Allstate Parkway
Markham, Ontario L3R 4T8
Phone: (905)-477-9700
e-mail: bookinfo@fitzhenry.ca

Distributed in the U.S. by
Consortium Book Sales & Distribution
34 Thirteenth Avenue, NE, Suite 101
Minneapolis, MN 55413
Phone: (612) 746-2600
e-mail: sales.orders@cbsd.com

Library and Archives Canada Cataloguing in Publication

Nickle, David, 1964-, author
Volk : a novel of radiant abomination / David Nickle.

Issued in print and electronic formats.
ISBN 978-1-77148-417-6 (softcover).--ISBN 978-1-77148-418-3 (PDF)

I. Title.

PS8577.I33V65 2017 C813'.54 C2016-907564-8
C2016-907565-6

CHIZINE PUBLICATIONS
Peterborough, Canada
www.chizinepub.com
info@chizinepub.com

Edited by Sandra Kasturi
Copyedited by Gemma Files
Proofread by Leigh Teetzel

Canada Council for the Arts Conseil des arts du Canada

We acknowledge the support of the Canada Council for the Arts which last year invested $20.1 million in writing and publishing throughout Canada.

Published with the generous assistance of the Ontario Arts Council.

Printed in Canada

Dedicated to the memories of

Sara Simmons

Helen Rykens

and Liza Ordubegian

ALSO BY DAVID NICKLE

Knife Fight and Other Struggles

The 'Geisters

Rasputin's Bastards

Eutopia: A Novel of Terrible Optimism

Monstrous Affections

The Claus Effect (with Karl Schroeder)

"Parasitism is one of the gravest crimes in nature. It is a breach of the law of Evolution. Thou shalt evolve, thou shalt develop all thy faculties in full, thou shalt attain to the highest conceivable perfection of thy race—and so perfect thy race—this is the first and greatest commandment of Nature. But the parasite has no thought for its race, or for its perfection in any shape of form. It wants two things—food and shelter. How it gets them is of no moment."

–Henry Drummond, *Natural Law in the Spiritual World*, 1883

DAVID NICKLE

VOLK

A NOVEL OF RADIANT ABOMINATION

TABLE OF CONTENTS

1927

Orlok

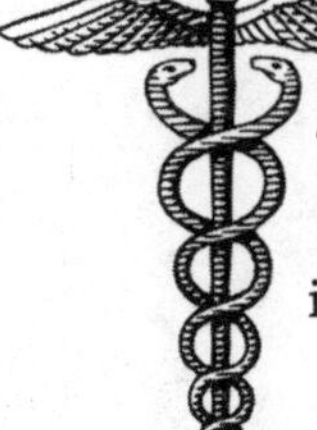

"Was he beautiful?"

As though he had just registered his own nakedness at that instant, Gottlieb blinked and covered himself.

"Beautiful? No. He was compelling. Huge. Very muscular."

"And you were sexually attracted to him."

"Of course I was."

The doctor allowed a dozen beats of the metronome before he spoke the obvious: "He was not like you."

"No."

Gottlieb was grasping at his penis. The doctor made no attempt to disguise his observation of that fact and noted with satisfaction that Gottlieb didn't seem to care. He was as guileless as a babe just then. Could a metronome tick triumphantly? The doctor let it, twice more.

"Describe to me the ways he was like you."

Gottlieb drew a deep breath and turned to the windows. They were open a crack to clear the air from the morning's session, and the sweet smell of apple blossoms wafted in. The doctor was used to the smell—this was a room in which he spent a great deal of time—but he noted it, along with the flaring of Gottlieb's delicate nostrils.

"How was he like you?" asked the doctor again.

"I don't really know," said Gottlieb. "I didn't know him for very long."

"Anything."

"All right. He was German like me. And he was my age."

"How old were you then?"

The slightest frown. "Twenty-two."

The doctor looked again to the window. A conversation was drifting in along with the apple blossom scent. Two of the girls—Heidi and Anna? Yes. He recognized Anna's lisp, and she and Heidi were inseparable. Ergo . . .

They weren't too distracting—they would barely register on the recording. If they lingered, or became silly, he would have to stand and shut the window, and risk disturbing Gottlieb. But the pair were on their way somewhere, and within four ticks of the metronome were gone. The doctor settled back.

"His hair was brown," said Gottlieb. "Like mine too."

Three ticks.

"And he was homosexual," said Gottlieb.

Four more ticks now.

"But not like me."

"Tell me how he is not like you."

"As to his homosexuality?"

"If you like. Yes."

"He is a masculine force. He looks at me and causes me to feel as if . . . as if I am not. Not masculine."

The doctor smiled. The last time Gottlieb had spoken of this moment, he'd immediately denied his homosexuality. They were progressing very well, at least as measured against their stated objective of delving into Gottlieb's neurosis. The doctor started to reach for a pencil where his breast pocket would have been, but stopped himself and settled his hands back in his lap. He spoke quietly, calmly, in rhythm. Like a lullaby. "He is looking at you now," he said.

Tick. Tick.

Gottlieb flushed and, as his hand came away from his penis, the doctor was pleased to see it was flushed too.

"In the beer hall, yes?" said the doctor.

Gottlieb stretched his slender legs on the chaise longue, and his eyelids fluttered shut. A breeze from the window lifted the drapes, raising gooseflesh as it passed. The air in the beer hall would not have been so fresh as this alpine breath.

"In the *Bürgerbräukeller*," said Gottlieb.

"What does it smell like?"

"Many things. Food . . . there is a basket of schnitzel nearby. There is some smoke. I mean from tobacco. And the whole place stinks of old beer. Men have been drinking all day."

The doctor waited until it seemed as though Gottlieb might drift off to sleep, before prodding: "Where is he?"

Gottlieb smiled. "Leaned against a pillar. By himself, across the hall from me. He is a very ugly man—his eyebrows meet in the middle of his forehead, so it seems he is scowling into his beer mug."

The doctor shifted in his chair. The towel he'd placed on the leather cushioning had moved, and in the warmth of the day the bare skin of his buttocks was sticking there. He fought to contain his discomfort, his growing impatience. The metronome ticked seven times more before Gottlieb was ready to continue.

"My friends are sitting with me at one of the round tables in the middle of the great room. There is Gunther and Alex and Haydn. Gunther is getting fat, somehow. His hair is still blond, but is starting to go up front, and in a patch at his crown. Alex is a little fellow—smaller than me. His moustache is long, and covered in foam from his mug. Black hair. Haydn? Always licking his lips. No foam there. Otherwise handsome enough. He works in a warehouse by the Isar. Keeps him strong and from getting fat.

"Are they properly my friends? Gunther maybe; we fought alongside in the War and he liked me well enough to have me at his wedding when it was done. Alex and Haydn were Gunther's boyhood friends from Augsburg. They were good fellows and tolerated me, but they preferred to reminisce with Gunther about this or that from when they were all bachelors. I didn't mind.

"We are drinking a round of lagers and Gunther is telling his story about the end of the War—after Armistice, but just by a few days. It is a little true, but for the most part a lie; he talks about how we met a company of British soldiers in No Man's Land. We shared our rations with them because they were so pitiable . . . nearly starving . . . literally begging for our aid.

"Gunther tells it boastfully, so as to illustrate his honourable nature. I remember the night differently—that we were all cold and hungry, and we all ate our own rations. It was still a good night—we refrained from slaughtering one another, kept our insults to ourselves. But no one begged. There was no . . . undue generosity. Not a whiff of charity, from Gunther or any of us.

"But I don't correct his lie. We are all becoming a little drunk, and this lie is preferable to political talk. Or a brawl.

"And yes. I am distracted.

"What is he wearing? It is . . . a grey shirt, yes, open-necked over a white undershirt. He has a cap, but he is not wearing it. It is stuffed into the belt of his trousers. I don't know what kind of trousers. Brown? Brown. A dark brown. I cannot see his boots, but later, I remember—

"All right. In the moment I cannot see his boots. There is a table of men in front of him, I think they are veterans too—two of them have helmets from the War, on the table before them. They are emptying their mugs quickly, having a very serious talk. I cannot hear what they are saying. But he is smiling at it, looking from one to the other as they argue among themselves.

"I imagine they are talking politics. Probably about the Weimar and the Jews, because of course later—

"Quite right, doctor. In the moment. In the moment.

"He looks up, and sees me looking. But he doesn't seem surprised. I think he has known that I am looking at him for a long time. Maybe since I started. Maybe he saw me even before.

"He grants me a little wink, then takes a deep drink from his mug. And he is gone.

"Disappeared into thin air? No. There is a commotion around him—nothing serious. A gang of men arrive—more veterans, I think. They crowd into the discussion, grabbing the shoulders of the men in the midst of talk. One of them has a platter of sausages and sets it down on the table, and by the time they've moved out of the way, he is lost in the crowd.

"Now Gunther claps me on the shoulder.

"'Hey, Markus,' he says, 'you look pale. Don't tell me you're done drinking.'

"On the other side of me, Alex empties his cup and grins at me. His moustache is dripping beer.

"I finish my drink. There is not much left anyway. 'Another round?' asks Gunther. It is his turn to buy. 'Fine,' I say, 'but I need to return some of this, first.'

"'Don't take too long,' Gunther says. 'Little Alex is thirsty. He'll drink his and your beer too if you dawdle.'

"I laugh at that and so does Haydn. Alex smiles, but I don't think he likes being called little. Or maybe he sees through my ruse. Because yes, maybe it is a ruse. I don't have to piss, or I don't have to piss very much. I get up and go, all the same.

"I cross the room. It feels as though the men here are looking at me as I go, but that is rot. Why would they? I become a little fearful, I admit, as I move through here, slip beneath the shadow of the balcony, past the pillars, thinking that I . . .

"I . . .

"I am outside now. In the beer garden. What is the weather? What kind of question is that? It is November. Just before six. It will get colder, much colder, but right now the air is pleasant enough—I can feel the gooseflesh on my arms, which are bare, but that is fine, because the cool air is just what I need. I have had too much to drink, maybe, after all. And part of it—a state of arousal, yes, that is part of it.

"The wind gusts. It is coming from the southwest. A winter wind. From the mountains. The few that are outside getting air like me look for shelter from it, back in the hall. Not me. Not him either.

"He is sitting on one of the tables, feet propped on the bench, spread apart, forearms resting on his knees. His forefingers and thumbs are rubbing together, as though to make warmth. His cap is on his head.

"Oh—I can see his boots now. They are old army boots. Laced up high. He has tucked his trousers into them. He is looking right at me. I look away, but only for a moment, because I cannot look away for long.

"'You are a Jew?' he asks me.

"I tell him I am not.

He points back at the hall. 'Your friends. Jews?'

"'None of us are Jews.'

"'Are you certain?' he asks. 'Have you sucked all their uncircumcised cocks?'

"How does that make me feel?

"Fearful.

"Angry.

"And helpless.

"And no, I do not care for any of those feelings. What sort would enjoy that? What a question. But I also know it for what it is: a crude flirtation, such as men make with one another. I despise this part, the beginning. But there is no other way.

"I tell him a joke: that they are all too busy sucking one another's cocks, and I must wait my turn. I laugh at it, my own joke, but he remains serious.

"'Come here.' That is what he says, then turns one great hand up and beckons me over. He might mean it as a command. I take it as permission.

"I am sitting on the bench where he is resting his feet, leaning back against the table where he is perched. He is saying something, but there's some kind of commotion from the street. . . . It sounds like a flock of great birds taking off. But that can't be right. . . . I cannot hear what he says because of it, whatever the sound is. His hand comes down on my shoulder and squeezes. He is looking down at me. I tell him my name, because maybe he was asking that. I think he was asking that.

"'Good enough,' he says. 'What town?' I tell him. 'Then what are you doing here in Munich?' And I tell him about the book that I am writing. He wonders why I could not write that book at home, and I tell him some of my story. He doesn't say anything to that, but his hand doesn't leave my shoulder. Aah, his grip is so tight.

"'I sometimes write,' he tells me, finally. 'Is your book true?' I tell him it is not true. It is a novel. 'Writing books that are not true is easy,' he says to me. 'True books are more difficult.'

"'That is not my experience,' I tell him. Fabrication is more difficult than just saying what's so.

"A group of men are walking past us, toward the beer hall. There are . . . maybe a dozen of them? Maybe less. They are dressed well. He loosens his grip on my shoulder, sits up as he looks over at them, but they don't seem to pay us any heed. 'Who are they?' I ask.

"'Who knows?' he says. 'I don't like them, though.' He slides off the table then, and slaps my back.

"'Inside,' he says. 'Not good to be outdoors right now.'

"We are walking back to the beer hall. He is opening another door than the one from which we came, an exterior door that goes directly to the cellars. We are at the top of a wooden staircase. There is one bare bulb lighting the way down, set in the wall. We are climbing down the stairs. I am first. He is . . .

"He is . . ."

Nearly sixty ticks of the metronome, and the doctor dared clear his throat. Gottlieb seemed to be dozing. But based on his experience, the doctor suspected something other: a phenomenon he had observed not infrequently, in the course of his work. In certain instances, the patient inhabited the memory so deeply that there would be no words for it. The patient might later recollect these deep fugues, might write those memories in a journal, might share that journal with a trusted psychotherapist. And that might be as near a psychotherapist would ever get to the nub of that deep, crucial memory.

The only thing to do until the fugue resolved, in the doctor's experience, was to wait.

The doctor reached and lifted the needle from the Dictaphone. He set about replacing the cylinder, which was more than three-fourths finished. Then, as quietly as he could manage, he shut and fastened the windows. Before he did, he drew in a last breath of the valley and regarded the circle of smooth-skinned girls and boys, sunbathing by the riverbank. The doctor savoured the breath, imagining he was capturing a last whiff of their virility . . . their fecundity.

From the chaise longue, Gottlieb gasped. The doctor didn't need to look to confirm: He had ejaculated.

"Herr Gottlieb," whispered the doctor, after he had set the needle back on the fresh cylinder.

Gottlieb's naked torso twisted, pale droplets of semen distending into ghostly rivulets down his belly, and his eyelids fluttered over a gaze still focused elsewhere.

"Tell me his name," said the doctor.

Gottlieb's lips parted so his tongue could wet them, because they were very dry.

"I cannot say now. I do not know it. He has not said it.

"We are deep in the cellar. I am lying close along his flank. My head is resting in the crook of his shoulder, my nose pressed into the damp fabric of his undershirt. I can smell him, even as his taste is still fresh on my tongue. . . .

"We are resting in the crook of two stacks of barrels. He has taken me to the darkest corner, past high stone arches and thick pillars. There is some light—from the far end of the cellar—and there is some sound . . . men talking, perhaps, at that end of the cellar . . . the noise of the beer hall above us? No. It is the scurrying feet of rats. That is what he says.

"'The true fathers of Munich,' he says. 'When those men are gone'—his hand leaves my shoulder to gesture upward, to the beer hall above us—'the rats will hold a feast.'

"'Do you not think they are holding one now?' I ask him, and finally he laughs at a jest I make.

"'It is true. I have never seen a starved rat. They have that advantage over us men: they will eat *anything*.'

"He pushes me away from him, just enough that he can straighten against the wall. He kicks away our trousers, where they are balled at our feet. Then he asks me: 'Do you know your blood type?'

"I do not know it, and he scolds me. 'If you find yourself in a hospital, needing a transfusion, you had better know. There is A, there is B, there is AB, and there is O. Mix it up, get the wrong blood in you . . . that's it!'

"'Why do you say this now?' I ask. I am thinking all of a sudden about *Nosferatu*—the moving picture. I had watched it not even a year earlier. The blood-drinking cadaver, who arrives in town on a ship of rats.

"Rats . . . blood type . . .

"'You can tell about a fellow from his blood type,' he says. 'Type O . . . I think you are Type O.'

"'I don't know what type I am,' I say. 'What type are you?'

"'I am Type AB.' he says. 'I can take any transfusion . . . most of the time.'

"'Most of the time? Have you done this often—taken blood?'

"'No. Hardly at all.'

"'What does your blood type say about you?'

"'It says . . .' he starts to answer, but seems to consider. He pulls me closer again, and takes my wrist, and pulls it over to his penis. It is hard again already. I tug at the foreskin with my thumb, and begin to caress it.

"'I can travel anywhere,' he says, 'speak with anyone, although I am never truly *of* anyone. I can see the truth of matters, when others are blind to it. As I saw the truth of you.'

"I ask him what that means.

"'You think that there is greatness in you—you have thought this since you were very small. But it is hard to discover, yes? You followed the Kaiser into war and thought there might be greatness there. But there was nothing but mud, and blood, and death. You write lies in a book that you hope others will read one day. Perhaps they will venerate you. Perhaps, through words bound together in a cloth cover, your greatness will be assured. But you know that words in a book won't carry you any further than deeds in the War did. Not so long as the only words you write are lies.'

"'I have a confession,' I say, and I kiss his throat, insinuating myself closer. 'I am not writing a novel.'

"'Ah,' he says. 'The truth of you. As I sensed. Thank you for that.'

"And now he takes my face in his hand and draws me nearer, and kisses me on the mouth. . . .

"And . . .

"Oh.

"Light!

"Light has filled the room—another bulb in the ceiling, switched on. There are three men. They wear brown shirts and ties. One has a stick, like a walking stick.

"One says: 'What is this here?'

"Another: 'My God—look there. A pair of deviants!'

"The third says nothing, but reaches down and grabs my shoulder, pulls me half to my feet. He has short hair, almost no hair . . . he is not much taller than I—but bigger around the middle. He has a wide moustache.

"'Look at this,' he says, and pushes me to the ground. 'Bare-bottomed, hey? You a man or a woman?'

"I try to get to my feet. The walking stick hits me. I fall.

"'We need to get them out of here,' says one. 'Tonight of all nights.'

"'Teach them a lesson.' The one with the stick. He strikes me again. In the chest this time. I feel a boot in my stomach. Another in my ribs. Someone laughs. I'm rolled over onto my stomach. The stick slaps my backside. I cry out—but not loud enough for anyone to hear.

"This has happened before, yes. In Stuttgart. Before the War. Then, it was a whipping. I am recalling it. How I was made to scream. Manfred and I! Manfred!

"I will not scream at this. No. No screams. Tears—nothing to do for that. But no screaming. Not from me.

"But there are screams.

"Two gunshots, first. Like little barks from a dog, a room away. Maybe from upstairs. In the beer hall. Men screaming upstairs—the scraping of chairs on the floor above us . . . something is happening upstairs.

"Then . . . a moment of quiet. But barely that before . . .

"There are screams *everywhere*."

Gottlieb's eyes were wide and he sat upright. Was he still entranced? Or had the recollection of the events in the cellar—the admixture of the beating in Stuttgart—pushed him back to consciousness, perhaps into a mania?

"Herr Gottlieb," the doctor said. "Markus. It is necessary that you breathe."

Gottlieb drew a deep gulp of air, taken as though he were preparing to dive beneath the river.

"Let the breath out slowly," said the doctor. "Slowly. And with it, let the memories of Stuttgart go too."

The doctor knew about Stuttgart already. They had discussed this shortly after Gottlieb arrived here at the estates. *Surrender your garments first, then your story*. And oh, Gottlieb may have been shy about those garments, but he told his story easily—how his father and uncle had found him and his cousin Manfred in an act of sodomy. Manfred denounced Gottlieb, and Gottlieb believed that because of that, the flogging had gone harder for him than Manfred. In fact, claimed Gottlieb, it had been Manfred who had instigated the encounter. Gottlieb was not blameless—yet nor was he guilty.

The doctor frankly did not care, one way or another.

"Leave Stuttgart," he commanded. "Return to the cellar. That is where we are."

Gottlieb drew another breath, lowered himself back to the couch, and although his eyes did not close, they refocused on the ceiling.

"The screaming," he said as the metronome ticked, "is everywhere."

"He has pulled one of the men to the ground, tripping him between his legs first, then grabbing his belt, then hauling him closer and grasping his head, by both ears. He holds it like an accordion, squeezing in. The man shouts. He twists. The man's legs twitch madly. It happens very quickly—so quickly the other two barely see what is happening before their friend is dead. This is a difficult thing to do, it is nearly impossible . . . to kill a man by twisting his neck. But he is very strong, stronger than anyone.

"The one with the stick swings at him now. But he catches the stick in one hand and twists it out of the man's grip. Then he stands, spins it in a blur, high enough to strike and shatter the light bulb hanging over us. It is darker again.

"And . . . *crack*! The stick strikes bone. A second man falls, nearly in my lap. Yes. I am turned over now, coughing, watching the third man—the one who took hold of me, I think—running between the pillars, shouting 'Help!' He runs after that one, very fast. They don't get far. He leaps on him, straddling him from behind as he draws the stick around the front of his throat, and kills him.

"I get to my feet. I find my trousers. The one who hit me with the stick might still live. I do not look to see. I do not care.

"I am not blameless. But I am not guilty either. He, after all, was the one who struck me.

"My . . . my lover, that is what he is, isn't he? He returns and bids me help him drag the third man back to the shadows.

"'The *Frauen* rarely come back here,' he says. 'It is filled with spiders and rats. We can leave these men for a time.'

"He gathers his clothing, does up his trousers. 'But we should be tidy,' he tells me, and I ask him what he means, and he shows me.

"He takes the man he just killed and hefts him into the crook of barrels, where we had just been. He takes the second man, and lays him next to him. The third man—the one who hit me—he we stack on top of the other two. As you would stack wood for the winter.

"'We ought to take our leave,' he tells me. 'It has been some time. Do you think your friends are still drinking?'

"'I don't want to drink with them.'

"'Better to do so,' he tells me. 'Unless they have chosen to leave.'

"We do not get to the beer hall—not right away," said Gottlieb.

"No," said the doctor. "That would have been difficult."

"We leave the way we came: back to the beer garden. But now . . . there are more men outside. They are dressed in the same coloured shirts as the men we left below. They are standing in a row near the gate to the street. Seeing them like this makes sense. They are S.A."

"Stormtroopers."

"Stormtroopers. One of them steps forward. He is very tall. He demands to know where we came from.

"We tell him that we were pissing. 'In the cellar?' he asks, and I shrug, drunkenly enough to convince him. But he is not finished with us, this one.

"'There is a revolution taking place,' he says. 'Inside, we have Herr Kahr. He is even now acceding to our Fuhrer's demands. The government will change. Things will improve for some. Others will get what is coming to them. You had better be ready for that. Now: Who are you for?'

"'Germany,' I say.

"'Clever answer. That can mean anything.' He stands close enough to smell us. 'All right, clever fellows. Tell us your names.'

The doctor leaned forward. He wanted to prompt Gottlieb: What does his mysterious lover say? But he knew better—drawing a sliver hastily simply embedded it more deeply.

A smile twitches across Gottlieb's face—oddly shaped, almost tentative, yet one of the few he'd spared the doctor since arriving.

"I tell him: 'I am Hutter. This is my friend Orlok. We are just here for a drink.'"

The doctor finished Gottlieb's session without the metronome—but the Dictaphone continued to spin. Gottlieb had laughed so hard at his own joke that the trance was broken for the day.

They spoke about the session, and the doctor allowed Gottlieb to talk about the things he believed he had learned from it, thereby generating his own theories. This filled the remainder of the cylinder. Gottlieb spoke at some length about the nature of his homosexual proclivities, and although it irritated the doctor, he held his annoyance in check. So far as Gottlieb was concerned, his homosexuality was a symptom of a disease of the mind, for which he sought cure here. And the doctor had given Gottlieb no indication that matters stood any other way.

So Gottlieb theorized that his homosexual attractions were a manifestation of the violence in his life, and finally concluded: "Had my father and uncle not beaten me so, I might have forgotten the sweet curve of Manfred's arse. And then . . . well there was the War . . . and that night at Munich, where we killed the six stormtroopers! It has cemented my erotic fixation, yes?"

"You said three," said the doctor. "Three stormtroopers."

"Three? Oh yes, of course."

"Were there others that night?"

Gottlieb shook his head firmly. "I meant to say three," he said.

"And you know that those three were stormtroopers how precisely?"

Gottlieb shrugged. "They wore the same coloured clothing. And stormtroopers surrounded the beer hall that night, while Herr Hitler riled up the crowd within."

"What did you think of Hitler?"

"Hitler? I'd seen him speak before. That night . . . he was very loud. Almost shrill. Ugly little man. Hard to look away from, though."

"And your friend? What was his name?"

"Oh, he never cared for Hitler. He thought Hitler was a liar. One night, after things had settled down and they'd put Hitler and his Nazis behind bars . . . he told me that he would like to fuck the lies out of Hitler, and would if he got the chance."

"Like he fucked the lies out of you?" asked the doctor.

Gottlieb appeared to study his hand, frowning at the slight webbing between his fingers as he held it to the light of the window.

"He never properly fucked those out of me, doctor. He went off long before that could happen."

"And you do not know where he went?"

"It was a sudden departure."

"Of course."

The doctor cleared his throat, and tried one last time. He put it to Gottlieb, directly.

"You know," he said, "it is interesting that for such an impression that this man left upon you, you cannot summon his name to your lips. Can you tell me his name, please?"

Gottlieb's fingers bent, then closed into a fist, casting a shadow across his face.

"I don't see what that has to do with anything," he said.

Daylight lingered over the grounds of the estate for some hours after Herr Gottlieb left the doctor's rooms. The doctor himself did not linger there long after. It was a beautiful summer's day in the valley where the estate stood, and the doctor thought to himself that he would not waste it, brooding over this troublesome patient.

He splashed water on his chest, beneath his arms, closed up his lavatory and then shut his office, and crossed the hall to the front steps. The outside air was cool, but welcome after the oppressiveness of the office, of his session with poor, broken Gottlieb.

As he walked, he passed Anna, her long blonde hair tied in braids that fell halfway down her naked back. She waved as he passed.

"Where is Heidi?" he asked, and she shrugged.

"I will meet up with her at supper," she lisped. "Will we see you at dinner, Herr Doctor Bergstrom?"

He patted his bare stomach. "I must watch my belly. But I will be there if you are."

She smiled—then glanced below his belly, and looked away from what she saw there. Now the doctor shrugged. Anna was a very healthy girl, despite her speech impediment, and she would soon become accustomed to all that her beauty inspired.

"We will see each other later, then, doctor," she said and hurried off.

As he watched her retreating backside, the doctor wondered whether Gottlieb would ever consider that one the way he contemplated Manfred's boyish rump. That was certainly Gottlieb's hope—that he could undo his nature, as though it were simply a neurosis, and take a wife with something approaching enthusiasm. The doctor remained a skeptic.

He set off through the orchards, which would lead to the riverbank, where the others here might be found, doing their afternoon calisthenics. And having contemplated that happy prospect, he turned his mind away again from Gottlieb, pondering his true patient, if one could call such as he a patient. . . .

The doctor smiled to himself and shook his head, as though to dislodge something that had fixed itself inside there.

He could not call that one a patient. He had never laid eyes upon him. The doctor could only list what he knew of him, on one of those index cards they used in America.

He was a huge man. Brown haired. A single eyebrow. Very ugly. But muscular. And fearless. With fantastical charisma. But a man with no name or identity yet—not one the doctor could decode, until he could break through with Gottlieb, or the amnesiac French girl, or perhaps some others as his associates in Belgium might uncover. For the time being, the doctor had nothing with which to find him . . . next to nothing beyond that description, and what was almost certainly his phylum:

Übermensch.

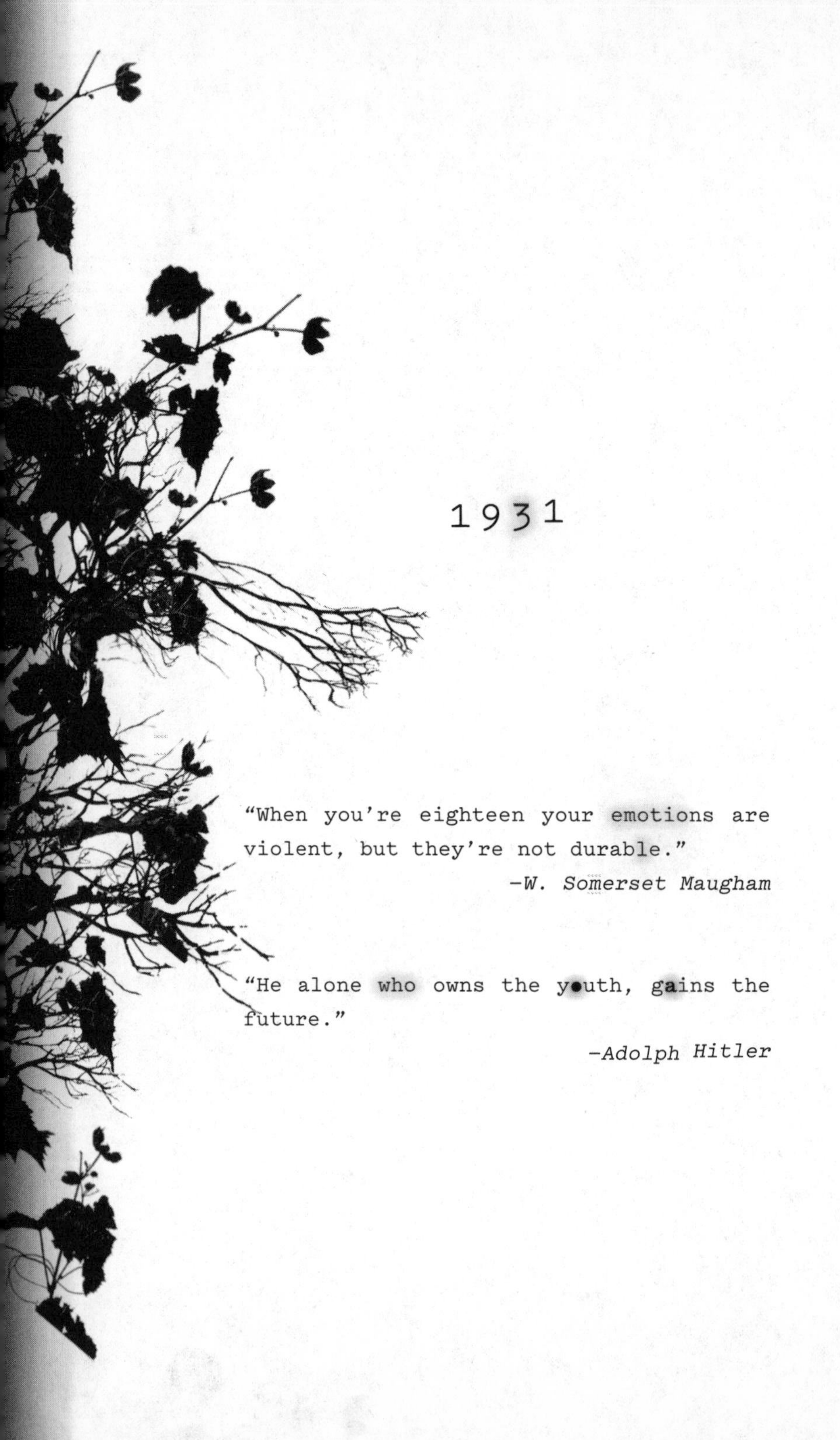

1931

"When you're eighteen your emotions are violent, but they're not durable."

–W. Somerset Maugham

"He alone who owns the youth, gains the future."

–Adolph Hitler

PART I

The Inferno Conundrum

One

A cold spring rain made for Jason's final night in the room at the *Hôtel de Badricourt* on *rue de la Hachette*. It came steady past the supper hour, washing up a wormy, familiar stink from the cracks between the cobblestones outside . . . a very Parisian stink, all dank and mouldering, like a year ago someone'd buried a privy, or maybe someone's aunt, under those stones. It would be good to be away in the morning; Jason didn't think he would miss Paris even a little once he took to the air. As long as the rain stopped, or at least let up a bit, it ought to be safe.

And even if it was a little stormy . . . there would be nothing to fear.

As he smoked in his room, he regarded the droplets forming on the windowpanes, misting in the street lamps outside. Jason thought about the first storm he'd flown in. That was over France too, in the Nieuport. It had nearly killed him and, in another way, it had surely saved his life. The Eindecker on his tail either could not match him as he climbed into the black cloud, or the pilot had lost his nerve as they rose to face sheets of rain that turned to daggers on their flesh.

Either way, Jason and the Nieuport climbed together and alone into the limbo of the storm. It was freezing and black, rainwater smearing his goggles, in a way that seemed without end.

But—it did end, in the brilliance of the sun, atop a mountain range of cloud, all gold, purple, and blue. . . .

Heaven.

He should not be sitting up smoking this late, and he knew it.

He would be flying again in the morning, and that was that. It wouldn't be a Nieuport. It would be a Latécoère 28, and he'd flown planes like it for many more years than he'd flown that tiny Nieuport, which in any case he hadn't flown for more than a decade now. The Latécoère was a big aircraft with a snug cockpit, and room for passengers and cargo in place of machine guns. It would carry him on a long, hopefully easy flight across the Mediterranean, not touching ground again until Algiers. And there he'd commence a new, or at least newer, life: an end to the long drought that had started for him in '29—which was, no fooling, two years gone now.

In the morning, he'd be a flyer again.

Jason finished his cigarette in three deep drags, and dropped the butt in the old teacup he'd been using as an ashtray. The pack in his shirt pocket had two more. He didn't have to check to know that but he did anyhow, and then he pulled one of them out and regarded it, and having done that, put it between his lips, which were dry like his mouth.

There was nothing to be afraid of out there.

Jason found a box of matches in his overcoat, and lit his second-to-last cigarette.

His room was on the first storey of the *Hôtel*, a floor up from the street, its window situated above a canvas awning. So from where he sat, he could not easily see what was going on at the front door. Jason did not know why that should make him uneasy. When he'd returned after an early supper, he'd had to ring a bell to get in, same as he had the past three days here. The place was safer than most.

The smoke burned down Jason's throat. He should sleep, but he couldn't sleep.

Was it really the idea of flying that was getting to him?

He played through the coming day in his mind. At a quarter of four, a truck would be waiting out front. Jason should be there first, his duffel packed and himself presentable. He'd climb in the back or perhaps in the cab, depending on whether the driver had gathered his co-pilot and mechanic first. They would make their way out of the city before the sun rose, and south, to a little airfield at Villeneuve-Orly, aiming to arrive near seven.

Then, they would see to the aeroplane that M. Desrosiers had acquired for his fleet. If the mechanic found no surprises, they would be in the air well before the noon hour. Then off to Algiers, to fly passengers and cargo and mail across the African continent.

This was not what Jason was used to. Whenever he hired on with a carrier, when they were flush enough to hire, he'd expect to billet the night at a cottage near the air field, or even in the plane itself. Once, he'd just used his duffel for a pillow and found a corner in a hangar. Nothing like that for Desrosiers and his flight crew. He'd made that very clear, on their second meeting. Desrosiers was a veteran of the Great War himself—an officer for France—and he got sentimental about it.

"You are going to be gone for more than a year in my employ. And Africa, whatever you may have heard, is not known for its comforts. So it pleases me that you enjoy the City of Lights for a few days. After all, I recall that you went to a great deal of trouble, to keep it from the Hun."

"As did we all."

"As did we all."

A flash of light caught Jason's eye and he turned to look at the wardrobe next to that little writing desk in the far corner of his room, all shadows, feeling a nervous little smile bloom around the cigarette. There was nothing and he knew it, but that didn't stop him from walking over and opening up the wardrobe, jangling the coat hangers, knocking superstitiously on the back panel.

He slammed it shut. Hands jammed into his pockets, cigarette clamped between his lips, Jason stalked back to the window. He leaned against the sill, then looked back to the wardrobe. He'd slammed it too hard, he must have, because the door of the wardrobe was open again, just a crack.

Jason pulled the cigarette from between his lips. It was burned down to half length. He would need more of these before they took off the next day. *If* they took off. Jason let a finger hover over the ember of the cigarette, feeling the heat against the cuticles as another idea formed.

"Don't need to go," he whispered. He could, he knew, just miss the truck, take the money that Desrosiers had advanced him—spend it on a train ticket instead. Hire on a steamer to New Brunswick. Or New York. Wherever. But finally return.

It would mean breaking his word. Worse than that. He would be a thief, effectively stealing Desrosiers' advance payment. And it would mean setting foot on ground Jason hadn't visited once in more than a decade . . . effectively resurrecting himself, in a country of nothing but drought and hardship.

He squinted through the strand of smoke rising from the cigarette. The wardrobe door was open wider now, yes? He thought it might be. And why not? The *Hôtel de Badricourt* was a better establishment than some in this part of Paris, but it was as old as any of them, and it was Jason's experience that floors in even new buildings warped soon enough.

I could just run, he thought, as the wardrobe door seemed to open wider still. . . .

Jason took the cigarette from his mouth, turning it his fingers. With his left hand he found a smooth spot, high on his throat, right under his jawline.

"Hell with you," he said, and jammed the hot end of the cigarette into the soft flesh there. The pain was exquisite—set his eyes watering so bad he thought he could feel his teeth loosening. Bad enough, he knew, to do the trick.

It was all right, he thought as he staggered over to the empty wardrobe, shutting the door again.

He could not just run. And there was nothing to fear, not in staying this course, not in the clear skies he knew awaited, above this storm. That place wasn't Heaven—but it was home.

It was his way, one of the few he might have left—to *go* home.

The rains had turned to fog five hours later, when Jason made his way outside again.

He huddled under the hotel's awning all the same, resting his duffel on the stoop, out of the puddles and the muck. His last cigarette had made it through the night, and he vowed it would make it through the wait too. Jason shivered in the pre-dawn chill, yawned, and thought not for the first time that although the river-stink of a Paris street after a heavy rain was not the very worst thing he'd smelled, it surely was rank.

The truck pulled up late by a quarter hour, announcing itself as it turned the corner with a backfire that echoed through the neighbourhood like artillery. Still, it was better than Jason had feared: it looked to be an old grocery delivery truck, with a wooden cover over the back. The ride would be dry, then, and that was something.

"M. Thorn?" the driver shouted, leaning across the passenger seat. Jason nodded, hefting his duffel onto his shoulder. The driver had a thick, greying beard and wore his cap pulled low over his ears. Just in case Jason were to get any ideas about riding shotgun, he pointed with his thumb to the back of the truck.

"Bien," said Jason and stomped around the worst of the muck, pulled the double doors on the back of the truck open, and pushed his duffel in. He stretched his shoulders, hoisted himself up and in, and shut the door.

"Good morning," said a voice from the dark. "You look like you had a bad night, now."

"It's all right," said Jason, although he knew what the fellow was talking about; he'd not slept more than an hour straight. He'd put a wet handkerchief on the burn on his neck, after washing it pretty thoroughly, but he'd been on this road before and knew infection was in his future if he didn't get it seen to. His eyelids had that sandpapery feel, and the skin of his face felt ticklish, like fly wings were bumping up against it in the dark. If he said any of this, the fellow across from him would likely tell him he shouldn't be flying, and wouldn't believe Jason when he explained that he'd flown like this plenty. So Jason just found himself a spot and settled on his duffel. The other fellow was sitting across from him. He was smoking a pipe. It filled the truck with a sweet smell that, along with the truck exhaust, almost covered the dank Parisian stench.

"My name is Albert," he said and reached across, offering his hand. "Zimmermann."

"Jason Thorn," said Jason. He took Zimmermann's hand and shook it. "You German?"

"Austrian."

"Barely can tell," said Jason. "Your English's good."

Zimmermann gave a chuckle and sat back. "As is yours."

"Vielen Dank," said Jason, in German. *"If you get tired, my German is not that bad either."*

"We are men of the world," said Zimmermann.

The truck lurched as the driver put it into gear and they began to move. Jason shifted the duffel around so it was more comfortable.

In the dark, Zimmermann fiddled with his pipe, reached into a pocket and produced a match, then struck it against the floor. In the brief light of the flame, Jason got his first good look at the man: slender, clean-shaven, with black hair slicked back close to his skull. His left cheek was marred by a line like a river on a map. Jason thought he might've had that scar from a sword fight, back in Germany, and if he'd got it that way, it meant that he went to a pretty fine school. His pipe was the sort you'd expect from someone who went to a good German school: a big porcelain thing, with a long ivory stem, and a picture of a man holding a sword in the air on the bell of it. That was as much as Jason could see before the flame disappeared inside it and Albert Zimmermann got his pipe going, but it was enough to give him a picture besides the one on the pipe, enough to make him wonder.

"They hired me as pilot," said Jason.

"So I have heard," said Zimmermann. "We will be flying out together."

"You're my engineer, then," said Jason.

"And your co-pilot. It will be a long flight. If you get weary . . ." Zimmermann paused. "Oh! On that subject—I apologize for my rudeness. Desrosiers has provided us a morning meal. I have already been at it, I'm afraid. But there is plenty."

Zimmermann leaned to the front of the cab, right behind the driver's seat, and dragged out a big wicker picnic basket. He flipped open the top, and then drew a tea towel away, and Jason peered in and silently agreed: there was plenty. There were four baguettes—three and a half, really—and links of sausages, and a steel vacuum canister that Jason strongly suspected was filled with coffee. There was a tall steel cup beside it, with knives and spoons, and a bottle of milk and, near the bottom, a jar of honey and another of mustard. The only thing that Zimmermann had touched was the one baguette. Jason couldn't hold that against him.

"Bon appetit," said Zimmermann as he pulled the half-baguette out and, moving his pipe aside, tore a bite from it.

Jason unscrewed the bottle and took two steel cups from the top, then opened it. He was right: coffee. He poured one cup for Zimmermann, another for himself, and took a gulp from it straight away. It burned the inside of his throat to match the injury he'd put on the outside. But it helped. Zimmermann sipped at his and smiled.

"A bad night," he said. "Did you spend it with one of Desrosiers' girls?"

Jason shook his head. "Never had a taste for that."

"For girls?"

"For prostitutes," said Jason.

Zimmermann shrugged.

"It is going to be a long time on this job. I am signed up for two years." He took another sip. "But I abstained also. Two years is a long time to suffer with the clap, yes?"

Now Jason laughed. "That it is," he said.

Jason drained his coffee, set the cup back on the flask and took a knife to one of the sausages. He offered the first two slices to Zimmermann but this time the other man politely refused. Jason put those and two more on some bread and ate them, until finally the food combined with the coffee and he began to feel himself again. Zimmermann, having finished his own coffee, returned to smoking, and Jason found himself wishing that Desrosiers had tucked a fresh package of cigarettes in the basket. He weighed the consequences for just a heartbeat or so before pulling out that last cigarette he'd been saving, clamping it in his teeth, and lighting up.

Zimmermann was peering over the driver's shoulder now, his absurdly ornate pipe dangled over one knee. The way was still dark—just the occasional lamplight, the glow from high windows. Jason wanted to ask Zimmermann straight: What in hell was he doing here on this job, him an Austrian fellow and Desrosiers a French patriot? But maybe that was a better question for Desrosiers.

"I will be very happy," said Zimmermann, "to be out of Paris."

"You have a bad night?"

"It was a good stay. Desrosiers is a very good host. He put me in an acceptable room, and offered presumably an allowance similar to the one he will have provided you. I enjoyed the fabled French wine and cheese. Strolled the banks of the Seine."

That wasn't what Jason had asked, but he decided that was all right.

"It is a good enough city. But I think it is a good time to be away from Paris and Berlin and everything else. Africa, now . . . a man can still make his fortune there. . . ."

"Desrosiers pays well," said Jason, "but it's not quite a fortune."

"For men such as we, it's a good start." Zimmermann took a puff from his pipe and regarded Jason.

"You flew in the *Luftstreitkräfte*," said Jason. "That so, isn't it?" Zimmermann shrugged, and smoked, and then nodded. "And you, Lieutenant Colonel Thorn, flew in the Royal Flying Corps. Two tours: one begun in 1915, lasting just under a year, and then again in the final push in 1918. You had a bit of a reputation. How many of our planes did you shoot down?"

"Fifty-two."

"One a week."

"Haven't heard that one in a while," said Jason, and as Zimmermann laughed, Jason drew a deep lungful of smoke and held it a couple of heartbeats.

"Desrosiers told me," said Zimmermann. "Your name."

"Didn't tell me yours," said Jason. "Or your service record in such detail as that."

"Didn't he?" Zimmermann shrugged. "Well. There is not so much to tell. I did not fly as long as you. Just for three months, as the war ended. As a consequence, I did not shoot down nearly so many of your comrades as you did mine."

"I'm sorry."

"It was war," said Zimmermann.

Jason had heard about the airfield at Villeneuve-Orly, but he had never visited it until that morning. As the truck pulled up in the grey dawn, it seemed like nothing so much as a farmer's field. They had come to it through a morning mist, past rows of cottages that were, so far as Jason could tell, completely deserted. The truck pulled up at a small cluster of buildings on the airfield's edge, and the driver climbed out, opened the back for them. He pointed to one building, a low wooden structure that looked like it held offices. A light burned in one of the windows. Jason and his co-pilot grabbed their bags, and at the driver's insistence left the picnic basket and the flask.

"Adieu," said the driver as he climbed into the truck and threw it into gear. He drove it in a wide circle and back out onto the laneway that had taken them here.

"So long," said Jason under his breath.

There were two other vehicles there: another truck, bigger than the one that'd dropped them off, and a Ford Roadster that Jason knew belonged to Desrosiers. Jason had ridden in it from the train station just a week ago, across the Seine to the hotel. It was a damn sight better than the back of that truck, he thought as he hefted his duffel onto his shoulder and headed to the door, just behind Zimmermann.

Desrosiers greeted them inside.

"I think this will be safe to fly today," he said as he led them down a short hallway to a larger room that might one day be a passenger lounge. Now it smelled of fresh pine sap, from interior walls that were halfway finished, and was filled with sawhorses and carpenter tools. The light came from an old oil lamp. This place hadn't even electric power. There were three other men in the room. They each of them were young, and muscular under their shirts. Ground crew, most likely.

"You've seen a forecast?" asked Jason, and Desrosiers nodded. Although it was warm, like a blanket after the rain, he wore a long coat over his slender frame, and to hide his diminishing hairline, a bowler cap.

. . . like old Sam Green had worn, every single day but the last one, in Eliada . . .

That—and the empty, half-built houses they'd passed on their way here, this dark and empty office, so much like his old town of Cracked Wheel at the end, gave Jason an unwelcome shiver of recall. He dearly wanted another cigarette. But his last one was long spent.

Desrosiers might have intuited as much. He reached into his pocket and pulled out a cigarette case, took one for himself and offered it to Jason and Zimmermann.

Jason took one and lit up as Zimmermann demurred.

"I think you'll find the aircraft in good repair," said Desrosiers. "My fellows went over it last evening. It is fully fuelled. And the cargo is all loaded."

"Good to hear," said Jason. "All the same, I'd like to take a look for myself."

Desrosiers picked up the lamp and led them through another door, and along a short brick-lined hallway into a space larger than the lamp could illuminate.

"I believe this will be a warehouse when it's finished," said Desrosiers. "Also, electrified. With any luck, we won't be flying from here again until it is. Tell me, M. Thorn. Did you see your friend?"

"My friend?" asked Jason.

"That Negro doctor," said Desrosiers.

"No." Jason wondered at that a moment: he hadn't told Desrosiers about Andrew Waggoner.

But he shrugged. Desrosiers had obviously had Jason checked out pretty thoroughly, before letting him fly. He wondered if he'd also figured out Jason's name change, the secret he'd left behind with the old one.

"Doctor Waggoner," said Jason. "I stopped by his place in Paris. Couple days back. He was out of town."

Desrosiers stopped in the midst of the space and gave Jason a queer look. In the lamplight, he almost looked angry. But Jason thought it must've been the light.

"But I'm certain you left a message," said Desrosiers. "Let him know you'd be gone awhile."

"I spoke with his wife, Ann. Another old friend. So yeah, I did."

In fact, Jason had been pleased to talk to Annie and not Andrew Waggoner. He'd been out of Paris at that tuberculosis sanatorium he ran, out near Vire, and it'd been good to catch up with her. Conversations with Andrew, when they happened, weren't nearly so pleasant.

Desrosiers smiled now and nodded. "That's good. You will be away for a time. It's important your friends don't worry. Did you see anyone else in town?"

Jason wondered if Desrosiers meant the cathouse he'd spoken of a week ago, as they drove from the train station. Jason, he'd said, was to go there, say who he was and ask for Eloise, who Desrosiers certified was clean as she was skilled. "The bill is already paid," Desrosiers had said. Jason had resisted. He thought now, though, that rejecting the hospitality might be taken as impolite.

"I had a fine time," Jason said. "Thanks for everything."

And so they resumed their crossing of the dark warehouse, and finally came to two wooden doors. Desrosiers handed the lamp to Zimmermann, pushed them open, and stepped outside.

The Latécoère lay ahead of them perhaps two dozen paces—half-submerged in a ground mist so thick that it might have been the crest of a cloud. Standing on the edge of it, Jason couldn't help imagining himself stepping forward, feeling that cloud light on his boots—feeling it give as it thinned, and tear like gauze, and then falling. . . .

He stepped forward. The cigarette, finished, dropped through the mist onto solid ground.

"She is fuelled," said Desrosiers, "and loaded. The weather reports—"

"—are good. That's good to hear." Jason approached the tail of the aircraft, and ran his fingers along its duralumin fuselage as he approached the forward hatch. Jason had crewed a Latécoère once before, although not as pilot. The chance to fly this one, fresh from the factory floor, was more than half the reason he'd taken this job. Zimmermann went ahead of him and ducked under the engine, and Jason reached to open the hatch. Desrosiers put a hand on his arm to stop him for a moment.

"M. Desrosiers?"

He smiled, weakly. "Oh, let us drop the formalities this morning."

"Emile?"

"Jason." Emile Desrosiers turned Jason to face him, hands clasped on both shoulders. "You will always have my gratitude, for your heroism. You know that?"

"All right," said Jason, and then, in French: *"Yes, Emile. I know that."*

"Good. I will, I am afraid, not be joining you out this morning. There are four passengers you will be carrying, and so no room for me."

"Your plane seats eight," said Jason. Desrosiers shrugged, and repeated: *"No room."*

That took Jason aback. The plan had been that Desrosiers would be along for the ride, to take care of all the formalities at Algiers. He had the language and, more importantly, the relationships. Jason didn't have the sense that Zimmermann had any of those things. He thought again, as he had the night before, and just as crazily, about walking away.

Desrosiers picked up on Jason's instinct, and told him not to worry, and then, in English: "Everything is in order. Do not fear. The men on the plane are my associates. They will take care of everything at the appropriate time; you are in good hands."

"They're already on the plane?" Jason peered back at the dark windows along the fuselage. Desrosiers nodded.

"Most of them."

"Early risers," said Jason. Zimmermann ducked back from the mist beneath the engine. He had somewhere found a torch that cut through the mist like a spear made from light. He flicked it off. "Is everything all right?"

"We got passengers," said Jason.

"Is that so?"

"That's so."

"I hope they are not fat," said Zimmermann, and he laughed sharply.

There were three of them who did not speak—they had settled into the wicker seats that were installed along the inside of the fuselage, forward of a stack of canvas bags. It was hard to even see them as Jason stuck his head in: just three hunched shadows in the dark of the passenger compartment. One of them was snoring.

The fourth arrived after Jason had settled in the cockpit, and he came up to say hello as they were preparing for takeoff. His name was Aguillard and he was a physician. Jason guessed him to be in his fifties. He had soft features, a rim of brown-grey hair around a bald head. He spoke to him in English.

"I am told that you flew in the war," he said.

"Yes sir," said Jason.

"You were very good at it," said Aguillard, to which Jason shrugged, and nodded. Aguillard smiled. "I suppose you would not be here today, if it were otherwise."

"No," said Jason, "I guess not."

Aguillard laughed at that, and turned in the narrow space to find his seat. That was fine with Jason. The ground fog had nearly burned off, and in a half hour, they'd be in the air. A few hours after that, high over the Mediterranean. Let Doctor Aguillard talk with his companions all that time, thought Jason, and let the pilots alone.

It was a little less than a half hour by the time Zimmermann joined Jason in the cockpit and the ground crew pulled the blocks from under the landing gear. The sky had cleared as well as the ground—the only clouds were formed in a high herringbone, pink with the early light. Jason took a breath, and almost of their own accord his fingertips found the cigarette burn beneath his jaw. It was healing, but still hurt when he pressed. He kept the pressure on as the aircraft gathered speed, and he dug in hard enough to draw a tear, as the landing gear bounced once and twice on the hard-packed turf. He finally put both hands on the controls only as the Latécoère took to the air and climbed over the roofs of the empty houses ringing the Orly airfield.

Jason took another breath and let it out slowly. The burn on his neck throbbed, but the pain of it was quickly receding. And for the first time since he'd woken up, he didn't feel the need for another cigarette. Whether on his neck or in his mouth. The controls of this new plane were pleasingly responsive as he guided it through a long, slow bank to a southwesterly bearing, watching as the ground below transformed to farmers' fields lined with tufts of windbreak trees and laneways. Paris herself—she was beyond his vision now . . . and with her the stink and the clattering noise, the disappointment. There had been a time, when Jason was very young, where cities like New York, Chicago . . . Paris . . . were a dream . . . mountains, he'd imagined, of brick and steel and light.

But they were also a nightmare. Who wants to be stuck on a mountain, after all?

Jason glanced over at Albert Zimmermann—who'd seemed eager

enough to get off this mountain as they drove from Paris. His Austrian co-pilot might have been smiling, but it might've also been a grimace of concentration. He was busying himself, marking his chart with pencil-lead as he read the compass.

Jason glanced at the altimeter. Soon, they would level off—and whatever cities they crossed would be far beneath their wings, and he need not look at any of them . . . just the sky, and the distant horizon.

Zimmermann looked up from the chart, then at the compass. He leaned across the cockpit, and said in Jason's ear: "Wrong direction." He tapped the bulb of the compass. "Southeast."

Jason shook his head. "Algiers is south."

"A change of plans," said Zimmermann. "Passengers want to make a stop first."

The pain at Jason's throat flared, and even as it burned he felt ice along his nerves.

"What in hell does that mean?" he said.

Zimmermann smiled and shrugged. "Doctor Aguillard gave me a new heading before takeoff."

"Where?"

"Southeast," repeated Zimmermann. "When we are levelled off I will show you on the chart."

Jason shook his head. "We'll change course once I've talked to Aguillard. He ought to've told me." And when Zimmermann shrugged again, Jason snapped: "*You* should've told me—" . . . *you Goddamned Kraut*, Jason nearly added.

He might as well have said it. Zimmermann drew back, his eyes narrowing. Zimmermann didn't say anything even as Jason levelled the Latécoère and unbuckled his harness.

"South," he said to Zimmermann as he handed over the controls, and snatched the chart from his lap. "Until I say otherwise."

Many years ago, as a boy, Jason had contemplated murder. The anger had come in consequence of fear, and at the time, he'd finally recognized them as conjoined. But for a while, Jason had thought about killing . . . a man saying he was a doctor, and a woman saying she was a nurse . . . both who'd lied and betrayed him, egregiously.

Jason was not that angry this time—not by a long shot—but he recognized the flavour of the feeling. The last time he'd let it get the better of him was the last time he'd flown for Imperial, and that'd ended badly. He did his best to push it down as he climbed down from the cockpit into the passenger compartment.

He found the men in their seats. Aguillard was in conversation with one situated in the first seat in front of him on the port side, while the two were distracted to starboard, looking out the windows and down at the French countryside beneath them. Jason didn't bother to wait for a break in the conversation.

"What is this?" he asked, showing Aguillard the chart. Aguillard blinked at it.

"Ah yes," he said. "Our new destination. There should be sufficient fuel, yes? It is not nearly as far as Algiers."

"M. Desrosiers set a flight plan. He needs the plane in Algiers."

"M. Desrosiers' beautiful aircraft will arrive in Algiers. We shall even top it off with fuel when we land." Aguillard took the chart and laid it out in front of Jason, with the morning sunlight coming in through his window illuminating the markings.

It was the first time that Jason had actually taken a serious look at it. It was a map depicting France and Switzerland and a slice of Austria and Bavaria. It was there, in Bavaria, that Zimmermann had placed his mark.

"There's nothing there," said Jason.

"Au contraire," said Aguillard. "There is a landing strip suitable to the Latécoère's needs. There is a farmhouse and buildings. There is fuel. There is, not far from there . . ." His voice trailed off and he shared a glance with his companion, who nodded at the unspoken command, and climbed out of his seat.

"You ought to've spoken to me about this," said Jason.

Aguillard looked at Jason appraisingly. "No," he said. "We could not risk it."

Aguillard's companion drew himself to a not-very-impressive height, steadied himself, and took the chart from Aguillard, then headed forward. Jason shouted for him to stay in the cabin, but the man ignored him, and Aguillard put a firm hand on Jason's forearm. He leaned close to Jason's ear, and spoke very clearly.

"You will not be travelling to Africa, Mr. *Thistledown*," said Doctor Aguillard, and tapped the map with his forefinger. "You have an appointment here. You might have been tempted to cancel it, had you known, and that would have been to no one's advantage."

The other two men had turned in their seats to face Jason and Aguillard. The morning sun and shadows shifted and turned in the cabin as the Latécoère corrected its course. Aguillard removed his hand, and with it motioned to his companions, and each of them nodded, and readied themselves, should Jason choose to do anything other than remain precisely where he stood.

Two

Of course Jason did try to get back to the cockpit and Aguillard's two men did manage to stop him. It wasn't much of a struggle. Jason stood up and shifted sideways to pull out of Aguillard's grasp, and one of the men, a baby-faced blond man who was tall as Jason and thicker by a third, grabbed hold of Jason's shoulder. Jason shifted again and broke free, but while he did, that first one's friend got around him and blocked the ladder. He wore little round glasses that he didn't bother to remove. He smiled and held both hands out and upturned, gesturing with his fingertips for Jason to come to him. Jason hesitated just long enough that the first fellow, the big one, could lay a hold from behind. Jason thought he might break it, but not without more of a fight than he wanted to have a couple thousand feet in the air. And he didn't know what he'd do after that.

So he just let himself be guided back to the seat. The pair withdrew to their own places.

Aguillard leaned over the seat back, so he could speak in Jason's ear. "Do not worry," he said. "Herr Zimmermann is an excellent pilot. My friend is an adequate navigator. It should be just a few hours before we arrive. You can stay put that long, yes, Mr. Thistledown?"

"My name's Thorn," said Jason. Aguillard made as not to hear him over the noise of the aircraft, clapped him on the shoulder, and sat back in his seat.

"Stay put!" he shouted genially.

Of course Jason would stay put. The Latécoère was on its way to 6,000 feet. Where would he go? Jason certainly had no allies if he wished to regain control of the aircraft—even Zimmermann had been more than happy to take Desrosiers' property on an unscheduled side trip to Germany before Jason had come back, and had now done so against Jason's orders. Desrosiers, for that matter, had not hesitated to abandon his plane and travel plans both.

And then there was that business of *Thistledown*.

That was a bad name. Bad to speak in general, and bad for these fellows to know.

The name had belonged to a killer, a man named John Thistledown, who'd run with other men as bad as he, from Oregon country through to the Dakotas. John Thistledown was a good shot and he wasn't shy about using that skill to kill men and women who crossed him. He did enough of that killing that people told stories about it, and he had an awful kind of fame for a while.

He had stopped eventually, met a good woman and made a 'stead in Montana, and that was where he'd sired Jason. But though he may have stopped killing men, he kept doing awful things—and it'd taken his wife to put him down.

Yet even in death . . . his name had brought more death to the farm, and the nearby town of Cracked Wheel . . . it had killed everybody there, and Jason's mother too.

And it had nearly doomed Jason, when Jason still used it for himself.

That was one reason Jason Thistledown vanished, in the spring of 1911, in the freezing waters of the Kootenai River—and why the next time he'd been asked a surname, he'd said "Thorn."

Andrew Waggoner had thought it was a funny choice, given the tenuous relationship between the down off thistles and the thorns on some branches. But it was easier to remember that way. And it didn't hurt that it was Lawrence Thorn and his family that'd first taken them in—when all of them arrived, on a disintegrating raft of mossy lumber and log, in such desperate need as they were.

Death preceded that raft by two days. Corpses, bloated and blue, their clothing slick tatters, floated down the Kootenai from Idaho, and more than half went past the Thorn farm. By Lawrence Thorn's firm order, not one of them got fished out. His boy Tom had spotted the first one—a lady, face down with her Sunday finery blooming around her like a swirl of pale algae. By the time Lawrence'd come to see, there were four others: two men, a Negro woman, and a corpse that'd encountered such obstacles that it was no longer possible to tell. The riverbank smelled worse than a privy.

"Go back to the house," Lawrence ordered him when Tom showed him. "This isn't wholesome."

They weren't wholesome, true enough. What Lawrence didn't tell his boy was he feared they'd bring disease. Lawrence's own father and mother had built the farm he owned in the very south of Alberta, and two seasons in, when he was but twelve years old, his mother had fallen ill and died. The dead folk in the river might've died like that, and might yet carry the sickness.

So he sent the boy inside, found himself a stout branch, did the work of dislodging the corpses as they caught in the river's edge—sending them onward downriver to whatever fate might have in store for them.

The raft came after the main flow of corpses had passed the farm. It was in the afternoon, a grey day threatening rain, and old Lawrence Thorn was still at the riverbank with his branch. He was in a state of some melancholy by that point, wondering whether he was doing right or wrong. His own family might be protected, but what of the souls of those dead in the river that Lawrence had let pass by without so much as a prayer for their passage to Heaven, never mind a Christian burial? What about the farmsteads downstream? The Blackfoot reserves, for that matter? If the bodies carried sickness, wasn't he just sending it onward?

It was in this temper, as the afternoon sun began to lower over the western mountains, that he spied the raft, with passengers on it, rounding the gentle bend in the river. It sat too low in the water, and listed badly to the right, where a tall young man stood, trying to keep it steady with a branch about as big as Lawrence's. A woman sat up at the opposite end of the vessel, cradling another woman's head in her lap. In the middle, a Negro sat clutching something in his arms, looking unwell.

A day prior, Lawrence might have had a mind to wave them all on, tell them to find somewhere else to put to ground. But—as he later explained to Jason, Dr. Andrew Waggoner, and Nurse Annie Rowe, over the sleeping form of Ruth Harper that evening—his aching conscience would no longer allow that choice.

"Come here, let me help!" was what he did say, and the young man shouted back: "We sure can use some," and guided the raft to the riverbank, where it came apart as soon as its bottom struck the round rocks there. Lawrence was amazed it had gotten them this far and said so; the raft was made of a wooden frame with four wooden planks nailed to it that looked as though they'd been through a couple of winters out of doors. They were weathered as barn board. By themselves they wouldn't have floated, but for a pair of logs that'd been lashed to the bottom on either side with hemp rope, and lashed badly; the logs rolled and slipped at just a bit of tugging, and the frame cracked as the passengers stepped into the water.

Lawrence kept his distance, and asked: "You look ill. So don't come close. I've seen what's come down the river."

The young man nodded and said something he had to repeat twice before Lawrence Thorn understood it: "Cave Germ," he said. "We don't have it. If we did, we'd be dead now like those other folk you saw."

"But you know about it." He motioned for them to come up. The young man helped the two women off first—one of them was in such awful shape she nearly had to be carried, then laid out on a soft spot of ground—then went back and helped the Negro up. As he stood, Lawrence saw he was about as tall as the youth and the thing he was carrying was a black leather case, as he'd seen doctors carry when they came to call from the mission.

"My name's Jason," he said. "This is Doctor Waggoner, and this here is Nurse Rowe, and this—" he ran a hand through the unconscious girl's light brown hair "—this is Ruth Harper."

"Harper?" Lawrence frowned. "From the mill town upriver?"

"That's right," said Jason. "From Eliada. But that place is gone now. It's just us, and what you saw come down that river."

Lawrence stood and thought about that a moment. Gone. He didn't have to speak for Jason to understand how he was mulling the implications of that statement.

"My name's Thorn," said Lawrence. "You're on my farm. If you're from Eliada you should know you've left America."

"Suits me," said Jason, and at that, Andrew Waggoner started to laugh. After a moment of that, Nurse Annie Rowe joined in. Jason kept a straight face until they were done, and Ruth—she just slept.

Lawrence Thorn and his family were good to them, and helped where it was needed most: by providing a swept-out, scrubbed-down room with good morning light, for Andrew Waggoner and Annie Rowe to work on Ruth.

Days before, they had all been at Eliada—where the creature that'd been named Mister Juke had taken over the hospital, and finally the sawmill at the middle of the town.

Ruth Harper's father was killed by it, along with the rest of the family, and Ruth—Ruth had been impregnated by the thing.

It wasn't truly impregnation. Doctor Waggoner said it was more like a parasitic infection.

But impregnation or infection, the cure was the same: an abortion procedure, similar but not precisely the same as the procedure that Andrew had learned when he studied at the Paris Medical School. Andrew had attempted it once, on a hill girl, but she was sick, and Andrew was injured, and she had not survived.

Andrew and Annie Rowe hadn't contemplated imposing that cure on anyone else as they escaped from Eliada in the waters of the Kootenai River. They fled far enough downriver to escape the Juke's effects, and finally stopped at an old trapper's camp. But when Jason arrived with Ruth, fleeing on the very heels of the destruction of that town, Andrew saw that he'd have to attempt the procedure again—and that the camp where they were resting was no place to do it.

So Jason went to work, and tore off the roof of the cabin, and with some rope he found and a couple of logs that had loosed downriver, did a barely adequate job constructing a raft for them all. And they set off, looking for exactly the situation that Lawrence Thorn and his homestead provided them: a clean, dry room with good light, and a host who would accept the things they would have to do there.

"I pray to God your Negro knows what he's doing," Lawrence said to Jason, as the two of them sat on the bunkhouse stoop. It was the cleanest, brightest place on the farm—clean because it had largely been shut up since Lawrence and his pa had built it—when they had thoughts that the farm might become enough of a concern to justify hired hands. It never really had—but they'd kept it swept and bright, repairing the glass in the windows as needed.

Andrew and Annie pronounced it fine, but they and Jason set to scrubbing it anyhow, with the help of Tom Thorn and his ma Susanna, while Lawrence hauled well water to the woodstove and then, once boiled, to the ever-more pristine bunkhouse.

And then Jason and Lawrence sat outside, while Andrew and Annie got down to the procedure and Tom and Susanna went back to the house.

"Doctor Waggoner isn't my Negro," said Jason. "He's his own man, and he's good at surgery. He learned his trade in Paris, France."

Lawrence huffed, squinting across the farmyard to their chicken coop. He was a tall man, lean-featured, and the years out here had carved themselves into the lines of his face.

"I apologize," said Lawrence. "But he seems hurt in one arm, and anyone doing a surgery needs both of them."

"That may be," said Jason.

Lawrence folded his hands together, and looked at Jason, nodding a little until Jason did the same.

"I already prayed," said Jason, "but I guess we can do that again."

It did not take long, and when they were finished, Lawrence spoke again. "Doctor Waggoner's not your Negro. I am guessing that Miss Harper is your sweetheart, though."

"I'm guessing."

Lawrence smiled and patted Jason on the knee. "You know, a good surgeon makes all the difference. My wife fell ill three years back, and we were blessed to have a doctor living downriver. My mother now—there were no doctors out here in those days. If there were, she might've lived to see my wedding."

"How old were you when she passed?"

"Fifteen."

"I was seventeen," said Jason.

"I'm sorry to hear," said Lawrence, and looked at him with dawning realization. "You're seventeen now, aren't you?"

Jason nodded through the tears, and Lawrence put an arm over his shoulders, and held him, and let him weep until it was done. Snuffling, Jason apologized, and thanked him.

"Do you have any other family?"

Jason wiped his eyes with his sleeve. "No," he said. "Thought I did, but she turned out to be a liar. And a murderess."

And thinking about Germaine Frost, and the people she worked with back in New York, he added: "You should know, that before long folks might come looking for us. Bad folks."

Lawrence slid away, and regarded Jason. "You on the run?"

"Not from the law."

"Then—"

"Who? The Cave Germ folks." When Lawrence didn't seem any less confused, Jason added: "Eugenics folks. They got me on a list, I reckon."

They didn't get to talk about that more until much later, because that was when Nurse Rowe, covered in dark blood and chest heaving, threw open the door and called Jason inside.

The Eugenics folks hadn't come to the Thorn farm in 1911. But twenty years on, it looked as though they'd come to find Jason Thistledown in France.

And they'd come to take him to Germany.

It should have panicked Jason—all the fears and worries that had kept him awake the night prior, they should have all come back to him. But terror is a strange creature—fiercer in the dark hours of uncertainty, timid itself in the face of calamity, when it often retreated, leaving a cold space, a calm. As the Latécoère flew on, Jason let his mind wander as he peered out the window at the clouds below. They stretched below in a long, flat plain—a sea of clouds. Under that sea was another world—a part of France where he might have flown the Nieuport, where he might indeed have met Zimmermann . . . on another flight to Germany.

He chanced a look behind him, where Aguillard sat—hoping that he might be dozing. Jason thought if he were, he might be able to get around and lay hold of him, strike a bargain with the other two men here and strap a parachute on, leap out the side of the plane. It was a mad plan—who knew what was beneath those clouds, really? But Aguillard smiled back at him, wide awake, erasing any notion of escape.

"You need to smoke?" asked Aguillard. Jason did—fiercely—but he shook his head.

"Well, you don't mind if I do?"

"Suit yourself," said Jason as Aguillard opened a small silver case and pulled a cigarette from it. He held it between his lips and turned the case over. It contained a butane lighter in one end. Once the cigarette was lit, he pulled it from his mouth and offered it to Jason. A curl of smoke found Jason's nose, and involuntarily, Jason drew it deep.

"Come now," he said. "You slept badly, and you badly need to smoke. I would offer you some whiskey, but I understand liquor is not your vice."

Jason took the cigarette.

"It is a good thing you are not flying," said Aguillard. "You are in no shape."

"I'm fine."

"No, no. You are not, really. The landing is not straightforward," said Aguillard. "We have done the best we are able to accommodate a runway, but it is not much more than a field, and shorter than you might care for. I believe that Herr Zimmermann will be better suited."

"How'd you know about last night? You been watching me?"

Aguillard pinched his own cigarette between his lips and held the case between two fingers, so he could clap, and laugh. "Not at all!" he said. "But I guessed it easily. It is good the Germans never captured you, Mr. Thistledown. You would have lost England the war."

"You keep calling me Thistledown."

"Yes, I do. It is your name."

Jason took another deep drag. He weighed some things—notably, his new job, with Emile Desrosiers, that had seemed such a lucky break . . . and now.

"Was I ever going to Africa?"

Aguillard replaced the case in his jacket pocket and puffed his own cigarette.

"You may yet," he said, "if you do as you're told."

They flew four hours and ten minutes altogether, and in that time, Jason smoked five more of Aguillard's cigarettes, after a while feeling not ashamed at all. The tobacco was good, better than Jason was used to and nearly enough to make him well-disposed. But the tobacco, from Turkey said Aguillard, was all they talked about after that. Jason wasn't going to give up anything else until he learned something new, so he decided that he'd just wait until they landed to do that, not trusting either Aguillard or—more particularly—himself with Aguillard.

After the fourth cigarette, the plane fell below the cloud cover. Jason peered out his window. They were flying over a low, tree-covered mountain range. He kept watching as the ground levelled, turning to forest and farmland. They flew over a lake, wide and blue. A town passed beneath them, and then a larger town, and at that, Zimmermann—Jason guessed it was Zimmermann—turned the aircraft and there were mountains again. They descended more rapidly, turning east and then north, crossing a valley. Here, they were low enough that Jason could make out structures—maybe a chateau, or something like it, and in the valley's middle . . .

Jason couldn't tell what it was at first. The structure looked like nothing so much as a marksman's target, drawn in a large clearing around a fast-moving river. He squinted. Could it be fencing? Long, high circles of fences—concentrically placed around one another? The span of them would have been huge—the largest, at least hundreds of yards in the radius. Enmeshed within it, a low, sprawling structure . . . like a factory, a military compound . . . that pushed against the riverbank.

Jason glanced over to Aguillard, who had been watching Jason as he pressed his face against the glass.

"Oh yes," said Aguillard, eyebrows raised, nodding, as though he could know Jason's thoughts on the scope of the thing, and agreed.

When Jason looked back, it was already gone, the aircraft cresting the peaks surrounding the valley, banking for what would be its final approach.

"Best strap in," said Aguillard. "It is not an ideal landing."

The aircraft flew low over sharp-tipped evergreens and lower across a meadow of tall grass and bright red wildflowers before the wheels touched down on a hard-packed pasture, where they bounced just once and finally rolled and stopped.

"All right if I stand up?" Jason asked, and when Aguillard indicated that would be fine Jason got up and headed to the cockpit. Zimmermann and Aguillard's man had unstrapped themselves and were climbing out of their seats. In front of them, the propeller was slowing its spin to a halt. Aguillard's man slipped sideways past Jason, offered Jason's old seat to him with a small smile. Zimmermann kept his eyes fixed on the instruments in front of him, so Jason reached over and waved his hand in front of him.

"Hey!" said Jason, and Zimmermann looked at him, and Jason looked back. Was he in on this thing, whatever it was? He sure knew Jason Thorn's service record before having even met him.

Did he know Jason Thistledown's? Had Aguillard told him all about that? Had Desrosiers?

"Did you know about this?" Jason finally asked.

"One does not argue with these fellows," Zimmermann said softly. Zimmermann gestured out the cockpit, where in the distance, mountains climbed to snow-tipped peaks, and nearer, a big farmhouse squatted, two long balconies facing them. Men seemed to be milling about in front of the building—maybe a dozen of them. As Jason watched, he saw a group of five split off and head toward the plane.

"What do you mean, 'these fellows'?"

Zimmermann pointed. "Do you recognize the uniform on those ones?"

Jason squinted and shook his head. The fellows were dressed in brown, with black caps. "Been a long time since I was in the service."

"They are S.A.," said Zimmermann quietly. "Hitler's men."

"The Nazi leader."

Zimmermann nodded.

"Your leader?" asked Jason. Zimmermann looked away at that. He started to say something, but Jason cut him off.

"Don't bother," he said, and climbed out of the cockpit, and then out of the plane, where Aguillard waited for him with his three companions, waving cheerily at the five who jogged across the field to join them.

Three

Three of the five wore what must have been the S.A. uniform—high black boots, brown denim shirts, the swastika symbol on an armband—and had pistols and daggers holstered at their belts. Jason had read in a newspaper that many of these S.A. fellows—stormtroopers, they called themselves—were veterans of the Kaiser's army. These three seemed about old enough to have fought in the war, but younger than Jason—too young to have fought in it for very long.

The other two were older, and dressed far more casually. One, a square-faced man with a mop of greying hair swept over a tanned forehead, wore a high-collared wool sweater and black trousers. His companion was the smaller—he barely reached to the first's shoulder—and balding, with glasses that clipped onto his nose. He wore a white shirt and a grey tweed vest that matched his trousers, tucked into high-topped hiking boots. With shorter legs and an ample gut, he came up behind the rest.

As they approached, Aguillard told Jason their names, and Jason blinked at the one.

"I once knew a Bergstrom," said Jason.

Aguillard nodded. "That would be Johannes's elder brother. Nils, yes?"

Jason didn't say anything one way or another. Aguillard was baiting him; he could see that the fellow was almost enjoying it by the twinkle in his eye.

"What's the little fellow's name again? Missed that," he said instead.

"Doctor Plaut. Jürgen Plaut," said Aguillard, and laughed. "The little fellow, eh? I must tell him about that. He won't be pleased."

And then they were there, shaking hands all around, talking quickly in German to one another. Jason kept his hands in his pockets and listened. His German was good, but not so good he could keep up with chatter in a crowd. He picked out words and topics here and there: there was a checkpoint at a mountain pass, a fellow all of them knew that seemed to be recovering, but not well, and an excellent strudel that had been set out in the house across yonder field. Plaut kept his head down, but old Bergstrom looked at Jason steadily—like he was studying him, taking stock. If he were anything like his elder brother, thought Jason, that would be exactly what he was doing. Jason looked right back, and held on until old Johannes looked away.

"It is all right," said Bergstrom to one of the uniformed men—and that was when Jason noticed that the two of them had their hands on their holsters, and the third had drawn his weapon, a Luger automatic pistol. He hastily returned it to his belt. Jason stepped back, and as he did so, the man with the gun became very still, watching Jason like he was a rattlesnake.

"All right," Jason repeated, and showed his hands palm out, slowly. The fellow stood straighter, looked to Bergstrom and then Plaut, and finally dropped the gun back into its holster. He didn't go so far as to fasten the cover.

Jason lowered his hands to his side, but kept them from his pockets, as it dawned on him: all of these fellows in the uniforms, with the guns at their hips, who not only outgunned but outnumbered him too—they were afraid.

"Let's go to the farmhouse," said Plaut, looking at Jason sidelong as he spoke with Aguillard. "The breeze off the mountain still has a chill to it, yes?"

Jason hadn't seen a farmhouse so large as this. It rose three storeys, and its walls were painted brightly, with Greek-style pillars drawn on each corner, and up top toward the peak, a mural that depicted something mythological; it looked to Jason like a dragon, fighting a man wearing old-fashioned mail armour. If they were in England, Jason would say St. George. Here, he was betting on Siegfried.

They led Jason across a wide porch, where more of the uniformed men lingered, leaning against railings and sitting on wooden chairs—through a large but simple kitchen walled in stained barn board and rimmed with a bench on the two outside walls—then down a hallway, its walls hung so close with antlers that it seemed like a forest pathway—and up two flights of stairs into a long sitting room that overlooked the meadow and the mountains beyond. Here, Jason was invited to sit, in one of three leather wing-backed chairs surrounding a low table made from a section of a huge tree. Bergstrom sat in the second, Aguillard in the third. Plaut stood. At some point along the way, the uniformed men had split away. Bergstrom crossed his arms over his chest and squinted at Jason.

"How tall are you?" he asked, in English.

"Six feet one inch," said Jason. "You?"

"Five foot and ten inches. Your weight?"

"Twelve stone." Jason raised his eyebrows in a question. "And you, sir?"

Bergstrom patted his belly. "I am sixteen stone."

"You are being rude, Doctor Bergstrom," interjected Plaut, in German. *"Welcome our guest. Herr Aguillard tells us he is a smoker. Offer him tobacco."*

Bergstrom shook his head. *"It is unhealthful."*

"It calms the nerves." In English, Plaut said: "Tobacco?"

"Yes," Jason said. "Thank you. I would like my bag also. And directions to the nearest town. I can walk it."

Bergstrom shook his head. "You may have tobacco. But I am afraid I must insist that you remain here. Too many have gone to too much trouble to send you on your way so soon." He stood and walked over to an armoire, from which he extracted a wooden case, stacked with cigarettes. As he returned and offered them to Jason, he continued talking.

"You have matured well, Herr Thistledown. Your features are even, you are well-muscled for one not an athlete. Your skin is clear. Your hair full. Your teeth, in spite of your deplorable smoking habit, are white and clean. No one would guess that you are nearly forty years old."

"Siebenunddreißig," said Plaut, and as Jason pulled a cigarette from the case and placed it between his lips, Plaut was there with a match. "Thirty-seven," he repeated in English.

"There's some argument on that, is there?" asked Jason in an exhalation of smoke.

"Not at all." Bergstrom smiled. "Born in Cracked Wheel, Montana to Helen and John Thistledown in 1894, in January. The fourth of January."

"Not much of a card player," commented Plaut. *"Look how red his face is."*

"I'm pretty good at German," said Jason, and looked at Plaut as he switched: *"I learned it in the war killing your country's children from the sky. I learned it very well I think."*

Jason continued in English. "All right, Herr Bergstrom. I won't play at cards. Your friend Aguillard tried to fish it out of me, and I held out because I didn't care for him. I'll come clean now, but not because I like you any better. I'm Jason Thistledown. That's my name. I was born in January, and Cracked Wheel . . . that town's gone now. Your brother, Nils . . . he had something to do with that. That, and some other things all this brings to mind, might account for the redness of my face."

Were these men afraid now? Since Jason had told Plaut about speaking German, the little man hadn't met his eye and had now retreated to one of the tall windows, where he appeared to be enjoying the mountain view. Bergstrom sat in his chair, hands folded in his lap, with a curious, attentive and unambiguously pleasant expression. Jason studied him, and Bergstrom would not look away.

"Yes," said Bergstrom. "My elder brother Nils did you a mischief at one time. Would my apology for your treatment at his hands have any meaning?"

"I didn't come here seeking one," said Jason. "I didn't come here of my own will at all."

"And you didn't really come to Idaho, and Eliada, of your own free will in the spring of 1911 either. You were tricked, yes? By Germaine Frost. She led you to a chamber of horrors—there is no other way to describe it, is there?—in Doctor Nils Bergstrom's lumber-town hospital. You very nearly perished there." Bergstrom leaned forward, gestured to the box on the table. Jason, noticing his cigarette was near its end, reached over and took another, lit it from the last one.

"A lot of folk 'perished' in Eliada," said Jason. "The whole town, by the time the Juke—"

"Yes?" prompted Bergstrom. "By the time the Juke . . . ?"

Jason dropped his spent cigarette into an ashtray on the table. "No," he said, "you tell me what I'm doing here first."

"Right now," said Bergstrom, "we are having a conversation about Eliada. I know it is upsetting to you. Among other things, it came at a time after you lost your mother, to the outbreak in Cracked Wheel. Might I remind you that I lost my brother. You grieve for her. I grieve for him. I also wish to understand about his death. We corresponded quite regularly until the spring—shortly before you arrived there. His last letters . . . they seemed to me to be indicating a growing psychosis—about this thing he called a Juke. Can you tell me anything else?"

"That's why I'm here? To tell you about Nils Bergstrom?"

Bergstrom produced a black leather notebook and a pencil from a satchel that only then Jason noticed, on the floor beside his chair.

"I know some of what came before," said Bergstrom. "I know what was found, after all had perished. I want to learn about the space in between."

Jason drew another three cigarettes from the box and set them on the arm of the chair. It was clear he wasn't going anywhere until he got through this.

"All right. I'll tell you what I know about your brother. You might not care for it."

Bergstrom raised his pencil, and set its tip to the notebook's first page.

"Your brother was the chief surgeon in Eliada. His boss, Garrison Harper, gave him quite a hospital. It was part of his idea about how a town should be made, and he spent a fortune making that idea real. It was right there in the town motto: 'Community. Compassion. Hygiene.' Your brother had nurses and equipment, and even another doctor to do work for him, and if anyone got too sick, a big quarantine building. But you know he wasn't just setting bones and sewing up cuts. He was also looking after the hill folk who lived outside that town. Paying special heed to the ones he thought weren't fit to breed. He had some friends in New York who were real interested in fixing those ones. You know about that part? Of course you do.

"I didn't know about that when I met him. I'd come up from Cracked Wheel, where nobody was going to breed. I was tricked into coming there, by a woman who called herself Germaine Frost and lied about being kin to me. What she was, was a friend of your brother Nils. She brought that sickness to my old town, and killed everyone there but me with it—even my ma—and thought me surviving meant something. Your brother seemed real interested in that too. You see now how I can say he had something to do with all that killing? That's how.

"First night, your brother locked me up in that quarantine. Tied me down like I was some sort of lunatic. There was something else in there with me. A lot of things. He called 'em Jukes. Things might've killed me, but I . . . managed to get hold of a scalpel and cut myself free before they did.

"Your brother was a lunatic himself by then. I could tell it. There were some folk in town who dressed up like the Ku Klux Klan. You know about them? They weren't truly Klansmen—they worked for him, or with him, or just listened to him. They thought those Juke things were Jesus. Just like your brother did. They weren't Jesus though. They were . . . parasites, is what they were. They could trick a fellow into believing anything.

"They were worse than that, though. They liked to lay their eggs inside folk, like a certain kind of fly will under the skin. But the Juke eggs, they liked it best in ladies' wombs. Your brother knew all about this and he didn't do anything, except one lady killed by it, he butchered, to see what it looked like inside. How 'bout that.

"That's what I knew of your brother, before he died. I . . . heard he had some of those things growing under his skin, and maybe that's what killed him, as they got bigger. I guess that must've hurt. But his mind was half gone by then, or so I'm told. He died an awful death, but he'd done awful things, so I guess that's about right."

Plaut had rejoined Jason and Bergstrom around the low table, and he looked at each of them—first Bergstrom, who squinted at Jason through the smoke that hung in the still air of the sitting room, and then at Jason, who busied himself lighting his fourth cigarette from the remains of the third.

"That is a nasty little burn at your throat," Bergstrom observed. "You make it yourself?"

"Using his neck as an ashtray," commented Plaut.

"That's near all I know about your brother," said Jason.

"It must be very painful," said Bergstrom. "Did you find pain helped you resist the . . . the Juke . . . when you met it?"

Sure it had. When Jason had been locked in the quarantine with the juvenile Juke, he'd sliced his hand on the scalpel while cutting his way out, and he later on realized that'd saved him. When Ruth Harper'd been in its thrall later . . . with its young in her . . . he'd fired a bullet into her foot, to bring her back to herself. How the hell would Johannes Bergstrom know that? Was he just guessing? Jason did his best not to confirm his supposition.

"I gather you thought it a great help to calm your nerves in the cockpit," continued Bergstrom. "Pain, I mean to say. That was why in 1915 your corps physician ordered you grounded, and sent back to England to train, yes? You were an exemplary pilot. But the cuts on your arms . . . must have seemed to some as nothing more than suicide attempts. To others as a kind of madness."

"You have my war record," said Jason.

"Easy enough to obtain," said Bergstrom. "You flew aeroplanes for Imperial Airways for three years, and they maintained clean copies of all your records for long after. If you had left under better circumstances, they might have been more diligent in protecting your confidentiality."

Jason wouldn't have expected anything other from Imperial. Hell, even Zimmermann seemed to have a good idea how Jason Thorn spent the war. What worried him more was how exactly Bergstrom and Aguillard and the rest of them connected Jason Thistledown to Jason Thorn, so long after he'd fled downriver with Andrew and Ann and Ruth. Had they got to Lawrence? Or Tom—wherever he was now?

"Do the cigarette burns help in the same way?" asked Bergstrom.

Cigarettes did help, and had for a while, but Jason knew that soon they wouldn't; like the incisions, the contusions, the nails . . . each only worked until his flesh learned the language of that particular pain. For now, the cigarette to the throat was still fresh enough to drive the demons away, to let Jason remain himself. As Jason thought this, it occurred to him that he had nodded. Bergstrom scribbled a notation.

"Your brother," said Jason. "He was a doctor of medicine. I'm guessing you're a doctor too."

"Astute," said Bergstrom "I am indeed a doctor."

"But not like your brother."

"I am what used to be called an alienist."

"A psychoanalyst," said Jason. "A head doctor."

"Yes."

"Are you psychoanalyzing me now?"

"No," said Bergstrom.

"Then what?" said Jason. "What are we doing here?"

"I am guessing, Herr Thistledown. You are a unique fellow. Perhaps you are, as Germaine Frost and my brother guessed, an evolved fellow. What I do know is that you are a member of a very select club. Of people who can turn away when . . . the Juke, as you call it . . . when it calls. I am interested in how you do so."

Jason shrugged and Bergstrom nodded. He was very different from his brother, or at least the way that Jason remembered him. Nils Bergstrom was skeletal—he moved like a marionette, which Jason supposed in a way he was. He was also a figure that Jason knew best from his nightmares; he had only known Nils Bergstrom in the flesh for a few weeks if that, when they met in Eliada. Were he to meet him now, as he was in 1911, Jason might not recognize him.

"But that is for another day," said Bergstrom. "What is important is that you *do* turn away. The work that the Juke does on you never lasts long."

Jason found himself nodding again—but this time he wasn't giving anything away. He was working it out.

Bergstrom must have seen it. He smiled in a way that seemed a little sad, and he nodded too.

"It is true, Herr Thistledown," he said softly. "We have one. Nearby. And that, to answer the question you posed earlier, is why we have brought you here."

"We are fucked," muttered Plaut in German. Bergstrom shushed him with a wave of his hand. With the same sweep, half-standing, Bergstrom reached across and plucked the cigarette from Jason's fingers, before he could jam the tip hard into his throat.

"Not now," he said softly, grinding the cigarette into the base of the ashtray.

"It is beyond that mountain," said Bergstrom, motioning out the window, across the fields. "There is a valley there. You may have seen it from the aircraft as you flew in, yes?"

Jason recalled the rings of concentric fencing, the deeply shadowed woods.

"It is there that we had a . . . a colony, one might call it. There is a great chateau there, and orchards. It is rugged land otherwise. But beautiful. At one time, the property had been in the Aurberg family, for what that is worth to you, but for as long as I have been alive, it has been a house of healing . . . of cleansing."

"Like Eliada," said Jason. "Its hospital, anyhow. Is that what you were trying to do? Make another Eliada?"

Bergstrom looked at Jason. "Not precisely."

Jason shook his head slowly and let out a low whistle. "But near enough," he said.

"We have not tried to duplicate Eliada," said Bergstrom. "That would have been a duplication of failure. My brother, and Mr. Harper and the rest of them had only discovered the creature months before you arrived. They embarked on a reckless experiment on their community without so much as a dissection to understand the thing they were dealing with."

"And you've done all that? You have it worked out?"

"To the greatest extent possible," said Bergstrom. "Much of its biology is beyond my expertise to properly explain. But in the simplest terms, it operates as a kind of parasite, pairing itself with humans. It tricks us, with secretions, into caring for it—into worshipping it, or some entity we imagine that it conducts. If it is allowed to breed freely, to feed its fill . . . it will overrun us. But first, ecstasy."

"That much, Eliada taught us," said Plaut.

It felt like Jason had swallowed sand. He wetted his lips, and stared between the two of them. When he had seen that thing as a boy, the Juke had done far more than overrun Eliada: it had raped women there, sending them into a nightmare that was like a pregnancy. It devoured infants in the womb to sustain itself. If a woman survived such an ordeal—and many did not . . .

Ruth.

He thought of her eyes as the thing grew in her, standing in the woods, glittering with the certainty of utter madness.

"So," continued Bergstrom. "We did not emulate Eliada—where my brother allowed juveniles—wild juveniles—free run, to attack and impregnate women . . . and as you say, infect himself. But a mature organism was cultivated for us. And brought here, to a specifically designed enclosure that would, we hoped, contain and channel the organism's effect."

"That being ecstasy," said Jason hoarsely, and Bergstrom shook his head.

"That being common purpose. When the organism engages with its human hosts, its only purpose is to have workers . . . helpers, as a queen in a hive. But the organism's needs are simple at that stage of its life."

"Calories," said Plaut. "It simply needs to eat."

Jason nodded. "Jukes have an appetite all right. You opened up something awful over there, didn't you?"

Plaut shrugged, and Bergstrom smiled sadly. He stood, and walked over to the windows, beckoned Jason to join him.

"Are you familiar with the term '*Volksgemeinschaft*'?" asked Bergstrom.

Jason shook his head no.

"The closest translation is 'people's community.' It is a way of living that is very much an ideal among the German peoples—and in the years since the war, it has become an ideal seemingly impossible to achieve. There are many reasons that this may be so. Our friends downstairs, in the uniforms . . . many of them say that we have allowed ourselves to be robbed by the Jew, seduced by the homosexual . . . weakened by the moor and the Asiatic . . . that our very bloodline is under attack. Maybe all this is so, although a more fundamental problem is this: we lack *Volksgemeinschaft*. We have since our terrible defeat in 1918. In the years since then, its absence has been filled with a psychosis."

Plaut arrived at the window at that point with two crystal tumblers filled with what smelled of brandy. Bergstrom took one, but Jason made an excuse it was early in the day. Plaut shrugged again, and downed it in a gulp. Bergstrom sniffed his and sipped more delicately.

"The organism was the last of many things that we attempted at the estate," said Bergstrom. "We set it, as I said, within an enclosure . . . guarded by rings of concentric fencing, tended by experienced caretakers who wore clothing and breathing apparatus that protected them from its secretions. At the outermost fence, nearly three quarters of a kilometre from the organism, the effect of those secretions had what we presumed was a measured effect on the population—"

"Population?"

Bergstrom looked at Jason levelly. "Nearly three hundred," he said. "A camp of young German men and women—all beautiful and strong and intelligent."

"Deutches Jungvolk," said Plaut.

Jason nodded. "They that youth club the Nazi Party set up?"

"Yes," said Bergstrom. "They are a branch of the *Hitler-Jugend*. Brave volunteers."

"What happened to them?"

"It is difficult to say specifically. We have not been able to successfully visit the site for several months. When we send in an expedition, it does not return."

Jason nodded, a trifle impatient. *"And so,"* he said in German, gesturing at Plaut. *"We are fucked."*

"The experiment was a success for many months," said Plaut.

Bergstrom nodded. "For many months, yes. But finally, it has been something of a failure. One beyond our ken, and, more importantly, our means to investigate. And that," he said, looking directly at Jason, "is why we have been forced to bring you here. We need you to go there, and with all your strength—as you have proven able—resist the call. Help us understand what has happened to our community. Perhaps then we can unmake this failure."

Unmake the failure. That made Jason laugh, and he didn't stop himself.

"You think I can help you 'unmake' a failure like that?" Jason wiped his forehead and looked straight at Bergstrom. "I only know one way to do that—one way in general terms. You got any more of that Cave Germ that Germaine Frost had? No? Well you Germans are good at finding other ways. That's a valley beyond yonder hills, am I right? Here's what you do." He leaned against the windowsill, until he got his laughing under control. "You take some o' that mustard gas you used on my old comrades back in the trenches in France . . . you dump it down there and you kill everything that draws breath. You have the stomach for that? I sure as hell don't, but if you want to 'unmake' your failure, that's what you got to do. A man named Sam Green taught me that lesson."

Bergstrom smiled sadly. "We could do that, of course. But we are no more mass murderers than you."

"I'm not going to help you," said Jason.

"You will be very well compensated," said Plaut, and Bergstrom nodded. "Ten thousand pounds sterling. When have you seen that much money?"

"Go to hell."

A smile flickered across Bergstrom's lips and extinguished.

"Herr Thistledown, are you afraid?"

He paused only a heartbeat—not enough time for Jason to answer, even were he inclined to. "I don't mean that as a taunt. It is reasonable to be fearful, returning to such an awful circumstance. There is no shame in this room. But you are a man who has conquered fear. You did so when you flew those deadly contraptions in the war, high over the trenches where your brother . . . well not really your brother, you have no brother . . . but that young man you watched grow up . . . who was killed in those trenches. That was why you went to war, wasn't it? To make sure that he didn't perish. In order to protect him, you conquered fear."

Jason didn't have anything to say to that, because he had to admit that there was something to it. Tom Thorn was seventeen when he volunteered without a word to his parents. Jason probably wouldn't have done so himself, but for the dismay he saw in the Thorn family: Lawrence pretended the tears were proud but Jason knew the old man well enough by then to tell they were more the grieving kind.

"Here is the situation," said Bergstrom. "There are very few people who have been able to turn away from the organism. There is you, of course. There is Dr. Andrew Waggoner, and his wife, Anne. They, however, at present are living in France, in circumstances that would raise questions, should they disappear for a time. But no matter. More conveniently, there is one other—who by happenstance, is nearer, visiting a family who is well known to us."

Jason felt an old vertigo, as though he were balanced on the edge of a deep canyon and beginning to slip.

"Ruth Harper," said Plaut.

"We could have her here in a day," said Bergstrom.

Four

Jason had hauled heavier packs on harder roads. This one was quite light by comparison: a powerful set of binoculars and a Kodak camera, loaded, with five extra rolls of film; a first-aid kit with additional tape and gauze; tinned rations; a canteen with water purifying tablets; a rough wool blanket and a tarpaulin with rope and four stakes; and a hatchet and a box of matches. So he didn't get lost, there was a map folded into a leather folio, and a compass. Strapped on the outside was a long bayonet knife. That and the hatchet were it for weapons. They weren't going to trust him with a gun.

Jason hoisted his pack on his shoulder and looked at Aguillard as he spoke with the men at the checkpoint. There wasn't much there: just a little wooden shack, a dozen yards from the rutted roadway that was the only way to the pass. There were four of them that Jason could see, but of course there could be more. It looked like the shack had a couple of rooms to it, and there was an outdoor privy a fair distance off. So you could put more inside.

Didn't matter. Jason wasn't going to try anything; these Germans had rifles slung over their shoulders, and they stood in a way that put Jason to mind of certain things. Didn't matter that Bergstrom and Aguillard had put all their money on Jason making it in and out of there alive. These fellows would shoot Jason, if he played it wrong.

And if they didn't, then Aguillard's two friends waiting with the truck would see to it Jason didn't get far off the path.

Aguillard finished with them and came back to Jason. The men regarded them warily, and Jason felt it best not to look back.

"They will be expecting you back in no less than twenty-four hours," said Aguillard. "Do you understand?"

Jason nodded. Aguillard and Bergstrom had gone through the plan with him the previous evening at the farmhouse. He was to enter the valley on foot, following the road to a point marked on the map, where it was advisable to take a footpath along the ridge. From there, he would proceed along this route until a point on the ridge, also marked on his map, that would afford him a view of the mansion that had until recently been the residence of Bergstrom and home to the troop of children. He was to mark down observations in the notebook they'd supplied him, reconnoitering to mark the movement of individuals over the course of a day. They had shown him several photographs from that vantage point, taken by the last group of stormtroopers who had returned from the valley, three months ago. There was a structure they had a question about: it looked like a teepee that the plains Indians might have made back in America, but taller—a steeple of tree trunks braced against one another at an apex that seemed to climb as high as the third-storey windows of the chateau. What was it that they had constructed? What was its purpose? What changes, from the last photograph?

What were the children who inhabited that place up to? What clues might there be to the fate of the previous expeditions?

What sign, if any, of the organism—the Juke?

"When you have finished those tasks," Bergstrom had said, "return to the checkpoint. Dr. Aguillard will be there to interview you, and conduct an examination."

If Jason either returned too soon, or did not return within two days, Aguillard explained to him what would happen next.

"Ruth Harper is currently visiting with the Dietrich family at their estate at Brandenberg. She has been there for several weeks now, we have been informed. Our associates there have contrived a plan to remove her similar in effect to the one we employed to obtain your services."

"There will be no question about it," said Plaut then.

At the foot of the pass, Aguillard asked Jason again if he had any questions. Jason shook his head.

"You know," said Aguillard, "you are a remarkably incurious man, given what you are stepping into."

"Curiosity isn't what you'd call a survival trait," said Jason. "I'll take your photographs and some notes and bring them back, like you told me. Then I'll go do the next thing you ask, because I don't imagine you'll let me get back on Desrosiers' plane after just this one thing. Long as I don't see Miss Harper here, we're square on that. Far as the Juke's concerned . . .

you fools don't know a thing about it more than I figured out as a boy. Less maybe."

"Mr. Thistledown," began Aguillard, but Jason stopped him.

"I will see you when I get back I guess," said Jason, and started to turn. Aguillard stopped him with a hand on his shoulder.

"If you could bring back one more thing," said Aguillard, and pressed an object into Jason's hand. Jason looked down at what was there.

It was Aguillard's lighter and cigarette case.

"The case is a favourite of mine. Please, return it when you're done. You need not bring the cigarettes back. They are for you," he said, and regarded Jason with an odd half-smile. It faded, as Jason pocketed the case and told him to go to hell.

Jason wasn't about to show it to Aguillard, but he'd be a fool not to admit it to himself: he was terrified climbing the steepening slope to the pass. He did know more about the Juke than Bergstrom and his biologist friends did—at least in the ways that counted. As he got closer to where the thing nested, he'd start seeing things. Faeries and gnomes in the trees, terrible birds in the sky . . . Folks from his past that he hadn't made right with or others he missed sorely enough to make a fool of him. Once, the Juke had made him see his old dad, Jack Thistledown, the gunfighter and reprobate, and the ghost of his ma too, and all that had nearly undone him. Whose ghost would he see now? He worried it might be Tom Thorn, his face torn half off by a German rifleman's bullet, wondering why Jason hadn't seen him safe in the trenches like he'd promised—why Jason had fled so swiftly, for the cockpit of his Nieuport and the skies over Tom's head.

Or he might see Ruth Harper, still living. The Juke had shown him that once—Ruth's pretty face on the head of a tiny Juke, mouth filled with teeth thin and sharp as a pike fish's.

Terrifying enough. He was more terrified of how it would go for Ruth, if he didn't do this job right, and they sent her hiking up this pass. He'd last seen her barely back on her feet, climbing into the back of Lawrence Thorn's wagon along with Andrew Waggoner and Annie Rowe, on her way to the Canadian Pacific station in Cranbrook. The surgery had been successful—Andrew had managed to remove the parasite, and she had lived—but it surely hadn't made her well. All the blood she'd lost had left her ghost-white, her once-plump cheeks drawn, her much-thinned lips with an uncertain twitch. It had been a week before she'd been able to stand, and she'd still needed a cane to steady herself by the time she left. And though she spoke, her words came softly and her thoughts were still a-jumble.

And when her thoughts formed, the things she said . . .

Ruth must be better off now. But what would the Juke pull from the depths of her damaged soul?

It was just past ten when Jason left Aguillard and the others behind. The day was already shaping up to be hot: a low ripple of herringbone cloud to the east that would do nothing to cool the sun as it climbed, and the air was still. Tall evergreen trees lined the roadway from a distance and climbed the slopes, but near the edges was just low scrub, so no shade there either.

Jason didn't care. He hauled uphill at a quick march, and when he looked back, the checkpoint was already out of sight. He took it a bit slower for a while; the slope was steepening and there was no rush. By the map, the hike was barely three miles.

It was a long haul all the same, or it felt long. It might have been a full hour before Jason found a path leading up the ridge—amid a tangle of bushes and low grass as the mountain slopes grew steeper—and he wasn't sure it was the right path, but it led to a fall of colossal boulders, newly enough shattered that climbing them was possible with just hands and feet. Beyond that, Jason found himself on a broad ledge, in the shade of tall pine trees on a forest floor covered in layers of rust-coloured needles. Jason flung off his pack and sprawled on his back. He could feel his heart hammering in his chest and his breath was rasping in his throat.

He didn't sleep, he was sure of it. But when he got up again, a cool breeze touched his cheek, and the air in the mountain pass seemed almost seasonally different. He squinted at the sky. The clouds had drawn nearer one another—as a net, pulling tighter. He opened his canteen and took a fast swig, screwed it shut and gathered his legs beneath him. Once he had his pack back on and the needles brushed from his trousers, he was off again.

The ridge climbed higher and the trees grew nearer one another. Between branches, Jason could see more tree and rock on the far side of the pass, as the slope there grew steeper and so also nearer. As the branches thickened, that view vanished for a time, Jason felt as though he were in a dark tunnel on the hillside—just trunks to either side, the barest sliver of sky peeking through overtop. Branches from the trees to either side of him encroached on the path such that he was bending and ducking, sometimes pulling one aside so that it whipped back as he moved through. The smell of pine sap grew thick.

The path, such as it was, grew steeper and also narrower, and Jason worried that he'd missed a branching, and somehow found himself on a secondary path that was creeping higher up toward the peak. He stopped at a point and pulled the map from his pack. It was little help: the path along the ridge was marked in grease-pencil, cutting a route that seemed too regular and straight, to the spot where he might observe the chateau. He could well have diverged, and he wouldn't know.

Jason dithered for longer than he should have, then decided to retrace his steps and see if there mightn't have been another route that didn't seem to be climbing so high.

He made it some distance before the futility of this course struck him, and it occurred to him that the path might indeed climb quite high as the slopes steepened, only to descend again. He was about to turn and make his way back again up the slope when his breath caught in his throat, and he froze. The hairs on his forearms were rising, and his mouth was suddenly dry.

He felt certain he was being watched.

He half-unslung his pack and slid the bayonet from its strap, pulled the blade from its sheath, and re-shouldered the pack. He turned in a slow circle, letting his gaze touch every branch, every shadow. There was nothing to see, but the instinct remained, and Jason was willing to trust that instinct over his sight. In Eliada, the Jukes could keep themselves well-hidden if they wanted to. He'd seen one disguised as his pa; Jason could believe that one might just trick him into seeing it in the shape of a tree, or a rock, and Jason wouldn't know until the thing was upon him.

Jason worked his tongue back and forth to get a spit going, then swallowed it. He dug into his pocket and pulled out the lighter, pulled a cigarette from the case and clamped it between his lips, and lit it. He drew deep, intending three more puffs before touching it to his neck for the familiar agony. He ended up finishing it, and grinding it under his boot.

A cigarette in the neck wasn't going to work anymore. He'd known it in his gut before he figured it out. He'd learned through hard experience that he couldn't rely on pain to which he'd become accustomed. In a month, or maybe even a couple of weeks, Jason could quiet himself with that trick again. If he were only facing German biplanes . . . He regarded the blade of the bayonet, and trembling a little, touched it to the palm of his hand. It was sharp, and it stung with the promise of liberating agony.

Jason peered around him, shivering now, as sweat evaporated from his brow, leaving him cold.

He might see what was around him, but with a sliced hand, he'd be no good for climbing. And whether higher up or back down, he would need to.

He couldn't keep relying on pain. Not every time he flinched. Before long, he'd whittle himself down to nothing.

"All right," he said aloud, and returned the bayonet to its sheath. More slowly this time, he started back up the path he'd already cut.

Behind Jason, nothing stirred.

It was good Jason spared his hand, because there was another climb before the ridge levelled out: this time, up narrow steps in the mountainside that were just a little too irregular to have been cut there by anyone. The trees spread farther up and down the slope at the ridge's height, and when it levelled out finally, Jason sat exposed on a wide ledge of a cliff face.

The valley fell away below him and stretched to the limits of his sight. Most of what he saw was treetops, first conifers as he'd seen along the pass, and further, a row-planted wood that Jason took to be orchards. The bowl of the valley seemed miles distant and was made of deep green meadow for a time, before the land dipped into a dark fold that Jason guessed to be the stream that cut through its middle. And the land rose again beyond it, from meadow to forest to slopes of mountains that climbed higher. There was sign of tillage, but from where he stood, Jason could see no structures—not even those circles of fencing that, he reminded himself, were made to contain the Juke. He was not yet in position to see the chateau, and whatever structures had been built up around it since the last German expedition, months ago. What might they've built there in that time, Juke-inspired?

The ridgeway continued further, creeping back and around an outcrop of rock that fell off the mountainside like a splinter. It seemed to be leading back down, at least somewhat, toward the valley. He drew a breath of the sweet and perfect mountain air—then squeezed his wound until the scent soured.

It shouldn't be far now.

The perch overlooking the chateau was well-hidden, but easy to spot from the path, by the remains of the Germans' camp. There was a swath of canvas, half-buried in pine needles and dirt, and not far from there three packs like Jason's, but emptied, contents strewn. Among the kit and the blankets, Jason spied a Luger automatic pistol. It was filthy, but had somehow avoided rust. Jason lifted it and confirmed that it was still loaded. He made certain the safety was set, and without another thought slipped it into his jacket pocket.

He rummaged a little more among the detritus, but found little else that he didn't already have, clean and packed in the sack on his shoulder.

He set that sack down then, in the shade of a low shrub, opened it, and removed the binoculars and the Kodak and the notepad. He went to work.

TEEPEE GONE.

Jason didn't think he'd forget to tell that when he returned, but he marked it down anyhow. There was no sign of the structure that had aroused such curiosity in his captors. The plot of ground where it had sat was covered in long grass, with spaces in it that may have accounted for its footings, but Jason had no clear view from this distance and height, even with the binoculars, and the depressions didn't seem to him to be properly placed to account for it. So he amended his note:

NO SIGN OF TEEPEE.

Jason set down the notepad and got the Kodak camera, and held it to his eye and took a picture. Then he set the camera down and picked up the binoculars. He scanned across the back of the chateau; over leaded-glass windows that reflected back the hillside behind them, up the single turret tower that was what made that mansion into a chateau, in some fellow's mind; down a drainpipe from the eaves that emptied into a stone cistern at the far corner; past a stout wooden door at the top of a short stone stairway that Jason guessed might lead into a kitchen. He paused there for a moment and scanned back, wondering if he might not have seen movement of someone near the cistern, but if he had, the person was gone.

He pulled the binoculars away from his eyes and let them dangle over his knee, as he sat back on the ground, and considered the structure as a whole. It was a big house all right, three floors and an attic, formed of whitewashed panels and dark wooden beams, in what Jason supposed to be the Bavarian style. Two tall stone chimneys sat at either end of the building, without a hint of smoke emerging from either of them.

Jason described all this in his notes, as he thought he was supposed to do, and wound the film in the camera ahead one more frame—and sat perched on the ridgetop that way for a time, looking down the slope. How long would he do so? Until he saw some movement, perhaps? He didn't think that Aguillard would be satisfied if he returned now, with a photograph of a quiet chateau and a cleared-up yard . . . particularly if he did so just a few hours after he'd set out.

Jason lined up another photograph through the viewfinder, this time focussing on the shingling of the villa's steep roof. He clicked the shutter, and lowered the camera to wind the film another frame, and then frowned, and lifted it again, and looked again through the viewfinder, and swore to himself.

There, next to the nearest chimney, were the tops of six great trunks, leaned and lashed together to form an apex of a narrow pyramid.

Jason lowered the camera and looked with his own eyes and swore out loud.

There it was, just as it appeared in the photo they'd shown him. The teepee was right there—stripped of furs—huge tree trunks, felled and propped up against one another in the grasses behind this chateau, as it must have been all along.

Jason stood up and looked back at the cistern, on the opposite side of the house. Had he seen something moving there again? He didn't know—and on a level knew that he couldn't tell. The camera slipped from his grip and landed with a disturbing cracking sound on the rocky ground.

He was in the presence of a Juke . . . the drug of that thing was working through him, making him see things that weren't there . . . or miss things that were.

Nothing moved by the cistern, but as Jason looked back along the building he saw that the back door to the kitchen now stood swinging on its hinges.

Had it been open before? Maybe it had. Maybe Jason had missed that just as he'd missed the giant structure. He dug his thumb into the burn on his neck, until the pain brought tears to his eyes, which he would not allow to look away from the house, the door, the thing alongside it. None of it faded, as it might if it were some hallucination—if it were a concoction of the Juke here, and that led Jason to conclude that the things he'd seen here before, the things he hadn't seen . . . those were the illusion. This was what was real.

He started to a sharp retort—coming from behind him, again and again.

It was clapping. Hands clapping.

Five

The fellow behind Jason was taller than he by nearly a head, and wider across the shoulder by a hand or more. Black hair that had grown too long hung in a curling shock over one eye; the other, blue as the sky, jittered up and down Jason, marking him. His beard was young, maybe a week's worth, and was lighter than his hair and his single eyebrow. His teeth were straight and white and grinning in the way of a picked-clean skull.

He wore no shirt, but his trousers were held up by suspenders slung tight over a scarred chest covered in bestial fur.

Jason's hand strayed into his pocket and his fingers closed around the handle of the Luger. The giant of a man looked at Jason's hand in the pocket and then his face and laughed and shook his head. With surprising speed, reached for Jason's pack—with its map and compass, its hatchet and its bayonet—and lifted the whole thing to one shoulder.

"Put it down," said Jason in German.

The man tilted his head, as though he hadn't understood. *All right*, thought Jason to himself. He slid the weapon from the coat pocket and lifted it to train it on the giant. He didn't quite get it into firing position before he worked it out—that he wasn't holding a Luger at all. He was clutching a piece of kindling—a dry piece of pine tree, bent a little bit like a pistol might be, like a child might imagine a pistol might be.

He tossed it away—to the bare ground, where the remnants of a camp might still be found, but far scanter than he had seen: no blankets, no kit, no sack.

Jason half imagined that the whole thing behind him—the teepee, the house, the whole valley—might just have been another hallucination, a fever dream.

"What is that, little brother?"

The man reached toward Jason, and with one immense hand grasped at

Jason's face. Jason pulled back just far enough that the fingers closed an inch from the top of his nose. He frowned, and grabbed again, and this time had hold of Jason's jaw, squeezing hard enough to force Jason's mouth open.

Jason grabbed his forearm, tried to pull it away, but it was no good. He was too strong, and with a turn of his wrist, forced Jason's head to one side. The pack dropped to the ground beside him as he brought his other hand up, and a finger to Jason's throat, as he studied it.

"Burns," he said, and pressed his finger into the tender flesh beneath Jason's jaw. The pressure was only slight, but it sent spikes of pain deep, through the inside of his ear. Jason jerked hard enough to break the hold, and also pull muscles in his jaw to create a new kind of pain.

The man's face did not alter in Jason's brief agony—as it would have, if this were a Juke illusion. He was solidly real. Jason's sudden movement had taken him by surprise, and he stumbled back, foot tangled in the strap of Jason's pack. Jason ducked and moved behind him, grabbed hold of the other strap, and yanked hard enough to knock him to the ground . . . as well, with enough force to tear at the cut he'd made on his arm. Jason howled, at the same time as the man shouted at the impact of his shoulder on the rock.

Jason kept going, half-running toward the steep slope of the ridge here, clutching the pack to his chest as he first ran and then tumbled, then righted himself and finally found himself at the base—at the rear of the chateau—which was no longer deserted.

A woman, slender and pale, stood in the kitchen doorway, her blonde hair tangling in thick curls over her naked shoulders, watching him as he righted himself and looked back at her. It wasn't only her shoulders that were naked. She wore shoes, and socks that had bunched at her ankles, but that was all.

She smiled a little tentatively, as Jason looked away, and up the slope to its empty summit. Was the man standing there? Was it the stump of a tree? Jason turned the pack over so he might withdraw the bayonet.

The woman must have moved very swiftly, for it seemed just an instant later that he felt her hand on his shoulder.

"Allons-y," she whispered, and tugged gently at his shirt. She pointed to the half-open doorway to the chateau. *"Rapidement."*

They hurried through the door at the back of the chateau and through a short hallway into a long room that might have at one point been a dining hall, but was now empty. She stopped in a square of light from one of the three windows along the wall.

Her body had a form that made Jason think of an animal. There was no softness to it, nothing pampered . . . a certain wary readiness. Her hips were narrow and muscular, as were her thighs, covered in downy fuzz that caught the sunlight like flecks of gold. Her pubic hair was darker, as was the hair that cascaded down her shoulders and half-covered the ropy tendons in her slender throat. She had small breasts that clung to her ribs like emptied change purses. Her face seemed deflated too, her eyes deep and sad over sharp cheekbones and jaw—incongruously voluptuous lips set in what might've been a permanent sulk. She had a smell that reminded Jason of the trenches.

There were high-backed dining chairs arrayed along the wall and she motioned for Jason to sit down. Jason didn't want to, but he did set his pack down on one. He hung onto the bayonet, but he didn't hold it in a way that'd frighten the woman.

"Who are you?" Jason asked in French.

She told him to call her Catherine. *"I am not certain it is my true name,"* she said, *"but it will simplify matters to say so."*

"How can you not be certain?" asked Jason. *"Of your own name?"*

She half-smiled and tapped her forehead. *"I forget many things,"* she said. *"When I came here the doctor tried many names to call me, and Catherine . . . it seemed to strike a chord, you know?"*

So the woman—Catherine—was an amnesiac? *All right*, Jason thought. When he was in hospital in England during the war, he'd met more than one fellow who couldn't recall his name, and probably one or two who weren't lying about it.

"And what about your name?"

"Jason," he said.

"You sound more certain than I," she said, and showed a glimpse of a smile.

They regarded one another in the uneven light of this room. Catherine looked at Jason steadily—something Jason couldn't reciprocate. He found his eyes flitting to the exits—there were two of them—and the windows, which looked out on a view that between trees led down slope, toward the mouth of the pass.

She stepped nearer, moving into shadow as she did so.

"It doesn't matter," she said. *"We are all reborn here, no?"*

"Of course—*bien sûr*," said Jason, remembering himself. "Why—*pourquoi—why do you say reborn?*" Catherine merely smiled, as though Jason should know full well why she said that. But Jason's mind was racing.

He did have a pretty good idea why she'd said reborn: she was under the influence, as were so many at Eliada in the end, of the Juke. She was looking at him and all around—likely seeing cherubs in those shafts of light, and when she looked outside those windows, Jason bet she saw Elysian fields. At the back of her ear, she'd be hearing songs that no one else did, and while those songs might've come from nowhere better than her own imagination—she would understand them as the clarion voice of God. Of a God. Telling her what to do next . . .

It might also be telling her what to see. Was she even aware of her own nakedness? Jason wouldn't have been surprised to hear that she thought herself to be fully clothed, in a gown . . . to think that this empty dining hall was filled with chirping fairies, tables covered in rich foods. Who knew what she saw even when she looked at Jason. She was inhabiting a lie of unimaginable scope.

And at that, Jason made up his mind: he, at least, wasn't going to add to those lies. There was no point.

"Listen, Catherine—*écoutez. I am here to look in on this place. Dr. Bergstrom and the Germans who used to be in charge here want to know what is going on. They asked me just to take some photographs and look at comings and goings. I met a fellow in the mountains. . . .*"

"We are in the mountains now. What fellow?"

"Very tall and strong. He was only half-naked."

"Only half." Catherine smiled. "He look in you?" she said, now in English.

"I guess he did," said Jason, and when Catherine looked puzzled, he just nodded. "Your English is as good as my French, I see."

Her grin widened and she measured a tiny invisible thing between thumb and forefinger. "A little better." She extended her hand so that he might take it. When she spoke again, she was back to French. *"They do not speak English much here so I do not practise. You have met Orlok. Better to stay indoors for the afternoon. Come."*

It was likely that the chateau here in the valley had been built by the same hands that made the farmhouse where Bergstrom and Aguillard were holed up. But the money was all in here. Catherine led him deeper inside, along a tall, wood-trimmed corridor flanked by carved doors, lit by candles set into iron wall-brackets. Jason tried to imagine the fellow that might live here, and could not help but think of Garrison Harper—the long dead lumber baron of Eliada—and his house there. When Jason walked those halls he was still a boy, and they'd seemed like a magical castle. Harper might have felt comfortable in this place, but he'd be outclassed.

"How is Dr. Bergstrom?" asked Catherine as they made their way.

"He's nervous," said Jason. "This thing got bigger than he wished, I think. He's been sending men in to see how big a mess he made. You see those men?"

"Men? Oh yes. Some men."

"Are they here?"

"No."

"You know where they are?"

They stopped beneath an archway, which led into a larger room with tall windows and whitewashed walls. Sunlight flooded across thick wooden floorboards, descending in columns through the dusty air. Jason could hear conversation coming from there. Catherine put a finger to her lips, and touched his chest. Jason took that to mean that he should keep quiet and stay put, so he nodded as she strode into the room.

As she did, a shadow appeared on the floor, and Catherine turned to it. She indicated back to where Jason was, whispered something that might have been in German. The shadow answered back, and she beckoned Jason come forward.

He stepped into a great hall. A staircase swept up from either side of the passageway, and the ceiling rose more than twenty feet above their heads. The conversation stopped as he emerged, and Jason could not see the source of the shadow either, which had vanished itself. Furniture was scattered about—as though it had just been delivered, but not arranged. There were three wing-backed chairs, facing away from one another, a long dark wooden table near tall doors that likely opened out of doors . . . a chaise longue, under one of the windows. Someone was reclined on it, knees tucked forward, covered in what looked like a blanket, or maybe a rug.

Jason peered up the stairs. Maybe the conversation had been coming from up there? There was a gallery at the top, and it was dark, so maybe . . .

"Hello."

The figure on the chaise longue had sat up and was getting to his feet—the blanket still wrapped over his shoulders.

"Markus!" called Catherine, and in German: *"Another has come to look at us!"*

Markus stood, a little unsteadily. He was a small man, maybe a head shorter than Jason, and although difficult to tell under the blanket, he seemed to Jason to be quite frail. Certainly, there was a timidity to the way he moved and held himself. He had a thin beard, and his hair, receding from his brow, hung long to his shoulders.

"Hello," said Jason. *"I do not want to make trouble."*

"You are not wearing a uniform," Markus observed. *"Not as the others did. You sound foreign."*

"He is English," said Catherine, and Jason nodded. That was close enough.

"What have you got in that pack?"

"Just my kit," said Jason.

"Food? Medicine?"

Jason nodded.

Markus stepped gingerly around the table and past the chairs. As he moved, Jason could see that he was just as naked as Catherine under the blanket. He was also thin, to a degree that seemed evidence of starvation. Jason set the pack down on the floor and opened it up.

"What do you need?" he asked. *"Food?"*

"Let me see," said Markus and knelt beside Jason to examine the pack. Jason caught a whiff from him—a similar smell to the one that Catherine gave off.

Jason reached in to help and pulled out the pack of rations—little tins of meat. Markus took one of them and studied it, squinting at the stamp on its lid. He didn't open it.

"Is that all there is?" asked Markus.

Jason nodded. *"I am not to be here for very long, so there is not much food. Do you not have food here?"*

"Very little," said Catherine. *"What there is . . ."*

"It is spoken for," said Markus.

"You have to feed it, right? The—"

"There are many hungry mouths," said Markus, interrupting.

Jason didn't need to finish his question: he thought he understood. If these folk were caring for a Juke, then all the edibles would be going there, to feed the beast as it grew larger and more voracious—while they happily starved near to death. Jason could smell it on him, now: not the battlefield, but a smell like apples, stale wine.

"Well, you both eat these," said Jason. *"I am not hungry."*

He pulled open the tops of two cans of meat, one for Markus and one for Catherine. They both exchanged a look and took the tins. Catherine sniffed at hers, but Markus was less timid; he reached in with two fingers and scooped out the awful grey-pink meat, and shoved it into his mouth. Catherine saw what he did and mimicked it. As Markus set into his food, the blanket slipped off him immodestly, and he crouched naked on the floor.

Jason could not look away.

Markus was emaciated—horrifically so. His shoulders were bones with scarcely more than skin covering them—his arms slender as tree branches—his back and flanks a xylophone of ribs. Jason could barely credit that the man was alive, except by the noisy slurping and gulping as he dug into the tin of meat. Catherine was thin, possibly suffering from similar privations—but not like this one. Markus was barely human.

Enough, he thought, and moved away to the base of the stairs that swung up in a grand curve to the gallery up high. There was a crest, presumably a family crest, affixed to the place where they met overtop the archway through which Jason had come. The crest showed two mythical beasts—lions with wings, and knights' helmets in place of their heads, astride what looked like a serpent, and holding something between them . . . a circular object, maybe meant to be a sphere. Maybe meant to be the sun? The moon? The world itself?

He couldn't really tell what it was, because it had been defaced. In the middle of the circle, someone had taken a knife or a chisel and carved what looked to Jason like a crude Nazi Party swastika.

Jason slipped Aguillard's cigarette case from his pocket, opened it and pulled one out between his teeth. He lit it with a flick. The smell of the tobacco blunted the stink of this place, and as Jason drew the smoke into his lungs he thought that more smoke might be better: putting the torch to this house would be a cleansing act—as good as dropping the Cave Germ amid the men and women made fools by the Juke in Eliada.

"Do not wander far."

Jason turned. Markus was standing now, smiling horribly through the grease that smeared his chin. His blanket was forgotten on the floor behind him, empty tin still clutched in one hand.

Jason shrugged and pointed at the coat of arms.

"I was just admiring the handiwork."

Markus looked and nodded, then turned his gaze back to Jason.

"The swastika," he said. *"It used to be everywhere here. On big banners hung from balconies! Now it is just bits of graffiti here and there."*

Markus drew closer to Jason. The smell of pork fat was mingling with Markus's own particular stink. Jason took a couple of steps back up the stairs, and Markus motioned no with a finger, shook his head. The tin clattered to the floor and he raised his other hand, made a beckoning motion.

Jason backed up two more steps, and held up his hand.

"Could you keep your distance please?"

Markus's smile grew. He didn't look away. But he stood his ground.

"Could you—could you cover yourself up please?"

Markus beckoned again. *"Give me a cigarette."*

"Then you'll . . ."

"Cover myself, yes."

Jason obliged and, once Markus had retrieved his blanket, lit the cigarette for him and one for Catherine too.

"These are great luxuries," said Markus. *"I have not enjoyed tobacco for . . . years now. It is not considered healthful by some."*

"That is a lie," said Catherine as she exhaled a plume of smoke.

Markus glanced at her and back at Jason. His smile was not entirely kind.

"I was not attempting to molest you," he said to Jason. *"You feared that I was, didn't you? No need to answer. You feared so."* He looked at the cigarette held between the bones of his fingers.

"You are nothing to fear," Catherine said to Markus, and then she spoke to Jason, in English: "No worry for you. Markus belongs to Orlok."

"Does he now?"

"As do I."

"I see."

"So you see there is nothing to fear from either of us."

Jason took his cigarette from between his lips and regarded the flaming tip of it, and looked from there into Catherine's glittering eyes, and then

Markus's, who had never looked away from him, and to the high, bright windows behind them.

"Because you belong to Orlok too," continued Catherine. "He marked you also. Now we are three."

Jason turned the cigarette around, and jammed its tip into his throat until the sunlight separated and spread into wings, feathered with beams of fire. Where they intersected, stood the man from the high ground—who'd called Jason *little brother*. . . .

The wings seemed to fold as he stepped forward, into the shadow of the room.

It was as though Jason were the only one of the three who registered his presence. Orlok had, since their encounter on the mountain, pulled on a coat, but it barely fit over his huge shoulders. He moved quietly for one so large, stepped lightly between Catherine and Markus, his hands brushing each of their shoulders in a way such as might be expected to gain their attention. Jason kept the cigarette at his throat. The big man, Orlok, held his gaze as he approached closer, then broke it as he climbed past him on the stairs.

Jason watched him climb a few steps higher, and then turn, and with one enormous hand beckon Jason to follow him, into the dark upper storeys of the chateau. Jason shook his head no.

"What do you mean?" asked Markus, in what sounded like genuine confusion, but Catherine seemed to understand. She looked up at Orlok, and at Jason. Was that terror in her eyes?

"Ah," said Markus, and on the stairs, Orlok smiled.

"All of you then," he said. "Come."

The three of them climbed the stairs, past the defiled coat of arms. Orlok led them through a room with windows covered in gauzy, reddish curtains, into another one furnished with dark wooden chairs and a long table in front of a huge stone hearth. Then to another staircase and finally to a bright room with tall windows that opened onto a balcony that judging from the light that filtered through the thick green tangle of branches faced the southwest.

The room was nearly empty of furniture but for one piece, against the northeastern wall: a Victrola, in a tall wooden cabinet. Orlok looked at it and then at Markus, and he hurried there and lifted the lid.

Orlok gestured with a nod, a thrust of his chin, and Markus reported: *"The song is called 'In a Small Beach Basket.'"*

"Well what are you waiting for?"

Markus turned the phonograph crank, and delicately lowered the needle. It was a summertime song, a foxtrot, very gay. Orlok smiled and his eyes narrowed, and he let one great hand sway in front of him as a conductor. Markus adjusted the volume, as Orlok drifted toward the balcony, his hips swaying in a little dance. He beckoned them to follow him, and Jason did.

Jason thought that stepping outside would quiet the music, that it would diffuse in the open air, but the opposite seemed to happen; the forest seemed to deepen it, enrich it. Was it a trick of the acoustics in that room? The sound bouncing around in that big space and coming out here magnified? More real?

Markus and Catherine joined them on the balcony. They too were swaying in time to the rhythm of "In a Small Beach Basket." Catherine stepped back, took Jason's arm and drew him forward.

You belong to Orlok too.

Little brother.

"No, no," said Jason. He took her hand from his arm and stepped back.

Jason did not belong to Orlok, would not belong to Orlok. What he might belong to, if he stayed any longer, was the Juke—he might soon start hearing its song through the trees, not this German music-hall ditty—and follow along like the rest of those who did so. He would not allow that to happen. He would not.

It wasn't to be a fight, though. Catherine shrugged, and clasped her hands above her head, and swayed. Orlok meantime was paying attention to Markus, who did not resist as Orlok placed a huge hand at the back of his neck, which he seemed to massage as he gently danced.

The music swelled with a final flourish of horns, and from inside, the needle clicked and hissed, signalling the end of the record. But the music didn't stop.

It rose up from the hills, from the trees—no horns, no clarinets . . . no piano. But a choir of voices, high and sweet that carried through the valley. Jason stepped to the edge of the balcony, but he saw only treetops.

Orlok swept his free hand in front of him, his fingers spread and trembling at the height of it. The song continued.

It was definitely coming from the woods, but Jason couldn't see anything down there. He turned to Catherine, intending to ask after it. But her eyes were shut. Markus, meanwhile, struggled weakly in Orlok's grip as he was pulled nearer. And the song grew richer still.

You belong to Orlok too, they'd said. He looked over the balcony straight down, did a quick calculation, and made up his mind.

Orlok might have sensed it. He looked up from Markus, and caught Jason's eye, and commanded: *"Come here, little brother."*

"No," Jason whispered. And without another thought, he lifted a leg over the low balcony railing, swung his other over, and clung to the railing for only a second before he dropped.

Jason landed well. The ground rose high on the foundations at this part of the chateau, and it was grassy enough, and although the drop might have been enough to break a bone, Jason prepared himself and tucked, rolled down the slope of it a few yards before scrambling to his feet and running. He held close to the wall, so he could stay out of sight of the giant Orlok, but far enough that he could move. He needed to be away, and now: he had been a fool to think that he could spend any time in the presence of a Juke before its song overtook him and he lost himself. The song was everywhere now—that idiotic song, with a thousand voices.

Jason clapped his hands over his ears, made fists and stuffed his forefingers in. He didn't expect that to have any effect . . . that the music would have moved inside his skull, and he'd hear it for as long as it played . . . louder . . . but it softened, and quieted, just as real music might. This was no fever dream.

He stumbled at the corner of the stonework, and rounded it. Here, the trees were closer to the foundations, pale thin spruce conifers. They nearly rode up the stonework, and Jason felt the soft branches whip at his face and shoulders as he hurried through, finally using his hands to clear them and letting the music in again. This suited Jason: having the foundation between him and the phonograph, there was nothing now but the voices. Alone, they seemed to Jason somehow sweeter—almost guileless.

Some seemed quite near, and as Jason continued he saw that some were very near indeed. Through gaps in the branches, Jason thought he could them. A flash of narrow, pale buttock, there for only an instant then gone. In a patch of sunlight, the long yellow hair of a girl, draping over sun-reddened breasts . . .

Ahead of him, Jason saw two boys—not boys, young men—in a clearing. They were well-muscled, light brown hair hanging to their shoulders. One was piggyback the other, who ran and stumbled in a small circle around the edge of the clearing. The rider was the only one singing—his head thrown back, as though he sang to the sky. Both were as naked as Markus and Catherine, and the sight of them brought Jason up short.

Before Jason could make sense of the scene, the horse-boy spotted him. His eyes widened, and he took off into the woods.

When Jason started moving again, he did so at a slower pace. As he stepped into the clearing, he saw the reason for it: there was a doorway cut into the stone, low, with a thick black-boarded iron-bound door blocking it. Leading from that was a well-worn foot path that led along a trail through the trees. Peering down there, Jason could see the buttocks of the young men, retreating toward a ridge of rock and perhaps a wider clearing.

Or something of a clearing: in place of the trees, there grew human forms—no, not forms, but humans—standing at attention, nude, faces turned toward the hot sunlight, sprouting . . . in great enough number that at a point, the substance of the forest seemed made of ruddy, sunburnt flesh.

Were some of them stepping nearer? As Jason stared, it seemed they were, slowly trampling saplings at the woods' edge. Jason stepped back, reaching for the wall, the door, but only grasped a sapling himself, and as he looked around saw that it was not them who'd come closer but he who'd walked farther: the foundations, that doorway, were a dozen yards back, visible through the arching branches over the trampled path. In the clearing, he saw a naked girl and a tall, tall boy step into view. They were covered in pine needles and soil, and grinned at him as they saw him looking. They held hands, and each reached out to take hold of branches at either side of the path. No, they were not branches; these were hands too, belonging to two nude boys—one barrel-chested with dark brown hair and another also tall, his hair shaven. The boys might have been behind trees, or hidden in them, or crouched down. . . .

But wasn't the opening to the house wider now? The sunlight brighter there as they moved?

Jason felt sweat burn away as that sunlight struck his forehead, and he realized: when the boys appeared, two trees had vanished. Had he mistaken them for trees?

"Mama," whispered Jason.

The sky overhead had no cloud, and the sun was cussed hot on Jason's skin as shade vanished by the branch. It was so bright that Jason shut his eyes, as his fingers found his wounds, and pressed them hard. The pain was like a splash of cool water, and Jason applied more of them in succession: jab! and jab! and jab!

And two more, until his finger was slick with sweat and blood, the pain was so awful he could barely stand. The ground seemed weak underneath him, and for a moment, he imagined it were cloud on which he stood—as if he were walking outside his plane, on that bounty of cloud.

He opened his eyes, to see how that was.

There was no cloud, below or above. He stood on a bare slope, looking down into the valley.

He was not in a forest. Not in a cloud . . . He stood in the midst of a vast throng.

There were more than a hundred of them. They were young, and slender, and still muscular. Most were young men. But there were girls too, as young and shapely as the men. The house was farther off than Jason remembered it being—maybe two or three dozen yards away, near the edge of the hillside.

And there was something else.

The teepee . . . that structure, that Jason had seen in photographs but not in fact—it stood, high on the slope.

Hanging from the apex of the structure was a thing that first looked like a collection of ragged sails. But it was bloody in parts, with sticklike limbs emerging from its middle, broken branches or the legs of a great spider. Other parts dangled like lengths of intestine, drooping nearly as far as the ground, ending in things that looked like nothing so much as mouths. Further up, there was a form like the torso of a man emaciated by starvation.

Although Jason had never seen one in person, he remembered what it was from Dr. Waggoner's explanations, those years ago at the Thorn farm.

"It is mouths. All mouths. And always hungry . . . That, in the end, I think, is all the Juke is—all any of us are. Organic machines for eating, and . . . and copulating . . . and eating some more. That is Man. That is God."

And this thing was all of that. But unlike the God that Andrew Waggoner saw, before he fled Eliada, borne in the icy currents of the Kootenay, but hours ahead of Jason and Ruth . . .

This one was dead.

PART II

The Decameron System

One

The Juke was a tiny thing.

Dr. Andrew Waggoner slipped it into the only clean Mason jar that Thorn had at hand and it fit with room to spare. Later, he would measure it and record it being just shy of two inches long—three-quarters of an inch wide.

He might have even kept it alive in the jar to let it grow a little larger. It was squirming in the forceps as he dropped it into the jar, and if he were to collect some of the blood and amniotic fluid that he'd spilled during the procedure . . . draped a layer of cheesecloth over the top of that jar and sealed it all in . . . the thing might've lived, and grown a little, and he might have had more samples, at least . . . more to finally work with.

But he didn't. He knew then a little of what those things could do when they got bigger—they had nearly taken him—so he put the whole top on and screwed it tight and let the thing suffocate. He might have crushed it too . . . he certainly wanted to, and Annie had thought it an excellent idea. But he wanted it in the jar. The creature he'd pulled from Ruth was too dangerous. He knew from recent experience that these things had teeth and they bit deep with them. This one, he'd later learn, had teeth comparable to a lamprey, ringing a mouth made mostly of very dense cartilage.

One of those only a little larger had bit his hand a few days back, and that hand still wasn't right. But next to the other things it could do, those filthy little teeth were the least of a man's worry. It wasn't just the teeth. It was the damn religion.

"Sure that's the only one?" said Jason Thistledown when he peered at the thing through the late afternoon sunlight that streamed in through the bunkhouse window.

Andrew shook his head. "The only thing I'm sure of is that Miss Harper is still breathing, and not bleeding."

"Can you go in again if there's another? No," said Jason, taking the answer from the expression on Andrew's face. "Too much blood."

There wasn't too much blood spilled, not by Andrew's reckoning, but Jason was right. Ruth was in no shape to undergo a second surgery any time very soon.

This was just the second time Andrew had attempted this procedure on a woman. The first was under open sky, in the middle of a filthy village square, when Andrew's broken wrist was worse than it was . . . and when Andrew had no notion of how the Juke and the unlucky woman who served at its host would respond to the knife. Poor, simple Lou-Ellen Tavish had died so that Andrew Waggoner might have some clue as to what he was up against . . . so that wealthy, bright young Ruth Harper might live.

Andrew was bright enough to know the hard lessons of Lou-Ellen Tavish's failed abortion were far from the only reason Ruth Harper was breathing now. There were other factors at play.

He had waited to perform the operation until he could find a clean room with good light, and this bunkhouse building, with its well-swept floor boards and high south-facing windows, was that. His hand was better. He had some time to think.

But even at that, the bunkhouse was no operating theatre, his hand was by no means restored, and there was never time to think enough. There would have been no hope at all, then, but for Ruth's major advantage—her great stroke of luck. This time, Andrew was not alone. Annie Rowe—cool-headed, competent, and nimble—was at his side. And so, Ruth lived.

"I guess we'll have to pray—*hope*, then," said Jason, correcting himself.

Andrew thought he caught something in the boy's tone, something low and insinuating that he didn't care for—but he let it pass, then. They had been through a hard time. The Thorns had fed them, but the hunger still haunted their bellies, their bones. As did the damn little Juke.

"Hope is good," said Annie. "You sit by her side awhile, Jason. Let her know you're there."

Ruth was laid out at the far end of the bunkhouse, half hidden by a reddened sheet that Annie had draped on a clothesline. From where Andrew and Jason stood, only her legs were visible—one of them with fresh bandages, covering the wound left where Annie had dug out a bullet, back at the riverside. Another sheet came down just below her knees like bloody skirts.

"Go on," Andrew said as he saw Jason hesitating. "She's asleep now. She can see you when she wakes and that will be good for her. You can tell her how fine she'll be."

Jason gave Andrew a rueful look that said he wasn't sure, but squared his shoulders and nodded. "Don't know why I'm so squeamish," he said, "after everything else."

"Nothing to be squeamish about," said Annie, and took Jason's hand to lead him around the curtain. The way he tiptoed, Andrew thought, it was as though he were going to see a corpse, and not his lady-love on the clear side of calamity.

Andrew looked at his own hands. He'd washed them clear of blood but his sleeves, rolled up past the elbow, were still red with it. The fingers of his right hand were swollen from the exertion, and his wrist and elbow ached in their splints. He inspected them again for little cuts or even nicks that might spell infection, but there were none: he'd been careful, and done most of his work with forceps and speculum. He hoped—yes, hope was the word, not pray, not again—that her uterus might heal well from the indignity. The fingers of his left hand—undamaged, unswollen—began to tremble as he worried about this, in a way they hadn't after Lou-Ellen Tavish perished. That, at least, had been certain: Lou-Ellen was dead, bled out, finished. The uncertainty, with Ruth Harper behind that sheet . . . Ruth, the girl who might yet die from any number of causes . . . it had bedevilled him.

Yet, she breathed—as Jason whispered to her, as Annie checked her for fever and blotted her forehead with damp washcloth, as Andrew examined her again as the sunlight crept away from the window and the afternoon waned . . . she breathed.

What remained of the Juke twenty years later was tinier still, withered in formaldehyde in the same jar—usually kept safe in the cellar room in the Waggoner household, on a shelf where the previous owners had kept their wine.

This night, September 21, 1931, the Juke was with Waggoner—in the middle of a table on the quieter upper rooms of the Liberty American Bar and Restaurant, bearing a prodigious collection of wine bottles, drawn (as was customary for the Autumn gathering) from its owner Bobby Grady's much better-stocked cellar below.

Around the table sat all the members of the *Société* who had been able to attend: only three of them. William Lewis was from Philadelphia, where he practised medicine and continued groundbreaking work on human mutation. He was a slender man, blessed with a certain agelessness, belied only by his receding hairline and white-flecked moustache. Manfred Kurtzweiller, the third member in attendance, had been the one to suggest Lewis for membership. His practice was in Vienna, where he specialized in gynecological medicine, but took a greater interest in the young biological field of parasitology. These days, most of his research went unpublished.

And of course, there was Andrew Waggoner: the chair and chief physician of the Vire Sanatorium, and also founding Chairman of the *Société*. He, who brought the Juke—who had come nearer than any of them to the organism's insidious nature.

They were getting older, the men of the *Société*, and so many of their seats were empty: Dr. Hebert, Dr. Johannsen . . . and the chair usually held by old Giorgio Molinare, who had stopped getting older rather definitively a month past.

Although Molinare was not entirely gone. He had left them his legacy: young Dominic Villart. He had been Molinare's student, and also assistant, taking care of the more strenuous tasks in the professor's inquiries on behalf of the *Société*. This night, he would become a member.

For the moment, Dominic perched where he always sat at these meetings, on the sill of one of the tall windows that overlooked *rue Delambre*. Sometimes there would be music coming up from the street, and Molinare had always complained that Dominic preferred that to the substance of their inquiries. But in a letter conveyed from his deathbed, Molinare had made clear he wished Dominic and none other to continue his work with the *Société*.

"Before we go further," said Andrew, "we should formalize the matter of M. Villart."

"Agreed," said Kurtzweiller, fingering his empty goblet impatiently.

"Do we even need to?" asked William Lewis.

"It's true," said Kurtzweiller. "We have the letter. And barely a quorum."

Lewis laughed. "A constitutional crisis, Dr. Waggoner?"

"Not at all," said Andrew. He lifted the jar from the table and held it aloft, like a glass in a toast. "There. A founding member. We are four now."

Kurtzweiller clapped and Lewis laughed again. From the windowsill, Dominic smiled uncertainly. Andrew beckoned. Dominic climbed down, Kurtzweiller motioned to the chair, and Dominic met Andrew's eyes, and Andrew nodded. And that was all it took for Dominic Villart to fill his old master's empty seat.

"Thank you, gentlemen. I will try to make myself worthy of the honour."

"A good start," said Lewis, "would be to open that wine for us."

Andrew shook his head. "Wine later. Business first. I think we're all very anxious to hear about Iceland."

"Yes!" said Kurtzweiller. "Iceland!"

Andrew set the Juke down and slid it along the table to Kurtzweiller, who passed it along to Lewis, who in turn placed it before Dominic.

"Iceland," said Dominic, and lifted the jar so it dangled between two fingers and he could peer at it. "Where to begin about Iceland?"

Dominic had been en route to Iceland when Molinare's illness became grave, his ship likely passing Gibraltar but possibly having gotten as far as the Orkneys. He did not learn of his master's death until much later, after he had returned to Reykjavik from the interior of Iceland, where the letter informing him of the sad news had waited for nearly a fortnight.

"I had all his other letters with me," said Dominic, "so until that one, that last one . . . it was as though Doctor Molinare was alive, and nearly alongside me."

"He was not," said Kurtzweiller. "Dismiss such ideas. Tell us what you found. Start with that. Was there a Juke?"

Dominic looked at the jar where he'd set it on the table in front of him. "No," he said and shook his head. He tapped the jar's lid with his fingertip. "Not like this."

Lewis sighed heavily and Kurtzweiller turned his attention to his empty wine glass. Andrew regarded the young man. Not so young as he had been, when he began working with Molinare and attending the *Société* meetings. He was lank and narrow then, effeminate in his youth. He had shed some of that in filling out, but not all. A thin moustache couldn't hide his full lips, the long lashes over his wide brown eyes. Early on, Andrew had speculated that beautiful young Dominic was more than an assistant to old Molinare and over the years he'd seen nothing to say he'd guessed wrong. But now, looking at Dominic handling the remains of the old Juke, Andrew reminded himself that affection between an older man and his young protégé didn't necessarily arise from scandal.

"There was very little conclusive to be found when we arrived," said Dominic. "The church was still standing, but there had been a fire."

"Yes. That much we read in the letter," said Kurtzweiller. Dominic had written a brief report on the investigation of the community that had fit the profile so well; the old church in the southeast, on a hot-spring lake near the foot of a towering glacier, had burned the previous summer. Prior to that, the stories of the Sigurdsson parish had occupied Molinare's curiosity considerably. This was one of the earliest Christian churches in Iceland, on a site believed consecrated in the 7th century by Irish monks and established permanently by King Olaf of Norway and landholder Ulfrid Sigurdsson three hundred years later.

Molinare had selected it for certain particulars.

The church had been very long without a priest. How long was indeterminate. Local stories went that the priests had been driven out by the little people—by faeries—who had claimed the church and as their own, although it may also have been Ulric Sigurdsson's change of heart. But the lack of priests did not mean the church was abandoned. It was on the lands owned by the old family and inhabited by a clan of shepherds, who sold their wool in Reykjavik—and kept the mutton closer to home at the instruction of their matriarch, whose name was Hekla and who did not meet strangers.

Molinare thought he had never found a cleaner analogue to the study of Eliada, and the hill people known as the Feegers at their mountain lake in north Idaho. He wished to go himself, but with his health failing as it was, he sent Dominic—first by boat, then on a truck hired in Reykjavik, and finally guided by a local man named Elmar on foot along shepherds' paths, to the foot of the glacier.

There, he found ruins. The church had been made of black volcanic rock, twice as tall as it was wide but for that no higher than two floors. The roof was gone but for a few charred timbers. The fire had not been that long ago; no word of it had reached Reykjavik, and Dominic's guide was visibly shocked at the sight of it—and the stench.

When they approached and pushed the charred doors off their hinges, they found its source. Among the pews were the carcasses of what they counted to be a dozen sheep, burnt to a crisp in the conflagration.

The church was not the only structure. There was a farmhouse, and a barn, and a bunkhouse. Dominic and Elmar searched them all, and all of them were empty, abandoned. Of the Sigurdsson's human inhabitants, the witch Hekla, all the rest, there was no sign. And so with the daylight waning, they bivouacked for the night in the bunkhouse—the only building that had anything resembling furnishings—and in the morning returned to the truck and Reykjavik, to summon help. And that was the end of Dominic's direct investigation: Icelandic Police occupied the site and, after interviewing Dominic and Elmar, forbade either of them from returning there.

That was the substance of Dominic's report, sent in a package accompanied by three rolls of undeveloped film containing the sum of the photographic account of their search. The photographs and the contents of the report were now contained in a slim folder in front of Lewis, who was the last to examine it before the meeting began.

"It was a fulsome enough account," said Lewis. "But it's not all of it, is it?"

"I didn't see a Juke," said Dominic. "I searched. We searched. . . ."

"Over the course of, what shall we say, eight hours?" said Kurtzweiller.

"I don't know how long we searched. The rest of the day."

"Did you enter the lake?"

"Lewis," said Andrew, "it was May, in Iceland. I don't think we'd be talking right now if he'd entered the lake."

"That's so. But really—just a day examining this place?" Lewis stood. "Not *even* a day? What would your late master say?"

"I'm sorry." Dominic pushed the jar away from him.

Andrew reached across and pushed it back.

"You omitted something," said Andrew, "from your report to Molinare. Didn't you now?"

Dominic said nothing for a moment, then nodded.

"I did not know he was dead, you see."

"What difference does that make?" demanded Kurtzweiller, and might have said more but Andrew raised a finger to hush him.

"What did you see?" asked Andrew.

"Molinare." He said it so softly that he had to repeat it. "Giorgio Molinare."

The men all bent forward at that. Kurtzweiller smoothed his moustache and fixed Dominic with a hard stare. Lewis let out a breath he had been holding. Andrew's eyes fell upon the Juke.

"I saw Giorgio," said Dominic, "moving between the bunks. He was walking very slowly, each footstep . . . making a rustling sound, as though he were moving through leaves."

"But there were no leaves on the floor," said Lewis, and Dominic shook his head in agreement.

"Can you describe him?" Andrew asked.

"He was unclothed. And he was not . . . not the same as when I'd left. He seemed more youthful, stronger. Younger even than when I met him."

"Did he speak to you?"

"No. He did pause, next to Elmar—who somehow remained asleep. And I called his name."

"And he didn't speak to you."

"No. He didn't even look at me. Just stood up straight and continued along the hall, then opened the door to the outside, and left. I did follow, but not quickly enough. When I stepped outside, there was no trace of him."

"It was dark. How could you know?"

"The Aurora Borealis—the Northern Lights—were bright in the sky. I suppose not bright enough to see by . . . but it seemed that the fires cast enough that I could understand . . . He was gone. I wondered if I'd dreamed it, and maybe I had."

"Still," said Kurtzweiller. "Why did you omit that from your report?"

Dominic sighed. "I didn't know that Dr. Molinare was dead. But I knew he was ill. I couldn't bear to tell a sick man that I'd seen his ghost."

Andrew tapped his finger restlessly on the table and pointed to the Juke. "Almost certainly you didn't see his ghost," he said. "What you saw was a Juke."

Dominic started at that, and looked at Andrew and then at the Juke in the jar.

"Of course," said Kurtzweiller. "The Juke, as we know, causes hallucinations such as this . . . to trick its hosts into letting down their guard. That is one of the species' primary adaptations."

"I know that," said Dominic, "but this . . . this was not that."

"What then?"

"It was Dr. Molinare." He sighed and shook his head. "It did not do what the Juke does. It didn't—didn't try to lay its eggs, not in me, not in my guide. It was—"

Andrew interrupted. "Did you have other sensations?"

"What do you mean?"

"The Juke—pardon me, Molinare—didn't lay hands upon you, correct?"

"It just told you—"

"It didn't touch you though?"

"No."

"Did you notice a smell—was there any sound?"

"No!" Dominic glared at Andrew. "Nothing!"

"Did you have—*an experience of transcendence, where the world fell away and a great void came upon you, and you felt that the world fell from beneath you, and you were borne aloft*?" Andrew shook his head and made himself clarify: "—a revelation?"

Lewis reached for a wine bottle and cast about for a corkscrew.

"It's obvious," he said when Andrew shot him a stern look. "The young man needs a drink."

"That won't help," said Andrew, but Kurtzweiller didn't agree and handed Lewis the corkscrew nearest him: the crude carving of a little Portuguese boy with a bandana, holding the screw where his privates would be. Lewis dug into the cork, and now Kurtzweiller raised his hand, to shush Andrew.

"That is all you have for us," he said softly to Dominic. "Isn't it?"

"I—" Dominic's skin flushed, and he squeezed his hands together.

"Perhaps another night," said Kurtzweiller, "or perhaps later this night, it will be different. You will unburden yourself, and tell the story in a manner that makes sense for you. I wonder if you have told anyone this story? Perhaps someone you met on the boat, returning from Reykjavik? No need to answer."

Lewis offered Dominic a glass of wine, then, as Dominic swallowed nearly all of it, poured three more, and slid one toward Kurtzweiller, another toward Andrew. This time, Andrew didn't object but lifted the glass, touched it to his lips and sipped, watching as Dominic helped himself to a second glass. Lewis rose to his feet and made ready to toast.

"To our newest member," he said, when Dominic and the rest stood. "Dominic Villart!"

"Arctic explorer!" said Kurtzweiller, and Lewis cried: "Scientist!" and Andrew barely stopped himself from adding, as their glasses clinked together over the table, the jar in its middle:

Oracle.

The four men hadn't got far—just the start of the third bottle—before the hammering at the door ended, rather prematurely, both the official and informal portion of the meeting of the *Société de la biologie transcendantale* for September, 1931.

When Andrew rose from his chair—only a little unsteadily—and opened the door, and he saw her, the gathering became something else entirely.

Two

"Miss Harper! My God!"

Andrew had not seen Ruth in long enough that he could not precisely say how many years it had been. But judging from her appearance, it could not have been as many as that. Her hair was shorter now than last time, but it had kept its lustre—her skin likewise showing only a hint of the passage of time. Had she gained or lost any weight in the span? She wore a tweed jacket and a long dark skirt, not as well-cut as some of her other ensembles, so it wasn't easy to be sure.

As to how she was? Andrew hadn't a clue.

"Not your God," she said, and smirked in her way. "Hello, Dr. Waggoner. I'm glad to see your *Société* still meeting here at the Liberty, and keeping its dates so assiduously."

"Of course," said Andrew. "It's good to see you. What, if I may ask, brings you here?"

"Discretion," she said, her voice low, and Andrew nodded that he understood. Only a few people knew that Andrew and the *Société* met here; fewer still, the nature of their business. Grady saw to that. If one knew the schedule—there would scarcely be a more discreet way to contact Andrew, or the other members, than to show up at an appointed time.

Ruth cocked her head and addressed the rest. "I hope I'm not intruding," she said and, not waiting for a response, touched Andrew's shoulder with a leather-gloved hand and stepped round him, into the apartment.

Kurtzweiller stood first, offering a little bow, and Lewis followed suit—"Of course not!" he said. Dominic was slowest to stand. But of course as the newest member, he had never met Ruth Harper, and would have only the vaguest idea of her importance here . . . and he had contributed more than his share to the murder of the first two bottles.

"No, madam," said Dominic finally.

"Hello." Ruth's face relaxed into a half-smile as she regarded the young man. *"Who are you?"* She turned to Andrew. "Who is he?"

"Dominic Villart," said Andrew. *"He's one of us."*

Dominic looked away. *"Only barely, I am afraid."*

"Recently," corrected Kurtzweiller. *"Only recently. You are one of us."*

Ruth nodded. *"Very good,"* she said. *"M. Villart, would you be so kind as to leave us for a moment?"*

"I'm sorry?"

"I'm afraid it can't be helped," said Ruth. *"You must leave."*

The three senior members of the *Société* regarded one another uneasily, and finally Andrew spoke to Dominic: *"Mr. Villart, this is Miss Ruth Harper. She is a valuable patron—"* he shared a glance with Ruth *"—a foundational patron. Why don't you refill your glass and find a chair in the Liberty for a while?"*

"Thank you, M. Villart," said Ruth as Dominic poured his glass and stepped out the door. "Mr. Lewis," she said, switching to English as the door closed, "see that he's not lingering on the stairs, would you?"

"I don't think there's any cause—" began Lewis, but Ruth raised a gloved hand, and he stepped to it, opening the door a crack.

He shut the door again and nodded. "It's good, Miss Harper."

"All right," she said. "Doctor Kurtzweiller—pour me a glass of that wine, would you?" She tugged the glove from her right hand by the fingers, then folded it and removed the left, and rearranged the wristwatch underneath. When she was finished, she accepted the glass and sipped, then took a bigger swallow and shut her eyes a moment and drew a breath.

"Something has happened," she finally said, "to Jason."

"Jason?" asked Kurtzweiller, and Lewis said: "Jason Thistledown," and Andrew stepped around the table, scooped the jar with the Juke into his coat pocket, and said: "Thorn. Jason Thorn." He pulled out a chair for Ruth, and tucked it back under her as she sat.

"What's happened?" he asked.

"Tell me, Dr. Waggoner—Andrew. Did Jason visit you earlier this year?"

"Not me," said Andrew. "Annie mentioned he called on her. She said he'd taken a job, in Africa. He'd be gone for some time."

"But you were not available?" Ruth twirled the glass by the stem so that the wine curled up toward the rim.

"No," said Andrew.

"That's a shame. I was hoping he'd lied about that. You two have always had a special friendship. Much more so than he and your wife."

"Lied? To whom? What happened to him?"

"Did he write you?"

"He didn't write me," said Andrew levelly. "You know how things are, Ruth—pardon me, Miss Harper. Now please—what's happened to him?"

"I do," said Ruth. "Well then. Mr. . . . Mr. Thorn has vanished. Not in Africa. And no, not dead—at least we don't believe so," she hastily corrected, perhaps reading the expressions of Andrew and the other two.

"We?"

She sighed at that, shut her eyes, and when she opened them, Andrew could see that they were damp.

"*We* believe," she said, "it is a Juke."

Andrew's fist curled around the jar in his coat pocket, and he looked to Kurtzweiller, and Lewis, and then back to Ruth. "Where?" was all he could say.

Ruth glanced down at her wristwatch, looked up again, and appeared to make a decision.

"Won't you all please sit?" she said. "I think the best way to proceed is according to your custom."

"Our custom?" asked Andrew.

"Pardon me. Your methodology. The Decameron System, isn't it?" She blinked. "I always thought that was a clever name for it. Don't you call it that anymore?"

They hadn't called it that, not at first.

But that was what got them through—Andrew and Ruth, Annie and Jason, in those days at the Thorn farm with the ashes of Eliada behind them . . . telling the story, the story of Eliada, in a rational order, in a way that made sense.

It was Jason who'd got it rolling, quietly in that bunkhouse with Ruth, as she recovered from the surgery that cleaned her of the Juke. The story he told came in whispers in her ear as he sponged cool water on her fevered brow: How they'd met, before either had set foot in Eliada that spring, and how well he'd enjoyed their conversation on the riverboat up the Kootenai to Eliada—which was to say not a great deal, as she kept wanting to talk about his no-good father's ill-gotten fame, a topic that he preferred to avoid. He told her a thing he never had before as her eyelids fluttered in the afternoon light—about how Dr. Nils Bergstrom had locked him up with a very young Juke in Eliada's quarantine, and how it'd seemed to have her face along with sharp claws and sharper teeth. He even told her that he was afraid it was going to rip his privates to shreds before he escaped. He cut his hand in that escape, and it hurt like fire, and that was how he learned that pain could stop that Juke magic from taking hold, or at least keeping it.

"So when you wake up, you'll be all cured," said Jason, "because I guess between your foot and your own privates, you'll be howling."

Ruth wasn't howling when she woke up. But she thought she might've been cured. She said she had remembered Jason's story, and told him that it was very sweet of him, and that it just might have helped.

"But darling, now that I'm on the mend, perhaps we could illuminate other mysteries than the legitimate reasons you had to put a bullet in my foot," she said when he asked her if she'd like to hear more.

She asked Jason if he might tell her what happened to her that night they decided to explore the quarantine, where they had become separated. Jason told her what he knew, but it wasn't much. He lost track of her that night at the quarantine, and lost track of himself too. "I thought I saw my pa, and my ma—I met a fellow who I think helped try and hang Dr. Waggoner . . . I think I might've done a murder. That Germaine Frost. I know at a point, you ended up in my arms. I know that moment for sure. But as to all of it? The order of things? I can't scarce make any sense of it."

By that time, Andrew Waggoner and Annie Rowe were hanging close, and Annie made an observation: "None of us are making a lot of sense of what happened, now, are we? Sometimes it feels like I came from that river, reborn. Now that's foolish. I know that's not so. I know my story. But there's another story too. And it's like it's trying to write me over."

Andrew thought that was a good way to describe it, the effect of the Juke.

"This thing tricks your mind into thinking it's God," said Andrew. "It needs you to worship. Not just fall down before it in a state of ecstasy. Not just to feel awe . . . but to *worship*, to deliver tribute. And how do you worship, without some Gospels to make sense of it?"

"Let's not say Gospels," said Annie, "please."

Ruth agreed. "Gospels are dreary things. And it's true. This Juke thing isn't God. It's a tapeworm."

"God is a tapeworm," said Jason, trying and failing to bring levity to the discussion. "The Juke sure does spin lies, though, and for some those lies seem pretty fine. Maybe we need to lay it out."

"From the beginning," agreed Andrew.

"But not Genesis," said Annie.

"Not Genesis," said Ruth. "The Decameron."

As it turned out, she was the only one in the room who had read Boccaccio's book of tales, and when pressed she hadn't the strength to explain it. But the next morning, when Ruth was feeling well enough to clarify, they all agreed that a system based on a crowd of Italians locked in a villa, telling stories to pass time as they waited out the Black Plague was a fitting way to describe their circumstance, there in the bunkhouse next to a river full of corpses.

And so, the Decameron system it was.

"I don't believe," said Ruth Harper, as Kurtzweiller refilled her glass and Andrew dug the cork from another bottle, "that any of us are in immediate danger. That is the first thing to remember, as the story I'm about to tell you might otherwise make you anxious. I have taken appropriate precautions coming here, and am fairly certain that no one has followed me. Your meeting place is safe.

"I was in a bit for a time, but I don't think that I'm in any more now. Of course, when I was in the worst peril, I'd no idea.

"My hosts were gracious and had every reason to see to my safety, so why would I think the anything but the best? I had been visiting an old friend and associate of my father's . . . Herr Egon Dietrich. Not to put too fine a point on it, he wanted money—in the form of a loan and perhaps investment, to bolster his textile manufacturing concerns in Potsdam. He needed that investment rather desperately . . . his American loans had come suddenly due, and like almost everyone in Germany he had no easy way to repay them. And of course you know that von Hindenburg, trying to help, only made things worse.

"Egon needed money, but he couldn't quite bring himself to request it in a cable. And so, I was the recipient of a handwritten invitation from his wife Bronwyn, to spend a few nights at their lake house. As it happened to be convenient—and as I recalled fondly the Dietrichs' visits in Chicago when I was a girl—I accepted.

"I should likely have known better. Egon and my father were great friends in the day—but of course . . . well, Andrew, you remember my father, his ideas . . . Eliada. Egon was a great admirer of Father's notions of a good, utopian society—and he and father also shared a close acquaintance with the people at Cold Creek Harbour. . . .

"As a girl, I didn't pay much attention to their talk of eugenics and utopianism. It was harder to avoid at the lake house, dining with adults. The first night, Egon insisted on throwing me a small dinner party with some, ah, friends. They were dreadful people. Couldn't stop talking about the Jews. The Jews who controlled the banks were strangling Germany. They were taking jobs and livelihood from good Germans. The Jews had ruined music, and art, and everything else that was right about the German Republic. They conspired with Freemasons.

"'Let us drink to Garrison Harper!' cried Egon, late in the supper after all had really had too many toasts to too many different things. 'And the great man's motto: Community! Hygiene!'

"'Also compassion,' I reminded him. 'There were three things in my late father's motto.'

"'Community—*Compassion*—Hygiene!' said Egon. 'For the lady.'

"Egon's friends were, so far as I knew, businessmen from Potsdam and Berlin and Frankfurt, who kept their own summer homes in the vicinity. That was for the most part true. But there were two who were something other. Arnold Hahn and Hugo Guttermuth were their names. I made a note of them so I wouldn't forget. They both stood out—they were much younger than Egon, and all the way from Munich, staying for the time being in an apartment over the Dietrichs' carriage house. I took it that they might have something to do with politics—*Munich* politics, if you take my meaning . . . as they seemed to approve rather too wholeheartedly of Egon's unfortunate anti-Semitism. And I guessed—given the time that they spent together, the way they seemed to attend one another—that they were, pardon me, homosexuals. I've no idea if they in fact were, and it doesn't matter now.

"I saw a great deal of them over the next few days, but we spoke scarcely at all. If I were by the water, they would be at smoking at the dock; in my room, I might look out the window and see one or the other standing on the green. When I played cards with Bronwyn in the salon, I would hear their voices in the hall. A hundred other moments like that. One of them, I think, would have ended with one of their hands over my mouth, their arms around mine—and then a long drive in a truck, to an airfield. . . .

"Well. I am here, not there. And why? I received a letter. It came on the morning post on my fifth day there. Let me read it to you:

"Dear Ruth,

"One day I hope I will see you and make good amends for the things my wounded soul has done. Right now you are in trouble. You have to get out of the house you are staying in. There are men there or not far from there with their eye on you. If I fail where I am, and I may, you must be well hidden for they will take you otherwise. Flee now. Do not tarry.

"Yours—

Ruth handed the letter to Andrew, so that he might see for himself.

"*Jason Thistledown*," read Andrew, and frowned. "That looks like his handwriting all right."

"It's distinctive," Ruth said, "isn't it?"

"You didn't read the postscript," said Andrew.

"What does it say?" asked Lewis.

Andrew read: "*Do not contact Andrew Waggoner or anyone else. Lay low. I will find you at* . . ." He looked up. The note finished with a drawing, a figure . . . of what, it was difficult to say.

"Crete," said Ruth.

"Really?"

"It's the Minotaur," said Ruth, and craned her neck and pointed. "See the horns?"

"The boy still can't draw. You went all the way to Crete?"

"It was a near thing," said Ruth. "But eventually, yes, I did."

"But he wasn't there," said Kurtzweiller, and Ruth shook her head no.

"A near thing?" asked Andrew.

"I did as Jason said," said Ruth. "Not as stealthily as I might have. I went to see Egon first—told him very quickly that the Harper trust would provide him a sum of capital as he required, and gave him the address of my solicitor in London—but that I needed to leave on a morning train.

"Did I not wish to at least know the sum, and to what use it would be put? asked Egon. When I told him that I trusted his sense of moderation to request only what he needed, he looked ashamed. Did I need to leave so quickly? Yes, I said. It was unavoidable. So he arranged to have me driven to the train station. With Herr Hahn and Herr Guttermuth, in their touring car."

"I can't imagine you would have stood for that," said Kurtzweiller.

"I shouldn't have. I had my suspicions about them—particularly given Jason's letter. I did insist upon riding in the front seat, though—and that's what saved me.

"Because they were kidnapping me. Just as Jason had warned. Just as I should have guessed.

"They turned off the main roadway to Potsdam a few kilometres away. A shortcut, said Hahn. I wasn't convinced—we were following a road winding through thick woods and up into the hills. I wondered how they were so familiar with the backroads around the lakes, having lived in far-off Munich. Herr Guttermuth, who was in the back seat, leaned forward with his hand on my shoulder and told me not to worry, that it would be fine—and Herr Hahn, driving at my side, added that I was very safe.

"In my experience, these are the things that men say to a lady when they well know that it won't be fine, and she is anything but safe. They want to see that the lady believes them when they say things like that—and so I did my best to convince them I did."

Andrew shook his head and smiled. "How'd you get out of it?"

Ruth allowed herself a little smile, extending her empty glass. Lewis poured as she explained: "It was absurdly easy. We were pulling through a small village. I simply reached over and turned the wheel—gave it a really good yank!—and Herr Hahn drove the car into the back of a beer truck stopped outside the petrol station. It made a frightful mess and a great commotion. No serious injuries, thank Heaven. While the men were sorting it out, it was a simple matter for me to go inside with a billfold of American dollars, and arrange a lift back to Potsdam. They didn't dare stop me in front of so many witnesses—and their car was in no shape to follow."

The gentlemen of the *Société de la biologie transcendantale* sat still and silent, as Ruth Harper took a long drink of her wine, drew a breath, and drank as much of it again.

"That was quite a leap you took," Andrew said. "Those two mightn't have been kidnapping you at all."

"You weren't there." Ruth's tone shifted, suddenly sharp. "And in any event—I wasn't wrong."

“I didn’t mean—”

“—to say I was lying? Or a fool? Of course not.” She looked down at her watch. “In any event, that’s what happened to me and that . . . is what I did about it.” She nodded inscrutably, and then looked up from her watch. “Yes, good. I think that should be enough time to be sure, one way or another.”

At that, Ruth put both hands on the edge of the table and pushed her chair back, and as she rose, she stumbled—the effect of her old injuries, endured twenty years ago, first at the hand of Jason Thistledown and then under Andrew Waggoner’s knife. Those injuries had saved her life. Maybe that car wreck, inspired by a letter from Jason Thorn, had done those things too: damage and salvation, all in one.

Ruth righted herself quickly, impatiently waving off offers of help from Kurtzweiller—and without another word, made her way to the door, down to the Liberty. When the door swung shut behind her, Andrew stood.

“She’s been through a lot,” he said.

“Perhaps,” said Kurtzweiller, and he gave a little frown. “I don’t know her as well as you.”

“Do you believe any of it, Andrew?” Lewis asked.

“The escape story? Yes,” said Andrew. “I do. That is Jason’s handwriting. Ruth—Miss Harper—has proven herself strong and resourceful enough through her life. After she escaped Eliada . . . prevailed against this—” Andrew withdrew the jar from his pocket and held it forward “—she managed to prevail against her late father’s partners to seize back the Harper fortune. Of course she was able to crash an auto, and escape from men she believed meant her harm.”

Kurtzweiller shrugged, and nodded toward the door. “One of us should go downstairs. See that she’s all right. Try and appease her.”

“Or if she’s left, at least fetch poor Dominic,” said Lewis.

“I was on my way,” said Andrew, a moment too late.

The door opened again, and Ruth Harper stepped back through, followed by two others: Dominic Villart, carrying a fresh bottle of wine, and a tall, dark-haired man with a white-flecked beard, hauling a brown fedora hat in one hand, an oversized porcelain pipe in the other.

“I passed the test!” said Dominic, grinning.

“Yes,” said Ruth. “I was worried young Dominic might have been . . . a spy, I suppose. If he tried to leave, or signal anyone . . .”

"You said you thought we were safe here," said Andrew.

"Safe enough," said Ruth. "If Mr. Villart had tried anything, Mr. Grady would have intervened. And if not . . . Herr Zimmermann would have seen to things."

"Herr Zimmermann?"

"Yes," said Ruth," I forget myself. Drs. Andrew Waggoner, Manfred Kurtzweiller, William Lewis . . ."

The stranger half-smiled and nodded at each of them.

"Albert Zimmermann," said Ruth. "Perhaps the last man to have seen Jason. I think that you will have a great deal to talk about."

Three

Albert Zimmermann took a seat next to Ruth Harper near the head of the table. Andrew asked if Ruth had explained the work of the *Société*, and he said yes: "You are hunting the Juke, correct?" which was near enough to true, although Lewis felt the need to add: "We are students."

"Of transcendental biology," said Zimmermann, giving a tight smile and shaking his head. "What a name for it."

"Don't mock," warned Kurtzweiller.

"Forgive me. I'm not mocking you. After everything I have seen . . . No. That's a good name."

"Herr Zimmermann was the one who sent along Jason's letter," Ruth interjected. "They were both in Bavaria. I think you—particularly you, Andrew—will find what Herr Zimmermann reports about that time to be of great interest."

"Bavaria? I thought Jason was going to Africa," said Andrew.

Zimmermann nodded. "So did I. That was the plan for both of us, so far as I understood."

"Both of you?" asked Kurtzweiller.

"Yes. Jason Thorn . . . Jason Thistledown was my pilot. He and I had both been hired on as crew in a new airmail service, flying out of Algiers, through Africa. We were to be gone a year, maybe more if all worked out as planned." Zimmermann shook his head again, and his smile returned. "I should best explain my role in this. It is not what I had hoped it would be, and as matters turned out, I am more than a little ashamed of it. I was a fool, twice over at the least."

"Don't be ridiculous," said Ruth. "Please, Albert. From the beginning, as you told me."

"Ah yes," said Zimmermann. "Your Boccaccio ritual."

"Boccaccio?" asked Dominic. "The Decameron fellow?"

"That one," said Andrew.

"They don't call it that anymore," said Ruth.

"We're going to hear a story," said Lewis to Dominic. "The same way you told us about Iceland. All in order."

"From the beginning." Dominic nodded, and Zimmermann did too.

"The beginning," he said.

"I learned to fly in the war," said Zimmermann. "A little later than Jason did. I flew for *Die Luftstreitkräfte*, and I survived my time, to be truthful, because it was so short. I surely would have been shot down, were I a year or two earlier to the game. . . .

"After the war . . . I continued to fly, but officially with the usual restrictions. Remember, the Versailles treaty dictated that Germany could have no air force. So I flew for *Deutsche Luft Hansa*, ferrying mail and passengers through Europe. And I taught—first in Germany, at small airfields with light and unarmed planes. But in more recent years—I frequently found myself in Russia. Do you know about Lipetsk?"

No one did. Zimmermann shrugged.

"It is a flight school . . . a place where many of my surviving *Luftstreitkräfte* comrades still teach young German men to fly and fight in the air—in proper fighting planes, in a place where Versailles does not reach. Outside of Germany, they are building a new *Luftwaffe*. Against the day that Germany has need of it, and Versailles . . . no longer applies.

"The Russians were amiable hosts—in no small part because they needed the skills we possessed—and we taught as many young Russian pilots as we did Germans. We were well-fed and well-paid, and we mingled. I taught there on rotation for five years. Happily, I might add. I might still be there now, were it not for the fact . . ."

Zimmermann took a deep drag from his pipe.

"Last spring, a man came to see me. A Russian. He said his name was Andrei, and would not tell me a surname. But he knew me very well, and my entire family. Including my great-grandfather on my mother's side.

"'Jocheved Calmsohn,' Andrei said. 'Of Salzburg.'

"'If you say so,' I replied—for the name meant nothing to me then.

"Andrei corrected that. Jocheved, he said, was a tailor by trade, of reasonable means . . . and considered by many to be a good man . . . 'A pillar of his synagogue.' I remember Andrei smirking as he said so.

"'And so we learn, that Albert Zimmermann, hero of the Fatherland . . . is a Jew!' said Andrei. 'What a secret you have kept all these years.'

"It was no secret—not that I had kept. For I had no idea. I was—I am—a Catholic, by both parents. I knew that my mother's family was in Salzburg. But she had never spoken of Jocheved, and he was long dead.

"When I protested, Andrei showed me documentation, which he had brought with him in a slim folio. 'Your career,' he said, 'might well be over.' And this was true. I knew of Jews who had flown in the *Luftstreitkräfte*, in the war. None flew, still. None—none that I knew of—taught at Lipetsk. You, Herr Kurtzweiller . . . you must have some idea how it is for the Jews in Germany."

"Not good," said Kurtzweiller. "But not so terrible."

"That is a matter of perspective," said Zimmermann. "In any event . . . Andrei offered me a bargain—which, he said, might both preserve my career and, he hinted, keep my family safe.

"'Report to me,' said Andrei, 'and to my masters.'

"'Report?' I asked, and he spelled it out to me. I was to spy for him . . . for Soviet Russia.

"'On Germany?' I said. I was aghast. 'That would be treason.'

"Andrei returned the documents to his folio, and shook his head no.

"'No,' he said. 'For now . . . we have need of you elsewhere. Who knows? This work might take you far enough away that Germany will be of no consequence.'

"In the end, this persuaded me. Andrei's interest was in a Frenchman. Emile Desrosiers. All I had to do, explained Andrei, was go work for him. He was starting a small airline in North Africa, and was need of experienced pilots for it. 'Sign up,' said Andrei. 'Keep your eyes open. You will be contacted from time to time, and sometimes asked to obtain something. But nothing untidy . . .'"

Zimmermann paused a moment to draw from his pipe, and stared through the smoke as he exhaled.

"And that is how one becomes a spy for a foreign power, against what one might have thought was one's will. The tiniest pressure applied in the correct place, and loyalties collapse and realign. It is an extraordinary thing. I resigned my position, gathered my effects and flew from Russia to Frankfurt—and then on a train to this place, to Paris. One of Andrei's operatives here met me, then took me to meet another, and that one had prepared a meeting for myself and Desrosiers on a suitable pretext. That is how it works. And it works very well: just two days later, I signed on with La Rose, Desrosiers' new airline.

"I met Desrosiers only three times. Once, in the lobby of a hotel—where I presume that he was staying. He was displeased to hear that I was Austrian, and that I had flown in the *Luftstreitkräfte.* He made sure I knew he had served as an officer for France—that we were old enemies, and he had not forgotten. 'I suppose you think that Africa will wash all that away,' he said to me. 'The dark continent is a great leveller, yes? All men made the same!' And more talk like that. Later I was called again to a dark suite of offices on the first floor of a building in Montparnasse—not far from here, in fact. There, I signed papers agreeing to a term of one year, and accepted a retainer—a generous retainer—in cash, along with a reservation at another hotel.

"'Enjoy the hospitality of La Rose,' said Desrosiers, 'and the wonders of Paris.'

"The third time was in that hotel room. Two days before we were to leave. Late in the evening. Desrosiers arrived alone, with a bottle and two glasses. Of our three meetings, it was the only one unusual enough to report to my superiors in any detail.

"'Tell me, Herr Zimmermann. Do you think you could fly a Latécoère-28?'

"'Of course,' I said. I had crewed on similar craft in Germany after the war.

"'I don't mean crew it,' said Desrosiers. 'I mean fly it. Alone.'

"'I suppose,' I said. 'But you do understand, sir, that the aircraft is designed to be crewed by two men at least. Do I not have a co-pilot?'

"'Oh, you do indeed,' said Desrosiers. He chuckled as he poured us out glasses of wine. 'You may even have met him.'

"'Perhaps. What is his name?' I asked, and Desrosiers laughed again.

"'Oh, I am certain you haven't been introduced. But you may well have met—over France. You will be flying with an old enemy. Jason Thorn.'

"He said it as though I should have known the name immediately, and as he related the details, my memory was pricked. A Canadian ace in the RAF, who flew two very distinguished tours—one in the midst of the war, and another at the very end. Fifty-two kills in as many weeks. 'No, we did not meet,' I finally said. 'Given his record, I think if we had I would not be here.'

"Desrosiers laughed aloud at that. 'Quite so!' he said, then leaned forward and became very serious.

"'I must take you into confidence,' he said. 'When the Latécoère takes flight two mornings from now, it is likely that you will have to fly it on your own. I hope this is not so. . . .'

"'Do you believe that Thorn will not honour his contract?' I asked.

"'Oh,' said Desrosiers, 'I am sure he will be there. M. Thorn has fallen on hard times. No. It is this. You will not be flying directly to Algiers, you see.'

"'I'm afraid that I don't,' I said.

"'You will be making a stop,' said Desrosiers.

"'Where, may I ask?'

"'I am not sure of that myself right now,' said Desrosiers. 'La Rose has . . . passengers on this flight. They will provide charts and instructions. I have been assured it is well within the range of the Latécoère.'

"'Will Thorn not be joining us on this detour then?' I asked.

"'He will,' said Desrosiers. 'But maybe not in the cockpit.'

"Before I could ask another question, Desrosiers reached into his coat and produced an envelope. It contained a stack of notes—at least twice as thick as the retainer he had given me. And unlike the retainer, which was in francs, these were American dollars. He placed it on the side table, and pushed it toward me. Under other circumstances, I like to think that I would refuse rather than participate in what seemed like a kidnapping, and would certainly be a betrayal. But of course I was not working for Desrosiers. I was working for men who were much worse. So I took the envelope, and told Desrosiers that there would be no trouble from me. I could fly a Latécoère alone as needed. I was, I lied, his man.

"Desrosiers left me the bottle to finish. I poured it in the sink, and sat down to write out my report. It wasn't a very good report: just a page, written, as per their instructions, in German, longhand, to a correspondent named Helmut—a bit of diversion that would implicate me as a spy for Germany and not Russia, should I be found out. I dropped it at the desk of another nearby hotel at just past two in the morning. One of my handlers—a woman I knew as Jean—met me the next afternoon during a walk along the Seine. She made it very clear that it wasn't a very good report and I would have to do better. I needed to learn the destination before we left, and preferably the names of the passengers. The unknown destination complicated matters, Jean explained, because her superiors had gone to some lengths to establish a network of contacts in Algiers—and they worried about losing contact. She reminded me, although she needn't have, that I could find no safety or solace in desertion. I might not be found, but my family would suffer.

"If it truly was a short detour, and I did land in Algiers, I would be contacted. If not—she dictated to me a postal address in Vienna, to which I should post a letter to Helmut, making my whereabouts clear. In the meantime, Jean said that her superiors were curious about Jason Thorn. Not because they knew anything exceptional of him—but because Desrosiers' mysterious passengers might. Jean handed me one piece of equipment that I was to put to use: a tiny camera. I have it still!"

Zimmermann dug into the pocket of his coat and removed what appeared to be a thick silver pocket watch. He handed it to Lewis, who passed it to Kurtzweiller who in turn showed it to Andrew. Sure enough, a tiny lens stood out where the wind-up knob should be. Andrew showed it to Dominic, who waved it away, so Andrew set it on the table.

"Ingenious, yes? It is a novelty item from the World's Fair in St. Louis in the United States. My masters did not waste resources. 'Take pictures,' Jean said to me. 'Of the passengers. Of Jason Thorn. Of your destination. When you are finished, turn the camera over in Algiers. Or mail it to Vienna.'"

"I take it you never arrived in Algiers," said Lewis. "Or found a post box."

"Jason," said Andrew. "We were talking about Jason."

Dominic handed the camera across the table, and Zimmermann slipped it back into his pocket. "Yes. I met him for the first time very early on the morning of the flight. I still had no idea about the nature of the passengers, or our destination. He seemed very—on the edge, I suppose you might say. I don't think he slept much the night before. I thought about asking him—did he know more than I? But of course I have seen men like your friend Jason before. A lot of them I flew alongside, in the war. They had seen men fall screaming from the sky, trapped in flaming cockpits. They had sometimes come very close to such ends themselves. Shell shock, they call it. As I looked at my co-pilot, fumbling cigarettes in the back of a truck, I thought it would have been wise to prepare for flying solo in any event. Your friend was in no shape.

"We met the passengers at the little airport at Orly at dawn. There were four of them. Three of them were Germans, and one was a Belgian. That one was in charge. His name was Hector Aguillard and he said he was a physician. Desrosiers made it clear: he was the one whose instructions I should follow. Jason, for his part, had no clue. As he inspected the aircraft, Aguillard and I spoke.

"'M. Desrosiers has spoken with you,' he said. 'You understand about the detour.'

"'I do,' I said, 'but only that much. Where are we going?'

"'Of course.' He reached into his valise and handed me a thick envelope. 'The chart in there is marked. We will be landing in Bavaria, as it happens.'

"'What is in Bavaria?' I asked, but that was one question too many and he changed the subject.

"'The landing strip is rough.' said Aguillard. 'A farmer's field. You are prepared?'

"'Yes,' I said, and he said, 'Good,' and that was the last he and I spoke alone before we landed."

"Where," said Andrew, "did you land?"

"As he said. In Bavaria. Near—but not too near—the town of Wallgau, south of Munich. We landed at a farm, near mountains. I did not spend the flight in Jason's company. When he learned of the change in plans, he became angry, and Aguillard and his men subdued him in the passenger compartment. One—a young Austrian named Gustav—joined me in the cockpit. Also a veteran of the war, but not a pilot. He had, he told me, survived the trenches, and that was something. It was during this conversation that I learned the other important thing about our destination. It was a project of Adolph Hitler's Nazi Party. Indeed, said Gustav, it was a project that might assure the future of the German people.

"Well. As you might imagine, this gave me little comfort. You know as well as I, Herr Hitler's views on the Jews. And here was I, not only a Jew, but a spy, for Russians. A Jew and a traitor, newborn.

"Jason would not speak with me when left the plane, other than to curse me. I couldn't fault him. Who knows what he might have done were we alone? But we weren't. We were greeted by a squad of Hitler's S.A. men, and Jason was taken off with them, to the great house, to learn what it was that required his presence.

"I was alone with the plane for only a few minutes before Gustav returned—alone as well. 'We will be having a short layover here,' he announced.

"This surprised me but I remained circumspect. The chart identified a town nearby, Wallgau. I asked about it. Gustav told me that it was barely a hamlet. There was a tavern, he understood, with some rooms, but although it was frequented by some of the S.A. men, he hadn't been there yet.

"'Perhaps we can travel there today,' he said, for it wasn't far, and he thought we both could stand for a strong drink.

"I had hoped to do so—where there was a tavern, I reasoned, there must also be a postmaster. But as it happened, we were not able to leave the farm for three more days, and I was kept under close watch at the farmhouse.

"For all that, however, I made use of those days. The house was much grander than one would think, more a mansion than a farmhouse . . . so I did not immediately learn what Jason's fate was—at least not first hand. I was set up with a bunk in a long dinner hall, converted to a barracks. Jason, I would later learn, had been placed in his own room on the second floor.

"I was able to wander the ground floor, and the kitchen, and step outside onto the porch, and to the privy, but forbidden anywhere else. Unless I devised some pretext to return to the plane, the men on duty would prevent me from wandering very far.

"It was not that I was made to feel as though I were a prisoner. Far from it: word had spread that I was a veteran of the war, same as many of the S.A., and all were courteous and respectful. Indeed, most of what I learned about the farm was talking with some of those fellows. It was the family property of the Visler family, in Munich . . . who had leased it—for a nominal sum—to the Nazi party . . . which in turn, had handed it over to the *Hitler-Jugend* . . . the Hitler Youth.

"'Where then are the youth?' I asked. 'Certainly not among the likes of you or I.'

"The S.A. man I asked this smiled at my joke in an uncomfortable way but instead of answering, pointed to the range of mountains, to the south. I had flown over that mountain before landing, and it wasn't very high—trees to the summit. Were they hiking?

"'Who knows?' he said.

"His watch-mate explained that there was another settlement, in a deep valley beyond those peaks, and that there had been some trouble there some months earlier. He wasn't there when it happened, and was sorry for it.

"'It was a nudist colony,' he said. 'Hundreds of naked, rosy-cheeked girls. Frolicking in the pines. Not bad, hey?'

"There is a small chateau there too, once the property of the Seckendorff family, but repurposed, just before the War, as a nudist colony and also a wellness spa . . . a place to allow the perfectible youth of Germany to flourish and mingle. The men I talked to thought it might have been overseen by the *Germanenorden*."

Lewis wondered what that was, and Kurtzweiller explained.

"A Teutonic society," he said. "Mystics. Theosophists. They put great stock in the purity of the Aryan race. It was popular in Berlin for a time. They met secretly, developed great plans—and told anyone who would listen about them."

"Eugenics," said Andrew. "We're familiar with the notion. What was the trouble at this spa?"

Zimmermann shook his head. "In time. Fräulein Harper told me about your Decameron system. I rather like it. We tell the story in the order it occurred. I can see the value in the exercise, for the men guarding the farmhouse had never put their thoughts in such order. I did ask about the troubles.

"One man told me: 'The children rose up, and refused to obey.'

"Another, who happened by in the midst of it, told me that a beast devoured them, and a third said that wasn't so. 'The Piper led them away.' What? The Pied Piper? Was he having me on? There was a serpent, said the first, but he wasn't sure that it hadn't fled from the beast. Maybe it hadn't.

"'In any event the children have become the forest,' he said. 'It is best not to wander too far.'

"'It is true, Herr Zimmermann,' said the original guard. 'We keep you here for your own safety.'"

"A Juke!" said Kurtzweiller. "A Juke dwells in that valley!"

"How did you escape it?" asked Lewis, leaning forward. "It is rare—"

Andrew lifted his hand and Lewis caught his breath. "The children have *become* the forest?" Andrew asked. "Is that what he said?"

"Indeed," said Zimmermann. "I asked him that too—did he mean they were transformed into trees? That would be quite a trick.

"'Think what you like,' was all he would say. 'Good German men have vanished there too. You don't venture far. Leave that to the American sorcerer you brought to us.'

"Yes, that was another thing that I learned: my co-pilot was a sorcerer! He had some magical ability to withstand the Pied Piper's song. That was why he had been summoned.

"It took me longer to learn about the men who'd summoned him. That took more risks on my part. My masters had girded me with more fear than training. I knew to lie, and step softly, and I knew if I were to fight a man in the dark, I best do it quietly and kill him in the end. Had I ever done any of those things? The first yes, the second perhaps, and the third—never. Nevertheless, on the second night, after the candles were snuffed in the barracks and the men were snoring, I stole from my cot through the main hall to the forbidden upper floors, where I was able to conduct a goodly search of the place. I learned the identity of some of the men who were in charge of the operation—written on the outside of envelopes addressed to them, discarded by a desk. There was a Dr. Jurgen Plaut; a Professor Hermann Muckermann; a Dr. Johannes Bergstrom." Zimmermann paused here, and made as if to study Andrew's expression. "Yes," he said. "Of relation to another Dr. Bergstrom, who died in America. Of Miss Harper's and your acquaintance. His brother, I believe?"

Andrew nodded. "I believe I know of Muckermann too. He's at the Kaiser Wilhelm Institute for Anthropology, isn't he?"

"He is in charge of it," said Kurtzweiller. "A Jesuit, I believe. I've met him."

"And Johannes Bergstrom," said Andrew. "I didn't know Nils had a brother. Particularly one who was a doctor."

"I'm surprised you didn't," said Ruth. "You might move in some of the same circles."

"We don't have as much to do with our German colleagues as we'd like," said Andrew, and glanced at Kurtzweiller. "Present company excepted. But I shouldn't be surprised, given the nature of the project, that a Bergstrom would be involved."

"Or a man like Muckermann," said Kurtzweiller. "As I think of it, I recall he has written fairly extensively on topics of breeding and eugenics. Doesn't care much for the Jews either."

"What about Plaut?" asked Lewis; to Zimmermann: "Who's he?"

Zimmermann bared his teeth in a humorless grin, and drew another puff from his pipe.

"I wish I could say," said Zimmermann. "I briefly met Dr. Bergstrom, and can confirm some things about him as a result. Tall, a little heavy in the gut . . . a square-faced man, maybe in his late fifties, early sixties. His hair was going white, but he had all of it. And yes, he was an alienist . . . a psychoanalyst. Muckermann was not in attendance during my stay there. I met Plaut only two or three times, much later on. A small man, stocky . . . in his forties, perhaps? A little older than me. As to his profession . . ."

"Yes?" prompted Andrew, after it was clear that Zimmermann had trailed off.

"It never came up," said Zimmermann. "We only spoke once . . . I suppose you could say we spoke . . . and then, there were other matters to attend to."

"Other matters?" asked Lewis.

When Zimmermann spoke again, it was very softly.

"There was so much blood. And under the circumstances . . . all he could do was scream."

Four

Lawrence Thorn stayed out of the bunkhouse for two days, until the screaming started up. He thought it was an animal, hurt or caught, when it carried across the meadow—and when he drew nearer the bunkhouse, he figured it for the sick girl, Ruth Harper, turning for the worse. But it wasn't. It was Jason.

Andrew Waggoner met him at the door to tell him what was what.

"The boy has been through hell and back," said Andrew. "He has nightmares. This was . . . a bad one."

"All right," said Lawrence, and fixed Andrew with a stare, "then let me see to him."

Andrew considered turning him away, but something in Lawrence's eye that early morning told him he better not. It was the fourth day they'd been there, and Andrew wondered how many more days their welcome would last.

He led Lawrence into the bunkhouse. The farmer had likely never seen the place tidier: Jason and Annie had scrubbed it spotless after the surgery. Jason was sitting on a chair near one of the bright windows, his back to the gold sunrise, staring down at his feet.

Lawrence lifted a chair from beside the door and brought it to sit by Jason.

"Leave us a spell," he said when Andrew made as if to join them, so he went over and sat by Annie and Ruth. He watched Jason and Lawrence—two farmers—hunched together, whispering, nodding, slowly shaking heads, occasionally looking up to regard Andrew.

After a few minutes of this, Lawrence stood and so did Jason.

"I'm going to the farmhouse," said Jason, "just for a little while. I'll bring back breakfast."

"You want some help?" asked Annie, and Lawrence shook his head.

"It'll be all right ma'am," he said, as he led Jason outside. "We've got things in hand."

The door closed behind them, and Andrew looked at the two women.

"Well," said Annie, "that was curious."

"I don't think he cares for us," said Ruth from her bed. "Mr. Thorn, I mean."

"I suppose we are an imposition," said Annie.

Andrew crossed his arms so he cradled his injured right in the crook of his left. "We are," he said, "but it's not just that."

Annie touched Andrew's shoulder, and nodded. It wasn't just that, and she knew it and Andrew knew it too. There was only so much forbearance to be had, in some white people—most white people, in Andrew's experience—for the presumed wisdom, medical or otherwise, of a Negro.

Ruth looked at both of them, and then straight at Andrew, and nodded.

"You," she said, firmly, "will never be an imposition to me."

Ruth Harper's and Andrew Waggoner's eyes met again across the litter of wine bottles, then they both turned to look to Albert Zimmermann.

Andrew thought that another man might have broken down—and maybe that was what Zimmermann was doing now, just not in a way that Andrew recognized. His chin tucked into his collar, as he set both hands on the table, bowl of his pipe clutched tightly in his left. It seemed as though he weren't breathing at all. Andrew reached toward him, but Ruth stopped him with a sharp shake of her head.

"Sometimes he's like this," she whispered.

Andrew motioned for Ruth to join him by the entryway, out of earshot.

"What did he see?" asked Andrew when she did.

Ruth drew a breath to speak, let it out, and drew another.

"There was a calamity at the farmhouse, finally," she said. "Definitely bloodshed. He has difficulty recounting it clearly. It's one of the reasons I took him seriously, when he arrived at Crete. Andrew, he was very ill, in the way that we became . . . ill, after we escaped from Eliada."

"Was he exposed to a Juke, do you think?"

"Not precisely," said Ruth. "No, I don't believe precisely, not like you and I . . . you and I and Jason were. But I had a sense of it when he arrived at the villa I'd rented. He knew he had seen something, and that it was terrible.

But . . . well, he has benefitted from our Decameron System. He continues to benefit from it."

"All right," said Andrew. "Is he going to be able to continue now?"

Across the room, as if he heard, Zimmermann rose from his chair. He shook his head, and set his pipe down. Ruth touched Andrew's elbow and led him back to their chairs as Zimmermann rolled his shoulders and resumed his own seat.

"If it is all right," he said, "I think I shall have that wine now."

Dominic emptied the remains of a bottle into a glass and handed it to Zimmermann, then set to work opening a fresh bottle.

"I got ahead of myself," said Zimmermann. "We are here to talk about Jason Thistledown, your friend. And mine, I suppose. I've told you enough about his captors."

Dominic topped up Zimmermann's glass, and looked around the table to see if anyone else wanted more.

"Jason did come back from his mission in the valley. Let me tell you about that."

"I was smoking at the front doors as the truck pulled up. Aguillard got out of the cab along with Gustav, and they summoned the guards. I joined at a distance to watch as they clambered into the back, and gathered the stretcher that bore Jason. They had strapped him to it at the chest and feet; his neck was covered in a thick swathe of bandage, as were his hands. His eyelids seemed swollen shut, his lips were chalky dry. His shirt was soaked with sweat and patches of blood. And he seemed as if he were convulsing—although that may have been a misapprehension on my part.

"'The door!' shouted Gustav, seeing me, and I hurried to it, propping it open as they hurried within. There was a sitting room—a smaller, finer one than the one where I was bivouacked, on the other side of the farmhouse—that had been remade as an infirmary, with cots and bandages and racks of medicine. I slipped in after Aguillard—and no one objected when I moved to help transfer him to one of the cots.

"Jason fought us as we undid the straps from the stretcher, and it was beyond us to bind him to the cot, so we had to hold him down while Aguillard prepared an injection. He was like a wild animal—pitiable in his way. Well, I took pity.

"As we held him, I leaned close and whispered, in English: "I am sorry, Captain Thorn. I did not know."

"And at that, he did calm himself. He let Aguillard approach with his syringe, and lay still as the needle pricked his forearm.

"'Go to hell, Albert,' he said finally. But he was smiling, and he added: 'That's right. You didn't know.'

"Aguillard ordered me out of the room, and Gustav escorted me back to the barrack hall. What had happened? I asked.

"'He returned,' said Gustav. 'That's something in itself. But he came back in the state you just saw him . . . filthy, raving . . . just past dawn today. He had lost the pack we sent him in with, and the camera we gave him.'

"'He's injured,' I said, and guessed: 'Did he do it to himself?' I mimed burning a cigarette in my throat, and Gustav nodded.

"'Dr. Aguillard believes the burns have become infected,' he told me.

"'Shell shock,' I said. Gustav agreed with that too.

"Now at this point, I should say that Gustav and I had visited Wallgau to attend the beer hall, and although I had found a postmaster I had not been able to get clear of Gustav long enough to post the letter to my masters. How much better my report would be, should I be able to include an interrogation of Jason Thorn! That night, I made to return to the infirmary."

"You were getting bolder," commented Kurtzweiller.

"It was not so difficult," said Zimmermann. "There was a watch placed at the front doors, and the main entrance to the infirmary. But there was also a passageway from the kitchens that led to the sitting room, and more than once I had seen S.A. men steal into it at night to filch some bread and honey. The Nazi S.A. . . . they dress like an army, but they are simple hoodlums at heart. Truly, something will have to be done with them should Herr Hitler ever gain power.

"So I did what they did: sliced a stub of bread, dipped it in honey, and when I was sure that I was alone, made my way into the sick room. I had a plan, should Jason be under guard, or care, to explain that I was simply coming in to check on my old pilot—and if Aguillard or any other told me to leave, well, I would. This was much simpler than my adventure in the upper floors.

"But as fortune would have it . . . Jason was alone. The straps had been removed, and he lay on his cot, smoking one of his cigarettes, feet crossed on the frames. He was utterly calm—and whatever drug Aguillard had given him, he was no longer under its influence.

"'Herr Zimmermann,' he said quietly. 'It's a bit late, isn't it?'

"'I thought you might enjoy an evening snack,' I said, and presented the bread. Jason sat up, with some difficulty, and took it from me.

"'You're sorry,' he said. 'I figured that out already,'

"As he bit into the crust, I set about to tell him part of the truth. I had indeed taken money to agree to the rerouting of the trip, but I had not been told the reason, or the risk. I had not known that Nazi Party interests were involved. I did not, of course, tell him about the Russians. I did not tell him the rumours I had gathered from the S.A. men here. When I was finished, I poured him a mug of water and when he had washed down his meal, he simply nodded.

"In time, I asked: 'Can you say what has happened to you?'

"'I can't,' he answered, and I motioned to his bandages.

"'Can you say how those came about?' I asked.

"'I did some of that to myself.' He held up his cigarette with one hand, pointed to his neck with another. 'Lit cigarette, pressed under the jawline. It's a trick I picked up . . . when I was younger.'

"'For the shell shock,' I said and motioned toward his bandages. 'You perhaps have learned it too well.'

"'Not for shell shock,' he said. 'Though I used it when I was flying. Nothing gets a man's attention like pain. For a time, anyhow. I don't think it's going to work anymore.'

"'You have become inured,' I said, and he nodded again.

"'It looks that way,' he said. 'Anyhow, your pal Aguillard tells me it's gone infected in there. So I'm taking some sulfa until I'm well enough to go back.'

"'Back to where precisely? Africa?' I asked, and that brought a quiet laugh.

"'No,' he said. 'Back beyond yonder mountains.'

"I asked him for what purpose, and he grew quiet again and finished his cigarette. He stubbed it out in a pan on the table by his bed and looked at me.

"'You say you're sorry,' he said, and now I simply nodded.

"'Now it's not I don't appreciate the bread and water,' said Jason. 'But I need you to do something for me.'

"'Name the task,' I said.

"'More than one task,' he said. 'First one's easy. Fetch me a pencil and paper. There should be both in that desk.' He pointed me to a rolltop desk by the window. While I found the items, he struck a match to light another cigarette and clamped it in his lips and beckoned. I hurried over with it. As I waited, he wrote a careful note—indeed, the same note that Miss Harper showed you. He folded it, and handed it to me.

"'Next job now. There's a lady named Ruth Harper. An American lady, real rich. Old friend of mine. She's staying with some folks she knows up in Germany. The Dietrichs, in Brandenburg. You find out the best way to post this to her, care of them. You don't show this to anybody here.'

"I unfolded the letter, and then read it when Jason nodded his approval.

"'This sounds very dire,' I said. 'The lady is in danger?'

"'That's what they told me here,' said Jason. 'If I can't do the job behind those mountains, they told me they'll go get Miss Harper and make her try.'

"'And we cannot allow that,' I said. 'Tell me, how is it that you trust me with this message? I could easily turn it over to Aguillard.'

"'That's so,' said Jason. 'But if you do, Miss Harper'll be in no worse straits than she is now. And if you don't . . . Well, there'll be at least one fellow in this place I know I can trust.'

"That is how Jason thinks," Andrew commented. "Very strategic when he wants to be. And I take it from your presence that you earned his trust."

"I did," said Zimmermann. "No one saw the letter at the farm. And although I considered it, my masters in Vienna didn't either."

"Now that's a risk," said Lewis. "If they'd found you were holding back—"

"—they might expose my ancestry. That is why I considered it. But I also considered the position in which Jason had been placed by the men there. It was very similar to my own: labour and loyalty, compelled by threat of harm." Zimmermann looked to Ruth at that moment. "To family and friends." Ruth nodded.

"And so it was that on my next visit to Wallgau, I brought two letters. One, to my masters—very circumspect—and another, to Ruth Harper, care of the Dietrich family, who were luckily well-enough born that the postmaster was able to find an address. It sounds absurd now—but it was important that I pass Jason's test."

"Not absurd at all," said Dominic, so softly that Andrew thought he might be the only one who heard, so Andrew amplified:

"It doesn't sound absurd, Herr Zimmermann. I hope Jason was happy when you reported your success."

"Happy enough," said Zimmermann. "Although it was not for some time—not for more than a week, when so much had changed."

"Albert," said Ruth, "you are getting ahead of yourself again." She shifted so as to address first Andrew. "Jason returned to the valley rather quickly, as you might imagine, Andrew." And to the rest: "Mr. Thistledown has never lain long in his sick bed. On the third day—"

"The second," said Zimmermann.

"The second day," said Ruth, "Jason left the farmhouse."

"At dawn," said Zimmermann. "I missed his departure. By the time I was up, the infirmary was open and the sheets on his cot were fresh. I did catch Aguillard at work at the desk, and asked him about Jason's whereabouts. Was he at the plane, preparing for us to leave?

"'Not today,' said Aguillard. 'We are guests here for a while longer.'

"'Pardon me for asking, but do you know how much longer?' I had spent very little time in Aguillard's company, and if Jason were gone, I reasoned it might be a credible time to press him for more information. 'Desrosiers must be wondering, after his investment.'

"'He and you have both been well-compensated for this delay,' said Aguillard. 'But I cannot say how long it may be. If Mr. Thorn's condition upon his return from his last sojourn beyond the hills was any indication, it might not be long at all.'

"'May I guess that he has returned for a second trip?'

"'You may,' said Aguillard.

"'What is he doing in that place?'

"'I shouldn't say," said Aguillard. 'But I believe you've already guessed. You must have, having spent time here among all these—' He gestured about him, with a short flourish '—these bumpkins.'

"'They call him the sorcerer,' I said, and at that Aguillard laughed.

"'Bumpkins,' he repeated. 'Thorn is no sorcerer. What he is . . . is unnaturally strong-willed. He is here because unlike you and I, Herr Zimmermann, he will not be bent. Yet he is going back to a place where everyone bends, sooner or later.'

"'That is the world as I know it, Doctor,' I said, and Aguillard laughed again, this time until he coughed and shook his head, finally reaching into his desk to produce a steel flask. Would I have a drink with him? Of course I would."

"What was Aguillard drinking?" asked Lewis. "Cognac?"

“Scotch whisky,” said Zimmermann. He looked puzzled at the question and Andrew explained:

“Dr. Lewis is helping drawing a truer memory than might otherwise exist.”

“Do you think I am fabricating?” asked Zimmermann.

“No,” said Andrew. “Not with your conscious mind. But our memories and the stories we tell . . . the lies . . . can sometimes intermingle. You’re a spy, after all.”

“It is an element of the Decameron system,” said Ruth. “A failsafe. I daresay, these gentlemen have deployed it with unusual discretion so far this evening.”

“Of course. Well, then. Scotch whisky was not what I would have expected Aguillard to have on hand, and not a drink that I often imbibe. So I had to ask him what it was, and that is what he told me. May I now tell you the other questions I asked of him?”

“Of course,” said Lewis.

Zimmermann set his glass aside and took a moment to relight his pipe. He made no effort to disguise his irritation, and finally, continued.

“I asked him about his own politics, to get that out of the way.

“‘Well I am not a supporter of Herr Hitler, if that’s what you mean,’ said Aguillard. ‘I am . . . let us say that I am a Perfectionist. In the formal sense of the word. And the men of Hitler’s Nazi Party do not fit with that, however much they might imagine themselves to.’ He paused, as though choosing what to say next. ‘It is necessary that we cooperate with them now,’ he said, at last, ‘particularly given the things that they have sacrificed for this . . . experiment. You are not, I hope, sympathetic?’ I assured him that I was not. ‘No need to tell any of those men these thoughts I am sharing, then.’

“‘Of course,’ I told him.

“Now, gentlemen, I can see by your expressions that you think this to be a very odd business. Drinking with Dr. Aguillard in the early morning—taking confidences such as those . . . One of you might want to ask me to provide another telling detail, to see if I’m not making it all up. Well. While I was thinking about what we were drinking, I might have forgotten to describe Aguillard’s state. Do you recall how I was, a few moments earlier? Quiet, maybe shaking—at a terrible recollection, a monstrous shame? At times, as Aguillard spoke, he was like as I might have seemed. His eyes would dart about the room, sometimes seeming to light on something . . .

but nothing that I could see. And then that would pass, and he would speak in a more ordinary way until it came again.

"I suppose . . . as I was telling this story, I suppose that I might have omitted those moments. They would have interrupted the narrative I was constructing . . . fabricating, if I have that correct, Dr. Waggoner."

Andrew folded his hands around the stem of his glass.

"Why do you think he was in such a state?" asked Lewis. "What thing was he recalling?"

"What indeed? I think that I know what it was now, but at the time, I would have had no idea." At this, Zimmermann allowed himself the tiniest smile.

"Well, what, then?" demanded Kurtzweiller.

"All right," said Zimmermann. "I will break the sequence of events and tell you. All through the night ending in Jason's departure, Aguillard had not slept. I learned later that he and Dr. Bergstrom had been in conference until the small hours. At issue was Jason's trustworthiness: Bergstrom was of the opinion Miss Harper should be extracted posthaste, and brought to properly motivate Jason. Aguillard thought that premature. They left one another in disagreement, and Aguillard stalked off to see to his patient. Aguillard spent the remaining hours with Jason, locked in the room. What transpired therein? It is not known. What is known, is this:

"Jason departed in the truck, accompanied by Dr. Aguillard, just past five in the morning. Later that morning—after Aguillard and I had finished our discussion, and most of his flask—I would learn that more than three-quarters of the provisions on hand in the kitchen were gone. I imagine that weighed heavily on poor Aguillard. For assuredly, as I learned later still, he was more than complicit—just as I was—in the schemes of Jason Thorn. Jason Thistledown."

Zimmermann drew deep from his pipe, and exhaled slowly into a haloed miasma.

"I had delivered a letter. He had delivered a larder."

Five

There was a sharp knock at the door, a rhythm familiar enough that Andrew shouted to come in. It was Bobby Grady, up from the bar. He stepped inside and left the door open behind him, long enough for the quiet from the Liberty to settle on them.

"Just thought you gentlemen ought to know, we're closed for the night now."

"Is it that late?" Andrew looked at his watch, and saw it was: close to three in the morning. "I'm sorry, Bobby. We got absorbed."

"So you did," he said and smiled. Bobby was an American expatriate, like Andrew from New York City originally, specifically Brooklyn. Unlike Andrew, a couple of decades on the continent hadn't dulled his accent. "You don't look like you're done either. Look at all those bottles with corks in 'em!" He gestured with one thick arm to the table, where indeed a good eight bottles of wine still stood untouched. "I don't mind if you stay past closing, but you gentlemen—and lady, pardon me, Miss Harper—got some work ahead of you."

Kurtzweiller lifted his glass in an exaggerated toast, but the attempt at levity didn't go far. He, like all of them, was mulling the implications of Zimmermann's story—of Jason Thistledown's return to the valley with a truck full of provisions. Just as one might, if one were worshipping, and feeding, a growing Juke.

"I think we do want to stay," said Andrew. "Not sure how much more wine we're going to have, though. This looks as though it's turning into an all-nighter. Do you have coffee down there?"

"Not made," said Grady. He deftly found his way around the table, picking up the empty bottles and tucking them in his arm—pointedly leaving the full ones. "I could fill the urn before I shut up, though. Not much trouble, Doc. You can fetch it yourself from the bar, if you don't mind doing that, and leave the back way. Might be best. Just lock up."

Andrew thanked him, and Grady addressed himself to Ruth: "Good to see you again, Miss Harper. Trust we're keeping the place to your satisfaction."

"It's your place, Mr. Grady. It's my investment, but I daresay you're keeping it better than I would if I owned it."

Grady laughed and shook his head.

"All right," he said. "Coffee'll be ready in a quarter of an hour. I'll leave a tray of mugs on the bar. And a key."

When Grady was gone, Zimmermann turned to Ruth.

"You have a stake in the restaurant?" he asked.

"A small one," said Ruth. "Mr. Grady was one of my father's . . . more sensible employees. Like Dr. Waggoner. And that meant, as things transpired . . . it was better he make himself scarce of America."

"Was he in that town?" asked Zimmermann. "Eliada? When it happened?"

"No," said Ruth. "Only Dr. and Mrs. Waggoner. And Jason and I. Only us."

"Mr. Grady was in Chicago at the time," said Andrew. "He's a good man."

"He protected my interests," said Ruth, and added, pointedly: "As you're doing now, Albert."

"Well." Zimmermann smiled. "Perhaps we can start an airline when this is finished."

Ruth smiled back. "With Jason."

"And on the subject of Jason," said Andrew, "what happened when he returned?"

"Did he return?" asked Lewis.

"Oh yes," said Zimmermann.

"It took longer than his first trip, though: he was gone for seven days this time, and when he returned, he was healthy and strong. This time, all the ill that came from his absence fell upon the farmhouse. The scouring of the larder was one cause—but not truly a serious one. It only left the company of S.A. men on rations for a day while the group arranged for more foodstuffs from Wallgau. I, of course, offered my assistance, riding in on one of the trucks to gather supplies once they were ready . . . and also, to take the opportunity to collect a letter from my masters in Vienna that was waiting with the postmaster. I had not told them everything—

but I had told them enough that they wanted to know more. What was the experiment in the valley? They demanded that I make my way to the site, and photograph it. They wanted to know more about the involvement of Hitler's party, and ordered me to ingratiate myself with the scientists there.

"Of course, I had already done so by this time, with Aguillard. The others . . . Muckermann was not at the farm during my stay, and Plaut, I learned, had departed shortly after Jason's first return. Dr. Bergstrom, meanwhile . . . he was not a man I thought I could deceive. He had a way of looking at you . . . as though he were listening very carefully, to things that you were certain you were not saying."

Andrew nodded.

"Even approaching him would arouse suspicion. So I kept a respectful distance. But I made a point of observing him, eavesdropping as fortune allowed, as I continued to talk with Aguillard. Bergstrom came downstairs twice daily at most, always wearing the same half-smile. Sometimes he would confer with Aguillard, but when this happened he would invite him out for a stroll in the field, or into the low hills. Aguillard would speak of many things—but not those conversations.

"Given Aguillard's state, I cannot help but think that Bergstrom was speaking to him as much as a patient as he was a colleague.

"Aguillard's state. Yes. The nervousness I'd seen during our conversation in the infirmary room only grew worse. He would lose the train of his thought frequently. To keep the conversation going, I decided to draw him out on politics—German politics, and the many flaws in the doctrine of Nazism. I was generally inclined to agree with Aguillard—but not for the same reasons. His loathing was that of a spurned lover . . . an ally, betrayed. For there was common cause between Adolph Hitler and Hector Aguillard."

"Never mind the politics," said Kurtzweiller, a trifle sharply.

"It is getting late," agreed Lewis amiably, "and we're too drunk for politics." He looked to Dominic. "Why don't you go downstairs and fetch the coffee?"

"Of course." Dominic rose and excused himself.

"My only point," said Zimmermann, "was that I could not extract a great deal from Aguillard, and he was . . . deteriorating. I began to wonder if that deterioration didn't have something to do with his daily routine. For each day, Aguillard would drive out to the checkpoint up in the foothills where

Jason was to rendezvous upon his return. He would spend several hours there. But to what end? It was manned by two S.A. men at all times—they had a radio, and would be able to signal should Jason return. What would Aguillard have to do there for hours on end?

"It was no good asking. I tried that one morning . . . the fourth morning, if you want some specificity, Dr. Kurtzweiller . . . and it was awful. Aguillard opened his mouth to answer, closed again, and so on, until he was gaping like a fish, eyes screwed shut . . . his voice a glottal sound, as much like retching, or choking, as speech. When he finally took control of himself, he was red-faced and breathing heavily. He wagged his finger at me, and coughed, and retreated to the kitchen to pour himself some well water.

"Some of the S.A. men rotated through guard duty there, and I asked them: what happens there? What does the shift entail? None of them offered Aguillard's response. But of course they had their own stories, and had already told me as much—of the children who'd turned into trees, and the serpent.

"'We guard,' they said. 'You are lucky you don't have to.'

"And it was in that conversation I hatched my plan to complete the second task my masters asked of me."

"Did you follow Jason into the valley?" asked Lewis, and Zimmermann shook his head.

"My masters in Vienna wanted me to do that, but I wasn't about to follow him there. I'm not a coward, but I'm no fool either."

"Of course not," said Ruth. "Tell them the story of the watch."

"The story of the watch?" Andrew spared Ruth a knowing glance. It was no accident that Ruth fell upon the Decameron to name the system they'd devised. Since he'd first met her, when she was really a child, she'd been enamored of stories . . . Andrew remembered that half the reason she'd given young Jason the time of day in Eliada was because she liked to imagine the gun battles his father Jack Thistledown'd waged in the Incorporation Wars from the last century. Ruth could not ever resist a tale.

Zimmermann merely shrugged.

"I persuaded one of the S.A. men to let me take his shift. His name was Gerhardt Holtz, I believe. He was older than the rest . . . not much, but enough. He was a complainer. That made it easy to convince him, and easier to convince his mates. 'Give Gerhardt a few nights off. Isn't Albert Zimmermann a good fellow for volunteering? Why not let him?'"

"So let me understand this," said Lewis. "The men of the S.A. decided amongst themselves the guard shifts? Who was their commander?"

"I wondered that myself, at first," said Zimmermann. "There was a *Hauptsturmführer* . . . like a lieutenant in the army, but of course the S.A. is not an army . . . but it seemed only in title. He, like the others, deferred to Plaut, or Bergstrom. But Plaut was away that night, and Bergstrom . . . well, he was preoccupied with his own matters. So yes. The S.A. men decided their own guard shifts. The *Hauptsturmführer* didn't care. So long as it was done.

"We marched up the road on foot, with packs of provisions and our rifles. It was less than a mile, not very steep but a very steady climb. There were four of us altogether. Shall I name the others? Frederich Stohl, Ernst Weber, a third . . . Peter . . . Janz? I am not certain. I didn't spend the full two days with them, as matters transpired, and their company was not the thing that I recall most vividly.

"The checkpoint itself . . . it was a small log cabin along a roadside, in a copse of evergreen. There were two rooms in it, and an outdoor privy behind it. One room was occupied with a wood stove, and cots. The other, with provisions—and rifles too, with ammunition, and a radio set.

"It was high enough in the foothills that the mountains beyond didn't seem as majestic. From the front stoop, it was possible to see the cleft through which the road passed, into the valley beyond.

"When we arrived, the men there were glad to see us. The weather was turning from an overcast morning to a stormy afternoon, so the eight of us waited it out around the stove while the cold rain pounded down. We were told things to watch out for. A brown bear was foraging in the vicinity, so we better keep the food shut away and always carry rifles outside—maybe just use the chamber pot at night, rather than chance the privy. The woodpile was getting low, and if we didn't cut some then the shift that came after us would have to. And we should keep an eye on the pass. One of the men reported seeing lights there the previous night—flames, he thought, from torches or lanterns. 'They were moving in a line,' he said, 'as if coming down from the pass toward us.'

"'But they didn't,' I said.

"'They vanished amid the trees,' he said, pointing up the hill.

"Did they investigate? No. Perhaps we might investigate now, I suggested. Once the rain had cleared up. 'Do what you want,' said another of the men. 'We will return to the farm for supper.'

"And return they did, in plenty of time.

"When they had gone, I attempted to form a party. I finally persuaded Frederich to join me on a hike. The rest had little enthusiasm for the adventure—none wanted to tarry too near the haunted pass—and I think Frederich only joined me when it was clear I would go alone if he didn't. We packed rifles and a hatchet, a pair of binoculars and an electric lamp in case we found ourselves on the mountain slope in the dark. Which, Frederich made clear, we would endeavor to avoid at all cost.

"'We will stay to the road. And we will not enter the pass.' He wagged his finger at me. 'Do not even consider it.'

"I promised solemnly enough to satisfy Frederich, and off we went, up the road as it wound up the slope. The sky was clearing as we went, but there was still plenty of cloud, some of it low enough that it collected in a steely mist that gleamed where the late-day sun struck it as it shone here and there. The binoculars were of little use, so I slung them. I wasn't sure what we were looking for . . . or rather, I didn't want to say what *I* was looking for . . . some tiny clue as to what was transpiring in the valley.

"As it happened, we found rather more than a clue. The road crested a low ridge, and to one side the land fell off into a rocky gully, carved by a fast-moving mountain stream that caught the sun here and there through gruel-thin mist that collected at the bottom. The far side of the gully was much higher than ours, the rock there nearly as steep as a cliffside. The road followed the ridgeline and after a few hundred yards disappeared again into trees. As we followed it, we began to hear . . . noises. Voices.

"High, clear voices . . . singing. I heard them first—I think. Frederich had little interest, at first just marching on with great resolve, as though he might overtake the song. But I convinced him to stop and we both crouched down at the edge, turning our ears to try and locate the singers. It was no good: the gully formed a natural amphitheatre, and the music echoed through the rocks so that it seemed to be coming from everywhere. I scanned the stream bed with my binoculars, again and again . . . but saw nothing.

"'Give them over,' said Frederich finally, and I was about to—but I caught a movement, upstream where the gully narrowed into a crevasse. I focussed, but there was nothing—and then, without warning, Frederich let out a cry and fell. He tumbled down the edge of the gully. I dropped the binoculars and turned, just in time to avoid sharing the same fate as Frederich.

"It was girl, blonde-haired and wild, filthy . . . naked but for shoes . . . she had pushed Frederich, and now her thin arms clutched at my shoulders. I let the binoculars fall, and managed to step back from the edge and swing her around over the gully. She scratched at my face, shrieking in a mad rage. I laid hold of her arm to prevent her from reaching my eyes, and with my free hand cuffed her ear. She shrieked again, and kicked out at my groin. She didn't manage to hit me, but it was enough of a distraction that I lost grip. She gave a last, half-hearted effort to push me into the gully, then turned and bolted, to the trees on the far side of the road.

"I gave a short chase, but not far into the woods. I unslung my rifle, shouting at her to stop as I stepped to the edge of the trees. But I hadn't a shot and she knew it as well as I. And of course Frederich had fallen. So I returned, thinking he might require aid. He was scuffed, but not badly cut and nothing broken.

"'Well,' he said as he dusted himself off, 'this has been quite a day. We survived a bear attack, and not many can boast of that.'

"At first I thought he was joking, but as we talked, Frederich insisted: the brown bear, possibly protecting her cubs, had swatted him and knocked him into the gully. I was lucky she had not torn me apart.

"There was nothing I could do to convince him otherwise.

"'Look at that cut on your face,' he said, pointing at me. 'That's not the work of a little girl.'

"Is that the cut?" asked Lewis, pointing to Zimmermann's cheek. Before Zimmermann could answer, Kurtzweiller shook his head no.

"That is from fencing," he said.

"The cut was on my jaw, and really nothing more than a scratch," Zimmermann said. "Frederich was in worse condition from his tumble. Still, he insisted it was time to return to the checkpoint. So we did."

"The singing," said Andrew. "Did it continue?"

"Oh yes," said Zimmermann. "I heard it echoing until we were well out of sight of that gully, and all the way back to the checkpoint I thought I could hear it still. I didn't talk about it, however, among the other men. Just as I did not contradict Frederich when he told the tale of how he'd faced a brown bear and lived. So we ate our evening meal, and I made certain to volunteer for the last watch of the night. The others would be sleeping deepest then, but I would be roused and be able to report any incident."

"To your Russian masters," said Andrew.

"To them. Yes." Zimmermann looked into the bowl of his pipe, and reached into his pocket to find more tobacco. "I was not sure precisely what I would be reporting. Frederich's delusion about seeing the bear . . . the presence of the girl . . . I presumed that she was one of the young, rebellious nudists from the valley. I guessed that the reports of bear sightings around the checkpoint might have sprung from a similar delusion. So I hoped that finding and perhaps interrogating that girl might offer up some better intelligence about the valley than a simple visit."

Andrew didn't think that was a good plan, particularly, but wasn't sure what he would've done in Zimmermann's place. "So what did you find, on that last watch?" he asked. Zimmermann struck a match and lit his pipe and puffed, watching the smoke rise before him. Ruth cleared her throat.

"I think we agreed it was an enormous man," she said. "Isn't that right?"

Andrew put a hand on Ruth's arm to indicate that she shouldn't be leading Zimmermann, but she brushed him away.

"Mr. Zimmermann has had difficulty recalling this moment precisely," she explained. "That is why, when he arrived to greet me at the house where I was staying in Crete, I was convinced of the rest of his story. He was addled."

"Addled?"

"In a way very familiar to you and I, Andrew."

"It is so," said Zimmermann. "Miss Harper has told me a fair bit about your Juke—the way it can insinuate itself into a man's perceptions, and perhaps worse, his recollections. This is what I have experienced, more and more, from that evening onward. What did I see that night? Miss Harper and I were eventually able to agree that the true memory was of a very tall, very powerful man. Fully a head taller than I. Twice as broad. But not fat. No fat at all. But he was also a great owl, whose wings blotted out the stars as they spread, or a woman smaller than a child, with razor teeth. . . ."

"But that wasn't right," said Ruth, coolly.

"No," said Zimmermann. "It was a man, as I described just now. I know this for certain, because I saw him again."

"Did he speak to you?" asked Lewis.

"Oh yes. I had elected to take my patrol farther from the cabin than the others suggested. I brought the lamp with me, and shone it up the road . . . into the woods to the side of it . . . My rifle at the ready—I knew there was danger, but I wanted to see what else ranged on this slope.

"I don't know how far I would have finally gone—the dark was absolute. But I didn't make it a long way. The light caught him where he half-hid, to the side of the roadway. He was crouched on his haunches. He was naked, but only from the waist. And hirsute. He grinned at the light, in a way that I first thought was just a squint. But the light didn't dazzle him. He stood, taking perhaps only two steps toward me before I lowered the rifle and ordered him to halt.

"'There is no hiding from you,' he said, and he laughed. A big man's laugh. Quite merry. It made me want to like him, I admit, so when he asked me my name I gave it readily.

"'The pilot,' he said. I didn't answer him this time so he elaborated: 'You flew the aircraft that crossed my sky a week ago. You brought the *Übermensch*.'

"The *Übermensch*. The superman," said Andrew.

"He was referring to Jason," said Ruth, and Andrew felt an involuntary shiver. It wouldn't have been the first time that someone had described Jason that way, and they all knew there was some evidence to back that up. But it never went well for him when someone else took notice.

"He spoke to me other things too," said Zimmermann, "but my recollection of those is less . . . reliable. I know that he asked me questions that I didn't answer, and others that I did. I did admit to being a pilot. I didn't tell him about my pact with the Russians. I told him how many men were at the checkpoint, but I think he knew that already. I told him everything I knew about Aguillard, and Bergstrom, and Plaut.

"And I told him finally that no one knew what to make of the valley, or the children who had disappeared there.

"'The men believe that the children have become the forest,' I said, 'and that there is a beast.'

"'Well,' said the giant, 'they are right. In both matters.'

"By then, we found ourselves back at the stoop of the checkpoint, and as we set foot there . . . I was alone." Zimmermann offered a thin smile. "I suppose that he might have just stepped out of the beam of my lamp, then hurried off. But if he did so, he moved silently and very swiftly, for I remember sweeping the lamp through the trees and up the road, even to the cabin itself. The giant was gone.

"I spent the remainder of my watch close to the cabin—as I'd been ordered to. Although I had really learned little from my encounter with the giant, I felt myself . . . drained of curiosity, of questions. It was a moment of peace . . . and of great awareness, I suppose . . . I can remember the smell of the pine needles, the icy breeze from the mountains . . . the emerging forms of the trees and the rocks under the pinkening sky. I didn't sleep. But I felt as though I were dreaming."

"And then," said Ruth, prompting after a moment's silence.

"And then," said Zimmermann, "Jason appeared over the rise. Jason Thorn. Jason *Thistledown*. He stood tall, and strong. confident. Better than he was when he left the farm . . . than he was, really, when I met him in Paris." Zimmermann drew deep from his pipe.

"And he was much better off than the man who walked beside him. That fellow, now . . .

"Herr Gottlieb. Markus Gottlieb. That was his name. . . .

"He was a wretch."

Six

"Jason's return ended my watch rather abruptly. Aguillard . . . well, he was not pleased to find me at the checkpoint when he arrived with the truck and his doctor's bag. I had created a minor commotion at the farmhouse in 'volunteering' to take a watch—and as I was then the only pilot there with skills to fly the plane, I suppose created a middling crisis in manpower.

"'What would we do, should anything happen? If we might have to depart?' he demanded, and when I suggested that he might simply turn the crank on that truck and drive off, he glared at me.

"'We mightn't get far,' he said.

"'I will stay close to the farm,' I said. 'I was merely trying to be of use. There is little for me to do, you will understand, Doctor.'

"Did he believe me? That I was simply bored? Perhaps. If he didn't, what did it matter? As Aguillard himself said: I was their only pilot." Zimmermann scratched his beard, and in a moment's pause pushed his chair back and rose to his feet. "I was *vital*."

"Tell them about Markus Gottlieb," said Ruth, who also stood—somewhat less steadily. "He was like the girl you saw."

"Yes," said Zimmermann. "Gottlieb arrived naked, but for a pair of boots . . . a filthy blanket over his shoulders."

"Just like that girl," said Kurtzweiller.

"Well she didn't have a blanket. And he seemed older, much older than the girl certainly. More weathered. Almost as if he'd been beaten, many times over the course of a long time. His hair was filthy, and hung below his ears, even as it was thin at the crown." Zimmermann patted his own forehead as he spoke. "Jason introduced him to me . . . the first thing he said as they strode up: 'Albert Zimmermann, say hello to Markus Gottlieb.' He seemed utterly unsurprised to see me, as though he knew that I would be standing watch that morning.

"Before I could say anything, Markus Gottlieb extended a wretched hand, and Jason said 'Go on, shake!' So I took the fellow's hand, which felt like a bundle of twigs in mine, and we shook.

"'How do you do, Herr Zimmermann,' Gottlieb said to me. His voice was strange, at once higher and rougher than I can impersonate. 'We are both veterans of the Great War—all three of us, excuse me. But I did not fly. It was the trenches for me.'

"He went on like that while we waited in the checkpoint for Aguillard and the truck—jabbering at whosoever met his eye. He was . . . I suppose you would say manic. While he interrogated Frederich, I pulled Jason aside and asked him about his new friend.

"'He's pleased to meet you all,' said Jason. 'Doesn't get a lot of conversation in the valley.'

"'So he is from the valley,' I said. 'I had guessed—'

"'—and now you know,' said Jason. 'He's not too well. We talked, and he agreed it was a good idea for him to come out and see the doctor.'" With a finger, Zimmermann tilted the back of his chair towards him, so it balanced on two legs.

"It was only when we returned to the farm that I understood it was not Dr. Aguillard of whom Jason spoke." The chair landed back on all four legs as Zimmermann let it go.

"It was Bergstrom."

"He intended to see Bergstrom? Did he know him?" asked Lewis.

"Oh yes," said Zimmermann. "Quite well. Gottlieb had been in Dr. Bergstrom's care, a long time ago. He explained this to any who would listen. Bergstrom had cared for him for a short time in that very valley, when the chateau served as a health spa."

"And a nudist colony?" asked Kurtzweiller.

"Just so," said Zimmermann. "Gottlieb arrived there in the vain hope of curing himself of . . . homosexual proclivities, one might say. Of course, he said, it was a good deal more complicated than that, and in the end . . . he left the valley spa, with Dr. Bergstrom's blessing, to return to the world and find what he only described as 'the source.'"

Andrew frowned. "The source of his homosexuality? That sounds absurd."

"Indeed. Gottlieb didn't illuminate matters during the ride back, but when we returned to the farm and Bergstrom met us, the nature of 'the source' became clearer.

"Bergstrom did not know who was accompanying Jason. Weber was quick to radio in a report of Jason's return with what he called a captive, but he didn't know his name. Bergstrom expected that he would speak to Jason first, and deal with the 'captive' afterward—so when Gottlieb climbed from the truck, Bergstrom kept his distance and let the S.A. men surround him, demanding Jason report. He did not recognize Gottlieb until Jason reminded him. 'Your old patient,' said Jason. 'How 'bout that?'

"It was only then that the reunion began. I cannot say it was especially joyful, not for Bergstrom. Although once Gottlieb was released, he was happy enough.

"'Doctor! You are looking very well!' he shouted, dropping the blanket from his shoulders so he stood nude in the midst of the men. He strode confidently over to Bergstrom, took the poor man's hands and shook them. This did not improve matters. The colour drained from Bergstrom's face and he regarded Gottlieb with what I might only describe as horror . . . the sheerest horror."

Zimmermann breathed deeply, his eyes focussed over all of their heads. His lips parted. Andrew started to say something encouraging, Zimmermann raised a finger, and continued.

"It is difficult to describe the moment, its impact. Perhaps if I employ your system. The truck . . . it was an old Büssing truck, crank-started. The cab was painted an awful yellow. At one time it had had doors on the cab but not anymore. It was stopped behind the house." Zimmermann's eyes fluttered and closed. "The door to the kitchen is open. A woman within, looking out and turning away. Seven men in total from the house. Gerhardt among them. The morning light was . . . brilliant. It seemed not to strike the world, but come from within it.

"Doctor Bergstrom wore . . . what did he wear? A pressed white shirt underneath a dark wool vest. He had shaved that morning, but badly. Flecks of blood on his jaw."

Zimmermann's eyes opened and he dragged the chair back, sat down again.

"'Herr Gottlieb,' Bergstrom said. 'I thought . . .'

"Gottlieb interrupted. 'You thought I might be dead?'

"''No,' Bergstrom said. 'But I am glad to see you are not. Still. I had thought we'd seen the last of you.'

"'Yes!' Gottlieb exclaimed. 'You sent me off, and perhaps thought we were finished. For a time we were. But I returned, see? You helped me—and now, I return to help you.'

"'Help . . .' Bergstrom seemed confused at this, so Gottlieb clarified.

"'The source,' said Gottlieb. 'I found the source. I found Orlok. And I have brought him here.'

Kurtzweiller frowned. "Orlok?"

"It is from the cinema," said Zimmermann. "A film shown a few years ago. *Nosferatu*."

"Ah," said Kurtzweiller, and nodded. "About the vampire."

Andrew steepled his fingers on his chin, allowing himself a smile.

"Orlok," he said. "Let me guess. Was Orlok the fellow you met in the early morning?"

"Yes," Zimmermann answered. "I believe that Orlok was that fellow's name."

"Was he a vampire then?" asked Andrew.

"Vampires are superstitions," said Zimmermann, a little sharply. "All I might say was that the name had an effect on Bergstrom—it seemed as though the word struck him bodily. He didn't say anything more to Gottlieb, not there. He ordered some of the men to escort him upstairs. When they did so, he followed, and Aguillard did too. Jason stayed back, came to me when the area had cleared somewhat, and when he spoke he spoke very quietly, and in English.

"'Did you get the letter sent?' he asked. I nodded yes.

"'All right,' he said, 'what's the state of the plane? Can it fly?'

"'I don't see why it wouldn't,' I said. 'There is plenty of fuel.'

"'Good,' he said. 'You might want to make sure you can fly too. Nothing to drink, right?'

"We walked around the house, and I asked him what he meant. Were we to escape?

"'Maybe,' he said. 'Depends on how that talk between old Bergstrom and Gottlieb goes.'

"I asked him what he imagined that conversation might entail. He admitted that he did not know exactly. But when I asked if it might have to do with Orlok . . . he said it might indeed. What—who—is Orlok?

"'That's between Bergstrom and Gottlieb,' said Jason. 'How much fuel's in the plane, you figure?'

"'More than enough to make Africa,' I said, and Jason nodded.

"'Then you'll be able to make Crete,' he said.

"The Greek Island? I would think so." I made a fast calculation as we walked. 'Yes. More than enough.'

"'Good,' said Jason. 'That's where you're going to want to go.'

"'What is in Crete?' I asked.

"'Miss Harper,' said Jason. 'You find her, tell her I sent you, she'll pay you well. Tell her what Desrosiers offered you, tell her I said to better it.'

"I asked Jason: was he not to be joining me? In answer, he named a villa, asked me to say it back and asked that I remember it, but not say it again.

"'That's where she'll be,' he said. 'If you're on your own, you'll need to go there. If it's us—well, I know the way.'

"I asked more questions. What happened to all the food that Jason took? Was it feeding a population in the valley? How many? What was the matter under discussion between Gottlieb and Bergstrom? And I asked again: Who was Orlok?

"'The food,' Jason said, 'got eaten by, yes, people in that valley.'

"The rest, between Gottlieb and Bergstrom . . . Jason was quite adamant, that it was not my affair. 'That's between a doctor and a patient,' he said.

"And as for Orlok?

"'That's something else again,' Jason told me. 'Orlok's . . . powerful. I'm pretty sure that Bergstrom and the rest would like to meet him. Gottlieb's sure. But I don't think Orlok's sure he wants to meet them, is the thing.'"

"You must have guessed," said Kurtzweiller, "that this Orlok was the man you'd met the night before."

Zimmermann smiled tightly. "I described to you my discussion in great detail just now. But that memory was hard-won. I didn't know what I'd seen then. I suppose that I intuited this might be so. But then . . ."

"You thought it might've been an owl," said Andrew, nodding. "This is all sounds very familiar, Herr Zimmermann. It took me a long time to put together what I really saw, those years back in Idaho. When I was in the Juke's sway."

"So I understand," said Zimmermann, glancing at Ruth. "I think that maybe Jason had a similar difficulty, describing the things that he'd seen in the valley. I only had a little time with him before Gerhardt came to summon him upstairs. He was notably unhelpful as regards any details of his time beyond those hills, in that mysterious valley.

"At first I thought he was being evasive, as I suppose he had every right to be. But as I think of it now, I believe he was embarrassed, and his evasion was not to protect a secret, but to mask his own ignorance, confusion—like a lazy student who arrived unprepared for an examination."

"When did you leave?" asked Lewis. "That night?"

"Oh no. I awaited Jason's signal, some clue that I should make a run—and for some opportunity. By the end of the day, our little farm became very busy. Word passed round the S.A. men with whom I still consorted, that a contingent of the *Hitler-Jugend* command would be arriving from Munich by the morning, and would expect to be seen to. I was pressed into service, erecting tents, moving cots and lockers there, as the bunkroom was cleared out to make way for the visitors. This was one of the few times where I met Plaut. You remember Plaut?"

"The screaming one," said Kurtzweiller drily. "You mentioned him."

"He had been staying in a house in Wallgau. I didn't see him often on his routine visits. He spent most of his time on the upper floor, off-limits to me."

"In the daytime," Ruth noted.

"This time, he made certain he was among us. He inspected the kitchen, the common rooms, as would a glowering butler . . . none of it was to his satisfaction. He made it known to Aguillard, but so as to be heard by all, that we were to be hosting a very important delegation of Nazi Party leadership, come to speak to the prisoner Markus Gottlieb and confer on strategy. He made certain to convey that to everyone before stomping upstairs, to speak again with Bergstrom and Gottlieb.

"The delegation turned out to be important indeed. Kurt Gruber was among them—do you know him? He is the chairman of the *Hitler-Jugend*—a very, very important official from Munich. I did not recognize him myself. But the S.A. were quite surprised and more than a little afraid. For the first time in my life, I raised my arm and uttered the words 'Heil Hitler.' It was made clear to me that it would go badly for me if I did not.

"He was accompanied by a guard of S.A. men, much younger and fitter than the ones at the farm. They were impressive. I counted twenty of them. When they exited their vehicles, they were met at the front doors to the farmhouse, by Plaut, Bergstrom, and Jason . . . and Markus Gottlieb. I barely recognized those two. They were dressed in S.A. uniforms themselves, scrubbed and sheared. Gottlieb in particular was transformed, his hair shaved to his skull, his beard to his sunken cheeks . . . his slight frame swimming in shirt and trousers that were too large by half. He looked ill, still . . . but there was a mischievousness in his eye, as Gruber and his lieutenants approached them. Neither he nor Jason saluted when the time came, and when Gruber turned to speak to Dr. Bergstrom . . . Gottlieb did a most unusual thing, and shouted a greeting.

"'Good morning to you sir!' as though they were old friends, he and this Nazi politician.

"Gruber might well have struck him for the insolence—he seemed that sort of German—and one could see his guard readying themselves for a confrontation. But he did not. Gruber removed his gloves, in the meticulous way that an officer does . . . then allowed himself a sharp but indulgent laugh.

"'Is this our prisoner, Doctor?' he asked Bergstrom, and when Bergstrom said yes, Gruber nodded genially toward Gottlieb and replied: 'Good morrow to you, Herr Gottlieb.'

"'It is good to see you again,' said Gottlieb.

"'I am not certain we have met,' said Gruber.

"'It would have been some time ago,' said Gottlieb. 'Were you not in Munich in 1923?'

"'Ah. I was much younger,' said Gruber. He leaned in, examining Gottlieb. 'So would you have been.'

"'You have aged better,' said Gottlieb, smirking broadly.

"'I am sorry, Herr Gottlieb, I do not recall.'

"'You may remember my friend better.' Gottlieb leaned nearer to Gruber as he spoke—and as he did, Gruber recoiled. Even from where I stood, I could see the mischief in Gottlieb's eye had shifted. I would not have let him get closer to me either.

"'He remembers you!' cried Gottlieb.

"Gruber's S.A. guard put a stop to any further conversation, stepping deftly between Gruber and Gottlieb. They might well have beaten him then—or at least taken hold of him. But they did not, simply stepping between the two as though separating brawlers at a beer hall. There was a deference toward Gottlieb that was uncanny, or so I thought at the time."

"It is odd that they brought Gottlieb out-of-doors at all," said Kurtzweiller. "He seemed a dangerous sort."

"The friend," said Lewis. "That was obviously Orlok."

"Obviously," agreed Zimmermann. "That, I recall, did cause me to draw a line between my encounter with the giant in the night, and the 'friend' that Gottlieb mentioned. I thought that they might well be the same, in part because of the glee with which Gottlieb spoke of him . . . and because of the flash of fear that showed in not only Gruber but also Plaut, and Bergstrom.

"The men withdrew indoors, for a meeting that was to last scarcely more than an hour. I attempted to follow, and got as far as the bottom of the stairs before one of Gruber's men made it clear I should leave. So I returned to the front doors, where the S.A. men from Munich were milling about, and waited with them there. They were not communicative, clearly a class apart from those assigned to the farmhouse—better disciplined, better bred. The men here were deferential, but suspicious of them.

"I didn't stay with that crowd very long. I had not seen to the plane since Jason had bade me leave in it, so I took the opportunity to wander in its direction, confirming it was indeed fuelled and fit to fly. Easier with a co-pilot, but I thought I could get it in the air on my own if need be. I even inspected the charts, and drew a course close enough to Crete to hire a boat.

"By the time I was done, so was Gruber. I could see him from the cockpit, marching along in some hurry back to his car along with those dashing young men of the S.A., who were loading into their own trucks. I waited until they were underway to return, yet when I did, I thought it might have been some trick; it seemed to me that the S.A. men had not left at all. There were as many outside the house as before. Twenty or so young men, gathered alongside the regular farmhouse guard.

"From a distance, it seemed as though it were the same men. They were wearing the brown-shirted uniform of the S.A. after all, and they were correct in number. As I drew closer, however, I could see they might not be. Those who didn't wear caps were unkempt, hair grown out, and sometimes bearded too. They didn't carry themselves the same way—Gruber's men were disciplined, stood straight and strong, as though they were a proper army. These ones leaned against posts and railings, slouching and smirking. When one of the S.A. men from the farm looked at them too long, they would stand a little straighter, almost defiantly . . . and that man would look away, find a fleck of lint on his shirt, shuffle away. As I drew close, one of the 'new' guards caught my eye in a way that seemed a challenge—and hoping to avoid trouble, I raised my hand again in the Nazi salute: '*Heil*

Hitler!' He raised his hand in return, lazily, as though he were mocking me—then said nothing, looking away as though bored.

"As it was clear no one would challenge me, I slipped indoors.

"The front hall of the farmhouse was empty. But the place wasn't quiet. I could hear the sound of intense conversation from the upper floors . . . sounds of someone cooking, or cleaning perhaps, from the kitchen . . . and from the infirmary, nearest me, beyond a door, cracked open . . . laughter. A girl's laughter.

"I sidled up closer, and peered in. I could not see the whole room—but there was Gustav, Aguillard's assistant, seated in a chair with his trousers pulled down below his knee, eyes shut, mouth hanging open in what seemed like a smile. The light from the windows flickered across him—shadows, cast no doubt by the laughing girl, just out of sight. I did not enter the room to see.

"I retreated to the barracks room that we had converted to a dining hall, thinking perhaps that Gruber would stay for a meal. The long tables there had been set, but only partly, as if the work had been interrupted: a cloth of deep red and some silverware was in place, a few candlesticks. As I stood there, the door at the dining hall's far end opened, and a girl entered the room. She saw me, froze in place—and for a moment, so did I.

"We recognized one another from the ridgeline, just two days ago. She was no longer naked—she had found a brown shirt, and wore it like a short dress, a belt clinching it to her waist. She had combed her hair too. Still, it was her. The cuts from her nails still itched. But she didn't attack again—I took a step toward her, and her eyes widened, and she disappeared into the kitchen. Before I could catch up, I heard the back door open and slam. And when I stepped into the kitchen . . ."

"There were corpses," said Ruth, after a moment's silence.

"What?"

"Yes, Dr. Lewis," said Zimmermann. "Fräulein Harper is right. There were two corpses there. I don't know who they were. Men of the S.A. I think. There was a great deal of blood. One had been stabbed. . . . I am guessing that the other's throat had been slashed, the blood pooled around his head on the stones of the floor. I didn't stay to confirm it, because seeing that girl . . . the carnage . . . the strange crew of doppelganger S.A. men outside . . . What perhaps should have been obvious was clear to me now. The great number of formerly naked . . . children, really, who had been living for months like feral animals in the valley, had come here, along with Gottlieb and whoever this Orlok was . . .

"And it was time to leave."

"So you abandoned Jason?" asked Andrew.

"In fact I did the opposite. I withdrew through the dining hall, up the stairs, to try and fetch him, bring him along. There was no one to stop me. The door to the infirmary was shut tight as I passed it, as were the front doors. I ran up the stairs and burst in on them: Aguillard, and Bergstrom, Plaut and Gottlieb . . . seated in chairs in front of the great window looking out over the hills . . . Jason, standing and smoking by the fire.

"Gottlieb had been expounding. 'His mother was a freakishly strong woman, that is how she lived,' he said. 'She bent bars and lifted pianos! No one could beat her!' He was sitting forward, gesticulating wildly. 'You were correct, Herr Bergstrom! He is a superman!'"

"Who was he talking about?"

"I don't know for certain, Dr. Waggoner," said Zimmermann. "One might surmise that he was speaking of the mysterious Orlok. But he stopped abruptly as I entered the room. All of them went quiet, and looked at me.

"'Hello, Albert,' said Jason. He stubbed his cigarette out in a candleholder, and pushed himself away from the mantle.

"'What are you doing here?' demanded Aguillard, and Plaut rose from his chair.

"'This is a private conversation,' Plaut said.

"I apologized, and turned to Jason. 'Captain Thorn,' I said. 'There is a matter of some urgency to which we must attend.'

"I caught Jason's eye as I spoke, and I think he took my meaning well enough.

"'All right,' he said, 'if you gentlemen—'

"Plaut's eyes narrowed and he stepped forward, swelling his chest in the way small men will do to make their presence felt.

"'No,' he said. 'Herr *Thorn* will remain here. There is nothing to be seen to. You have overstepped.'

"Aguillard stepped between us then.

"'Go back downstairs,' he said softly, and took me by the arm, trying to turn me around.

"I did not let him. I took him firmly by the wrist and pulled his hand from my arm. He let out a little shout—I must have twisted, it must have hurt. But I recalled the corpses downstairs . . . the girl . . . the guard, surrounding the front door like a street gang. If any of you have survived a war, you learn at a point to sense when matters become dire. And so I stepped back, fast, beckoning to Jason to follow.

"Jason understood it was time to leave. 'I got to see to this,' he said to Aguillard, and started across the room. But it was worse than either of us had guessed. Gottlieb stood, uttering . . . I can only describe it as a shriek. Wordless and high, like an animal in terrible distress, or rage. He started across the room to us, his hands held like claws. I reacted with a shoulder that sent him hard into one of the little tables. His thigh hit it with a crack that I am sure was not breaking bone—but he sprawled over it as though it were, tumbling to the floor. Plaut, I believe, shouted for guards. Bergstrom, in his own panic, reached into a drawer, in a fumbling way that I have seen men who are new to combat do.

"Jason saw what was happening. He moved very quickly across the room to intersect with Bergstrom as he removed a Luger from the drawer, began to raise it. Jason tackled him before he could get a shot. The gun went off—and Plaut cried out. The bullet had grazed his leg . . . the left, I believe. Jason took the gun from Bergstrom's hand and stuffed it in his belt, ordering Aguillard to see to Plaut, and Bergstrom to take his seat."

"And they did?"

"They did, Dr. Lewis. Even Gottlieb, on the floor, seemed to calm himself, rolling onto his side and looking to Jason, obsequiously. I was surprised, but Jason took it all in stride. 'All right,' he said to me, 'we need to get going.'

"We hurried down the stairs and got as far as the front hall before we saw anybody. There, we saw two men—young, thick-bearded, one stripped to the waist, the other wearing a brown S.A. shirt. They greeted Jason as though he were an old friend but I had not seen either of them before.

"'Where is Markus?' demanded one. 'Upstairs?'

"Jason told them that was where he was.

"'Who shot the gun?' that one asked, pointing to the Luger in Jason's belt. 'You?'

"Jason said no, and when the other asked if there were more guns up there Jason said he didn't know. Then the pair disappeared up the stairs.

"'They are killing people,' I said, when we were alone. Jason gave me a puzzled look, as though he did not understand. I told him about the corpses

I had found in the kitchen. Did he need to see them? He shook his head no. 'I believe you,' said Jason. 'It adds up.'

"I demanded to know what he meant, but he wouldn't say more. And so we set out for the plane—right out the front door, where I had left the mysterious stormtroopers.

"There were more now—more than twice as many. They weren't in uniform at all, and some of them were nearly naked. Young men, some young women too. And yes, there were the old S.A. men too, the ones I knew from the farm—many of them by name. They stood in the midst of these new people, straight and still—as though they had stumbled into some gathering of the dead, and hoped not to be noticed. The new people stared pointedly at them, sometimes stepping close as though they had spotted some blemish, other times stepping back and simply looking, like artists framing a portrait.

"Jason took my arm to hurry me across the field.

"It was I would say three hundred yards from the steps of the farmhouse to the Latécoère. We started out simply walking, so as not to draw attention . . . and then, less than half the ground covered, a gunshot persuaded us to run. More gunshots followed, followed by screaming. . . .

"I tried to look back, but Jason would not let me. He stayed just behind me, and every time I slowed he pushed my shoulder—not hard enough for me to stumble, but hard, so I kept running until we reached the Latécoère.

"Jason climbed inside first, his hand on the Luger, and bade me follow once he pronounced it clear. Before I climbed aboard, I did look back. The gunfire had stopped, but it was impossible to say who had been firing. It had certainly done nothing to disperse the crowd; indeed, it might have grown, nearly five-fold. They milled between the farmhouse and the tents.

"'These are the children—the *Hitler-Jugend* you were sent to observe,' I said. 'Obviously,' Jason agreed. 'And Orlok?' I asked, and he repeated back to me: 'And Orlok.'

"'What exactly are they doing?' I asked, as he took his seat in the co-pilot's chair.

"'I'm not exactly sure,' he said. 'But I know they been living badly in that valley. There are orchards, and the water's not a problem. There are deer in the woods that they sometimes catch, but they're bad hunters. So it's apples and water, the occasional deer, maybe a hare, and whatever stores they've managed to plunder.'

"'They have returned to the farmhouse for a good meal?' I asked, and Jason laughed at that.

"'Logistics, sure.' Then the laughter ended, and his face fell. 'They had to get away,' he said. 'Like you.'

"He did not say more about Orlok. He said some things—intimate things, regarding Fräulein Harper, which I will not repeat. But I took them greatly to heart, and told Fräulein Harper all of them, when we finally met.

"Then he stepped outside as we started the engine, and he hauled the blocks from beneath the landing gear."

Zimmermann drew deep and drained his glass.

"That was the last time that I spoke with Jason Thistledown."

Seven

As Albert Zimmermann finished that last piece of his story, it left them all quiet. It had come out raw and wounded . . . with tears . . . and there were implications that set them all thinking.

Kurtzweiller had opened another bottle, and as he filled everyone's glasses, Lewis wondered aloud what had happened to Dominic, who had still not returned with coffee. Andrew agreed that was a good question, and rose to call downstairs: "Dominic! Do you need help?"

When no answer came, Andrew stepped to the bend to peer down. The lights were dim, but not dark; Andrew could see the end of the bar, and seated at one stool, Dominic—or who he presumed to be Dominic, the view of his shoulders and higher blocked by the ground-floor ceiling.

Andrew turned back to the room. "Drink up," he said, and went downstairs to see about the *Société*'s newest member.

"Do you need help?" asked Andrew again. He leaned on the bar beside Dominic, lowering his head so he could meet the other man's eye. Dominic had helped himself to a cup of the coffee, and was staring into it, his hand shaking. He sipped it noisily.

"I did see a Juke," he said, "in Iceland. Didn't I?"

"Yes," said Andrew. "I think you did."

"I'm sorry," he said. "I lost the trail . . . I ran. There was more to learn, and it should have been obvious to me. I failed you, didn't I?"

Andrew sighed. "You did," he said. "Sure. You lost the trail. You ran. You failed. Just like we all have. We've been trying to investigate this for years . . . decades, some of us. We were better at it, we'd be closer."

Dominic smiled wanly. "You knew that Molinare and I were lovers," he said.

"Sure. We all understood that."

"Do you think that fellow Zimmermann and Jason were lovers, too?"

"I hadn't thought about it. From what I know of Jason, he's not that way."

"Because of his affection for Miss Harper?" Dominic set down his cup. "That might mean less than you think. But I don't know about Jason. I've heard Molinare speak of him, and the adventure that you and he had in that dead town when he was barely a man. But I did talk with that Albert Zimmermann fellow, when Miss Harper sent me down here."

"Did he tell you something?"

"No. I had a sense of it. Possibly."

"Well," said Andrew, "I'll make a note of that." He thought for a moment. "Were you listening just now? To the story about the watch?"

"No. Why?"

"There were some things Zimmermann said . . . just now. As I think about them . . . Maybe you're right. But what of it, if you are?"

"I wasn't entirely truthful you when I told you about my journey in the north." Dominic sighed. "The night in that bunkhouse, that wasn't the only time I encountered Molinare's ghost."

"You saw him again, afterwards?" Andrew didn't see the trouble with that. "After the business in Eliada, with the Juke . . . many nights I'd awake, remembering the things that it made me see."

"I did see him afterwards," said Dominic. "But I also saw him before."

"Before?"

"Before I arrived in Iceland. But after . . ." Dominic looked at Andrew directly, with a chilling clarity. ". . . after the day I now know that he died. I heard his voice in my berth on the steamer, from England. I saw him at the edge of my vision."

"There are no ghosts," said Andrew. "You know that."

"Of course," said Dominic. "But there is the experience of them. Just as true, to the man who feels that. And II think that that Zimmermann fellow is seeing ghosts. Perhaps also Miss Harper. They both love that Jason fellow."

"As you loved Molinare."

"Just as I loved Molinare. Would you like some coffee, Dr. Waggoner?"

Dominic rose and circled the bar, retrieved the percolator, and filled a cup.

"When was the last time you saw Molinare's ghost?" asked Andrew.

Dominic set the cup down before Andrew.

"Just now," he said. "Just a moment ago. He was at the bar, over there."

Dominic pointed to the far end of the bar, toward the Liberty's street entrance. "He warned me, as he often does."

"What did he warn you of?"

"Calamity," said Dominic. "Always calamity."

"Well," said Andrew, "whether you saw him or not, I wouldn't doubt the prediction. Based on Zimmermann's story, I think that's just what we're going to be faced with."

"What did he tell you happened to Jason?"

Andrew thought about that a moment. Zimmermann

"Zimmermann, got out of there, finally. Flew out of there in that plane. He got far away. But he wasn't with Jason. He thought he would be flying with him; Jason gave him every indication that that's what was going to happen. But it didn't work out that way."

"No? Why?"

Andrew drew a breath and held it a moment, as he thought about what to say. "It was right as they were getting ready to leave. Some awful things happened at that farmhouse . . . like the things that you said you saw . . . at that old burned-out church in Iceland."

"The dead sheep," said Dominic, and Andrew said, "But not sheep."

Dominic looked into his cup.

"Jason had got the props spinning and pulled the blocks, which was when he should have hopped back into the plane. But he didn't. He saw someone, you see."

"Who did he see?"

"Zimmermann wasn't clear on that. Just like you weren't, when you were trying to tell your story."

"A ghost?"

Andrew smiled and shook his head. "A vampire. Or a fellow named after a vampire, from the moving pictures."

"Bela Lugosi?"

"From *Dracula*? The talkie? No. The one from *Nosferatu*, the silent German movie. Orlok. That's who I think it was, although Zimmermann's not too sure of anything. What he saw from the cockpit was Jason standing straight up after he pulled the block, looking back to that house and nodding at a big fellow who was running up, shouting something at him. Zimmermann couldn't hear what, but he saw this fellow . . . take hold of Jason in one big hand, grabbing his jaw, and looking deep at him for just a moment. Then he let Jason go—and Jason just looked over at Zimmermann, and waved. Zimmermann got out of the cockpit and climbed down to the hatch, shouting after him. But by then, Jason was already walking away, side by side with this giant man . . . this Orlok.

"Zimmermann finally got back into the cockpit, got the plane going again and left that place, flew to Crete where he scuttled that plane, so he'd seem dead to his masters. He left Jason behind."

"With his lover, perhaps?"

"I don't know enough about that Zimmermann fellow to say. But I don't think Jason is a homosexual," said Andrew. "I think Orlok's a Juke. I'm pretty damn sure he's a Juke. Right over in those mountains, in Germany. Bavaria. Not far from us now."

"A Juke. And your old friend Jason . . . he found it." Dominic finished his coffee and slid the cup away from him. "It found him. What will we do?"

Andrew drained his own cup. It was cool and bitter, and it suited him. Just like his own recollections of Jason's own fare-thee-well those many years ago, in Canada.

"We're going to have to check Zimmermann's story. Professor Kurtzweiller knows people in Berlin who might be able to shed some light on the goings-on in Wallgau. Dr. Lewis has contacts of his own here, and abroad. In a few hours, I'll need your help transporting Zimmermann and Miss Harper . . . back to Vire, I think, for the time being. That will be as safe as anywhere. Safer than anywhere else. And it's . . . it's a place I can think."

"Of course," said Dominic.

"But as for Jason and Orlok, the Juke . . ."

"Yes?"

"Sooner or later," Andrew said, "we're going to have to do something about that."

PART III

The Elysium Deception

One

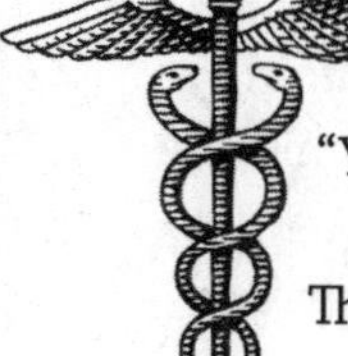

"You are looking very well, Mrs. Waggoner."

"You," said Annie Waggoner, "are being quite formal, Mr. Thistledown."

"Mr. Thorn," he said.

"*Lieutenant Colonel* Thorn. You're not fooling anyone," she said.

Jason Thistledown lifted his teacup and took a sip. His hand didn't tremble, but Annie had an eye for these things, and could tell that hand wanted to. He was going to fly again, off to Africa . . . the last thing on earth he should be doing, and the hand knew it.

They were sitting in the parlour room of Annie and Andrew's apartments in Paris, sheltered from a misting spring rain that fogged the windowpanes and drained what little life there was from the wan afternoon light. Just the two of them.

Andrew could well have been there too; Jason had wired to say he was in Paris for some time, and they'd arranged the date days in advance. Annie knew the schedule at the Sanatorium de Vire, and she knew he could damn well be here in town if he wanted to be.

"I think I'm fooling folks well enough," said Jason. "How're you two doing?" And then he thought about that and laughed. "I'm sorry, Annie, I didn't mean to say—"

"—that we're fooling folks?" Annie smiled at that. "We're fooling folks fine, thank you. And other than that . . . well, we're doing all right for ourselves. The sanatorium's in its fifth year. We're seeing to . . . forty-six patients now."

"Do they get better?"

"Not enough do," said Annie.

"Same as ever I guess."

"Same as ever." Annie drew a breath. "How about you now?"

Jason blinked, a little too quickly. "What about me?"

"You're not well. Too thin. You're not smoking right now, but I'm going to guess it's only because you smoked your last on the way here. And stubbed it out there." She leaned forward, and with a finger indicated the glistening flesh between collar and jawline. "That looks bad, Jason."

"You don't mince words."

"No."

"Well, all right," said Jason, "no sense in denying it. I remember when you sewed up my hand, back in Eliada. You sure knew what you were doing."

"I recall that Andrew was the one who sewed your hand," said Annie. "I only helped."

"Well, it's not infected," said Jason. "I know from infected. I clean it, and when it gets bad enough I slap a clean bandage on it."

"You maintain your wound," said Annie. "That doesn't give me a lot of comfort."

"It's not about comfort," said Jason, and took another sip of his tea. He set it back down, and the saucer betrayed a rattle. He sighed. "Sure," he finally said, "I'm just not right. It's been hard times. Work's been scarce to none since Imperial Air sent me away. But I do believe things are turning around. This job in Africa . . ."

Annie regarded him, and felt a pang. For that moment, the hardness of the years sluiced off and Jason became that wounded boy she had met in the cellars at the Eliada Hospital—who'd just escaped, bleeding and terrified, from Mister Juke's lair in the quarantine. Rescued by Andrew, maimed himself. Both of them—the farm boy, and the Negro doctor Annie would eventually marry—were each on the cusp of something monumental back then. They showed it in their eyes . . . in a terrible innocence that crossed Jason's gaze again, right as they drank their tea.

"It's certainly far from here. Have you ever been?"

"No," said Jason.

"I have. We have."

"You and Andrew? Where now, in Africa?"

"The Congo," said Annie, and at that Jason laughed.

"Lookin' for the Cave Germ?"

"Something like that," said Annie. "Andrew had a theory."

"He always did," said Jason. "When'd you go there?"

"Oh, years ago. The War was still on."

"That's how I missed it," said Jason. "Did you find the Cave Germ?"

"No, thank the Lord. Mostly what we found was how bad an idea it was for a white woman to be travelling there with a Negro," said Annie.

"There and most places, I expect," said Jason, and Annie agreed that was so, and thought a moment—although not, she soon concluded, long enough.

"It's not as bad here," she said. "France is not a bad place at all, for folk like us." She leaned forward. "We have room, you know. If you're going to Africa because times are hard, I don't think there'd be any trouble finding you a place to stay here. At Vire. Wherever you choose. There's room."

It was an absurd invitation and she knew it as soon as she offered it. Jason's cup rattled against the saucer and he lifted it to draw a sip. He set it down and put the saucer aside.

"That's kind, Annie," he said gently. "But I think you and Doctor Waggoner got your hands full with those tubercular folk. You help them get better. That's what you've always done best. You've a knack for it. I'll be better in the sky. Always was, always will be."

She should have pressed the invitation, or offered it differently to begin with. Given what she learned when Andrew returned to the Sanatorium de Vire in the company of Ruth Harper and her Austrian hobo, Mr. Zimmermann . . . it would have been better if Annie had dug into her store here, and offered Jason a strong sedative dissolved in his teacup. He would be far safer drugged and kidnapped by Annie Waggoner than he would as a guest of Nils Bergstrom's brother and the Germans, in the sphere of the Juke.

He would be far safer, Annie thought darkly, as she too often did these days, if someone had finished the job—maybe her and Andrew, if they'd managed to find another batch of that Cave Germ, and brought it straight to Cold Creek Harbour.

Andrew arrived at the Sanatorium de Vire late in the afternoon following the night of his meeting with his biology club—which was earlier by five days than Annie was expecting him. He was to have arrived by rail, and he came instead by car . . . or rather, in an ambulance driven by a young Italian man. Andrew made a great show of tending to two tubercular patients, newly arrived from Paris. When Jean-Pierre, the intern on duty, ran out from the hospital building to meet him, Andrew waved him away and shouted to have Annie—and only Annie—meet him at the *Maison du soleil*. That was, of all four of the quarantine buildings, the one with the fewest patients at present: just three, in a house with three dormitories and a dozen private rooms. It tended to get more use in the summer months.

Andrew apologized when she arrived, dressed for the sick rooms and full of questions: Why hadn't he called ahead? Allowed time to prepare for intake? Why summon her from the residence, and not let Jean-Pierre or some of the other staff, take care?

"We have guests," he said. "An old friend, and a new one."

And as he and the driver opened the back of the ambulance, and after Andrew made it clear that tuberculosis was a ruse, Annie and Ruth Harper embraced.

"I'm sorry we didn't call ahead," said Ruth. "We couldn't risk an operator overhearing." She rested a hand on Annie's arm. "Our past is catching up with us."

Annie wasn't sure what Ruth meant by that, but put questions aside for the moment, and gave a quick nod as though she did. "We'll get you both inside, then." She looked at Zimmermann, to whom she had not yet been introduced. He seemed an upright enough fellow, but Annie couldn't approve of that beard. "Two rooms?"

"If they're available," said Ruth, "thank you." Annie looked between the two of them, Ruth and Zimmermann, and blinked.

"Oh," said Ruth, "I am sorry. Mr. Albert Zimmermann, Mrs. Annie Waggoner. Mr. Zimmermann has provided us a great service."

Zimmermann gave a bow of his head and a little smile. "It is a pleasure to meet you."

Andrew offered his own apology. "It's been a long drive and I'm feeling it," he said, "but that's no excuse for rudeness. Annie, Mr. Zimmermann probably helped save Ruth's life."

"Something you and Mrs. Waggoner have in common," commented Ruth.

"And he knows where Jason is," said Andrew.

"In Africa?" asked Annie.

Zimmermann sighed. "Would that it were so."

"We believe he's in Germany," said Andrew. "Bavaria."

Annie frowned, and shivered. "We'd best get indoors," she said. "You can explain it all when they're settled."

"Yes," said Zimmermann. "Thank you for the lodging."

"You should save the thanks for after you've seen your room," said Annie.

None of the rooms in the Sanatorium de Vire's five buildings were much to look on. But they were clean, and designed to be easy to keep clean, with walls and floors tiled, chairs hard-backed, beds steel-framed, tables made from steel too. The mattresses were wrapped in rubber, and the linens changed daily. The only added luxury at *La Maison du soleil* was in the views. All the rooms faced south, through a break in the trees that surrounded the sanatorium looking down the gentle sloping fields toward the rooftops of Vire, some three kilometres off. But even that was in service of the sanatorium's singular purpose: to help the tubercular patients who rested here to defeat the bacterium that was otherwise slowly killing them.

Sunlight, clean air . . . as matters improved, some limited exercise in the paths through the woods that enclosed the facility . . . most importantly, clean air . . . there lay the cure.

Mr. Zimmermann didn't complain about any of it but the last, at least as it related to his pipe and tobacco. But he understood well enough that he couldn't smoke in a house where other patients were recuperating, and even neglecting their health, he couldn't expect to hide very effectively either. And so, sighing, he surrendered his pipe and tobacco to Andrew, and set about to make himself at home in his tiny room, as Andrew explained to him the protocols of the sanatorium.

Ruth Harper required no such explanation. She had, after all, financed the purchase of the land and the construction of the sanatorium six years ago, when Andrew and Annie finally decided to settle in France and resume their professions. . . . She had approved the plans, setting a generous budget which assisted in obtaining the necessary permits. She had in every respect seen them well-established here in lower Normandy, and knew the place as well as they.

Still—Annie sat with Ruth for much longer than Andrew did with Mr. Zimmermann. He stuck his head in on his way out, and again to bring them meals an hour later. Stars were emerging, and the two had finished their dinners and were sipping tea by the time Ruth had finished telling about her improbable adventures in Brandenburg, along with Zimmermann's more outrageous story of what had become of Jason near the Bavarian Alps, and how he had found his way to Ruth Harper.

"Why didn't you come right here?" asked Annie. "Why go to Paris?"

"We couldn't be certain that whoever is behind this wasn't keeping an eye on Vire," said Ruth. "Dr. Waggoner's and your practice here is no secret—that was rather the point of it all—and if the people who tried to kidnap me and did kidnap Jason were on the hunt, they might well be watching this facility. The *Société* meetings . . . well, they are kept to a maniacal schedule. I knew that Andrew would be there. And I knew that the people who could best help . . . that they would be there too."

"In a public tavern."

Ruth shrugged. "In a private room. In a very discreetly run tavern."

"Who do you think the people . . . the ones trying to get you are?"

"Nazis?" Ruth had been sitting on her bed, and now she fluffed a pillow and leaned back, setting it behind her head. "Certainly men associated with Nazis. A band of hooligans, that's for sure."

Annie got up and drew a sheet to cover Ruth, then set Ruth's discarded shoes by the door.

"It does come around," said Annie, "doesn't it."

"How is that?"

"I was just thinking," said Annie, "about the Klansmen at Eliada. How they . . . how they tried to hang Andrew."

Ruth nodded. "Just before we arrived that spring. I remember."

"They weren't truly Klansmen," said Annie. "They wore those sheets, because they thought they needed to be *something*. But they weren't nothing . . . anything. They weren't anything."

"I'm not sure if it's the same, precisely."

"The same as what?"

"As the men who came for me. As Nazis in Germany. The men in Eliada . . . they were addled by Mister Juke. They thought they were in contact with God."

"Nazis don't think that?"

"That they're talking to God? Oh no. I don't believe that they do. From my time in Brandenburg . . . listening to Egon Dietrich and his friends . . . I think they have a very good idea of what they want and who they are. I don't think they're addled at all, and I don't think they have anything to do with God." She paused an instant, frowning. "They are hooligans, though. They've that much in common."

"I spoke with Jason before he left, you know."

"I know. Andrew told me so."

"He wasn't well," said Annie.

"Albert . . . Mr. Zimmermann agreed with your assessment, when they met." Ruth stretched and pulled the sheet higher.

"But Annie, Jason has never been well. Not since Eliada, or just after. Do you remember how it was when we left the Thorn family?"

Annie did remember. They'd remained there for just a month, and for most of that time, once Ruth was clearly going to recover . . . Jason kept away from them. From Andrew, from Annie. Even from Ruth . . . especially from Ruth. By the time he left, he spent all of his time at the Thorn farmhouse, and would barely make eye contact with Andrew, or Ruth. The rejection had left both of them brokenhearted, each in their own way.

Annie thought she was able to see through what it seemed—the spurning of a fallen lover, the sudden shame in befriending a Negro—to what it was. Jason was collapsing on himself, finally . . . the death of his mother, the horrors of Eliada. . . .

When he told them, at month's end—as Ruth was preparing to return to her home and inheritance, and Annie and Andrew, to simply move on—she wasn't surprised. Of course he would stay here on this farm, with Lawrence Thorn and his children. Of course he would abandon the Thistledown name once and for all, along with all its associations. The name was dangerous—the Eugenics Records Office, or the people who'd worked with Germaine Frost and Nils Bergstrom, would be more interested in their superman Thistledown more than ever. If not that—Thistledown was a killer's pedigree. He needed to disappear.

And he needed some time to heal. More time, really, than the onset of war would ever allow him.

"I wanted to keep him here," said Annie. "Like he was still a child."

"You didn't know him when he was a child," said Ruth. "It's true to say that no one living did."

Annie nodded. That was so. Everyone Jason Thistledown grew up with, everyone he'd known, had been taken by the Cave Germ.

"I hope that the Thorns were good to him. I think that they were," said Ruth. "Maybe better than I would have been to him, if he'd let me. It hurt badly, leaving him behind, but I truly don't think that I'd have been a good wife to him, if he'd joined me. For I was certainly a child then."

Annie didn't disagree.

"You'll be fine for him now," she said after a moment, and then corrected herself: "I mean, assuming you still wanted to."

Ruth gave a little laugh.

"And assuming there's a chance," she said, "at anything."

Annie found Andrew back at the house they kept adjoining the main hospital building. He'd cleaned away his dinner plates, but lingered in the dark sitting room with a glass of brandy that was certainly not his first. He had that jar of his out, set on an end table, next to a candle burning down to its base. In the murky formaldehyde, what remained of the Juke floated.

"Is there any left for me?" she asked, indicating his glass. Andrew lifted the bottle from the floor by his chair so as to indicate yes, and she fetched a glass from a cabinet and let him pour.

"I'm sorry," said Andrew.

"For what?"

"I surprised you," he said. "Maybe put us in danger."

"That's true. You did, and maybe we are. But all's forgiven," said Annie. She took a sip of the brandy. "It is Ruth Harper we're talking about. You couldn't very well turn her away. Not after everything."

"And Jason," said Andrew.

"And Jason's friend. Herr Zimmermann."

"She told you his story," said Andrew. "I heard her going over it with you. Ruth likes a good yarn, always has."

"Yes," said Annie, "she did. It's quite a tale."

"Do you believe it?"

"I think so," said Annie. "Yes."

Andrew chuckled and drained his glass. "You're one up on me, my love. I'm not entirely sure."

"You think Zimmermann's lied? Or Ruth?"

"No," said Andrew. "No one's telling things they don't believe are true. But the Juke . . ." He lifted the jar from the table and let it swirl, so the flesh of the tiny thing inside caught the dim candlelight in turns. "The Juke spins lies," he said.

"That is so," said Annie. "What are you meaning to do?"

"We're already doing it," said Andrew. He reached into his shirt pocket and pulled out a little disk—it looked like a pocket watch.

"Zimmermann took some pictures with this," he said.

Annie squinted. "That's a camera?" she said, and Andrew unfolded the little rangefinder.

"So I'll run them through the lab, see what he got," said Andrew. "Dr. Kurtzweiller is back in Berlin, or should be soon. He's going to make some inquiries . . . about Wallgau, the things that might be going on there. Dr. Lewis is staying on in Paris, looking into this Desrosiers connection."

"And Molinare?"

Andrew poured another glass for himself. "Molinare is dead. I thought I'd told you."

"Maybe you had," said Annie.

"He died," said Andrew, "some time ago. But his assistant is with us now. Dominic. Good boy. You met him."

"Oh?"

"Just now, driving the ambulance. I set him up in a spare room at the hospital, but he'll be off in the morning back to Paris. He'll be helping out Bobby Grady."

"At the Liberty? Doing what? Tending bar?"

Andrew smiled and shook his head. "No. Planning some logistics."

"Logistics?"

"For the event that Zimmermann's story holds water. It's not as easy as you'd think," said Andrew, sniffing at his brandy, "for a Negro to cross over from France and into Germany." He sipped, and then took a deeper drink. "Especially not these days."

Two

The Sanatorium de Vire helped to ease two pressing health matters near to Annie's heart. The greater of them was the tuberculosis epidemic, which was emerging as workers from Vire finished the first of the sanatorium's structures, only to bloom to its full fury in France three years later, as money from Paris assisted in further modernizations, and the construction of the final two.

The lesser was Andrew Waggoner's. Since Eliada, Andrew's capacity as a surgeon remained diminished—while his interest, and talent, as a researcher grew keener—and like Jason, like Annie, like Ruth Harper herself, the horror of Eliada loomed behind everything he did. The Sanatorium was no more a cure for that horror, that evil, than it was for the suffocating symptoms of the tubercular patients who came through their doors. But it was a salve for both. It helped.

Annie also understood that the Sanatorium was a good place to hide . . . better than one might think. For within the hospital building, a massive structure partly made from the original manor house on the land, Andrew had hidden amid his microscopes and centrifuges the equipment he used to further his studies on the central mystery of their life: the Juke, and the strange biochemical means it used to bend minds and hearts toward its ends. The folk from Cold Creek Harbour and their friends had not yet visited here, not once—and if they did they would find nothing to indicate the work that Andrew had done over the years in parasitology, neurology—theology.

If they came looking for Ruth Harper and Albert Zimmermann—Andrew and Annie, along with the Sanatorium's small staff, would see to it they left still looking.

Over the next day, Annie met with all of the staff singly and in pairs, to tell them about the new patients, who would be in her direct care. All were impressed with their need for privacy, and all of them said they understood. From time to time, the sanatorium hosted patients for reasons other than tuberculosis.

Only one of them, Luc Curzon, learned their true names, and that was by necessity. Luc had maintained the gardens and grounds since before the lands were acquired—and he was the only one of the seven who worked the Sanatorium who had ever seen Ruth Harper in person, four years earlier when she visited the newly built hospital and hung a portrait not of herself, but her father Garrison.

"She is in hiding, with a gentleman? Ah." Luc smiled. "A scandal."

"Not exactly that. Not that at all in fact."

"I see. Well it doesn't matter. I will not betray Mademoiselle Harper if she wishes to remain anonymous."

"I know you won't," said Annie.

"If I may say, Madame Waggoner," said Luc, "I don't believe any of the people working here would. They are all worthy of your confidence."

"So they are," said Annie. "But they don't deserve the burden. I just didn't want you surprised."

Luc said he understood, promised to keep the confidence and otherwise help any way that he could, and when he left Annie felt a momentary lifting of spirit—as though for a moment, she were not alone, the burden of this was shared. It was fleeting, though; the burden, all of it and like always, was square on her shoulders.

Andrew spent the first day in his study—which is to say, that suite of rooms in the cellar of the main hospital building that he'd managed to rope off for his own purposes.

The rooms were built for the eventual installation of an X-ray machine, but so far the only nod to such a use was a photographic dark room that Andrew and the *Société* used to process film from their far-ranging investigations. As Annie was speaking with Luc and the other staff members about discretion surrounding their visitors, Andrew was using that room and its equipment to unload and process the contents of Zimmermann's novelty spy camera. There were fifteen exposures on the roll, and although only a few of them were useful he made prints of each of them. By the time they were dry and Andrew had returned to the residence with them, Annie was just back from making afternoon rounds and seeing as best she could to the needs of the legitimately ill patients at Vire.

Andrew arrived clutching the prints in a leather folio, and when he established that it was just the two of them, he set them out on the dining room table. It was late in the afternoon and the sun hit the table directly, lighting the pictures with an otherworldly luminescence.

"Look these over," said Andrew. "I want to talk with you before I go see Zimmermann."

"All right." Annie squinted. There were four photographs of what was surely the farmhouse where Zimmermann and Jason had been held captive. It was big—bigger than Ruth had described, nearly the size of their hospital building. In one photograph, there was a truck parked out front . . . in another, a half-dozen figures, standing around the steps to the porch. A third photograph was likely the same building, from a different angle and farther off. It was nearer dark in that one, and a bright light shone from a window on the uppermost floor. A fifth photograph was darker still, and blurred by movement in the camera.

There were photographs of what seemed like a high street in a small town. Definitively a German town, in Bavaria. The cobblestones were slick, as though it had just rained. "Wallgau?" she asked aloud, and Andrew said that it was likely.

"But look more closely," said Andrew, indicating an awning, under which a pale figure stood clutching its shoulders alongside another, seated on a bench. Annie squinted, and Andrew handed her a magnifying glass.

"Oh!" They were two girls . . . or perhaps boys, with blond hair grown long like girls.

They appeared to be nude.

"Yes," said Andrew. "I'd have thought that Zimmermann might've remembered seeing that. Might've mentioned it in the telling."

"Being as he took the picture, yes." Annie drew the glass over the rest of the photograph. "Where was this picture on the roll?"

Andrew indicated the top corner, where he had written "4" in grease pencil. Annie noticed that all of the photographs were numbered.

"Four of fifteen. So before these." She motioned to a set of photographs that were of people. Number eight was of an older, heavyset man in a cable-knit sweater, standing on the front porch. Bergstrom? There was a resemblance. Number six was of a man in a badly fitted uniform with a swastika on his left armband. Who was that? Annie wouldn't be able to guess. Photograph seven was definitively of Jason. He was standing outdoors, looking at a map, with a small pack on his back. There was another man standing near him—not quite as tall as Jason, moustachioed and round-faced, losing his hair . . . he might have been smiling, or he might just have had the sort of face that feigns a smile even in repose.

"No need for the glass on that one," said Andrew. "Nothing but Jason . . . and maybe that fellow Aguillard?"

But Annie disagreed and kept the magnifier. "Look at Jason's neck," she said, and Andrew leaned over to peer through the glass. Jason's throat was pockmarked with burns that swelled like insect bites.

"I know," said Andrew softly.

"Hurting himself did help," said Annie, "back in Eliada."

"Back in Eliada," said Andrew with a snort. He slid the photograph aside and drew another one—number twelve. It was of another person, and also candid. But it was far bolder than the others. This was of a man, black-haired, with a lean face, and shirtless, lying asleep in a cot, lit by the dimmest light of the moon crosshatched by windowpanes. Although the light must have been dreadful for the purpose, this photograph was sharper than the others—as though Zimmermann here had taken the time to hold very still with his little camera, to capture the image of his dozing subject perfectly.

Whoever he was, he slept on his side, an arm beneath his head driving his dark hair onto his bicep. Annie took the magnifying glass from Andrew and studied his features more closely—to make sure she saw what she thought she saw.

"That's right," said Andrew. "It's a Heidelberg scar, right there on his cheek."

"You're not—"

"I am. Add a beard and an inch more hair," said Andrew, "and see?"

Annie set the glass down and steadied herself with a hand on the table's edge.

"That's Albert Zimmermann," she said.

"Sleeping like a babe," said Andrew.

Andrew and Annie brought supper to their guests, but didn't stay for long. Both were asleep when they knocked, and had been through the day. Ruth joked that this stay in quarantine was so far more pleasant than the last time. Zimmermann asked if Andrew had had any luck with the photographs. Andrew surprised Annie by lying, saying "Tomorrow." On the way back, Annie asked him why, Andrew didn't have a good answer.

They ate their own dinner alone at the house, and when it was finished, sat down again with the photographs. Annie was prepared to leave him to it—this was business for his *Société*, a group in which she was pleased not to be included—but Andrew asked that she stay.

Annie thought that he might want to discuss the pictures further—maybe try to parse them with Zimmermann's story, or guess at the story that Zimmermann might have been hiding . . . or might well have been hidden from him.

"Who do you think is lying?" he asked.

"I'm sorry?"

"Somebody's lying," said Andrew. "I don't think it's the camera."

"Somebody doesn't remember," she said, then specified. "Mr. Zimmermann doesn't remember. Or he didn't even see to, begin with. The Juke does that."

Andrew shook his head. "The Juke does something *like* that. Not precisely, not in Eliada. The nature of that thing . . . of its chemistry . . . is to make you see things—things that'll draw you to it. Make you worship it. At a point, makes you want to copulate with it. That's how it lives, how it reproduces. It becomes God. Nobody worships a God they don't understand to be there."

"There's millions of Roman Catholics who'd disagree," said Annie. "Faith, darling."

Andrew shook his head, and slid the picture of Jason under the light for a heartbeat before moving it aside, replacing it with one of the farmhouse pictures. "Or a big old Juke, at the heart of the Vatican," he said.

Annie laughed. "Covered in stigmata," she said and Andrew laughed too.

"Better write the Pope," he said.

"I'll fetch the stationery later," said Annie. "I'm not sure you're right about the Juke's nature though. At least the one we saw in Idaho."

"It sure took me for a ride," said Andrew.

"Yes," said Annie. "It showed you a kind of Heaven. But it didn't show me that. From me—it hid."

"That's not so," said Andrew. "You were well aware of the Juke that

Bergstrom kept in the quarantine. I asked you about Mr. Juke, and you told me what you knew."

"I knew it was a hermaphrodite," said Annie. "I'm pretty sure that I even had a look at it—and if I'd been looking at it properly, I would have seen that it wasn't that at all. But that was the problem: I didn't look at it properly. I made up my mind as to what it was . . . and managed to ignore everything that told me what it really was . . . and I did that for months—until things got bad enough that I couldn't ignore it anymore. When it was too late."

"But you did see it," said Andrew. "You didn't miss things. You didn't fail to see people, as they walked past you in the street. You weren't blind to it."

Andrew pushed all the pictures out of the light, leaned back in his chair, and looked at Annie.

"I don't think that Zimmermann's lying," said Andrew. "But I think he's been tricked."

"Just like Jason." Annie put a hand on her husband's shoulder. "Maybe just like all of us."

Andrew's damaged hand reached up to touch Annie's, but he didn't say anything, so Annie continued.

"Sometimes I think that we are all unhinged," she said. "Susceptible." She smiled, stroking the back of Andrew's hand. The skin was dry and cool, tight over his knuckles like an old man's—not like a surgeon's, not since twenty years ago.

"Suckers," she said.

"I don't think we're suckers," said Andrew.

"We're hunting someone named after a picture-show monster," said Annie. "Based on a story you and your friends heard from a hairy-chinned Austrian fellow you'd never met 'til then, during a night of heavy drinking in Paris."

Andrew chuckled at that. But Annie wasn't done.

"All to find a man you won't even take the time to speak with, who maybe doesn't want to be found. In Germany. Maybe the one place in the world that's worse for a gentleman Negro than the United States of America." She lifted Andrew's hand from hers and stepped away. "And I should stop you from going. You're my husband, and I should keep you safe here. But I know that I can't."

"You could," he said, but Annie shook her head.

"You know I can't. We're suckers, darling. You and me both." As she turned to draw the curtains against the quiet dark, Andrew laughed one more time.

Mail came the next afternoon from Berlin, with news from Dr. Kurtzweiller. It was a long letter; Kurtzweiller had been busy and diligent. Still, it offered very little news. He had been unable to meet with Professor Muckermann—"I confess we are the barest of acquaintances," he wrote, "so it is not surprising that he could not find the time."—but confirmed that the professor had only recently returned to Berlin, after a long stay in Munich.

Kurtzweiller also confirmed that there was some talk of troubles around the vicinity of Wallgau, over the summer—but details were difficult to ascertain and he thought he would need to travel to Munich himself in order to learn much more than he heard from his contacts in the *Reichstag*.

"There was indeed a large *Hitler-Jugend* troop staying there for some time, in a mountain valley. It had come to my contact's attention because boys from some Berlin families were among them, and they had lost contact with their sons. The matter was properly one for the *Bayerische Polizei* in Munich, however, and my friend did not know what had come of any investigations they might have conducted. To my mind this does confirm Herr Z.'s account to a very great degree, although obviously not entirely."

Kurtzweiller said that he might learn more in Munich, where he expected to be ensconced by the time this letter arrived at Vire. He offered a post box number where Andrew could send a reply, along with whatever he had learned, and promised to write again once he was settled in suitable rooms.

"Eventually," he wrote, "I believe that we must meet there. It is the nearest city to Wallgau, and also the town where the *Hitler-Jugend* and the *Sturmabteilung* are headquartered. It is not likely to be safe. Even in Berlin, the Nazi Party makes its presence very well known, and the *Polizei* does not seem a match for it. I cannot think matters are much improved in Munich, particularly for men such as yourself, or the Jew Zimmermann."

That same day, Andrew did bring the photographs to Zimmermann, and to Ruth. Zimmermann had bathed, and made use of scissors and a razor to shave his beard, and he rubbed his freshly bare chin as he flipped through the photographs, and put names to the faces. "Yes, that is Aguillard with Jason. Those men on the porch? S.A.," and he listed some names.

"That is Wallgau," he said as Andrew showed him the photograph of the high street. "I remember that day—early on, the first trip into the village... before I even found the postmaster." Andrew tapped the image of the two nude youngsters, and Zimmermann drew a breath.

"I did not see them," he said.

"They appear hard to miss," said Ruth, who sat beside him at the little table in his room. Zimmermann shook his head.

"That's not all you missed," said Andrew, and removed the last photograph from his folio: sleeping Albert Zimmermann on a cot. Zimmermann's hand moved from his chin to his ear, and over it, smoothing his still too-long hair against his temple.

"Wer hat das fotografiert?" he whispered, and Ruth translated: "Who photographed this?"

"Do you have any memory?" Andrew asked. "Might you have mislaid the camera in the barracks at the farm, when you slept?"

"It could have been taken by one of the S.A. men," said Ruth, "who shared the room."

"It could," said Annie. She rested a hand on Zimmermann's shoulder, then withdrew it abruptly at the panicked look in Zimmermann's eye, as he turned at her touch. "I'm sorry Mr. Zimmermann. It could be innocent. A prank."

"It was not." Zimmermann took the picture by the top corner, flipped it over, then tapped the back of it. "This was not innocent."

"How do you know that? Does any of this help your memory?" Andrew had moved over by the window, leaning against the sill, his shadow cast over Zimmermann, who shook his head. His hand moved to his forehead, and he looked down at the back of the photograph.

"Have any of you ever flown?" he asked.

"I have," said Ruth. "Not in the pilot's seat."

"Of course not. But tell me, did you feel safe?"

"To be honest, no. I was terrified the engines would die, and we would fall like a stone into the ocean."

"That might have happened," said Zimmermann, "and you might well have died. But it was not likely that your peril would arise from a badly tuned engine. Do you know what was the greater hazard?" He tapped his temple with his finger. "Your pilot. And his inner ear. You see, when one is flying, particularly in fog or the night, it can happen that one loses oneself.

In a cockpit . . . there are instruments that help against this: gauges that show air speed, a compass, an altimeter which shows how high we are flying . . . an inclinometer, to show how level the wings are. There is even a watch, so we might know that time marches forward and not the other way. A pilot needs these things. His own wits are not enough. They will trick him. They will tell him that up is down. And because that is not so . . . he will crash." Zimmermann turned the photo over again, and looked on his sleeping self.

"In the war, we flew in daylight and nearer the ground. But if we weren't careful . . . if we did not mind our instruments . . . we would lose one another. And we would be alone in the sky, each of us an easy target." He made a loose fist, and tapped his sleeping self.

"Having lost our way, we could be shot, so very easily, and never know until our death was upon us."

Three

Clouds had moved in from the south through the afternoon, and with them came rain. It announced itself by huge droplets on the windows, then rivulets and then a stream. By the time they were finished, it was coming down hard enough that even taking broad black umbrellas from the vestibule, even dashing from those steps to the main hospital building, in the end Andrew and Annie were soaked to the waist, shivering.

There was not time to change clothes, not right away. As they stepped through the doors to the entry hall, they were greeted by the day nurse, who said that Doctor Thomas needed to speak with Doctor Waggoner immediately.

"It concerns Madame Pierrepoint," she said. "Matters have taken a turn."

Andrew set their umbrellas in the stand and they both sloshed up the stairs. Doctor Thomas—Bertrand Thomas—was in the east-wing recovery room, where Madame Lucille Pierrepoint was evidently still resting following her surgery.

Thomas had done the surgery himself, that morning: a *plombage*, to collapse the patient's right lung, by the insertion a few grams of paraffin wax in her upper thorax. He had asked Andrew if he wanted to observe, and ordinarily as chief physician, Andrew would have done so—but of course he was seized by the greater mystery of the Juke, and so he waved it off.

It ought to have been a simple procedure, and Madame Pierrepoint ought to have been out of recovery and resting in a room in the hospital now, and as they climbed the stairs to surgery Andrew swore under his breath. Doctor Thomas was young—just twenty-eight years old—and an able enough surgeon, trained as Andrew was, at Paris, and he had done the procedure many times. . . .

But he was young.

They saw Doctor Thomas through the glass of the recovery room—hidden behind mask and gown, at Madame Pierrepoint's bedside. She was the only one in recovery, and she looked impossibly small in her bed, pale and bandaged. She was only thirty-seven years old, but the ravages of tuberculosis had wasted her, and she seemed twenty years older. Her eyes were closed and her mouth hung open.

Annie tapped on the glass, which made Doctor Thomas start. He stepped away and came out, pulling the mask from his face and his gloves free.

"What is the problem?" asked Andrew, speaking French.

"Yes," said Thomas. *"A problem indeed. Madame Pierrepoint appears to have fallen into a coma."*

"She was awake this morning," said Annie. She had seen Lucille herself, just prior the noon hour, groggy but alert as the anesthetic wore off.

"She was," said Thomas. *"She was doing well in fact. She had taken some broth and was able to speak a few words as of twelve hundred. At fourteen hundred hours, she seemed to have fallen asleep. Three hours later, at seventeen hundred and a quarter hours, when the nurses came around to check on her, she would not wake. She has been unresponsive since."*

Andrew nodded. "So we're dealing with a blood clot," he said in English.

"That's what it likely is," replied Thomas. "She may well have suffered a stroke."

Of course it was a blood clot, formed during the surgery this morning; of course it had made its way to Lucille Pierrepoint's brain; and of course, this was the cause of the coma. Annie had seen this often enough over her years—decades, really—assisting in surgeries and tending to their aftermaths.

Doctor Thomas had taken some steps to deal with this one already—small doses of strychnine and atropine—with no effect.

"Well let's look at her," said Andrew. "Another pair of eyes, yes?"

"Yes," said Thomas.

And then, finally, they went off to surgery, to change from their wet clothes into surgical gowns and masks and scrub down before entering the recovery room.

"I'm going to stay here tonight," Andrew said as he hung his jacket, "whatever we find."

"I'll tell the kitchen to make us a meal then," said Annie.

"That sounds fine. But you don't need to stay. Go back to the house. Get some rest."

"I'm all right," said Annie.

"You are all right," said Andrew, and smiled. "You've been carrying this place . . . without any help from me. At least not lately."

Annie stepped behind Andrew to tie his mask behind his head, then tied her own.

"Lately you've had other things to do."

Andrew filled a basin with hot water and soap, and scrubbed his hands. "Finding Jason. Finding the Juke. Or Orlok." He made room for Annie beside him as she scrubbed. "Drinking the night away," he said.

Annie raised an eyebrow and half-nodded.

"Looking out for our old friend Ruth Harper," she said.

"Drinking the damn night away." Andrew reached for a towel and patted his hands dry.

"Well, come back in with me, see what's what, then order a plate of food for here and one for yourself. But after that—go home to bed."

"Andrew—" she began, but he raised a finger to shush, and handed her the towel.

"Get some rest, Nurse Waggoner. Because something tells me in the morning, there'll be another surgery. You'll want your wits for that."

By "another surgery," Andrew meant a trepanning—or as the procedure had become to be known this century, a craniectomy. If chemicals weren't going to ease pressure on the brain, then a burr hole in the skull might do the work.

"That'll cure her or kill her," said Annie, and Andrew peered up at one of the skylights, rattling with the rain.

"If it is a stroke and the drugs don't help her, then it's death anyway. Death or worse."

He shook his head, and opened the door to the recovery room. Doctor Thomas was there, and offered Andrew a stethoscope.

They talked and examined Lucille Pierrepoint—listened to her wheezing breath, shone lights in her eye, redid all the little tests that Doctor Thomas had conducted through the afternoon—and then the three talked some more. It wasn't long, but enough time to convince Annie that Andrew was probably right.

She would need her sleep.

The rain was, if anything, coming down harder when Annie left the hospital—enough so there ought to be thunder and flashes of lightning accompanying it, or a wind. But the air was still and it was quiet, too; nothing but the water, spilling from clouds that perched, still and patient, overtop Vire. It was a short walk through the gardens this time to the house's porch, and the umbrella was up to the task. Annie arrived home as dry as when she'd left.

She flicked the umbrella open and closed the door, then set the umbrella on the floor of the entry hall to dry. It was in so doing that she noticed something she might otherwise have missed.

She had set the umbrella down in a pool of water.

Annie stepped away from it and turned on the hall light.

The water made a trail, down past the stairs and toward the kitchen.

Annie put her hand on the doorknob back outside, and cracked it open—so that if need be, she might run.

"Hello?" she called. "Who's there?"

Through the kitchen doorway, another light switched on and bathed the hallway in a yellow square.

"Nurse Rowe?"

Annie shut the door again. "Been a long time since anyone called me that name."

"Are you alone?"

"Yes, Ruth," said Annie, sighing. "I'm alone."

And there was a shadow down the hall, and then stepping into the hallway . . . there was Ruth Harper—soaked through and through . . . hair streaking down her face like she'd been pulled afresh from the Kootenai River. And then she was walking down the hallway—running down the hallway—right toward Annie, and before Annie could get her hand back to that doorknob, she had wrapped her arms around Annie's waist.

"I can't be alone," said Ruth Harper, and she was sobbing: "Please. *Please.*"

Annie got Ruth back to the sitting room, started up a fire in the hearth, and ordered Ruth to strip off her clothes.

"I'd like to get you in a hot bath," said Annie, "but that'll take time to draw. So we'll get you out of those soaking clothes. Do you need help?"

Ruth shook her head no, but she did need some help with the fasteners on her blouse, her hands were shaking so badly. Annie crumpled up paper, lit it underneath the pyramid of logs she'd made, then got Ruth started with the top two hooks.

"I'm fine," she said after that, so Annie opened up the trunk and selected a thick woolen blanket. By the time she brought it over Ruth had stripped to her undergarments. Annie draped the blanket over Ruth's shoulders and led her to the sofa.

"Now sit," she commanded, and when Ruth obeyed, Annie poured brandy from a decanter that Andrew had left on the mantelpiece. Two generously filled glasses. Ruth accepted one of them, but didn't drink.

"No one saw me," she said.

Annie sat beside her on the sofa. *You didn't see anyone see you* was what Annie thought, but what she said was: "Well that's good. Even if they had, in this rain I don't think they'd have gotten enough of a look. . . ."

"No one saw me," said Ruth again. "I'm sorry I left my room. I know it created a risk. But I couldn't stay there. In that *quarantine* . . ." She looked into her glass, and then lifted it to her lips. "Where's Andrew?" she asked.

Annie explained, and Ruth listened carefully.

"Andrew doesn't do surgery, still?" she asked.

"No," said Annie. "Not when he can avoid it. Which is pretty well all the time. Doctor Thomas is able enough."

"Not able enough to keep that poor woman safe," said Ruth.

Annie sipped her brandy, and Ruth finished hers.

"It's the damned quarantine," she said. "It has me . . . seeing things."

Annie rose to get the decanter, but Ruth took hold of her arm, so Annie sat back down.

"I know that this isn't a quarantine. But do you remember when we decided on this place? We joked."

"I remember," said Annie. Ruth had made a joke that the Harper Foundation was long overdue to pay for a proper quarantine, after botching it so badly in Eliada. It wasn't properly a joke—but they'd laughed at it, loud and long, all the same.

"Do you know," said Ruth, "that I had only ever been in the quarantine at Eliada the once? And that time—that time . . ." She lifted her feet from the floor to the lip of the sofa, and let go of Annie's arm to wrap her own arms around her knees.

"You know, all these years, I've had such a hard time remembering that night. I remember it began as a lark: Jason, that sweet, handsome, and very sad boy . . . an outlaw's son . . . had told me stories of that quarantine. Quite fanciful. I didn't really believe them at the time. But oh, I liked stories. And I liked a mystery.

"I remember that we had just gone through his hateful aunt's things, to solve a bit of that mystery . . . and sure enough, found a mysterious letter. In French. We left that with my friend Louise, the only one who had a hope of understanding it. I think she was cross about that. She had teased me about Jason. He was interested in me, that was very clear. And I was interested in him.

"I was, by that point, attempting to seduce him—that's really what I was doing . . . creeping off with Jason Thistledown, to find a quiet place in that quarantine . . . and seduce him. Make love with him. I kissed him on the way there. Made my feelings plain as I could." She smiled wanly.

"What a dreadful girl I was."

Annie protested that she was not, and to that, Ruth held out her glass.

"For a long time, my last reliable memory of the quarantine was as we approached. I remembered seeing some activity around it—men in white robes and hoods. I remembered seeing a scurrying thing. . . .

"After that . . . my recollection was . . . sensual, I suppose. I had always understood there to have been a gap, a time when I was inside the quarantine, that was simply lost to me. Because if I were to make a sequence of it, I would say that I next recalled Jason's touch. His handling . . . his penetration of me. We joined together, in the cellar room at the hospital. That sounds like awful poetry, but it is how I remember it. . . .

"I am sorry. I'm being very frank, Annie."

Annie reminded her that she was a nurse and appreciated frank talk. She poured another finger of brandy into Ruth's glass and sat back down.

"I was fond of that memory," said Ruth. "It was a memory I'd often return to, even after Jason . . . well after he left me, left all of us, at that farm in Canada. Really, it was never far from my mind."

"That boy leaves an impression," said Annie, and at that, Ruth laughed bitterly.

"I'll agree with you on one point: an impression was left," said Ruth. "The question is, what left it?"

The fire dimmed a moment as the last of the paper burned out, but the logs had caught well enough, and announced combustion with a pop and a geyser of sparks that made Annie start.

"I know this sanatorium isn't a quarantine, or it isn't *that* quarantine," Ruth said. "But hiding in it, alone through much of the day and all of the night, as I have been . . . it offers up something of a portal, do you understand?"

Annie didn't, so Ruth elaborated.

"The hours I spent in the quarantine at Eliada . . . they weren't a blank time. I didn't forget. As I think of it, I can recall precisely how that went. Jason had sighted a woman, in the woods. He motioned to her, and I saw her . . . she was on the ground, in the dirt, in the embrace of something small but strong . . . like a raccoon but without any hair on it . . . and with jaws that were very different. If that makes any sense. Or even if it doesn't. That's what I remember seeing. And it frightened me! Oh, it gave me such a terror. The poor woman writhed underneath it, as though she were in terrible pain. Which no doubt she was.

"I ran. I turned and ran, left Jason to face that . . . I ran toward the light, the torchlight from the guard around the quarantine. There were men guarding it, but I managed to find my way to a door before any came round a corner. And I slipped inside, and shut the door behind me . . . and I remember, now, feeling such the fool. Here, I'd goaded Jason into this dangerous adventure. Only half-believing the whole of it. And I'd abandoned him. So what did I do? I called out for him, in that pitch black space within my father's quarantine. 'Jason!' I said. 'I'm sorry!' I said. And although I didn't know what that word meant—I still don't, not really—I called out that I loved him. And do you know, Annie—do you know what happened?"

Annie shook her head.

"He came to me," said Ruth. "He came to me, in a halo of golden light . . . tall, and so beautiful. He . . . he reached out a hand to caress my face, and he smiled . . . he smiled. And he said that he loved me."

"Jason came to you."

"Yes," said Ruth. "And he loved me."

"Oh, Ruth." Annie put a hand on Ruth's shoulder. But she shook it off so violently as to nearly cause Annie to spill her brandy. Ruth apologized.

"I was thinking about his touch," she explained. "Recalling it. In such vivid detail. Your touch . . . was too much."

"I'm sorry," said Annie.

"Don't be," said Ruth. "You were offering comfort."

"When did you start remembering this way? So vividly?"

"I can't pinpoint it," she said. "For some time I think. It is possible . . . it's possible that I've been remembering the Juke, from the beginning. I wonder if I wasn't remembering it when Jason and I finally did make love to one another. I'm wondering if it's not the Juke that I remember, when I recall Jason."

Annie didn't understand and said so.

"I think," said Ruth, "that on one level or another, I've been remembering that . . . that rape, my whole entire life. Although it's not precisely a rape, is it? It's an infection."

"In a way," said Annie, "I guess it is. But the way that infection's delivered . . ."

"It makes quite an impression," said Ruth. "And do you know what that impression is? Not revulsion. Rather the opposite."

Ruth clutched the blanket close around her and stood. She walked close to the hearth, and finally, let the blanket fall so she stood nearly naked before the fire.

"Jason was a very handsome boy," she said. "But the world . . . it's filled with handsome boys. Do you not think it odd, that after twenty years, he is the man that I think of, when I think of men? My first lover, it's true . . . who left me, two decades ago. Who came back to me, so briefly, after the war . . . and left again.

"Isn't it strange, that when I receive a letter from him—the simplest, most hastily written letter—that I should follow its instructions without question?"

Annie had always thought it was love that made a girl do that sort of thing. But she thought about it again.

"Oh," she said.

And Ruth looked over her shoulder and echoed:

"Oh."

She knelt down and lifted an iron poker from the rack, poking it into the embers at the heart of the fire.

"I'd intended to go with Doctor Waggoner, with Zimmermann, to

Germany. To rescue my *love* Jason Thistledown from the Juke. Or from Orlok. Because of course, Jason had written me. He had professed his love for me. And I do want to go. More than anything. I want to go to *him*."

She pulled the poker from the fire. Its tip was glowing a faint pink, and she brought it close to her left hand.

"I wonder," she said, "if I would feel the same if I burnt my palm, right now. The pain worked for Jason, when he wanted to get out from under the spell of a Juke. What do you think it'd do for me?"

Andrew returned to the house just past three in the morning, and found Annie dozing on the sofa beside Ruth Harper, back in her blanket and curled up there. Annie, a light sleeper, awoke as he stepped into the room. She put a finger to her lips, and indicated that they should meet and talk in the hall.

"How is Madame Pierrepoint?" asked Annie, before Andrew could question Ruth's presence, and Andrew explained the news was good.

"She came to an hour ago," he said. "She did suffer a stroke—there's partial paralysis, on her left side, and her speech isn't back yet. Though part of that's the *plombage*. We'll keep a close eye on her for a couple days. I think there's a good chance she'll come back. Now what—" He indicated with a thumb toward the sitting room.

Annie guided Andrew into the kitchen as she thought about what to say.

Finally, as they sat down at the table, Annie took Andrew's hands in hers and looked him in the eye and told him straight up: Ruth Harper was in no shape to go to Germany, and neither was Albert Zimmermann.

Four

Bobby Grady knew some musicians in Paris—jazz men who played the Liberty some nights, just drank there others—and some of them he trusted, so he called on those ones. Just a few of those were not ill-disposed to the idea, as he explained it. So it developed into a plan.

Annie thought it was idiotic when she heard it first, but she warmed to it.

Certainly she was convinced of Grady's assertion that she and Andrew wouldn't be able to travel in Germany together, and surely not to Munich. Not into a city of brownshirt thugs, rallied around a leader who dined out on the disparagement of lesser races, and fomenting terror of miscegenation. Travelling there absent his white wife, Andrew would be safer, but still not safe. Not on his own.

Bobby's plan rested on his friend—a Negro trumpet player name of Ozzie Hayward—and Ozzie was up for it. Ozzie had come to Paris by way of Louisiana, eventually fronting a jazz quartet known in Europe as *Le Noir Qui Danse*: The Dancing Negro.

It wasn't a particularly descriptive moniker: not Ozzie, nor his drummer Pete Norland, nor piano man Bill Colbert, nor sax player Charlie LeFauvre did more than tap toes in time to their music. They were all *noir*, though, and unlike the general run of Negros, Germans—at least the class of German that listened to jazz music—liked them well enough.

"Tolerate's a better word," said Ozzie, swirling a glass of whiskey in the ground floor barroom of the Liberty, where Andrew and Annie met him for the first time on a bright Tuesday afternoon, before the crowd showed up. "They like the tune well enough . . . hum along, cut the rug with the Fräuleins, all that. German folk need that now—happy songs, sad songs. Any kind of song. Maybe they need the Negro too. But not for nothing but someone to whip, you dig?"

There wasn't much whiskey in his glass, and Ozzie drained it.

"They need nice music more than a Negro to whip, and we sure do make nice music. So we're all right."

They were sitting around the table with Bobby, Ozzie, and Dominic Villart, the Italian boy who had driven the ambulance and inherited Molinare's seat at the table upstairs. To Annie's eye, both Dominic and Ozzie were nearly children—smooth-cheeked boys, wet about the ears. But not really; olive-skinned Dominic was quite muscular, his hair creamed back, a shadow of beard across a well-cut jawline. Ozzie used cream too, more of it and probably a different brand, to plaster his kinked hair nearly straight and flat against his scalp. A part like an arrow ran along the right side of his skull, back past the crown. Ozzie was rail thin, so Annie didn't think he'd be any good at all in a fight, but maybe that was all right. She liked him. She thought others might too, especially sad German boys, deciding whether to whip or sing along. And that was good for Andrew.

"It sounds like you know a lot about the Germans," said Andrew.

"We been through Germany four times now," said Ozzie. "Couple times in Berlin. One time up in Frankfurt. One time down where you want to get to, Doc: Munich. That was two years back. We accompanied a heeler show, naked ladies being part of that. Scooped some heavy sugar over five nights, but I'm guessing half of that was for the ladies. More than half. Different crowd than Berlin."

"How is that?" asked Annie.

Ozzie shrugged. "Berlin's different than everywhere, and that's something. But Munich . . . Munich especially. Not a jazz town. More a beer hall town. Oom pah pah . . . Wouldn't have thought we'd ever be back there. But here we are, thanks to my man Bobby. . . ."

Now Bobby shrugged. "It was high time," he said. Bobby knew musicians, and the people who booked the musicians too. And he'd pulled some strings with the manager of a little cabaret he knew, along the Isar. . . .

"Time indeed. So here we are, booked for a week, less'n a week from now. And lo 'n' behold, my quartet got itself a fifth." He grinned and tapped the table in front of Andrew.

"Afraid I'm not much of one," said Andrew, "but I'll try and pass."

"Don't do that," said Ozzie. "They might ask you to play a tune, or dance. And you can't do either of those things I'm guessin'.

"Just keep your hat low when anybody asks anything, particularly one of them brownshirts. They ain't police but they act like they are, and that makes 'em worse. And they're all over Munich. One of them asks you anything, you don't speak German, even if you do. You're just a dumb *Neger*. You know what that word means?"

"It's German for Negro."

Ozzie shook his head. "Not when they say it to you. They mean 'nigger,' then," he said. "Important distinction. That's what we are there, Doctor. Just like back home."

Andrew would meet up with Ozzie and *Le Noir Qui Danse* at Gare du Norde station two days hence, packed for a roundabout trip to Munich. Dominic would meet with Dr. Lewis and board the same train but in First Class. It would take a day and a half, and they would need to change trains once, in Stuttgart. Thus Andrew Waggoner, the chief physician at the Sanatorium de Vire, would enter Munich as a tone-deaf jazz man who couldn't so much as make eye contact with anyone until he was well away from the München LFF station, and safe at Dr. Kurtzweiller's rooms.

The absurdity of it all came up several times that evening at home, in Andrew and Annie's Paris flat.

"You know, I could probably get away with it," said Andrew. "Just buy a first-class ticket, sit up front with Lewis and Villart, and tell the stationmaster I'm a doctor. In German! *Ich bin Arzt!* Who'd be bothered?"

"Probably no one," said Annie. They were in their bedchamber, and Andrew had undressed for the night. Not Annie. She sat in front of the vanity, unpinning her hair, and she could see Andrew's reflection behind her, his good hand behind his head, his bad . . . rested on the sheets over his chest. "But if the wrong person was bothered . . ." She pointed with the tip of a comb at the reflection of that hand.

Andrew apprehended the gesture and lifted his hand from his chest, drew the fingers toward a fist. He grimaced as they froze in a loose cage over his palm—as close as his old maiming would let him make to a fist these days.

"Can't afford another bang like that one," he said.

"Couldn't really afford that one," said Annie, and they both laughed, gaily, as though they were spending an ordinary night in Paris before an ordinary trip, making light of old hardships with no care for new ones.

"I'll be good," said Andrew. "Careful, I mean. I just . . . I just resent it, that's all."

"I know. We came here to France so we wouldn't have to," said Annie. "Be careful, I mean."

"We always had to be careful," said Andrew. "There are parts of this town where we can't really walk together."

"And there are parts where we can," said Annie.

"So there are."

Annie set the comb down and went to the bed, slid under the covers beside Andrew.

"I don't like seeing you off like this," she said. "I understand why it has to be done. But I don't care for it."

"Remember," said Andrew, "when you saw me off from Eliada? Got me a medical kit, a coat and a knife . . . that intervention saved my life."

"It did," said Annie. "But you know it was old Sam Green who tipped off Jason, who did the work of getting that bag to you . . . and getting you clear of town."

"That's so," said Andrew, and he fell quiet.

"What are you going to say to Jason, when you find him?" asked Annie finally.

Andrew pondered. "I'm probably going to give him hell," he said.

"You could've done that this spring, when he came by to see us."

"Yeah." Andrew leaned back, and shut his eyes. "I do regret missing that opportunity."

Annie propped herself up and pushed Andrew's shoulder. "Hogwash," she said. "You haven't wanted to so much as look at that boy since he waved goodbye at the Thorns' farm. Twenty years ago. When we did see him, that time after the war when we were all in Lyon—you proved it." Leaning in close, Annie made to look all over the room, everywhere but at her husband . . . the way he had at the little Armistice dinner Annie had arranged for them all, pretending desperately that Jason and his chest of medals was not in the room.

Andrew looked away himself, not smiling now. "Jason abandoned us," he said quietly. "Abandoned Ruth."

"Abandoned you," said Annie.

Andrew pushed himself up against the headboard, so his eyes were level with Annie's. "Well I'm not going to abandon Jason," he said. "When I talk to him—if I can talk to him, if there's anything left of him—I'm sure I'll point that out. If he can't figure it out for himself."

They slept late, and when they woke, they made love. So it was just past noon before they set foot outdoors, and Annie at least was famished. They found a bistro, half underground and floored with brick, and took a table near the front where they dined on omelettes and pastries, washed down with thick dark espresso coffee. They considered a bottle of wine, but Andrew suggested they wait until later. They paid their bill, then judged the day warm and sunny enough for a stroll along the banks of the Seine—taking a familiar route that Andrew had first shown Annie just prior their wedding, one he had discovered as a young medical student, more than a decade before that.

They didn't speak much, either at breakfast or during their walk. That was fine; silence was a familiar and not-unwelcome aftereffect. For her part, Annie found she drew into herself—into a little globe of satiety, a space all her own. It had been that way every time they made love, even that first time—sooner than either of them had ever admitted; sooner, Annie sometimes worried, than Andrew even knew.

They fell into the shadow of Pont Mirabeau and considered, silently, whether to climb onto the bridge or continue on the riverbank.

They had been on another riverbank, then—the west bank of the Kootenai River—and had only recently undergone a miracle. Two miracles really.

The first was a lie, magnified in the shadow of the Juke. They did talk about that lie—that miracle—at great length. For Annie, the lie was almost absurdly banal. It was a lie of omission. The lie Andrew told himself was the lie of the city where they were now, the steps to the bridge that they quietly agreed to eschew . . .

They had leapt into the river in a shred of time where they'd been allowed to escape, underneath the hovering mouths of the Juke in the temple it had made of the mill at Eliada. They'd emerged, downstream, a good way's off . . . and there, found bare shelter in the ruin of a cabin, its roof staved in by bad winters and rains. It was bare, but it was enough. . . .

And there was the second miracle, the one they made the most use of. There was wood and some scraps of cloth, which Annie used those to re-splint Andrew's broken arm, and there was some line and a hook in an old tackle box, which she used to find them supper from the river. She made a fire, too, to cook it all.

And as they sat by the fire she'd made, Andrew had reached for her. First he touched her face, the backs of his fingers drawing along her jawline, down her throat to the nape of her neck. The touch was . . . thrilling, in its way. She was surprised at how soft his hand was, at how easily she could differentiate between the ridge of a knuckle, the smoothness of a nail. At a point, she took hold of his hand and turned it, drew it lower, to her breast, and she drew closer to him and kissed him, and reached down and found him hard for her.

Such detail! On the banks of the Seine, she reached over to take Andrew's hand now, and squeezed it, remembering . . . well . . . everything. When she had climbed on top of Andrew, she felt as though she were reclaiming something—as though she had come back from that absurd delusion inspired by the Juke. She thought that same thing might have happened for Andrew, in their first moment together.

She had always assumed so.

But of course they didn't speak afterward then, and rarely did later. And for a moment, as they stopped to look across the Seine, she thought about the story Ruth had told her, now days ago, and she wondered whether it *had* been that way for Andrew—or if when she was looking at him, he might not have been looking at some Heavenly version of this city; some other, tricky version of herself?

These thoughts did not occur to her much in those earlier days. She had had other worries: the arrival of Jason and Ruth, not even a day afterward, made for immediate medical emergencies, and the particular emergency of Ruth's infection also stirred another fear—that Annie might be in Ruth's state, fertilized and infected too, and in need of a similar surgery.

Andrew's train left that night, at half-past eight. They ate an early dinner in their rooms, and Andrew stepped out at just before seven. There was no need to accompany him there, in fact Dominic and Bobby advised against it. Andrew would be using his own passport—the risk of getting caught out on a forgery was worse than the risk of a border guard recognizing Doctor Waggoner's name out of the blue. But there was no sense in advertising their connection. So Andrew would leave alone, and Annie would return to Vire in the morning.

They said their farewells when the taxi arrived. He said something reassuring, and she said something encouraging, and an hour later, as the last of the twilight disappeared and the street began to light up outside her window, Annie found she could scarcely remember what either of them had said to one another.

She made quick work of the dinner dishes. She tried to read a novel she'd brought with her, a Hemingway book about ambulance drivers about which she'd heard good things. But she couldn't concentrate enough to enjoy it. She made up the bed, retired early, but slept badly and woke at a point in the dark hours, convinced that someone was watching her. She knew it was absurd—that photograph of Zimmermann, in Zimmermann's camera . . . it was clearly spooking her—but she flipped on the bed lamp and made sure.

There was no one there, in one way, but in another—of course there was. Jason Thistledown, with his scalpel-cut hand and his cigarette-burned throat, was there. She couldn't begrudge Andrew going off to find him, as dangerous as it was. But she could begrudge herself—for not doing something that day in the spring to persuade him . . . even to compel him . . . to miss that flight. To stay at Vire, where Ruth Harper and Albert Zimmermann now hid, and become well again.

Annie did get back to sleep, and the second half of the night she did sleep better. Indeed, she slept well enough that she awoke late, for the second day in a row. It could well have been late enough that she'd miss her eleven o'clock train into Normandy, but she was woken by the ringing of the doorbell, at just past nine.

"Bonjour—Madame Waggoner?"

The apartment was on the first floor, and because Annie was not dressed she didn't go downstairs but half-stepped onto the small balcony, just enough that she could see. The visitor was a lone gentleman, wearing a wool overcoat that matched his dark blue bowler hat. Annie said *"Oui,"* and asked if he minded waiting a moment while she dressed. He doffed his hat and said of course he didn't, and a moment later, as Annie ran a brush through her hair and stepped into a frock, she tried to place him. She did recognize the face—round, with a long moustache, balding, middle-aged. But from where?

She opened the window again, and saw that he had lit a cigarette and was leaned against the lamppost, smoking it. He looked up and waved, and said something that she couldn't quite make out. So she waved back, and went downstairs to the lobby, and opened the front door and bade him good morning.

"I am to take it," he said in English, "that Doctor Waggoner is not present?"

"I'm afraid not," said Annie.

"Well that is a great shame," he said. "I had been informed that you were both staying in the city. I had hoped we might finally meet."

So they hadn't ever met. Annie squinted in the morning light and shaded her eyes.

"Well," he said, "perhaps you can pass along my greetings." He reached into his coat and produced a calling card. "Do you expect him back soon may I ask? I would like very much to speak with him, on a matter of mutual interest."

Annie took the card, and turned it over to read it. She read it twice, looked at the visitor and read it again. Then worked saliva into her mouth, it having suddenly gone dry.

"My apologies for the intrusion, Madame. I will be on my way then," he said, and turned to leave.

"No apology necessary," said Annie, "Doctor Aguillard."

He paused in returning his hat to his head. Annie continued.

"Why don't you come in and sit? I'll make a pot of coffee, and we'll wait for him together."

Doctor Hector Aguillard smiled gratefully.

"That would be splendid, Mrs. Waggoner," he said.

Five

"You're not from Paris, are you?"

"No, Madame." Doctor Aguillard accepted the cup and saucer Annie'd prepared, and Annie poured more coffee for herself from the percolator. Unlike Aguillard's, hers was pure black. "I am from Brussels originally," he said.

"But you've travelled since then. Recently, maybe?"

Aguillard answered with a genial shrug. He had removed his coat and his hat and hung it in the hall. He wore a grey tweed jacket, the sort that had a belt sash stitched onto the back, and under it a white shirt that was also turning to grey, and a green bow tie. He might have arrived straight from the train station. Right off a barge.

Annie sat down on the sofa across from him. She had drawn the curtains when he came in, so that although the morning was clear and bright, in here the electric table lamp was the only illumination.

Aguillard took a sip from his cup. "I was just in Zurich in fact, briefly, before coming to Paris."

"Zurich's a beautiful city." Annie lifted her own cup to her lips and took a sip. She recognized him from the photograph from Zimmermann's camera roll—of course it was him. But he seemed slimmer, maybe even a little older, than the photograph portrayed. This caused her to briefly wonder if the picture might not itself have been older than Zimmermann had indicated.

"Is something wrong?" asked Aguillard then, and Annie saw that she had been looking at him too hard—too speculatively. She smiled and set her teacup down in its saucer.

"Nothing, sir. I'm just trying to place you."

“I doubt you would recognize me,” said Aguillard. “We have not met. I am . . . a colleague of your husband’s. A peer, one might say.”

“A peer,” said Annie. “Do you work in pulmonary medicine?”

Aguillard smiled wanly and shook his head. And now he paused and looked at Annie. As though he now, were trying to place her.

“Your maiden name,” he said, “is Rowe, is it not?”

“It is,” she said. “Haven’t used it in a long time. How do you come to know that?”

“Well,” he said, drawing himself straighter in his chair. He patted his jacket pocket and withdrew a cigarette case. “Do you mind?”

Annie brought a basalt ashtray from the mantelpiece and set it on the coffee table between them. He removed a cigarette from the case and Annie struck a match to light it.

“You were a nurse,” he said, “working for Doctor Nils Bergstrom. Ann Rowe.”

“In Idaho,” said Annie. “That’s right.”

“Doctor Waggoner worked there also.”

“That’s right too.” Annie dropped the match in the fireplace and resumed her seat.

“I can only imagine the things you must have seen.” Aguillard crossed one leg over the other and let the cigarette dangle from fingertips over his knee. “In Eliada.”

“Is that so?”

“That is so,” said Aguillard. He drew deep on his cigarette. “I have never met Doctor Waggoner, or yourself. I do not work in pulmonary medicine, as you describe it. But we are nevertheless peers. We have an abiding interest in the same phenomenon.”

Annie finished her coffee and set the cup back in the saucer.

“Do you remember anything from Eliada?” he asked.

“Oh yes,” said Annie. “Hard to forget Eliada.”

“You remember the patient Mister Juke then.”

“Yes indeed,” she said. “He was an odd one.”

Aguillard sighed. “Madame Waggoner,” he said, “let us drop the pretenses. I think we both understand what Mister Juke was. Not a he, or an it, but an . . . organism. It was an organism that got the better of Doctor Bergstrom. And Garrison Harper too. And somehow . . . its presence led to a terrible massacre.”

Somehow, thought Annie. What she said was, "Terrible."

Aguillard rested his cigarette on the edge of the ashtray, and took another sip from his cup, deeper this time, then set it down too.

"I am being very forward," he said. "I apologize. I suppose I am overanxious—I've been waiting some time to speak with Doctor Waggoner on these matters. . . ."

"On your common interest," said Annie. "Peer to peer."

"And now I have intruded upon you. Drawn up old memories." He drew himself farther up in his chair and then fell forward, his elbows resting on his knees. "Do you expect Doctor Waggoner back soon?"

"Soon enough," said Annie. She leaned forward too, far enough that she could get a good look at Aguillard's eyes, see about his pupils.

"Doctor Aguillard," she said, having satisfied herself, "I don't pay the same degree of attention to your common interest as my husband does. But I think I can keep up. Now why don't you tell me where you really were last. It wasn't Zurich."

"No. Not Zurich."

"Where?" Annie reached to slide the ashtray away from Aguillard.

"Bavaria," he said. Annie took his cigarette from the ashtray's edge and stubbed it out, and when Aguillard complained that he wasn't finished with it, she told him to relax and try to remember. She didn't tell him that the generous dose of sodium amytal that she'd infused in his coffee would help him with both of those things. She didn't need to; Aguillard, no fool, was figuring it out. He blinked, and felt his forehead with a hand, ran the slick of sweat that came away between his fingers, and started to rise. He did not quite reach his feet; halfway up, dizziness overcame him, and steadying himself on the coffee table he sat back down. His eyes cast down, and to the side, and finally set, wide and incredulous, on Annie. *What have you done to me?* they asked her.

"Doctor Aguillard," said Annie softly. "Don't fear. I am a trained nurse. I know my business. I know how much is too much, and how little is not enough. Now. Could you be a bit more specific?

"Where?"

"Wallgau, in the south . . . a village near the border with Austria, near the mountains. Have you a map? I could show you. . . ."

"No need. I know it. Now what were you doing there?"

"Ha! Good question. Very good question. When I got there I thought we were looking after a Juke. But not at all, as it turned out. *La bête était morte. Depuis longtemps."*

Annie switched to French, along with Auguillard. It was likely easier for him, in his current state. *"The Juke that you were looking after . . . was dead?"*

"Murdered, it so happened."

Annie affected a demeanor of shock.

"We were furious when we learned. The specimen was a rarity, and moving it to Wallgau—to the valley beyond it . . . was a complicated feat."

"You moved it?"

Aguillard nodded drunkenly, then shook his head. *"Not I,"* he said. *"But . . . we did."*

"From where did you move it?"

"Oh, Eliada. That is the only place where one could find a Juke. Where God watches over. That is the only place. Ever, anywhere . . ."

"Eliada is gone. Jukes are big. From where did you move it?"

"From Eliada."

Annie leaned forward and gave Aguillard two light slaps on his cheeks.

"Did you collect it at Eliada yourself?" she asked, switching to English. Aguillard was too comfortable speaking his native tongue.

"Not me," he said in English. "But men from the office did. And it was not terribly large. It was tiny in fact. And very well-protected for the journey." Aguillard smiled lopsidedly. *"Au sein de la mère."*

"Its mother," said Annie. "Inside a woman?"

"There were three women, carrying Jukes. The only survivors of the contagion. Aside from yourself, Doctor Waggoner, Miss Harper, and Mister Thistledown." He frowned. "Tell me, what have you given me?"

Annie told him, and he nodded. "It feels as though you gave me quite a large dose."

"Large enough to keep you out of trouble."

He laughed at that, and nodded again.

"You are, if I may say, a less-than-gracious hostess." He pronounced it *hos'ess*.

"You're one to talk." Annie stood. "Those women were at Eliada twenty years ago."

"And they are all long dead, nearly as long as that." He shrugged. "Fragile things. Their children . . . are hardier."

Annie fought back curiosity. She could dig into Aguillard's memories for hours, days, and that curiosity wouldn't be sated. What did they do to the women? How did the "children" survive, and how did Aguillard's people manage to control those children . . . keep them from turning the tables?

But she didn't have hours . . . not by the look of Aguillard, whose forehead was now slick with sweat . . . whose hands fell loosely in his lap. She had a few minutes.

"Why did you come from Wallgau to talk with Doctor Waggoner?"

"To enlist his help."

"Help with the dead Juke?"

"No. With the one that killed it."

"What killed the Juke?"

"Who, you mean?"

"Orlok," said Annie—and at that, Aguillard's hands made fists, and he lifted his head, and Annie's heart sank. She'd tipped her hand. Aguillard—no fool—had seen it. He knew, now, that she knew more about Wallgau than how to find it on a map.

"Orlok," said Aguillard. "Yes. You and your husband . . . are better informed than I thought. And that is why . . . you poison me. Has Jason . . . Thistledown contacted you?"

Annie kept her voice level. "Who is Orlok?"

"You are asking the questions."

"I am asking the questions."

"Who knows who he is? He is someone that our . . . hosts . . . our hosts had been looking for . . . for many, many years. You know our hosts?"

Annie didn't answer, so Aguillard went on.

"Well they are Nazi Party. Idiots. Plaut, the fat fool. And oh . . ." He looked to one side, as though he'd seen something there, and blinked. ". . . someone you might know! Bergstrom! Johannes Bergstrom! You worked for his brother, in Eliada!"

Annie didn't bother to feign surprise. She just nodded. He laughed.

"Nils Bergstrom was a surgeon. Johannes . . . an alienist. But a eugenicist. Still. Like his elder brother in America."

"Like you."

"Like me, yes."

"All working from the Eugenics Records Office?"

Aguillard nodded, a lolling head-bob, and laughed. "Cold Creek Harbour.

That's part. Twenty years ago, when all that occurred . . . we were mostly working for . . . them. For Cold Creek Harbour."

"Tell me about Orlok," said Annie.

"Oh yes! Orlok! Well Bergstrom'd been looking for him, for years."

"So you said."

"So I said. Orlok . . . he is the vampire, yes? From the old moving picture. But obviously not a vampire. No such thing! Still. That's what he calls himself."

"Did you meet him?"

Aguillard nodded once more.

"Tell me about him."

"Big. Very big. Not handsome. But beautiful. Like a mountainside beautiful. Just as they suspected . . . A superman. They could not find him for years of looking. And then . . . when they had ceased to look . . . when they brought the Juke, I think . . . then, he arrived!"

"How."

"Like Christ to Jerusalem," said Aguillard. "How else?"

Annie leaned back on the couch and regarded Aguillard. His mouth was turned up in a grotesque smirk, even as his eyelids fluttered and his breathing grew shallow. Time was growing short.

"Did you tell anyone you came here?" she asked, and he said no, he hadn't. "Not your masters with the Eugenics Records Office?"

"No," he said. "Came here firs'. You . . . your husband . . . I'd wanted to bring him there all along. Before Jason. But idiot Nazis . . . wanted a white."

"Did you contact your Eugenics Records Office?" she asked again, and again.

"No."

"What is it you wanted to ask my husband?" she asked.

"Well. I wanted to confer. Just as I told you. We know that he had maintained . . . an independent inquiry . . . into *biologie* . . . *transcendantale* . . . And I wanted to see . . . if he had ever encountered . . . a hybrid."

"What do you mean?"

"I wanted to know . . . if he could explain a mechanism in which a Juke . . . could, in its pupal state . . . mingling with a living foetus within a uterus . . . also become a man."

As the drug completed its effect, English became too much for poor old Hector Aguillard, and even French was a morass. But Annie satisfied herself on several important points. First: she satisfied herself that Aguillard was here alone. He had not, for a reason that he couldn't make clear, contacted any associates in the Eugenics Records Office since departing Wallgau . . . since fleeing Wallgau. On that last point he was very clear. Wallgau and its environs had become a hazard to him and his person. Which made sense, given Zimmermann's account of his own departure. He had also not contacted Emile Desrosiers, which was more of a relief; it had only occurred to Annie after the drug took effect that she might have to deal with the local businessman—possibly gangster—once the interrogation was done.

The interrogation was interrupted by an aspirating event—some of the coffee and a foaming dose of bile found its way to Aguillard's windpipe—and if Annie hadn't been there, that might have ended matters right there for the poor doctor. But she managed to clear his airway and lean Doctor Aguillard forward so that he could cough and vomit into a bucket that she hastily fetched from the kitchen.

She was able to nurse him back to a state where he could, briefly, answer the last set of questions that she had—and also to confirm that he had, in fact, abducted her friend Jason Thistledown and placed him in such a dangerous situation. To that, he offered his last coherent words in answer. And after Annie allowed those words to sink in, she moved Aguillard to the sofa, and let him lay down.

She arranged her skirt then and kneeled beside him, watching as his eyes fluttered half-shut, and listening as his breathing slowed . . . as he slipped into unconsciousness . . . coma . . .

Setting her mouth, Annie touched his cheek with her fingertips, and then brought thumb and forefinger to his nostrils and pinched tight as she placed her hand over his mouth.

Forty-two years, Annie thought as she sat there next to Aguillard's still form, *and now I'm a murderer*.

A murderess.

Murder was something that she had thought about, every now and then over the years since she and Andrew had escaped Eliada, fled North America, and finally taken up hiding in plain sight in France. Fleeing was the intelligent thing to do, she knew that . . . Andrew wasn't safe in America—not as a Negro practising medicine, or trying to . . . but also not after having escaped the horror at Eliada, knowing that the people who'd wrought it . . . Germaine Frost's, Garrison Harper's masters . . . knowing they existed as a specific and ever-present menace.

It was sensible to leave, but it was not a thing that always sat easy with Annie. She felt as though she were running from a fight, letting a war go, and that allowing those men to persist . . . that was a kind of abrogation too. She had wondered how it would have been, to open up one of the jars of contagion that Germaine Frost had brought, in the panelled rooms where the eugenicists at Cold Creek Harbour met to discuss their idiot notions . . . to watch them all choke on the fluids bubbling up in their lungs. . . .

To cull them.

Annie checked the clock that hung over the mantel. It was still early—just half-past nine. There would have been plenty of time to make her train, had the morning gone differently. But of course she wouldn't now. She was going to need some help for the next part of this, help from someone she could trust, and she was sure she could trust Bobby Grady.

But she wouldn't be able to raise him at this hour . . . they'd have to wait until two in the afternoon to meet with Ozzie and Dominic. He didn't keep a telephone at home, or at least hadn't supplied Andrew with an exchange, so she would call him when he arrived at the bar.

In the meantime, she would have to try and telephone Vire—get a hold of Luc Curzon, see if he might be able to put Ruth on the line, or at least deliver a message to her. And Annie would also need to compose a wire to Andrew. That would have to wait until he arrived in Munich, at Herr Kurtzweiller's rooms there. Annie hoped it would catch him. He needed to know . . . Ruth needed to know . . . matters had changed, rather dramatically.

Murder! She shook her head—in disbelief? No, looking down at Aguillard—his face already pale and gray—there was nothing to do but accept what she'd done.

But there lay the surprise. Maybe that's what made Annie laugh, as she did.

Annie had always imagined that her innate goodness, her *morality*, would draw in on her, prick her conscience, were she ever to commit such a thing. That was what she would tell herself, when she would imagine Charles Davenport, wheezing and coughing and choking on his deathbed, put there by Annie's own vengeful doing. It stopped her, this . . . this ghost of kindliness that she had always imagined haunted her.

Perhaps it still did . . . it might yet come for her in the night, and wake her with shrill accusations. Did you not vow to preserve life when you entered the medical profession, Annie? Don't you know that there is nothing worse—nothing!—than taking a human life? Doesn't revenge taste so much worse inside you now than maybe it smelled, when you were thinking about it?

Maybe revenge would taste worse tonight. But now, as Annie held fast on Aguillard's mouth, his nose . . . it tasted just fine.

Aguillard was a fiend. He had at the very least participated in a decades-old scheme to murder the tiny town near which Jason Thistledown grew, murdering in the process his mother. He was culpable in the obscenity of Eliada—even if he hadn't unleashed the contagion there . . . the Cave Germ.

After he had stolen Jason Thistledown's family . . . after his organization had driven Jason from his home, to the bosom of the Juke . . . Hector Aguillard had come to personally rob Jason of the rest of himself.

She might have spared Aguillard, for all that . . . simply let him drift unconscious, ask Mr. Grady to see that he was driven to some location far off and left to come to, forgetful that anything had happened.

She might have, until she asked him specifically about Jason's well-being, and heard his answer.

"Oh Jason, yes. He is very much alive. You must watch that one."

"Why is that?"

"He is monstrous," Aguillard had said, his words slurring, his breathing slowing. *"Utterly monstrous. If you see him . . . do you want my advice?"*

And with just two words, Aguillard convinced her.

"Tue-le."

Kill him.

I won't kill Jason, she thought.

But monstrous things . . . For killing those, there is an argument.

Annie removed her hand from Aguillard's mouth, and let go of his nose. The nostrils stuck closed for a moment, and then the elasticity of the cartilage asserted the glue of mucous, and first the left and then the right popped open.

A murderess, she thought—and *A murderess*, again, as breath hitched in Aguillard's chest and he coughed, and as she put her hand back over his mouth and pinched his nostrils once more, she concluded:

A murderess.

PART IV

The Syncopation Gambit

One

Andrew Waggoner and the august members of *Le Noir Qui Danse* had five seats together on a coach just up from the baggage car. The seats were hard, and too small. But the company was good, and leaving Paris, they had some room to stretch their legs. There just weren't many folk heading to Germany in the night, on that night.

"Why'n't you take the window, Doc?" Ozzie suggested after they'd stowed their bags and settled in.

"For the view," said Andrew, and Ozzie laughed and said, "Some view." The sun was already below the horizon as they were underway, and mostly what the window did was reflect back the lights in the car, the faces of Andrew's fellow travellers.

Bill Colbert, the piano man, was up on his feet and smoking a thin hand-rolled cigarette, toe-tapping, looking guilty as hell, of something-or-other. Pete Norland, who played drums, sidled in beside Andrew, tipped his hat over his eyes and made to pretend to sleep. Ozzie sat down beside Charlie LeFauvre, the saxophone player, who had a cloth-bound book in his lap that he didn't open. It was *Ben Hur.* Ozzie had a bag with sandwiches in them, and he pulled one out and dug into it after the conductor had come around to take a look at their tickets.

Once the train picked up speed, they got to talking. LeFauvre wondered about Munich, and the venue—the Cabaret Imperial—and made it clear just how much he didn't care for the German cabaret tradition these days, "with the boys dressed up as the girls and the girls not dressed at all . . . and all that political bull*shit*."

Colbert lit up another cigarette and agreed that he didn't like that business when the Germans did it, but added he didn't like very much of anything that the Germans did, and Ozzie said he didn't want to hear any of that once they came to the border and Colbert told him not to worry. "I'm entitled to my opinion," LeFauvre said, and picked up his book.

"Hey Doc," said Pete Norland, to get the topic changed, or at least moved on, "what do you think of the cabaret?"

"Haven't ever been to one," said Andrew.

"Well you're gonna be in for a treat, then," said Norland. "You speak much German?"

"Enough to get by."

"I speak it pretty well," said Norland. "'Enough to get by' will mean a lot of their jokes go right over your head."

And then Norland got into a long talk about grammar in German—how simple music hall jokes that might fly in England or France just didn't work, because the language used so many compound words, and puns didn't necessarily play the same way . . . but they did play in a different way, and a fellow had to speak and understand German better than Pete obviously thought Andrew did. "And anyhow," said Pete finally, "they don't even speak proper German in Munich. It's all Bavarian there."

"Well then looks like I'll be completely lost," said Andrew. "You tell me when to laugh."

"A rimshot ought to do it," said Ozzie, and at that they all laughed, even LeFauvre who was supposedly deep in *A Tale of the Christ*.

"Doc's not going to be in the Cabaret for long, if at all," said Ozzie. "He's up to his own business, ain't that right?"

Andrew nodded, and LeFauvre and Colbert nodded along, because they had an idea.

The whole band had more of an idea as to what business Andrew was up to than he'd have liked—Dominic had given Ozzie an altogether too honest short version of the problem in Wallgau when they first met—and Ozzie'd shared it with his band, so as the train pushed eastward through the dark fields of France, they all had their questions.

Colbert wanted to know about the Nazis, which Dominic had indicated were going to be a problem for them all, and not just because the colour of Andrew's skin.

"You got a friend stuck in there with them stormtroopers," he asked. "You figure he's one of them by now?"

Andrew allowed as he didn't know exactly what Jason's predicament was, but from what he knew of Jason and had heard of Nazis, he didn't think it likely Jason would've signed up. He wasn't even sure that Jason was in the company of the S.A.

"That's good," said Colbert. "Speaks well of him. Speaks well of you too, going in to help him out."

Andrew didn't have a good answer for that, but Ozzie mentioned that it wasn't only to help out Jason Thistledown that they were bringing in Andrew along with the other two.

"The march of science," he said, and winked.

Dominic had told Ozzie a little bit about the Juke too. LeFauvre put his book face down on his lap and asked about that. He'd been given to understand that they were looking into a bug that made a man pray more, and he didn't like the sound of it.

"Like a rash," said Norland. "Itchin' for religion."

"Man should pray because it's the right thing to do," said LeFauvre.

Andrew said he agreed on that point.

"Trouble is," said Norland, "what if scratching an itch is also the right thing to do?"

Ozzie told Norland he was a thoughtful fellow as well as a smart-mouth, which Andrew hoped would end that line of questions, but it didn't.

"You a praying man?" LeFauvre asked Andrew.

"Sure."

"Sure," said LeFauvre, and at the look he gave, Andrew smiled a little sheepishly, and shook his head and apologized.

"I'm not really, no."

"All right."

"I wouldn't be either," said Norland, "I knew about this bug. What'd be the point?"

"God's still there," said LeFauvre. "Bug or no bug."

Andrew said that might be so. "But one thing's sure," he said. "Sometimes, it's definitely the bug. If I don't pray, ever . . . the bug never has a chance to trick me."

LeFauvre looked skeptical, and for a moment, Andrew felt awful, naked in his own flip cynicism. The train pulled faster through the night, and the silence between them stretched likewise.

"Well," said Norland, finally, "good luck with that, Doc. Gonna bet you're in Charlie's prayers, if not your own."

And that did it. They all laughed, even LeFauvre before he shook his head and picked up his *Ben Hur* and let it go. A minute or so after that, Andrew figured it was all right to go stretch his legs in their near-empty car.

They had to change trains in Stuttgart, and it would be a considerable wait; the *Deutsche Reichsbahn* train to Munich wasn't due in the *Hauptbahnhof* for four hours after they arrived, at a quarter to eight. There weren't many folk there given the hour, but there were some: maybe ten who'd come in on the train with them, and had other trains to catch rather than appointments in Stuttgart, spread out through the long hall and a couple of fellows in uniform that Andrew thought might be *Polizei*. A woman and a man, smoking and conversing quietly, sat on a bench next to a large wheeled trunk and a pair of smaller suitcases. By the stairs to the ticketing hall, nearly across the concourse, a group of five or six men sat and stood among a clutter of duffel bags in a way that made Andrew think of a group of soldiers.

The band unloaded their bags, and Ozzie's trumpet and Charlie's saxophone, Pete Norland's elaborate drum kit, spread over three cases . . . and they took over a bench along the edge of the cavernous platform concourse. William Lewis and Dominic did not precisely join them, but they sat in easy sight. Ozzie tipped his hat to them, then settled back, his trumpet case next to him. It was quiet here in the small hours, a good time to sleep, he said.

"You won't get much on the next leg. You know what they call the German rail cars? Thunder boxes. All metal, from wheel to seats."

Andrew didn't think he would sleep, but although what he felt like doing was walking, he knew enough not to. This was a big station, and here in the small hours of the morning it was all shadows, broken just by a few pools of electric light here and there . . . but mostly, shadowy places, where it'd be easy for a wandering Negro to find himself on the receiving end of a beating.

He did stray over to sit by Dominic and William. Dominic had brought a deck of cards, and they were playing hands of gin rummy, using William's trunk as a sort of table between them. But they folded them up when Andrew sat down.

"Ozzie says we ought to sleep," said Andrew.

"Bad idea," said Dominic. "Don't want to miss our train."

"Did you have an easy time of it at the border?" asked Lewis.

It was, in fact, absurdly easy. The conductor had spent more time with the band members' American passports than with Andrew's French papers, and hadn't even bothered to ask about their business in Germany. No one had troubled any of them when they got off the train and wrestled the luggage off the platform to the concourse—although neither had any porter lifted a hand to help them with the load. Andrew once more wondered if it wouldn't have been easier just to travel up front, get a sleeper coach car with Dominic and Lewis, and use the time to discuss their plans once they got to Munich, and then Wallgau. Dominic tapped the side of the deck on the trunk that Lewis had brought, slid it back into its box then swapped it out for the package of cigarettes in his jacket pocket. He offered around, and Andrew and William both partook.

What the hell were they going to do, in Munich . . . in Wallgau? Three days ago, Ruth Harper had demanded to know, as they sat alone in her room at the sanatorium. Andrew laid it out for her as best he could.

"Kurtzweiller will have settled in. He'll talk to people. Hopefully he'll have more of an idea what the situation is in Wallgau. The farm's owned by a family in Munich . . . the Vislers. He's looking them up. They might know a bit more. And then . . . there's the Nazis."

"He's not going to talk with the Nazis, surely . . . ?"

"Not directly, about Wallgau I mean. But why wouldn't he? They're running an election now I hear. People running elections do like to talk."

"He's a proper detective, is Dr. Kurtzweiller."

"He speaks the language."

Ruth stood up and went to the window, but only looked out an instant before she turned and leaned against the sill.

"How will you even keep your own wits about you?" she asked. "Any of you?"

"We'll take precautions," said Andrew.

"Really?" Ruth's tone was withering. "What precautions? Did you ever manage to replicate that hill-people concoction that didn't quite see you through the day in Eliada?"

"No," said Andrew.

"Are you going to cut yourself? Some other methodology?" She pointed to her foot, into which twenty years ago Jason had discharged a pistol.

"Dr. Lewis is gathering equipment."

"*Equipment.*" She laughed bitterly, and shook her head. "Andrew, I would have a better appreciation for the decision we made, that Albert and I stay hidden in this . . . this prison, and not join you to Wallgau . . . if you could make it clearer to me exactly how the *Société*'s plan is any better."

Now, Andrew regarded the trunk that Dr. Lewis had packed. In it were various things: two new Leica cameras and more than a dozen rolls of 35-millimetre film, sterile jars of various sizes and a jug of formaldehyde, instruments for dissection, binoculars, electric lamps. And for protection: wartime gas masks, double-filtered with activated charcoal and a mechanical gas treated for chlorine, and oil-cloth coats and pants . . . rubber gloves . . . all roughly sized for Andrew, Dr. Lewis, Kurtzweiller, and Dominic.

Andrew had brought along in his own bag of supplies from Vire, such as nurses used when interacting with tubercular patients: gloves and masks and goggles . . . Andrew also packed a case of phials of extracted wasp venom, adrenaline and several hypodermic needles . . . these on the conjecture that adrenaline might be the agent of distraction that Jason and he had activated in Eliada with sheer, searing pain, to break the Juke's spell. And if it didn't . . . well, there was the wasp venom. The efficacy of which was a conjecture too.

That was the trouble: all of their measures were conjecture. Fact was fact. It had been twenty years since Andrew or anyone he knew had encountered a living Juke.

"Oh dear," said Lewis, and when Andrew raised an eyebrow he nodded toward the band. Two of the men from the stairs had crossed the concourse, and were talking to them. Andrew tapped the ashes from his cigarette and straightened to listen. Dominic put a hand on his arm.

"Don't show interest," he said, and Andrew nodded and dragged on his cigarette.

They were speaking German, in pleasant tones. One—a short heavyset fellow with greasy blond hair—appeared to be asking about the drum kit. *Was ist das, mein Herr?* That kind of thing. Norland put his hand on the bass drum kit possessively—maybe too possessively—and the other fellow, who was a head taller than the first, he took issue with that, and said something else in German that the echo of the station rendered incoherent.

Andrew dropped his cigarette to the floor and, shaking Dominic's hand off, stood. Two other men from that group were on their way over, walking at a brisk pace.

"I'm supposed to be with the band," he said. "That's how we get through."

Dominic rose too. "You can't help," he hissed. "Sit back down."

"No point now," said Andrew. He'd caught the smaller man's eye and, smiling, that fellow beckoned Andrew over, and Dominic too.

"Kommen sie her!"

As he'd been advised, Andrew feigned incomprehension, so the man repeated, more loudly, beckoned with his whole arm. *"Kommen sie her!"* Come!

Andrew nodded and walked over.

"Welches Instrument spielst du?" What instrument do you play?

"He does not understand what you are saying," said Ozzie, interjecting. *"Speaks no German."*

The man turned to Ozzie. *"But he is with your orchestra?"*

"He plays piano," said Colbert, and mimed chords.

"Where is his piano?" asked the tall one.

"We can't take a piano on the train," said Ozzie. *"He'll make do with whatever they've got."*

"But you carry your other instruments." The tall one bent down to look at the drum kit. He identified them one by one, by their cases: *"A trumpeter. One who plays an alto saxophone. A drummer."* He pulled the leather cover off the front of it, and read the illustration—a silhouette of a man, legs akimbo in the middle of a dance move, and in cursive script the name: *Le Noir Qui Danse.*

"What does that say?"

"Der tanzende Neger."

"Which of you Neger is the dancer?"

Ozzie smiled wide. *"None of us dance."*

"Is that name meant to be a joke then?"

"We play music to which one can dance," said Ozzie. *"Who wants to watch a Neger dance?"*

The other men had arrived, and gathered staring curiously at the band.

"Fellows!" said the tall one to the others. *"We have a dance band here!"*

"Can you play us a song?" asked the short one.

Ozzie indicated that they weren't really set up for it, but one of the others—a wide-shouldered youth with too-long blonde hair—corrected that by snatching Ozzie's trumpet case, opening it and, plucking out the mouthpiece, blew a raspberry into it. The cover from the bass drum was already off, and the shorter fellow fumbled with the trunk containing the snare. The band members shared a worried glance through wide, ingratiating smiles, and Ozzie finally nodded.

"We can play some music. But we have no piano," he said again, and Andrew looked down. It had been quick thinking on Colbert's part—it let Andrew sit this out with some grace—and if they got out of this—when they got out of this—he'd thank him for it.

Pete Norland managed to convince them not to unpack the whole drum kit—he could make do, he said, with the snare. Ozzie Hayward retrieved his mouthpiece, wiped it on his handkerchief and got his trumpet ready, and LeFauvre licked the reed of his saxophone and put it in place. The men drew back a respectful difference, and Ozzie nodded around once they were all ready.

Andrew didn't recognize the song, but Dominic did—"Confessin'," and he mentioned the title just before Colbert cut in with the lyrics, in English, confessing his love, and going from there. He did a pretty good job crooning, particularly for a piano player—and so did they all, playing without a piano. Ozzie led the band with noodling trumpet work, weaving in and out of Colbert's vocals, which soon lost the lyric and fell into a kind of inspired gibberish that shouldn't have worked but elevated the music and sent it off in another direction. Lewis made his way over beside Dominic, and when the song wound down, he tried to lead a round of applause, elbowing Dominic to do the same.

Would that the Germans had felt as good about the performance. The short one did clap, along with two others, but the thin one and the broad-shouldered blond man shared a glance and shook their heads.

"Do you know any German songs?" he asked, and before anyone could do anything but nod, the blond fellow asked: *"'In Einem Kleinen Strandkorb?' What of that song?"*

Ozzie wiped his handkerchief over his forehead. *"'In a Small Beach Basket?' I think I've heard it, but—"*

"I will remind you," said the blond man. He stepped forward, and began to sing. He spoke no lyrics—just "Da da-da-da da dat daaa!" and "da-dataaa!" and so forth. But his voice was beautiful, high and clear, and he did not miss a note, or a beat. He stopped and looked at Ozzie, and said: *"Why don't you play that for us?"*

"To be honest," said Ozzie, *"I don't think we know that one. Sounds like it's a foxtrot, though."*

"It is," said the singer. *"By Eric Harden. Do you know Eric Harden?"*

"You must know Eric Harden," said the short one.

"We can play you a foxtrot," said Ozzie.

"We need to hear the Basket song."

"We don't know it," said Ozzie, then quickly added, *"but we can try."*

He indicated to Pete Norland, to lay down a foxtrot rhythm, then put his trumpet to his lips, and blew a few bars that more or less approximated the song that the big blond fellow had sung a moment ago. It was close, but not near enough for the German's purposes—so he started singing again, and conducting, and as Ozzie followed more closely, LeFauvre came in on the saxophone.

This pleased the Germans more. The tall one swayed with the music, and put his hand on his smaller friend's shoulder to indicate that he should too. The others who'd come round went further: one, a bearded man in a thick dark sweater, took hold of the man next to him and started to dance, to foxtrot.

Ozzie's trumpet handed the melody off to LeFauvre's saxophone entirely, and he held the trumpet to his breast, eyes closed as LeFauvre followed the singer and Pete Norland kept the tempo. Lyrics began to emerge in the singing, as though the music had spurred memory—and Colbert joined in, offering a contra-punctual harmony. Ozzie, head bobbing, put his trumpet back to his lips and stepped back in.

Others were gathering. Those others still here from the train from Paris had risen from their benches, and craned to hear. The couple who'd been keeping to themselves and smoking together, abandoned their trunk and luggage and crossed the hall to better hear. Ozzie, maybe sensing the attention, lifted the horn of his trumpet to the dark wooden rafters of the *Hauptbahnhof*, and eyes tight shut, cheeks blown out like a frog's neck, breathed a string of notes that ascended to a sustained shriek so clear it made Andrew shiver and seemed to freeze everything in the moment: the men dancing, the couple walking . . . the song. It was as though they were all suspended in air at that terrible height, before gravity took hold.

But it was a trick. Norland picked up the beat, tapping his stick on the back of the bench like it was a wood block, and LeFauvre took over, and so did Colbert, picking up the melody with that gibberish lyric he seemed to favour—taking the song away from the German boy altogether . . . and bringing it to new level, the same time as it hauled them all back to Earth.

Andrew was watching the couple, standing at the edge of a circle of light, long shadows covering their faces. The woman stepped around in front of her husband, and rested a hand on his shoulder, enfolded her other hand in his—and he tilted his head, and stepped to the side . . . and they were dancing too, twirling across the station floor, into and out of the pools of light beneath the hanging lamps.

They weren't the only ones. The men were all in motion now, two of them paired off—the others, swaying on their own—heads tossed back, eyes on those dark rafters.

Andrew felt a touch at his arm—and turned to say no thank you, but it wasn't a dance.

It was Lewis. He'd opened the trunk, and pulled out a pair of gas masks. Back at the bench, kneeling in the trunk's shadow, Dominic had already put his on.

"Come on back," said Lewis. "You know what's happening."

Andrew took the gas mask from Lewis and followed him back to their bench, past it, into a darker corner. Lewis pulled the mask over his face, tightened the straps. Andrew waited a moment—looking back at the dance that seemed now to have overtaken the whole station, everyone who was here.

"No," said Andrew. If he put on the mask, the same kind that Dominic and Lewis were wearing . . . any cover as a musician would be blown. They may as well head right back to Paris, assuming he could avoid arrest.

Andrew set the gas mask down on the bench.

He stepped away, back toward the music . . . the bacchanal that was going on before them. Someone else had taken up singing now—a woman, it sounded like, maybe that woman dancing with her husband—and it echoed joyfully through the great chamber.

Andrew looked around him. It was the train station—only a train station, imposing and vast as train stations are . . . but there was no vision here . . . nothing like he'd seen in Eliada, in the hills, when the Juke properly had its teeth in him.

That woman's voice now . . . was that the voice of someone gone oracular? He didn't think it was: she was singing well, in a way that projected and filled the hall . . . but she was laughing, and he could see her husband laughing too. They'd just had a moment of happiness. A moment of joy.

As for the young men? Now that was something else. Watching them gathered round the musicians, Andrew thought that they might be a little different. They were more like the men in Eliada who'd come to hang Andrew that night, dressing up like they were Klansmen . . .

At least they were when they approached, with that dangerous geniality . . . just wanting to hear a song, making it clear by their presence that if they didn't hear a song—that song . . . that things might not be so genial. That there might just be a beating.

It hadn't played out that way, though. Fact was, they weren't hearing exactly the same tune that they'd sung . . . they couldn't have, because Ozzie Hayward and *Le Noir Qui Danse* didn't know it.

By all rights, that should have started the clock ticking again, on that beating. Andrew knew these types.

But it hadn't. The music, imperfect though it was . . .

They were lapping it up. The pair who were dancing alone, now linked arms at the shoulder and were swaying fast, while the men dancing with one another had drawn closer, lost in the improvisations.

Andrew squinted at them. They were far away—farther than he thought they ought to be. He had wandered . . .

"Excuse me."

Andrew stepped to the side, as the married couple—surely they were married—as they whirled past his shoulder. He stepped aside, and looked back to the band—now at the far end of the hall. He stood at the steps of the ticket hall, the duffel bags abandoned by the dancing men just a few feet off. Seated among them, squatting really, on his naked haunches . . . Doctor Giorgio Molinare grinned at Andrew, and stood, and waved a greeting.

"This isn't my friend," said Andrew. "What is it now?"

He looked up to the high ceiling . . . squinted when he saw nothing but the hanging lamps. He looked back down, and Molinare shrugged. The thing that was playing Molinare shrugged, rather. It was an important distinction and Andrew made sure to keep it top of mind. He'd been wrong . . . should have taken the gas mask. He was sliding into a delusion that could only be from a Juke—but for the subtle differences. He didn't feel that his will had fled in the face of any magnificence.

Molinare was far from magnificent. He was the same gangly old man that Andrew remembered from the last time he'd been in Paris for a meeting. Andrew had never seen him naked, but he was as Andrew imagined . . . sagging pectorals, arms with pale flesh hanging from bone like wet towels on a rack; a small, uncut penis dangling from a whitening nest of pubes.

It was interesting that it was Molinare. The ghost of Molinare.

And a very different ghost than was shown to Molinare's young assistant and lover.

"As soon as I get home," said the ghost, "I am going straight to my warm bed."

He turned then, and went into the ticketing hall. Andrew stepped around the duffel bags and followed.

There was a row of counters, all of them but one dark, and that one was empty for the time being. There was a policeman by the doorway. He paid no heed to naked old Molinare, nor, more incredibly, to Andrew Waggoner as he followed the spectre to the middle of the hall.

"Warm bed," said Molinare's ghost. "Lie me down to sleep." It raised an arm to beckon Andrew to step closer. As though Andrew might want to sleep too, which as he thought about it, he did—and why shouldn't he? He'd been awake through the trip from Paris, and for—how long, here at Stuttgart?—and he was exhausted, in that insects-on-the-skin way that happens during an all-night vigil in post-op at Vire.

He shut his eyes a moment, just an instant, and opened them again, and wasn't entirely surprised to see another spectre standing in Molinare's place.

"Madame Pierrepoint," he said aloud.

His patient, grey and sagging, a sutured scar bisecting her chest, but smiling radiantly . . . naked as Molinare . . . as Molinare's spectre . . . as the Juke . . .

"Madame Pierrepoint is alive in France," said Andrew, and her ghost shrugged, and coughed, as if to say: How was it to know? And Andrew wondered at that: How was *he* to know? Was she alive? He had watched her eyes open, and tested her along with Doctor Thomas, and found her vital signs satisfactory, her responses encouraging . . . but who knew how she was doing now? Things could have taken a turn. He might have lost his patient—this might be her shade . . . coming to talk to him, deliver the sad message like Molinare's shade in Iceland, announcing his passing to young Dominic.

No. Not ghosts.

Andrew might have said it aloud, but he couldn't be certain. He did know, on a level, that there was no point in saying anything aloud. The apparition was not a real thing, it could not interact with him on the level of language—in its particulars, it could not interact at all. Not there.

Likely it was nothing at all in front of him. Andrew craned his neck, to see if he could spy the ceiling of the ticketing hall. There, if anywhere, would be the thing . . . the swirl of dangling maws . . . the great mass of the Juke.

He had no trouble telling there was nothing there. There was no need to squint. Golden sunlight caught the beams, sending sharp, narrow shadows across the expanse. . . . There was nothing there.

Nothing but the light.

The sun had risen. And it lit the *Hauptbahnhof* like a great, brick hearth, the growing crowd of travellers that had now filled the ticketing hall.

Madame Pierrepoint was not, he saw, among them. And neither, he saw a moment later when he left the ticketing hall for the concourse, was *Le Noir Qui Danse*.

The train to Munich arrived on time, at a quarter to eight, and Dominic and Dr. Lewis insisted that they board it immediately—leave the band behind.

"They left us," said Lewis. "There's nothing to be done."

The band had left the train station an hour ago, when a train bound for Berlin arrived and left again. It was not clear to Andrew that they had done so by their own choice, but Dominic insisted that they had.

"Those men . . . persuaded them to join them to Berlin," said Dominic.

"Persuaded them. How?"

"They bought them tickets," said Dominic. "I don't know how they persuaded them."

"Perhaps Berlin is a more welcoming place for their kind," said Lewis.

"My kind too," Andrew said, and Lewis nodded.

"In any event, they've gone now. And Doctor Kurtzweiller will be expecting us."

They had packed up the trunk by the time that Andrew returned, so it was simply a matter of hauling it, along with their regular baggage, to the platform itself and leave it to the porter. Andrew took hold of his own bag, with its still-unused ampoules of adrenaline, and followed them. Should they have stayed, while Andrew determined just what had occurred with the musicians?

The truth of it was, they should have. But none of them this morning was in a state to investigate that. Andrew . . . he had lost himself for hours. Neither Dominic nor Dr. Lewis, even swaddled in masks, could account well for the time after the music began.

As they settled in—seated together this time, Andrew was through masquerading—and the German-made train rumbled its way to the south, all Andrew could think was that they had to do better in Munich.

They had to do much better in Wallgau.

Two

Ruth Harper's return to Chicago in the autumn of 1911, October 3, came as a surprise. She might have wired ahead, and her father's lawyers would certainly have appreciated it. Mr. Lester Keegan, who was in the process of handling what he had until that afternoon assumed to be the Harper estate, told her that in as many words: "It would have been a courtesy to inform us. We might have assisted, Miss Harper."

Keegan was a big man with a florid complexion, his whitened hair slickly oiled directly back on his skull . . . and although Ruth had seen him at the house in Astor from time to time, he had never spoken with her directly, until she arrived at the firm's offices unannounced. Which was fair enough; she hadn't spoken to Keegan either. Why would she? She was a child then, and children kept their peace, particularly among their fathers' employees.

"Thank you for the lesson in manners, Mr. Keegan," she said. "I have suffered some privation, you will understand. Assistance might have been welcome. But I managed."

"Of course." Keegan opened a thick folio on his desk. "Well. You shall not have to suffer that privation any longer, Miss Harper. Your father's will stipulates a generous allowance that will keep you in school and, dare I say, in comfort."

"An allowance?"

"Until," said Keegan, adjusting spectacles on the thick bridge of his nose, "you have reached an age of . . . twenty-five years, at which point the entirety of the estate will become yours. Unless, of course, you marry earlier. . . ."

"And until then, who will be managing my fortune?"

"Trustees," said Keegan. "Including myself . . ." He produced another sheet of paper and read off a list of names that Ruth didn't recognize—

but most of whom had also visited the Astor house at one time or another while she was there, and also, to whom she had not spoken during those visits.

Over the coming months, she would remedy that . . . speaking not only to Keegan—to whom she'd speak extensively—but to each and every one of the trustees managing her late father's affairs, as often as necessary. It was true that there was nothing that she could do, at the age of nineteen, to get the fortune, and her father's business and philanthropic interests, back under her full control.

But if she couldn't control them, she could exercise such influence as to be nearly indistinguishable. And in the end, she gained control years earlier than the will her father wrote had stipulated. She didn't have to marry anyone to do it either.

In the fall of 1931, on the 12th day of October, Ruth Harper—on her own accord, and against the advice of both Annie Waggoner and her own better sense—left the Sanatorium de Vire and set out for Bavaria, accompanied by Albert Zimmermann.

Luc Curzon, the old groundskeeper, had taken them to Vire after dark, in one of the ambulances once again. It wasn't likely necessary . . . the staff at the Sanatorium had been remarkable in their discretion. But Ruth wasn't sure about the townsfolk, whatever Annie thought.

That afternoon, she had taken a telephone call from Annie, in Paris, saying that she was quite certain that there was no one of consequence on their trail . . . that she had met a gentleman that Ruth understood to be Aguillard—and he was alone, and ignorant, and easy to deal with in the end. Ruth wasn't sure that she understood what that meant, but wasn't about to press it on the telephone—safe or not. Annie said she would be leaving to join her husband. "I sent a telegram explaining about the gentleman. And I've got one back from him just an hour later."

The return telegram simply said, GOOD NEWS STOP COME AT ONCE STOP GOOD NEWS HERE TOO.

"So I'm heading off."

And at that point, Ruth became more forceful:

"We will meet you in town," said Ruth, "for a drink . . . at supper tomorrow . . . and all set out together from there. I'll arrange the tickets."

Annie didn't think it was a good idea—not given Ruth's "anxieties" as

Annie put it. But she was in no position to refuse, and their circumspect discussion made it unlikely.

So in Paris they met: not at the flat, but at the Liberty. Ruth made a point of arriving a couple of hours early—she wanted to speak with Bobby before Annie. Bobby wasn't in that day, however, and when she asked after him heard that he wasn't in yesterday, and wouldn't be in today either.

"Mr. Grady is on holiday," commented Zimmermann as they sat down and he stuffed tobacco into his pipe.

"That would be a first," said Ruth.

"Well, it is good to be back in a tavern," said Zimmermann. "It feels like a holiday, after that absurd prison."

"Not a prison," Ruth said. "A hideout, Albert."

Zimmermann struck a match on the edge of the table and set it to the pipe bowl. "Prison," he repeated.

It was just past four, but on that count Ruth ordered them a bottle of decent Beaujolais and a baguette, and they did their best to limit themselves to that bottle before Annie arrived. After storing her bags behind the bar next to Ruth's and Albert's, she sat down with them, and was able to explain at least somewhat more fulsomely.

"It was Aguillard," she said, after Albert guessed it might have been. "He came by the apartment. The morning after Andrew left."

"Just dropped by?" asked Ruth.

"Just dropped by. Like that," said Annie. "He was alone. He'd come from Wallgau." She allowed herself an odd little smile. "He wanted to consult. With another expert on the Jukes . . . which he knew Andrew to be."

"That's odd," said Albert. "Aguillard was a member of another society, who also knew of the Juke. Why would he seek out Dr. Waggoner?"

"I think it went badly in Wallgau," said Annie, "after you left. And I'm not sure just how much he was talking to that society, like you call it, when he got away."

"What happened there?" asked Ruth. "What exactly did he flee?"

"The same thing that you did," Annie said to Albert. "Orlok. He had a theory about Orlok that he wanted to discuss with Andrew."

"Yes?" asked Ruth.

"He believed that Orlok might be part Juke."

Ruth thought about that, and thought about ordering a fresh bottle of wine. "The Jukes are a different species," she said. "That's like a fish being part dog. You can't be serious."

"He was serious," said Annie. "But you're right. Species from such different phyla don't hybridize. So that's probably not what he's talking about. But it's something close. He seemed to think this Orlok fellow did things to people like a Juke might. But he's a man."

"That does fit with your story," said Ruth, and Albert corrected: "My experience."

He tapped his pipe into an ashtray and put it away in his coat pocket.

"How did Aguillard develop this theory?" asked Albert.

"He didn't. Orlok told it to him."

They took a light meal at the Liberty and did order another bottle of wine, Ruth expending some considerable effort, trying to persuade Annie to imbibe. It did no good: Annie was set on moderation.

Her determination worried Ruth. Annie was telling Ruth and Albert a great deal in one sense, but nothing at all in another. What had happened between her and Aguillard? Why was she certain that they were, in fact, safe? Where was Aguillard now?

"We spoke," Annie said. "He was alone," she said. "I'm not sure exactly," she told them.

She spoke at some greater length about Orlok, and his story—which she readily admitted made little sense.

"Aguillard said Orlok told him about himself one night at the farmhouse, him and Bergstrom. He fought his twin in his mother's belly, and by the time he was born had eaten him up. And this gave him great strength he said."

"How mythological."

"Or how biological," said Annie. "That was Aguillard's guess. That Orlok, this man . . . was somehow the intermingling of a juvenile Juke."

"One that didn't devour the foetus."

"But the other way around."

"That's absurd," said Ruth.

"Maybe," said Annie.

"Who can say?" Zimmermann offered to top up Annie's glass, but she slid her fingers over the rim.

"Did you explain all of this in your telegram?" asked Ruth.

"Not all of it."

"Did you explain about Aguillard?"

Annie speared a green bean from her plate and popped it in her mouth.

In this way, she remained impenetrable through dinner, and afterward, as they summoned a taxi to the *Gare de l'Est*, and when the train arrived, settled into their separate cabins. Annie remarked that it was likely quite a bit fancier than the train that Andrew had taken with the musicians, and also direct.

Keeping to the spirit of things, Ruth decided not to tell her how much she'd paid for the tickets.

Her belly hurt, like it sometimes did in the dark hours, but Ruth stayed in her berth through the night and didn't raise a fuss. There would be nothing that Annie or anyone else could do for it because Ruth knew it wasn't real pain. It was a ghost of pain—of the worst pain she'd ever experienced—but it was nothing but a reminder, a memory made tangible in flesh. It had flowered in reality, in the days after Dr. Waggoner had removed the Juke from her . . . the tiny, vicious thing that she understood had in fact devoured whatever innocent seed she and Jason had fertilized in Eliada.

The phantom pain in her belly tended to awaken with the genuine pain of memory.

"You got to go back on your own," Jason had said. "I don't want you no more, all right?"

Those were his words, but were they his feelings? His face was red as they spoke, on the banks of that river, the day before they'd all planned to go to the train station, get back to Chicago—and his eyes were wet. Ruth thought that he did want her, and she wanted him too.

And then he said a cruel thing, a thing that when she thought of it, always brought that belly pain back in full force.

"That's not real what you're feeling. You're tied up with that thing, the Juke from your womb . . . it's telling you what to feel—" and he paused, and stepped back "—because you're a weak female, and don't know better."

Ruth didn't go for help, but she did switch on the electric lamp, and look at the note that Zimmermann had brought her from Jason, and read it again and again: *One day I hope I will see you and make good amends for the things my wounded soul has done.*

She didn't have to read it very many times before the pain faded. She wondered about that—about the draw of him, after all these years. In spite of herself, she wanted to see him—rescue him—take him home, to Chicago finally.

"Weak female that I am," she whispered aloud to her otherwise empty cabin, as the train bore down on the Bavarian border through the black night, and with those thoughts in mind, eventually she slept.

But not long. Ruth woke early in the morning, just as the sky was lightening outside her window, by a quick knock at her door. Ruth wondered if that might have been a customs official. But it was Albert.

"Guten morgen," he said, and continued in German: *"May I enter?"*

Ruth was momentarily taken aback. They had done this once before, on another train from Athens—early in the morning, with a knock at a cabin door, followed by a wordless embrace. It had been an instant. So far as Ruth understood, one that they both regretted. Certainly one they had never repeated, despite ample opportunity.

Albert must have read her expression.

"Not that," he said. *"I wish to speak."*

Ruth stepped aside and Albert stepped in. He slid the door shut behind him and faced Ruth.

"It is concerning Frau Waggoner," he said.

"Oh?"

"She knocked on my door. Very late. And no," he added, *"not for that."*

"Then what?"

"It was very odd." Albert sat down on the bench under Ruth's bunk. *"Frau Waggoner was . . . a little agitated. She asked me if I had killed."*

Ruth raised her eyebrows. *"What did you tell her?"*

Albert gave a wry little smile. *"Never, to my direct knowledge."*

"An excellent answer." Ruth sat down in the seat opposite Albert. *"And why did she want to know?"*

"I wonder this too. May I smoke?" Albert was dressed as though the train were due in Munich in just a few minutes—in an overcoat with a light scarf and wool trousers. From his coat, he pulled his pipe.

"No," said Ruth. *"Frau Waggoner will wonder why this cabin smells of your tobacco if you do."*

"And we don't want that," agreed Albert. *"She did tell me why she wanted to know. I asked her this myself and she answered. But I am not sure I believe her.*

She said that she had been thinking about her time—all of your time—in that town of Eliada. She said that she believed that the disease . . . that killed everyone . . . not the Juke's disease . . . that it might have been a blessing. And that by allowing it to spread through the town, killing them all to a child . . . that this might have been a service. A good killing. What evil might they have wrought, had they been permitted to survive?" Albert looked at the pipe in his hand with a certain regret, and slipped it back into his pocket. *"She wondered if I had felt that way about the enemy that I killed in the War."*

"And you don't believe her?"

"Why would she come in the night, to ask this of me, my opinion concerning a twenty-year-old question that she must have given thought to long ago? Why would she not have asked me this during those times at Vire, when she brought in a plate of dinner and waited quietly until I was finished?"

"She is going to join Andrew, in a hunt for Jason Thistledown and the Juke. Or Orlok, the hybrid. And she is thinking that something similar must happen when she finds them? Perhaps she is steeling her will for that?"

Albert shook his head. *"Perhaps,"* he said, *"she has blood on her hands already."*

Ruth nodded.

"Perhaps," she said.

The train pulled into the *München Hauptbahnhof* at half past nine in the morning. There was a misting rain coming down, and—after changing a few francs for an absurd amount of Deutsche Marks—Ruth purchased umbrellas from a vendor near the front steps, and handed them around while they hunted for a taxi. Annie had an address on *Rottmannstraße* for Kurtzweiller, but none of them, not even Albert Zimmermann, the only one of them who had spent time in Munich before, had any clue as to how far it was from the station.

Albert stepped close to Ruth, and whispered in German: *"Frau Waggoner does not seem to have slept."*

Annie joined them before Albert could say anything more.

"I think there is a stand for taxis there," she said, and pointed across the crowded cobblestone plaza to a line of long black autos curbside.

What Albert said was true—she did not look rested. She had applied makeup and combed her hair, but that couldn't hide the jittery look in her eyes, or the entirety of the dark rings beneath them.

They made their way across the plaza, through the crowd of mostly men. Their attention was mainly drawn to a small podium at the centre of the plaza, where a small wooden platform had been erected, and another group of men were gathered. Some of them, Ruth noticed, wore the red armbands and swastikas of Nazis. It looked as though they were preparing for a rally, but the preparations were early. Certainly, no one among them looked as though they were prepared to give a speech. As they passed a message post, she saw that handbills had been posted. Only one of them seemed like it was from Nazis: *National-Solzialismus* it read. *Der Organisierte Wille Der Nation*. With three stern-looking fellows in profile—much fitter looking than the stooges setting up their podium—occluding a swastika.

The organized will of the nation. Ruth shivered. Just what her father had fancied he was creating, in Eliada.

Maybe Annie was right. Maybe killing them would be a service.

They were soon near enough the taxi that the drivers spotted them, and the one from the second car sprang from the vehicle and shouted an offer to help them with their bags. The driver from the front of the line shouted at the second to stop, and summoned them to his car. Over the objections of the other driver, it was this one that Ruth led them to. The driver was a dark-haired man of middle age with a thick handlebar moustache and curling hair barely controlled under a navy blue cap. His white shirt collar needed cleaning, and his breath smelled from the row of yellowed and decaying teeth he revealed in a wide smile.

They loaded their luggage into the boot and piled into the car. Annie read off the address for Kurtzweiller's flat. The driver asked for it again, then asked if she was certain.

"*Ja*," said Albert, "*We are certain. How much?*"

"*Mein Herr, I cannot take you right there*," said the driver. "*I would not recommend that you go there at all in fact. Not with the ladies.*"

"*Why is that?*"

"*There was a battle on Rottmannstraße. Brownshirts and Kommunistische gangs. Last night. You are not from Munich, Mein Herr?*"

"*No.*"

"*Munich is the home of the Nazi Party and Herr Hitler. We do not treat Kommunistische interlopers kindly. It has become a matter for the Polizei. But they and the brownshirts . . . not so far apart.*"

Ruth started to translate for Annie, but she shushed her with a touch. "My German's not good, but I get the gist," she whispered.

Then to the driver: "*Can you take us close by?*"

Albert repeated the question, and the driver shrugged, and named a price.

The driver left them outside the *Münchener Polytechnische Schule*—the Munich Polytechnical School—and gave walking directions to the address on *Rottmannstraße.* The rain was coming down harder, and perhaps they should have sought shelter there, but none of them suggested it or even seemed to consider it. Bags in hand, they set out along the broad high street of *Gabesbergerstraße.* It was lined with shops and offices, and some of them were open—but there weren't many about on the street outside them this morning. At first, Ruth thought they might explain that with the rain, which was cold and steady and utterly discouraging.

As they drew nearer *Rottmannstraße*, it became clearer that there was something other at work, and Ruth understood the taxi driver's reticence. The neighbourhood seemed to be in a state of emergency. The street itself was barricaded, with men who were obviously *Polizei* stationed beside wagons, and alongside them, other men who were obviously not *Polizei* . . . who by their brown shirts and caps like the ones Ruth had seen on the poster . . . were Nazi brownshirts. Several of them carried rifles.

Beyond, Ruth could see more police wagons, and also what looked like a fire wagon, affixed with a massive water pump, and hauled by a team of powerful draught horses. As they approached, two of the *Polizei* and three brownshirts were talking with a pair of young men just this side of the checkpoint. It did not seem, to Ruth, to be particularly cordial. Albert suggested that they pause and perhaps reconsider.

"This is unusual," he said. "Why would they barricade the whole street?"

"True. A battle between Nazis and Communists," said Ruth, "is not that unusual, I understand. I wonder what's different?"

She stepped forward, and motioned for Albert and Annie to follow. Albert shook his head no, but Annie nodded and continued forward.

They'd made it to within a half-dozen yards of the checkpoint when one of the brownshirts noticed their approach, and cried out for them to halt.

"*We will wait until you are finished, Mein Herr!*" said Ruth, and stopped, adjusting her umbrella.

Ruth noticed that as they approached, the conversation between the young men and the *Polizei* had stopped. They all looked now at the three newcomers. The brownshirt who'd shouted was a young man himself, with an unfortunate string of acne crossing his cheek between his left eye and jaw. He had a rifle, but it was slung over his shoulder. He looked to the others, who shrugged, then stepped forward.

"Guten Morgen, gnädige Frau," he said.

"Good morning," said Ruth. *"What is the trouble?"*

"Not a concern for you," he said. *"The district is closed. Be on your way, please."*

"Forgive me. We have just arrived in Munich, on a train overnight, yes? We are very tired. The family we are visiting . . ." Ruth motioned beyond the barricade.

One of the *Polizei* came over. He was older, with a well-trimmed beard. He looked on Ruth kindly.

"Where are you staying, gnädige Frau?"

"On Rottmannstraße."

The *Polizei* looked over at the young men at the checkpoint. The kindness drained from his face.

"I am sorry to tell you, gnädige Frau. There is nothing there for you."

"Nothing?"

Behind him, one of the young men smirked—and seeing this, a brownshirt drove the butt of his rifle stock into his belly. The man doubled over, and his mate raised his hands in defence.

"I think," said Ruth, *"that I need to speak to someone in authority."*

Three

"Andrew! You've arrived!"

"All of us have," said Andrew, and stepped back so that Kurtzweiller could see into the hallway. "Almost all."

It was late in the morning of October 12th.

"Well yes," said Kurtzweiller. "I had expected you two." He indicated Dr. Lewis and Dominic, who stood on the landing. "But Dr. Waggoner—I thought you would be at the cabaret tomorrow evening. We were to meet there. . . ."

"I thought so too," said Andrew. "But . . ."

"We should come inside," said Dr. Lewis. "There's much to discuss."

Kurtzweiller stepped aside and bade them enter. Dominic gamely took hold of the trunk and hauled it into the long hallway connecting the rooms that Kurtzweiller had found for the *Société de la biologie transcendantale.*

"We had an incident in Stuttgart," said Andrew.

"An incident?"

"A Juke incident," he said. "Hallucinations. At the train station. We all disassociated. Lost time. The musicians—"

"They are gone," said Dominic.

"They left us there," said Lewis. "They went to Berlin with a group of men. They went willingly, might I add."

"Maybe willingly," said Andrew. "But the Juke—"

Kurtzweiller held up his hands to interrupt. "Let's talk about this in time, when we can be more discreet," he said. "You are not the only ones with things to report. Let us retire to the sitting room. There is a gentleman here, who I think may help clear matters up."

Kurtzweiller led them along the hall and through a doorway, and into a small and sparsely furnished sitting room. There was indeed a visitor. A slender fellow, small with hair that was cut very close to his skull . . . dark, with tiny flecks of white. He wore a wool suit, and sat on a wing-backed chair with one leg crossed over the other. He plucked at the fabric of his wool trousers, and didn't rise when the men entered the room—but he did smile broadly.

"Andrew Waggoner, isn't it?" he exclaimed, in a high, delighted voice.

"Yes," said Andrew. "I don't believe we've—"

"—met? No, no, we have not. But I have heard all about you. Not you other gentlemen . . ." He blinked, and pointed a narrow finger at Andrew ". . . but you, Doctor Waggoner. A great deal about you."

Kurtzweiller stepped around into the middle of the little room. He beamed, first at Andrew and the others, and then at his visitor.

"Allow me to introduce to you gentlemen," he said, "Markus Gottlieb."

No one said anything for a moment. Lewis looked at Kurtzweiller with an unreadable expression that might have been a glare, or just simple astonishment. Dominic retreated a step back into the hallway—as though he were preparing to bolt back out the door, and calculating how easy it would be to get round the trunk in the hall. Andrew shut his eyes for a moment . . . for an instant, fearful that the dreams of the Juke were intruding again, and this entire place were simply another hallucination. It was finally Gottlieb who broke the silence.

"Excuse me, Doctor Kurtzweiller. I know Doctor Waggoner. I would be only guessing which of these two is Dominic Villart, and which Doctor William Lewis."

Andrew shook his head as though to shake cobwebs off, and Lewis spared Kurtzweiller having to speak, and introduced himself.

"And Herr Villart," said Gottlieb, motioning to the doorway and smiling. He leaned forward to shake hands—still sitting, legs still crossed. Lewis took his hand and then Andrew did. Finally, Dominic re-entered the room and shook hands too.

"It is good to see you all." He sat back and pressed his hands together in front of him—a gesture that might have seemed like prayer but in context seemed more one of delight. "And all so shocked!"

Kurtzweiller cleared his throat. "As I was, yesterday when you arrived, Herr Gottlieb." He turned to Andrew. "I wish I could say that I had discovered Markus through my investigations. I am afraid that instead, my investigations caused him to find me."

"It is so," said Gottlieb. "Doctor Kurtzweiller made some inquiries at *Braunes Haus*. Excuse me. You three are foreign. That is the Brown House. The Nazi headquarters, the new one on *Breinner Straße*. Before that, he called on Heinrich Visler in Bogenhausen. In both cases, he asked about Wallgau, and the Visler farm and estate. . . ."

"I believe I was discreet."

"Discreet enough," said Gottlieb. "For the old days. Certainly, yes. But to be truthful, you could not be discreet enough to slip past Orlok. Not in Munich. And so . . . so we came to find you, Doctor Kurtzweiller."

Andrew crossed his arms. "We?"

Gottlieb shrugged.

"We are many," he said. "Now forgive me—I could not help but overhear as you entered. You had an, I believe you called it . . . an incident, in Stuttgart?"

"We did," said Lewis. "What do you know about it?"

"Not much," said Gottlieb. "Just what you blurted out at the threshold. But it does excite my curiosity. You were travelling with *Neger*, more *Neger*, yes? And they abandoned you?"

"Yes," said Andrew. "We'll talk about that in a minute. First: how did you know my name? All of our names?"

"I learned all of your names from Doctor Kurtzweiller. I learned yours from your old friend. Jason Thistledown."

"Where is he?"

"It is good to hear you ask after him. He is not far."

"And he's safe?"

"Oh yes." Gottlieb nodded. "He is safe. Soon we will all go to see him."

"Why can't he come here?"

"He's not coming here," said Gottlieb. His voice lowered. "Not here. Because here, Doctor Waggoner, is not as safe as that." He smiled. "As you should know, having wisely decided to travel hidden among a *Neger* jazz band rather than take a chance alone, as you are. The countryside is bad these for good *Volk*, is it not? Now, you tell me. How was your journey—and how did you come to misplace, what are they called? *Le Noir Qui Danse?*"

Andrew didn't tell Gottlieb very much more about the Stuttgart "incident" than he'd told to Kurtzweiller in the hall. But Gottlieb didn't seem to be that curious about the details. Or rather, about nearly all of the details.

He didn't care what Andrew saw when he wandered through the empty spaces of the station. He didn't care that there were other people in the station, or how many, and his eyes wandered around the room when Andrew ventured there.

What he was interested in, was the music—specifically the song that the German boys wanted to hear so badly. What was the title? Andrew didn't know; Dominic thought it was something about the seaside. Lewis said that it was a German song. None of them could hum it, even though Gottlieb asked them each to try.

"Music is very important," said Gottlieb. "It is what binds we *Volk* together. When we sing, when we dance . . . when we hear the sweet voice of a girl . . ." he shook his head with a wistful smile ". . . or a young boy . . . singing a sweet song . . . we join together. This is what happened in Stuttgart, Doctor Waggoner. A particular song drew good *Volk* together. You included among them."

"I can't hum the song," said Andrew, although as he thought of it, he understood that to be a lie. He could hum the song. It was right there in his head . . . he remembered how the band played it, even some of the lyric—about a small beach basket. But if he did hum it . . .

It would be like opening a door.

"Well that is unfortunate," said Gottlieb. "Perhaps we will hear it again, in our travels, and it will come back to you."

"Maybe," said Andrew. "Now you tell me, Herr Gottlieb, what is happening here?"

"In Munich?" He laughed. "Nothing good. So many people out of work. The Deutsche Mark is weak. And the Nazis have a grand new home! Kurtzweiller went to see it." He spared Kurtzweiller a wry look. Andrew stepped in.

"What's happening in Wallgau then? With Jason, and with this man Orlok."

Gottlieb looked down at his hands, which he had folded over his knee. "Well. Something hopeful, I think. Yes. Very hopeful. It is good that you are here. A happy coincidence. We had hoped to go and fetch you in France. Did you know that?"

Andrew shared a glance with the men of the *Société*. "I didn't. Why would you do that?"

"You are all so very clever. The *Société de la biologie transcendantale*. Transcendental biology." Gottlieb unfolded his hands and set them on the armrest, and uncrossed his legs, and for a moment it looked as though he were preparing to rise. "Things are moving a bit more swiftly than we thought. As I said—we hadn't expected you to be here quite so early—not all of you."

Gottlieb looked at Andrew as he leaned forward onto the balls of his feet, and pushed himself up.

"You will excuse me, Doctors Kurtzweiller, Lewis . . . and Waggoner. I must go and make some arrangements. Please do not attempt to leave. I will return, hopefully shortly, with transportation."

"Transportation to where?"

"Why to Wallgau, of course, Doctor Lewis. Where else would you be going, knowing what you know?"

They did try to leave. Dominic tried the front door, down two flights of stairs and coming out alongside a tailor shop. It was no good; there were a pair of young men standing guard there, and before they ushered him back inside, he thought he caught sight of three more, watching the door from a café across the road. The apartment also had a fire escape, coming out from a wide window in the kitchen. But looking down into the alley, Andrew saw four more men, loitering in full view of the window and the ladder. As he stepped out onto the ironwork walkway, they caught his eyes and motioned no, back inside. Andrew waved back and retreated.

"What have you done?" he demanded of Kurtzweiller when they shut up the window.

"I'm sorry," said Kurtzweiller. "Perhaps we ought to have simply gone to Wallgau—to the farm. Not tried to sneak around Munich. I'm not good at sneaking about, I am afraid."

"On the other hand," said Lewis, "this does seem to get us to Wallgau, and the farm, and the valley."

"It does get us there," said Dominic. "Not of our own volition though." He looked at Andrew. "This is the calamity," he said, "that Molinare speaks of."

"No," said Andrew. "It's *a* calamity, but no one speaks of it. Leave that out of your thoughts, Dominic. Come on—let's put some coffee on." He turned to Kurtzweiller. "You do have coffee here?"

"Of course," said Kurtzweiller, and opened a cupboard to find a tin of coffee. He filled a pan with water and set it by the stove.

"We can't go anywhere," said Andrew. "So we'll sit tight. We do need to get caught up."

"Of course," said Kurtzweiller.

"Let's go through it then. You went to see the family that owns the farm. . . ."

"Heinrich Visler," said Kurtzweiller. "That's right. I visited him at his house. A gracious man. Very much a supporter of the Nazi Party. Friend of Adolph Hitler, or so he told me."

"How did you manage to see him? What did you say?"

"I said I was a friend of Muckermann."

"The eugenicist fellow who wouldn't see you in Berlin?" asked Lewis.

"The same." Kurtzweiller lit the gas burner and set the pan atop it. "Visler likes Hitler, as I said. Quite a lot. Enough to give Hitler and the Nazis the run of his farm. 'It is for the youth,' he explained. 'The youth are our future. But Herr Muckermann will know more about that than I. For he has visited the place since work began. It is best that I stay here.' He knew about the Seckendorff property. But he said there was no point in talking to him." Kurtzweiller tapped his temple. "Addled, for many years now. And it was long ago that the place was deeded to the spa, which in any case Visler understood was also under the control of the Nazi Party for the purpose of training the *Hitler-Jugend*."

"So far, nothing but what we already know," said Lewis.

"Quite so. But it was a pleasant conversation. And at the end of it, he called ahead and also wrote me a note on the back of a calling card—and so it was that I was able to visit the Nazis, as a guest at the Brown House."

Kurtzweiller peered out the window, through the bars of the fire escape railing and down into the alley. He made a tsk sound with his teeth.

"So. Yesterday," he said, "I visited Kurt Gruber in his offices."

"The belly of the beast," said Andrew.

"Indeed. It is quite a belly. It used to be a mansion. Owned by a British woman, if you can believe that. The Nazi Party bought it from her and renovated it. It is their offices and a shrine to their Führer too. Gruber showed me a room where they keep the flag they bore in 1923 at the beer hall. It stands on a pedestal, in a room by itself. They have not washed out the blood . . . which I suppose is the point of that flag. They had enough other ones hanging throughout that building."

"He gave you a tour?" asked Andrew.

"Yes." Kurtzweiller poured a measure of coffee into the water, as it was beginning to boil. "He had reason to be proud I suppose. Gruber was there with Hitler and the rest at the *Bürgerbräukeller*, the night they tried to take the government. He was very young then, barely twenty. I don't think he fought in the War. So this was the moment that made him." Kurtzweiller smiled. "The hall for the flag was also a more impressive room than the offices that they afforded him. He was in a small annex on the first floor, far from Hitler's office and near to Ernst Röhm's."

"The head of the S.A.," said Lewis.

"Yes. His superior now. We sat down there, with coffee that was far weaker than what I am making you now. And we talked about Wallgau." Kurtzweiller raised a hand. "I was not being indiscreet, Andrew. He believed that I was there on behalf of Herr Muckermann. I did nothing to dissuade him. From the moment that we met, I was surprised to notice that he seemed more than a little afraid when we spoke, and I wondered if he might not be in some trouble—either with his superiors, or with Muckermann and some others. Indeed, before I could ask questions as to the state of the town, he raised the matter, with a tone of apology."

"Apology?" Dominic had gathered mugs from a cupboard and set them on the kitchen table.

"He understood himself and the *Hitler-Jugend* to have let Muckermann down. The plan for the estate . . . and for the experiment . . . was twofold, you see. Muckermann was, for the most part, interested in finding the best among the young men and women of Germany. The strongest . . . the *Übermenschen*. But Gruber admitted that he had been persuaded to expand the experiment—in part because of his own promises and ambitions. 'I was not convinced, you see, that we were finding the best of the German youth. Certainly not enough of them.' That was what he told me. And that, he said, was why he permitted the introduction of . . . of the experiment. The *Hitler-Jugend* needed to grow. He had been under instruction to see to it, in fact, that its numbers doubled." Kurtzweiller turned down the burner to a faint blue ring. "Absurd. The fool wanted to stage a recruitment drive like no other. And so . . ."

"The Juke?" said Lewis, and Kurtzweiller nodded.

"The Juke. Although Gruber did not name it, that's what it was. Small wonder that Herr Zimmermann never met with Muckermann when he was in Wallgau. He had stopped attending the farm shortly after the work there began. And he had written of his worries in several letters to Ernst Röhm. He was convinced that it was ungodly. Not surprising. He is, after all, a Jesuit. I think that is why Gruber was so pleased to talk with me—he imagined that I might convince Muckermann of his remorse, if not his competence."

"By the Grace of God," said Dominic. Kurtzweiller ignored him.

"I also asked him about the missing children, particularly the ones that I'd learned of in Berlin. He showed me carbon-copied reports, in a file folder, of the investigations, of which there were twelve. 'As you can see, *Mein Herr*, we are cooperating fully,' he said to me. Those files were more than I had been able to obtain on my own visit to the *Bayerische Polizei*, so I read them through. And I saw . . . that it was not much more that I could learn from them than I knew already. They were dated in the summer months, most of them in July. Seven boys, five girls. Five of them were blue-eyed, two green-eyed, three hazel and two brown. Some blonde hair, some light brown hair. No red. No brunette. Ages between fourteen and twenty. Photographs were on file for six of them, but not in this file. All of them, missing in the vicinity of Wallgau, Bavaria.

"All of them, members of Gruber's *Hitler-Jugend*.

"And then, I did something that you might call indiscreet. I asked him about Orlok. In the broadest of terms. 'What news of Orlok?' I asked. I imagined that this would draw him deeper, and he would reveal more of the true goings-on in Wallgau. It might have also given me away. But neither thing happened. Gruber looked puzzled, and stared out his window for a moment and became quiet. When I asked him again, he shook his head, and apologized once more for inattention. He said that Orlok was a name that he had not heard for some time. Then he laughed, and asked if I was talking about *Nosferatu*."

"He didn't know who Orlok was?"

"No, Andrew, he did not. He knew that the experiment in Wallgau had gone badly. He knew that steps needed to be taken, and he understood that they were out of his hands. 'Men closer to the Führer than I are managing Wallgau now,' he told me. Still. He apologized for any damages that might have happened to Herr Visler's property, or might yet. And he apologized again through me, to Herr Muckermann.

"But of Orlok? He knew nothing. I left his office not convinced of that: that Orlok had remained secret to the farm, and Wallgau. But I was also convinced he was not lying to me. His reaction . . . it was consistent, with some of the things that Herr Zimmermann described to us, among the men who stood guard at the farm. Herr Gruber should have known about Orlok. He should have, given everything else, been worried that he didn't. But I believe something was preventing him from knowing fully."

"Or he simply didn't know," said Dominic.

Kurtzweiller found a ladle hanging by the stove, and used it to skim the top of the coffee. Then he dipped it in and filled each mug.

"I am a terrible detective," he said as he poured, and raised an eyebrow at Lewis. "I am a better transcendental biologist."

Andrew took a mug and sipped at it. It was very hot and ferociously strong. "When did Markus Gottlieb catch up with you? And how?"

"He rang the doorbell," said Kurtzweiller. "Yesterday evening. He introduced himself, and invited himself in."

"And how?"

"I think I was followed. Probably by men—by boys—like the ones in the alley. They are all over, these . . . youth . . . if you look."

"But they are easy to overlook," said Andrew. He thought about the pictures of the young people that Zimmermann had taken, without apparently knowing he had done so. About the photograph of Zimmermann, sleeping in the barracks.

"I wonder if we might have met more of the children of Wallgau," said Lewis, "at Stuttgart."

Kurtzweiller snorted. "The children of Wallgau! That is a good name for them."

"Why are we going to Wallgau?"

Kurtzweiller looked to Dominic. "Such a scowl!" he said. "We are going as guests, Herr Villart."

"Prisoners you mean."

"We were going to have to travel there one way or another," said Kurtzweiller. "It—" They all looked to the front hall as the doorbell rang, and Kurtzweiller nodded. "Ah. Perhaps our transportation has arrived."

It had not.

They were met in the stairwell by three people—two young men and a girl. The men wore coveralls. Their hair was too long, and one of them had a fuzzy moustache such as a boy might grow. The girl wore a long skirt and a wool high-necked sweater. She had blonde hair that was tied in a bun, and her face was sunburnt. She spoke in English.

"We have seen to the visitor," she said. "No need to worry."

"Who was it?" asked Andrew.

"It was a telegram. Not to worry. We have already sent a reply."

"May we see it?"

The girl considered. She withdrew a piece of paper from a pocket in her skirt, waved it in the air and returned it to her pocket. Then she curtsied and turned to retreat down the stairs.

"Soon," she called over her shoulder. Her companions didn't move, though, until Kurtzweiller shut the door.

"Prisoners," said Dominic, and looked to his right a moment, and then, stepping through the door into the sitting room, said to no one apparently: "That's right, my love. You were right all along."

Andrew looked to the others, and motioned for them to wait in the hall, and he followed Dominic into the sitting room.

"Who are you talking to?" Andrew asked, and Dominic pointed to the wing-backed chair, where Molinare sat, naked. His eyes were wide and round as a fish's. His penis was rigid against his belly. He grinned and gave a nod at Andrew, and beckoned him over with one thin arm.

"Calamity," he said, and as he began to stand, Andrew drew a breath—and plunged his left thumb into his coffee cup.

It was not quite scalding—but it was hot enough. Molinare sat back down, and as Andrew watched, he faded into the upholstery, and vanished.

"Stuttgart," he said as he stepped out of the sitting room. "Again."

Andrew laid out four syringes on the kitchen table, and the *Société* lined up and, one after another, rolled up their sleeves for a dose of adrenaline. Andrew administered the last shot to himself.

Did it work? Did it drive away the hallucinations that that a Juke could bring about? Andrew and the *Société* had theorized that it might, in that intense and sharp pain had worked for Jason and Andrew in Eliada . . . but there had scarcely been opportunities to test it.

And as for this test—Andrew couldn't say, not at first. As he felt it work through his system, attenuate his nerves—with an almost electric shock—he leaned against the windowsill and looked outside into the bright alleyway—and watched as a half-dozen young men, no longer just three, stood around a seventh man, who lay bleeding on the ground.

Andrew's heart raced and he gasped, as he watched two of the men lift that seventh, and haul him to a doorway in the opposite side. One of them looked up and perhaps saw Andrew at the window, but may not have.

The entire incident might have been a vision—a lie.

Andrew summoned Lewis to the window and pointed, and asked him if he could see that too. But by that time the man—the body?—was obscured, as the men had gathered around the doorway. Lewis just laughed—high, mirthlessly—and stumbled away, into the hallway. Kurtzweiller, meanwhile, was occupied; Dominic had taken ill, and was vomiting into the sink, and Kurtzweiller held his shoulders.

"It's all right," said Kurtzweiller, "it's all right."

Andrew looked out the window again, and saw that now four other men had entered the alleyway. They were in uniform—not police, but with caps, brown shirts and swastika armbands. They carried batons.

They used them, rushing at the six who stood there, hammering down blows on upraised arms, ribcages . . . a skull.

Andrew could not look away. Although his heart still hammered, his breath felt short in him, he was struck then by the terrible quiet of the brawl below. The Nazis—the brownshirts, surely that's what they were—came upon the men in the alleyway matter-of-factly, as though they were at work on a farm. And the men under attack did not cry out either, although first one and then a second fell.

One of the men did manage to get around the brownshirts, and kicked him in the side of the knee, or more properly stomped. *It's broken*, thought Andrew as the brownshirt collapsed sideways. And finally someone screamed.

One of his comrades saw what had happened and swung his baton, but it was an awkward swing and it threw him off balance. He staggered away from the fight, and into the middle of the alley. He held the baton in front of him in two hands, and then stepped forward, swinging again, this time connecting with the man, once in the forearm, again on the shoulder. No screams this time.

Andrew stood away from the window. His hand was cradling his right elbow—which twenty years ago, a man in a sheet had smashed with a tree branch . . . while Andrew Waggoner fell to his knees and watched others string rope, for him, and for a Juke. He hadn't screamed either, or he didn't remember it. He'd just taken it, and next to him, the thing called Mister Juke dangled from another rope, the same branch. . . .

Andrew leaned over and opened the window. He had a crazed notion, for just an instant, that he might throw the pan of coffee over the fire escape, and he went so far as to reach for the handle, and then recoil at the burn. It wouldn't help. And as he turned back, he saw that he might not need to.

The girl from the hallway ran into view. Her hair had spun out from the bun at the back, and it flew behind her, along with her skirt. She had a long knife, and matter-of-factly, she plunged it once, and twice, and a third time, into the back of the brownshirt. When another turned to face her, she slashed his face, and he cried out again, clutching it. In the meantime, the remaining men in the alley pressed in on the remaining brownshirt. One grabbed his arm and pulled the baton from it, while the other took him by the throat. The girl turned on him and plunged the knife into his chest.

Andrew fell back against the kitchen table—hard enough that the legs made a precarious groaning sound against the floor. Dominic was sitting on the floor, propped against the doorjamb. Kurtzweiller had left the room.

"He is gone," said Dominic. He was bathed in sweat, and stared at his hands, which trembled. "He is gone."

Andrew stood away from the table. He was shaking too, and his throat felt raw, as though he'd been shouting.

"He'll be back," said Andrew, and stumbled to Dominic's side, but Dominic shook his head.

"No," said Dominic. "He is dead."

Andrew frowned, and then nodded. The test was a success; adrenaline worked, as well as any mountain-made potion in north Idaho. As well as pain and nearly as fast, and looking at Dominic, Andrew thought it might work nearly as deep.

Because it wasn't Kurtzweiller that Dominic was missing, that he mourned. It came upon Andrew in a flash of insight.

"Ah," said Andrew. "That's true my friend. Molinare is dead."

He put his arm around Dominic, and held him tight.

Manfred Kurtzweiller, alive and well, stepped over Dominic's legs into the room a moment later. With him was Gottlieb, who wore a new overcoat, and carried a black leather folio under his arm.

"Doctor Waggoner," he said, "Herr Villart. We must find Doctor Lewis. A car waits outside, and under the circumstances, I think it best we leave Munich now.

"Time, I fear, is short. And I think you will be interested in what awaits us at Wallgau."

Four

The fighting had gone on for a day. There was a fire, in a dress shop that had spread to the floors above it and two neighbouring buildings on *Rottmannstraße*. Some looting too. And there were deaths. Fourteen members of the Nazi Party's S.A. Seven Communists. One member of the *Polizei*. And fifty-three injured badly enough to require a physician. The *Polizei* were still rounding up suspects, which meant that they were at once very busy and also interested in speaking with the foreigners who wanted details about their missing friends on *Rottmannstraße*. Ruth Harper was able to speak with a senior officer, but not the most senior: *Oberstabsfeldwebel* Walter Fischer, originally from Nuremberg, readily agreed to sit with her and tell her what he could. The address that Kurtzweiller had supplied was in one of the fire-damaged buildings, and not accessible. The building had been evacuated along with the others. But visiting the apartment would not be necessary. He had at his desk updated lists of the dead, injured and detained.

"*Nein*," he said. "*None of them were Neger. And among those identified: no Waggoner, no Kurtzweiller, no Villart . . . no Lewis. This is a very interesting mixture of friends, for a lady such as yourself.*"

"*How is that?*"

"*An African. A German. An Italian and an Englishman.*"

"*An American*," said Ruth. "*Two Americans in fact. Both Waggoner and Lewis—*"

"*Right, of course*," said Fischer. "*Well the happy news is they are not among the dead or the injured. Not those we have identified. And your . . . American friend Waggoner will not be among them. That is very lucky—I was not stationed here at the time, but this is the worst incident of its kind since 1923.*"

"*The Hitlerputsch*," said Ruth.

"*No putsch this time*," said Fischer. "*And the news appears good for you and your friends, gnädige Frau. With that said . . . we do have some photographs.*

There were four who perished in the battle that we cannot name."

"Do you think . . . ?" said Ruth, in English, and Fischer shrugged.

"It is unlikely. They do not seem like a match from what you have told me. And the photographs are ugly," he said. "If you would prefer—"

"No," said Ruth. "I will look."

It was mid-afternoon when Ruth left the *Polizeipräsidium München* headquarters and rejoined Annie, where she waited at a café. While Ruth was conferring with the police, Albert had gone off to check into the cabaret where *Le Noir Qui Danse* was to perform tonight. And Annie . . . well, she made it clear that she preferred not to deal with the Bavarian police if it could at all be avoided. When Ruth stepped inside, Annie was sitting in a corner booth, her hands warming around a tea pot, a plate of biscuits half-eaten beside it.

"Andrew wasn't there," said Ruth as she sat down. "Or if he was, he wasn't hurt, and wasn't arrested either. The same goes for the others."

"Thank God." Annie lifted the teacup and sipped from it, set it down and shook her head. "They are such idiots. My husband and his friends."

"They're not idiots."

Annie smiled. "No. They're suckers." She looked at Ruth. "I'm sorry. That's a private joke between Andrew and me."

Ruth ordered tea for herself, and tried to order more biscuits but Annie said she could have the rest of hers. She had nearly finished both when Albert arrived, with news of the Cabaret Imperial.

"They didn't show up," he said as he sat down and shrugged off his overcoat.

"What?"

"The show is cancelled," said Albert. "I managed to speak with the doorman. The management is quite angry about it. They did not send word—they simply didn't arrive. He told me that it is likely the last time that the cabaret will let *Neger* musicians play there. What did you learn from the *Polizei*?"

Ruth told him.

"They are not here. *Le Noir Qui Danse* is not here either. Do you think they may not have arrived at all?"

Annie reminded him about the return telegram.

"And Kurtzweiller was certainly here," said Ruth.

"Did you tell the *Polizei* about Wallgau?" asked Albert. "About Orlok and Jason and the rest?"

"Of course not."

"Good," said Albert. "Because I think we can all agree, that is where we need to go next."

There was an electric train from Munich to the town of Kochel, which was most of the way to Wallgau, and it got them to the little lake town by lunch. It was still fourteen miles to Wallgau from there, and Ruth despaired of being able to hire a car given the recent goings-on. But it turned out not to be difficult at all. They found a driver at a lunch counter by the lake, and he agreed that once they'd all eaten, he'd take them south.

It was all very easy, and it made a part of Ruth feel deeply uneasy. She had to remind herself as she admired the blazing orange and red hues of the turning leaves, that she had until a few days ago expended considerable energies to keep clear of Wallgau, of the farm and the valley. Would Jason have wanted her now to drive up to it, in a taxi from a quaint resort town, along with Albert Zimmermann who he'd sent to rescue her?

Oh, hang it, she thought as they pulled out of town and onto the lakeside road to Wallgau.

It didn't matter what Jason thought.

She wasn't going to leave him to that place—not any more than Annie Waggoner was going to leave Andrew and his friends to their fate.

"Where will you be staying?"

They pulled in from the north, along a two-lane roadway through golden forest and foothills, that opened finally onto a broad, flat valley, and rows of low houses and stretches of farmland, and so it was they were in Wallgau.

"We don't know," said Ruth. "Can you recommend—"

The driver looked back over his seat. He was an older man, with thick mutton-chop sideburns that had gone entirely white. He seemed amused. "There's an inn," he said. "I will take you there. I will wait if they do not have rooms."

The inn was called the Isar, after the river, and it did have rooms. Several of them had only recently been vacated, and the innkeep was delighted to see them occupied again.

When Ruth came back out to tell the driver he could leave, and they were fine, he had already gone. A young woman, blonde hair, very thin, was standing at the edge of the road.

"Je lui ai dit qu'il pouvait y aller," she said when Ruth looked about.

"I am sorry? You told the driver to leave?" asked Ruth, switching to French.

"Yes. There were rooms, right?"

Ruth agreed that there were. The young woman—she looked no more than twenty in one sense, far older than forty in another—stepped close to Ruth for a moment, as though brushing by. She was wearing a long dress, down nearly to her ankles. Her hair was tied tight behind her head, in a bun. She seemed almost skeletally thin; her eyes were enormous.

"How did you know?" she asked, and the girl smiled wide.

"I was in the taxi with you," she said. *"All the way. Do you not recall, Mademoiselle Harper?"*

The girl reached over and took Ruth's hand. Her fingers were like sticks, like a tree-branch—cold, and rough—and her nails were black with dirt. Ruth's blood went to ice as she realized: the touch was familiar.

She did recall.

"You were in Munich. In the café," Ruth said. "When we checked into the hotel, you followed . . ."

"Nous avons dormi comme des soeurs!"

We slept like sisters.

". . . to my room." Ruth shook the girl's hand off as she recalled: opening the door to the hotel, standing aside for her guest . . . going to the washroom to clean herself up . . . sliding between the sheets on the right side of the bed, feeling breath at her neck, her hair brushed aside, before she slept, as though she were alone, and safe . . . as though she were asleep with a sister . . .

She looked around for Albert, or for Annie, or for anyone on the street in Wallgau. But there was no rescue for her. She and this girl were alone.

They had travelled to the *München Hauptbahnhof* in one taxi—the three of them squeezing in the back, while she sat up front, plucking at her dress and humming—and Ruth had purchased four tickets, not three. The girl had followed them onto the train, wafting restlessly up and down the aisle. She hadn't needed to present her ticket, no one else seemed to notice her either. It was a waste of Deutsche Marks to have bought it.

But Ruth had bought it all the same. Because while Ruth, like everybody else, had failed to notice her they had continued to account for her. Zimmermann had made accommodation for her on the train. The waitress had brought her tea at the café.

Ruth had made room for her in her bed.

"You are from the valley," Ruth said, then repeated it in French, and added, "Orlok." The girl nodded solemnly.

"Jason," she said. "Jason too."

"Jason Thistledown?"

"Oui! Le fils d'un tireur!" She clapped and grinned. *"He is like Orlok! A great fighter! I belong to him! Just like you, Mademoiselle Harper! We are Jason Thistledown's!"*

And that, God help her, was when Ruth knew she could hold back no longer. She made a fist and hit the girl, in the jaw, hard enough to knock her to the ground.

The girl had left a deep scratch across Ruth Harper's forehead and down her right cheek, kicked her in the stomach hard enough to leave her gasping, and nearly bit through the skin of her left forearm before Albert and Annie were able pull her off. Annie finally got hold of her, arms wrapped through her underarms and clasped behind her head, so she struggled and kicked and swore, while Ruth regained her feet, and Albert looked at her curiously.

"I know you," he said.

The girl spat. Albert turned to Ruth, and as he studied her injuries, told her. "I know her. From the mountain pass. And the farmhouse." He ran a finger down Ruth's scratch, not quite touching it, and produced a handkerchief. "Now she has marked us both."

Ruth took the handkerchief and held it to the scratch. She looked around. The melee had attracted some attention—a pair of men on the other side of the street, one of them pushing a wheelbarrow, had paused and were watching with interest. Another woman watched from the first floor window above a butcher shop.

"I am all right," she called, and said it again in German.

The girl struggled briefly and then glared.

"You may as well let me go," she said in English.

"What is your name?" asked Ruth.

She looked to one side and shook her head—as though the question were foolish. "Call me Catherine."

Ruth turned to Albert. "She has been with us since Munich."

Albert blinked, and Annie's grip weakened so that Catherine could shrug out of her grip—and could probably have run off, if that was what she'd wanted to do. Albert and Annie were distracted enough—just as Ruth had been—as the memories that had always been there sorted themselves. Ruth thought she would help them along.

"She spotted us at the checkpoint," said Ruth. "She had been waiting at the polytechnical school, and saw us asking questions. She followed along as I visited the *Polizei*. She sat with us over lunch in the café. When we went to the hotel, she came too."

Annie looked at her. "You went to sleep with Ruth," she said. "I saw you go into the room together."

"We only slept," said Ruth.

"And then . . . you were there at the train station, on the train, with us. . . ." Albert chuckled and looked at Ruth. "It is all suddenly very clear. The Decameron System to the rescue."

Ruth turned to Catherine. "Why did you follow us?"

"Jason sent me," she said.

"Jason?" Annie looked wide-eyed. *"Où est Jason?"* she said. *"Is he here?"*

"No. He is at home. But not far."

"Can we see him?"

Catherine put a bony finger to her lower lip, and looked first to the left and then to the right, as though trying to make up her mind.

"You have all travelled such a long way," she said, and pointed at Albert. *"Particularly this one. Back and forth so many times like a pendulum. I wonder how Jason would feel with him back in the fold?"*

"Let me ask him myself," said Albert.

"No, no," said Catherine. *"Jason told you what to do. You listened to your other master, did you not?"*

"I came back here to see Jason."

"You came back with Mademoiselle Harper," said Catherine, *"for your own reasons."*

Later, the three of them would agree that the roadway had been far more crowded than they'd thought, than they noticed: that all along, they had been surrounded by as many as two-score people . . . young people, *Hitler-Jugend* perhaps.

"There were five of them at least in here, watching while we booked our rooms," said Annie. They were sitting in the dining room of the Isar, with tall mugs of pilsner in front of them, in full sight of the desk. "All men, or male. One of them was pretty young."

"Yes," said Albert. "He could not have been more than fourteen years old. Thin and soft. He was shirtless, and his chest caved in. He was watching from the door."

"Two stood very close to me," said Annie. "They were watching me sign into the guest book. I guess to figure out my name."

"That makes sense," said Ruth. "What were they wearing?"

"Which one?"

"The one looking at your handwriting."

"A brown shirt," said Annie. "Yes. *That* kind of brown shirt. But it didn't have the armband. And it had a hole in it in the arm, and a browner stain. . . . I'm going to guess blood." She nodded. "I seen enough blood in my time. So yes. Blood. Down about where the ribcage ended. It didn't fit him so well. Think he took it from another one he killed?"

Ruth nodded. "There were more of those shirts outside. On boys . . . and men, I mean. They were there when we got out of the taxi. But not all close by."

"Where were they?" asked Albert. "Details please."

Ruth closed her eyes and rhymed off as many as she could name: the three of them who were sitting by a rain barrel next to the dry goods shop, another two who lingered in the doorway of a chemist's . . . two of them, a boy and a girl who might have been siblings, sunbathing nude on the sloping roof of a house at the corner . . . and on. And on.

"Thirty-seven," said Albert finally, who'd been marking off the descriptions down on a sheet of notepaper. "That was how many we saw before they moved on us. Agreed?"

"Agreed."

"Now. Was that the same number as afterward? Were there more?"

Ruth looked into her beer and concentrated. "I don't believe so."

"I'm not sure," said Annie.

"All right Albert," said Ruth, "what do you remember?"

"We were in the middle of a crowd. They were humming a tune. Two of them—no, three—held me so that I would have to struggle to move. Looking around . . . I saw a man holding onto each of you, firmly . . . but not so as to hurt either of you. The girl, Catherine . . . she turned and walked away, surrounded by people . . . such as we had seen before. So in answer to my own question: I don't believe there were many more than we had counted from our own memories. I don't think there were any more. They were all humming. That I remember."

"Good," said Ruth. "But what did she say?"

"I'm sorry?"

"She said something," said Ruth, "just before she turned away. Do you remember what it was?"

Albert frowned. "She said . . . to wait until the morning. That we could see Jason then. That he was . . . dealing with the others?"

Annie shook her head and frowned. "I don't think that's quite right," she said.

"That's what I remember," said Albert, and Ruth nodded.

"I think that's what she said," she said. "And then the fellow let go of me, and the three people let go of you, Albert . . ."

"And I got loose," said Annie.

"They walked off," said Albert, "up the road in the direction of the farm. I've taken that road many times myself."

Ruth nodded. "That makes a good deal more sense than Catherine simply vanishing."

Annie frowned and shook her head.

"Not really sure about that," she said.

It had been a clear day, and it was a clear night too, nearly moonless, and after dinner, the three of them stood at the banks of the Isar, and considered setting out for the farm then—before the youth returned for them. The only light was starlight, so it would be easy to lose themselves, even following a roadway. Albert thought he could manage it, having travelled the route before, and Annie was willing to try it. Ruth worried.

"They could be standing by right now," she said, "guiding us to where they want us to go."

"Ja," said Albert. He took a deep, crackling puff from his pipe. "They could be. But who do you think they might be 'dealing with'?" He looked at Ruth. "Doctor Waggoner perhaps?"

They stood quietly for a moment, thinking about that.

"You've walked this before?" asked Annie, and when Albert said that he had, she nodded. "Let's go," she said, and that was that. The three of them set out under the stars for the house where Jason Thistledown now lived.

PART V

The Delirium Objective

One

Rain was sheeting down as the truck pulled up in front of the farmhouse. It had been raining since they left Munich, and water had leaked through the canvas covering and into the back, where Andrew and the *Société* were seated along benches surrounding their luggage—notably, Lewis's trunk, which Lewis had opened to distribute the gas masks. Gottlieb sat up front with their driver, a young man he had introduced as Dieter, so it was only when the truck stopped at the farmhouse that he remarked on the masks, that each of them held in their laps.

"Did you think you were back in the war?" he asked. "Bad fumes from the engine?" And he laughed. "Come inside. Leave them here with the luggage."

Andrew left the mask but brought his doctor's bag, and held it over his head as he stepped out of the back, into wheel-rutted mud. The truck was not the only vehicle here. There were two other similar trucks, a larger truck that looked like a delivery vehicle . . . and a Ford town car, painted a deep red. The farmhouse was nearby: three storeys, with Greek-style columns at either side, and a mural, depicting what looked like a dragon, across the span of the facade just above the front doors. Gottlieb urged them to hurry, and they did—but when they stepped inside, they were all still drenched.

They found themselves in a bright, warm front hall—opening on rooms to the left and the right, with a great staircase climbing to a first floor, and a passage to the back of the house alongside it, hung with antlers on high. A young woman waited there with towels, and handed them out to each of them.

"You should remove those clothes," she said in English. "So wet."

Andrew peeled off his overcoat and the others did the same, and towelled off.

"I'll be fine," said Dominic, and Kurtzweiller nodded gruffly.

"Upstairs," said Gottlieb after they'd dried themselves.

"What is there?" asked Andrew, and Gottlieb only smiled and beckoned.

They climbed into a large room—it looked to Andrew almost like a gentleman's club, with leather chairs and sofas . . . desks here and there . . . small side tables for drinks, and newspapers . . . and a broad row of windows, looking out over a wide field.

There would be mountains farther off—they were rendered invisible by the rains, but Andrew knew they would be there. This was a room very much as described by Zimmermann . . . the one that he had snuck into in the night to read mail . . . the one where he and Jason had met, before he left and Jason stayed behind.

There were four men in that room now, and they each regarded Andrew and the *Société* silently as they entered. One of them, Andrew did not recognize: one, slight, black-haired, with a high forehead, wearing a dark double-breasted suit, was standing by the window, hands at his hips and elbows held outward. A second one, Andrew thought he might know: square-jawed, older—maybe sixty—with a mop of white hair, and a look about him that was disconcertingly familiar . . . he thought that might be Johannes Bergstrom, long-dead Nils Bergstrom's older brother. He sat in one of the chairs, legs and arms crossed as though he were holding something in.

The third, Andrew was fairly sure about. He stood more than a head taller than the first fellow. He was broad about the shoulders, narrower at the waist; he wore a pair of trousers with suspenders, and a workman's shirt that fit too tightly over a lean and well-muscled torso. His hair was dark brown . . . and was crudely cut. He had a single dark eyebrow over eyes that seemed to burn.

He stood behind one of the chairs, his hands holding the back of it like a shield, and when he looked at Andrew, he grinned. Surely, thought Andrew, this was Orlok.

As to the fourth, sitting in the chair in front of the man likely to be Orlok? There was no question.

"Hello, Doctor Waggoner," said Jason Thistledown. He smiled too. "You ought to get out of those wet clothes. Goin' to catch yourself a death."

"Sprechen sie bitte Deutsch," said the stranger, and Jason obliged.

"Of course," he said in German. Then he looked up to the giant looming behind him. *"These are the ones,"* he said.

"And you are Orlok," said Andrew.

The giant—Orlok—reached down and patted Jason on the shoulder, and nodded his head.

"Call me that," he said. *"You are Waggoner then? The Neger physican. Yes."*

"I am Andrew Waggoner."

Orlok lifted his hand from Jason and waved a finger at Andrew and the rest. *"I will want to talk with you later. We have a thing in common . . . in what we have defeated. And I am most anxious to learn what you know of that."*

"I am anxious to talk also," said Andrew.

The stranger looked Andrew up and down. *"What is the worth of that?"* he demanded, looking to Orlok. *"This Neger is a distraction, Herr Orlok."*

At that, Orlok laughed—a surprisingly quiet chuckle, given his impressive size. Andrew would have thought his laughter the sort that would boom across the valley.

"Herr Goebbels," said Orlok, addressing Andrew, *"does not think highly of you Waggoner. Do you know why?"*

"We have not met. I do not know why."

"You are a degenerate," said Orlok. *"From Africa. That is why. He thinks you are sub-human."*

"You've been called worse things," said Jason, and then glancing at the stranger—Goebbels—repeated himself, slowly, in German.

"But Herr Goebbels," said Orlok, *"should not toss around insults like that. Do you know that he can't even climb the stairs? Not with ease. A bad foot. Born that way. Degenerate."*

Goebbels took his arms from his hips, crossed them and, put a fist to his chin.

"Still," said Orlok, *"he comes from a very long way off. All the way from the City of Berlin! That is nearly as far as Paris, where you have come from. Maybe not quite as far. I should be more gracious. He brought a great store of food for us, a whole truckload. And we are always hungry here. But it is a peace offering—am I correct, Herr Goebbels?"* He looked to Goebbels, who nodded. *"And as such . . . it buys you consideration."*

Goebbels lowered his hand to the crook of his arm. *"Herr Orlok, would you prefer to continue this conversation later?"*

"No, Herr Goebbels. We were doing very well I thought." Orlok grinned. *"I am sorry, Waggoner. We should introduce ourselves. You have friends with you here."*

Andrew introduced the *Société* such as were present, and Orlok introduced the others properly. The man in the chair was indeed Johannes Bergstrom. He did not meet Andrew's eye when he was introduced. Orlok continued.

"And Herr Joseph Goebbels. He is a politician. With Hitler and the Nazi Party. He has an election coming up next year and he would like very much to win it."

"For my party, my Führer to prevail, yes."

"So. That is what we are discussing." Orlok stepped around the chair and approached Goebbels more directly. To the small man's credit, he didn't cringe as Orlok drew closer—he returned his fists to his hips, and stood straighter.

Orlok spoke to Goebbels. *"Waggoner knows about the thing you brought here. The Juke. He knows what it does. He knows how it does it. Better than Bergstrom. Maybe better than me. We will talk about it now. And you will be respectful."*

Goebbels stepped back from Orlok. He shook his head.

"I did not bring the thing . . . this Juke here," said Goebbels and gestured to Bergstrom. *"That was you, Doctor. We only gave you money, and this place to do the work. And our youth . . . to bring the heart of Germany together as one. The experiment is something that I for one would never have supported."*

Bergstrom shook his head and started to speak, but Goebbels raised a finger and continued.

"There are other ways of convincing the people to support us in the vote, and well beyond that. We have our own science of persuasion and I for one trust it . . . newspapers, and rallies, and simple example. Propaganda. It is at the least, something that we can control."

"And this," said Orlok, *"you cannot control."*

"I do not believe that you can control it either," said Goebbels.

Orlok shrugged. *"Believe what you like."*

"I believe it to be possible that we can exercise control," said Goebbels. He held his hands forward, in upraised fists—as though he were grasping a rope, or the handles on a heavy trunk. *"But together, Herr Orlok. Not opposed as we have been."*

Orlok turned to Andrew. *"Do you see how well this discussion is going? How long do you think we have been talking, Herr Goebbels and I? Two days! Well, not all of that time. He went to sleep back in the town and then came back to talk again today. He is so determined. And as you might guess . . . I have not granted him his wish. And yet he persists."* He turned to Goebbels. *"Why do you persist?"*

"It is to our mutual advantage," he said. *"You are a great man, Orlok. We know how to reward great—"*

"No." Orlok said it quietly, but he stopped Goebbels as surely as if he had shouted. *"I accept your offering, Herr Goebbels. Not your terms."*

"We can reward your loyalty," said Goebbels.

Orlok shook his head.

"We can ensure your safety."

Orlok laughed again, this time at a volume suiting his frame.

"Talk to Waggoner," he said. *"Respectfully. Convince him of your party's virtues. Perhaps over a meal, of the food that you brought for us. A meal with the degenerate Neger."*

Goebbels sighed, looked to the floor, then back up at Orlok.

"I will go now, I think," he said. *"Remember that I am offering both a reward, and a peace."*

"You," said Orlok, *"are begging for help. Now come. Beg at the Neger's supper table."*

Goebbels flinched only a little. He was quiet for a moment, looking at his boots. Finally, he merely shrugged, and offered an icy smile.

"I think you may have overestimated my persistence at last. Leb wohl, Mein Herr," he said, and started toward the stairs.

Orlok was right—the little Nazi did have a bad leg. He managed well enough for it, Andrew thought, as he made his way down the stairs and to the front door—only a little more slowly and awkwardly than dignity would allow.

"I expect we won't see him again," said Jason.

He got out of the chair as soon as they heard the front doors close below them, stretched, and ambled over to the windows. Had he lost weight? From the photograph that Zimmermann had of him, it looked to Andrew like he might have gained some. Andrew was wondering how the burns were on his neck when it occurred to him:

Here he was, in the farmhouse at Wallgau. There was Jason Thistledown, who he had spent nights wondering whether was alive or dead.

"You're alive," he said.

Jason turned and looked at him. "You're a smart one."

"I don't know about that," said Andrew. "I'm here, aren't I?"

Jason regarded him a moment. "Where's Ruth? She here too?"

Andrew shook his head. "She's safe."

"You know that for a fact?"

"I know that for a fact."

"Thank you."

Jason rubbed his chin and crossed the room to Andrew, until he was right in front of him. He looked Andrew in the eye, and reached out with a hand. Andrew frowned, and took his hand, and Jason clasped that one with his other hand, and so did Andrew, and they shook.

"I'm sorry," said Jason, and Andrew said, "I am too," and although Andrew thought they might speak more of it later, that was as far as they got, that first day at the Wallgau farm.

There were not even apologies on that last day, at the Thorn farm.

In the pre-dawn before they were to depart, Andrew watched as Annie held onto Ruth, who was not weeping. She might have been . . . it would have been better if she were. She was sitting on the edge of her cot, staring at her hands that pinched at the fabric homespun skirt that had once belonged to Lawrence Thorn's dead wife and now covered her. Her face was like a death mask. Her words came on the faintest wind, flat and cold.

"Jason won't come," she said. "He won't even come to Cranbrook, to see us off. We are an abomination. No. That is not precisely what he said. *I* am an abomination. That."

"No," said Annie, and repeated it: "No, no, no," and so on, nearly as softly.

"No," said Andrew, in barely a whisper. Annie looked up at Andrew, and wordlessly—with the widening of her eyes, the raising of her brow—made her wishes clear.

Leave us be.

Andrew went off looking for Jason. He guessed that the two of them had just spoken, so thought he might find Jason lurking around outside the bunkhouse, or up at the pen tending swine, or just lingering by the Thorn house. It wasn't so. Jason was abed, and it was Lawrence's boy Tom that Andrew finally found, in the front of the farmhouse with a bucket of well water in each hand, hauling it up the steps to the kitchen. He stopped, set the buckets down, when he saw Andrew coming up. The sun was just coming up by then, just a little pink of it, and it lit his face. He was glaring.

"What you want, Nigger?"

"Doctor," said Andrew, and when Tom said, "What?" Andrew repeated: "Doctor Waggoner. That's my name, son. Don't call me *nigger*."

"Well you scat," said Tom. "This is the house."

"You seen Jason?"

"Sure," said Tom.

"Can you fetch him?"

"What for? Jason's got no need to talk to you," said Tom, "not you nor your nigger-lovin' friends. Father'll take you to town later."

Andrew took a step toward Tom.

"Son, I just need to see Jason. I can find him myse—"

He didn't get a chance to finish. As he grew closer, Tom set his mouth, reached down and picked up one of the buckets, and flung it in Andrew's face. The water struck him first, in a freezing sheet—and then the bucket itself, heavy and steel, struck home in the worst place—his elbow, still in a sling.

"You get! You get!" shouted the boy, and probably Andrew should have done just that. It was, he would often reflect, an idiotic moment. Tom could not have been more than twelve years old. He was small for that. If he'd been in Andrew's care, he would have examined him for worms, or kidney disorder.

He wouldn't have hit him, with a half-made fist in the side of the head. He wouldn't have brought that fist back—fully formed—in the other side of the face while the child was reeling with shock from that first hit. Tom fell to the steps, knocking the other bucket over and spilling the water all down his trousers, and he let out a keening wail.

The front door to the farmhouse swung open at that—and there he was.

Jason, half-dressed. With a shotgun in one hand.

"What in hell," he said, and Tom looked back and then pointed at Andrew.

"Shoot him!" he screamed. "Shoot the dirty nigger! He tried t' kill me!"

Andrew raised a hand to Jason, waving what he thought was calm. "Jason, it's not—"

Jason held the gun at his waist. He didn't point it, but he didn't move to put it away either.

"Did you strike my brother?" he said quietly.

"It was a misunderst—"

"You did."

The sun had finally topped the trees on the other side of the Kootenai, and rays of it struck Jason's brow, for years afterward, that would be the memory that he carried of Jason Thistledown: a young man painted gold by the morning light, his eyes narrow with contempt and pity, as cold as the light was warm.

"Jason," said Andrew, "please. Ruth—Miss Harper—you hurt her badly—"

"That's about enough. Go back to the women. Mr. Thorn'll take you to where you need to go."

And then, in the golden dawn, Jason Thistledown raised the shotgun to his shoulder and aimed it just above Andrew's head.

"Don't ever hit my little brother," he said.

"Jason—"

"Now get back."

"Joseph Goebbels," said Orlok, as they all sat down to feast hours later, *"is a man that I would not ever fuck."*

Kurtzweiller and Lewis exchanged what they must have thought was a tiny glance at that, but it caught Orlok's eye. He looked at Kurtzweiller, and then Lewis, then Dominic and finally over at Andrew, who was seated across from them at one of the long wooden tables in the farmhouse's dining hall.

The room was long and narrow, and from Zimmermann's tale, Andrew guessed this had been used as a barracks for the S.A. guard just a few months ago. It certainly showed signs of wear—there were ugly scratches in the dark wood framing doors and windows, and the bare board floor was scuffed with the dragging of furniture. At one end, a banner with a swastika hung crookedly off the wall. They all sat on low wooden benches at either end of the table.

Between them were heaped platters of food: potatoes, roasted in fat and salted, glistening hocks of pork, likely cooked in the same oven, and more platters filled with fruits—apples and oranges. Strewn among them were tins, half-opened, with meats and vegetables, pickled mushrooms. At the far end was a great bowl of carrots, badly peeled and boiled too long.

It was a feast, but one prepared by children. Starving, wild children who had spent too long on their own and barely knew how to operate a stove . . . and who had forgotten how to dress themselves.

There were perhaps two dozen of them, maybe more at times, in the dining hall along with Orlok and his entourage of Jason, Bergstrom, and Gottlieb. Some sat at the table, with plates of food that they cleaned with bare hands. Others hovered behind them, either waiting for a space to open up or simply shovelling food onto plates and eating standing. They were young . . . not really children, but youthful . . . adolescents, and very young men—and women . . . and they were for the most part naked.

"Goebbels thinks you are not human," Orlok said to Andrew, and Andrew nodded.

"You were saying," he said.

"Well, I would fuck you," said Orlok, *"before I fucked him. Why are you squirming?"* He was looking at Dominic, who was indeed shifting, rubbing his arm.

"Bad arm," said Dominic, and Orlok nodded.

"You all have bad arms," he said. *"You think you are tricking me."*

They did think that. Before they had come to dinner, Andrew had pulled each of them aside and administered a pinprick of wasp venom . . . barely a drop each, but more than a single sting would ever inject. The pain was enough to bring tears, and it lingered. Even through dinner, where Andrew noted a little sourly, there was not a drop of wine to blunt it.

"They are just keeping a clear head," said Jason, who was seated beside Orlok. *"Like I used to."*

Orlok nodded. *"Burning cigarettes in their necks?"*

"No," said Jason, switching to English, "something else. Isn't that right, Doc?"

Andrew sighed, and rubbed his arm so it hurt more. "Something else," he said.

"You finally manage to get that hill-folk concoction right?"

"No," said Andrew, "just pain."

"Deutsch sprechen!" shouted Orlok.

"Es ist nur Schmerz," repeated Andrew.

"Ah. That is brave. But stupid. Why do you hurt yourself?"

"I do not wish to fall under a spell," said Andrew. *"None of us do."*

Orlok raised his brow. *"Why not?"*

"We do not wish to lose ourselves." Andrew gestured around him. *"We want to see what is here. Not some fantasy."*

"And how can you be sure that you lose yourself? Could you not be finding your better self instead?"

"No. We have seen this before. It does not lead to our better selves."

"You have not seen this before," said Orlok, gesturing to indicate the room, the shifting crowd of people. *"But you have seen a thing that I have seen too. We have both fought it. So I understand your fear."*

At this, Lewis interjected. *"You fought the Juke?"*

Orlok grinned and nodded. *"I devoured it,"* he said, and then he laughed. *"How did you kill yours, Doctor Waggoner?"*

"Everybody died. And it starved," said Andrew, and Orlok laughed.

"That is a good story," he said. *"Fast. To the point."*

"How did you devour a Juke?" asked Kurtzweiller.

Orlok turned to Kurtzweiller. *"My brother Jason tells me you like to hear stories. That is how you understand your world. You tell a story to others, with their wits about them, and ask them to see if it is strong. And so you can say what is true and what is . . . fantasy."*

"The Decameron System," said Jason and, in spite of himself, Andrew smiled.

"Doctor Bergstrom relies on something similar. He calls it psychoanalysis," said Orlok. He reached over and put a hand on Bergstrom's shoulder, and when he tried to flinch away, gripped hard enough to make him cry out.

"Decameron System. Psychoanalysis. Telling a good story. To find the truth of it. Maybe I will tell you one now. About fighting the Juke, yes?"

Orlok stood, so that he loomed high over the table. Bergstrom, to one side of him, visibly shrank away, and even Jason slid down the bench.

"Here we go," he said under his breath, in English—this time, without drawing rebuke.

"My struggle," said Orlok, and he grinned wide—as though he had made an exceedingly clever joke that none understood but him.

"It begins—"

Two

"—before I can remember in words.

"I have memories, but they are of the senses not of the words—and why should they be? I was in the womb, suckling through the nabelschnur . . . sated and growing. I remember that. I also remember, just before that, terrible pain. And yes, struggle. My earliest memory is of struggle . . . of an understanding that I might indeed die before even being born . . . the idea burst upon me like a great flash of light. I do not think I had such ideas before, and I did not again for long after.

"This idea of my death was bright. It did not frighten me. How could it? I had no other ideas before this one. It was neither good nor bad—but everything. I simply knew that I might die, and also that I might not. I knew that I came very near to it. I knew that an enemy was near. And that one of us might die. And I did not die. Instead, I became sated.

"Look at you, Doctor Kurtzweiller. You already think this is a bad story. You know something about the foetus, and the womb, and you know that a foetus is liable to remember nothing of that time. Doctor Bergstrom might disagree with you. He might say that we are all formed by our time in our mothers' wombs, and memories from there have even greater power over us than the memories we make in the cradle. This is what I remember. Maybe I dreamed it all, yes?

"But the story is not only me and my memories. It is also those of my mother, whose name was Maja. I do not know what town she was from originally. She was with a circus you see. My mother was very strong. Big. Like me. She performed feats of strength with the circus, and travelled with it everywhere it went. She gave birth to me near Vienna. I was conceived in Bulgaria she told me. My father was probably still there. But she was not sure. She did not recall even his name. He was a tradesman, from Pleven. Not very handsome, she said . . . it was from him that I inherited this single eyebrow . . . and not willing

to take on a wife from the circus. Maja took many lovers in those days prior, but my father was the last. . . .

"The second-to-last.

"There was another, although she would not call him a lover. This one came upon Maja in Bulgaria too . . . two months later, in another town . . . Vratsa . . . near mountains, much like this Wallgau.

"It is in Vratsa, Maja told me, that she met the dhampir.

"What is a dhampir? Not a vampire . . . not a Nosferatu. But near to it . . . a creature said to haunt the darker corners of Bulgaria, the Balkans. It is a soft thing, perhaps the child of a vampire and a human . . . and it comes to women, often virginal women, to deflower them.

"My mother was not that . . . she was with child, with me, and far enough along that she would soon not be able to perform her feats of strength. The dhampir appeared to her as she readied for bed after the second night at Vratsa. It may have been in the audience—she said she thought she remembered it, a pale creature with a face like a full moon, eyes black as the night . . . dressed in dark rags. . . .

"And it was the same, in her wagon, where it slithered under the cover and into her bed. She remembered how weak it was—she easily could have overpowered the thing, for it seemed to have no bones, nothing like muscle . . . it was all flesh, she said. Flesh, nearly liquid.

"This was the opposite of me. I was born with great strength, unusual strength, and it showed even before my first year. The circus owners were so impressed with me that they tried to make me a part of the show—have me lift up chairs and small tables, snap tree branches before I was even two years of age. I did not do that for very long. For I was a disobedient child and prone to tantrums and, in the ring, I could not easily be controlled. The only thing for me would have been the sideshow, in a metal cage, where strangers could watch my display of mighty anger safe on the other side of thick iron bars. Maja would not allow that. For even though it might have been a help—after my birth, she found herself going to fat, and not so strong as she once was—Maja loved me. And I loved her.

"We worried about each other too. I worried for her. Maja was getting fatter and weaker . . . maybe keeping up with my ferocious appetite, she overate? Got lazy like a mother can? It was not just that. It was said that my birth took away her strength and put it in me. Her strength and her beautiful fury. All in me.

"She worried about me because of those things. I was a beast of a child. Too strong. Too angry. I could not play with other children, because I might harm

them. Or worse—I might persuade them to do harm. I did not take instruction, but others did follow mine. Children, and men, and women too. None said no to me.

"This talent of mine did help us. Maja grew fatter, and then she grew thinner, and weaker. The Italian who owned our troupe might have tossed her out . . . the circus is no place for the infirm. But I would not allow it, and so he would not consider it. And we travelled with the rest, often doing nothing to earn our keep.

"Maja was not as grateful as you might expect. She worried about me, but she also worried about what it was I had become. She loved me and also feared me. She told me again and again, the story of the dhampir, and the night it had taken her—and, she feared, taken me too.

"'Ah, mein Kind,' she would say, 'you have been poisoned by the dhampir!' And I would say back: 'Ah, meine Mutter, I have eaten it up!' This would make her laugh, but as she wasted, I came to understand it as a truth. When she died . . . I was not more than ten years old then . . . it was a certainty.

"I had fought a dhampir once. And I would do so again.

"I fled the circus. I climbed on board a freight train. And then another. And another after that, and finally a truck. And in that way, I made my way to Bulgaria. To Vratsa.

"A dangerous journey for a child? Perhaps. But not for me. There was always food and shelter when I needed it. No one moved to harm me when I took either. As for rapists and pederasts? I was very strong and fast. I had nothing to fear.

"I arrived in winter. It had snowed the day before and the roads were thick with drifts of it. I remember that . . . trudging through the clogged streets . . . stopping at a tavern, and taking food from the plates of diners there . . . I slept in a church pew for a time, and remember a priest.

"But that earliest memory—that of the senses, not of word—grew to my present experience. And that is what I recall the most about Vratsa: the cold, the satiety . . . and the call.

"When dawn broke, I left the town and climbed into the hills and up the slope of a mountain. And there, I found the opening of a cave. I had not received direction, or even a hint. . . . No one in Vratsa had told me about the dhampir that preyed upon them. I did not know the way to the cave. But I arrived. And although it was dark, I clambered within. Blind.

"But not blind at all. I felt that I knew where I was going . . . I felt I was going . . . to a kind of home. It was . . . like faith.

"And soon enough, the faith was rewarded. There was light—a firelight—that I only came upon after creeping through the darkest of caverns. I did smell smoke, but only as I was nearly upon it . . . a well-stoked firepit, in the middle of a high chamber with an icy pond in its middle. Stacked around the fire were carcasses, of goat and fowl . . . and also baskets of vegetables. Stoking it, and tending to this winter store, were three girls.

"Not girls really. Women. Strong. Maybe sisters? They had the same blonde hair. Muscular. One of them was pregnant. And that one . . . she commanded the others.

"I tried to speak to them but it was no good. I could only say one or two words in Bulgarian that I had learned on the way and I did not even know what they meant. I tried to get close and that was worse. They threw stones at me and shouted at me to go. One of them picked up an axe, and waved it at me.

"I became very angry at that. And I picked up rocks and threw them back. I was better aim, and hit them in the faces and arms and bellies . . . and this drove them away from the fire and into the dark of the caverns.

"I did not give chase. I did not care about these girls, and I could tell in my heart, that I was already upon the creature I sought—the dhampir. It lurked nearby. It would soon reveal itself, I was certain. So I sat down to warm myself by the fire, and eat some of the food that was there. That is one sensation that I recall in the hours before we confronted one another: the ferocious hunger. It was a depraved hunger, a lust for the foodstuff, to not only consume it but possess it.

"I saw the dhampir, when I came to the edge of the pond of water, to drink and clear my throat. There was a splash, and a rippling, and it—or a piece of it—emerged. It was nothing as Maja had described to me: no moon-faced man with black eyes. It was rather a great serpent, or first a great serpentine thing, that slid from the water, with a terrible wide mouth. I remember that mouth moved close to me, and breathed air that was sweeter than anything I had smelled, even as it widened and I could see the rows of teeth.

"I snatched it, with both arms around its neck—thinking that I could pull it out of the water, or at least squeeze its throat and kill it. The throat collapsed easily in my grip, and the mouth opened wider so that it had nearly turned inside out. And I did pull it from the water. But of course it was not a neck . . . it was only one of many mouths, and it did not come from the depths of the pond . . . it had been drifting there, dangling on a long throat, from high among the stalactites.

"How did I kill such a thing? Again, I remember sense, not words. I know that I was lifted from the ground. I know at a point I was submerged in icy water. I

know that I bit and tasted flesh. At a point, hot smoke filled my lungs. And I felt a powerful erection . . . and a sexual release, not my very first . . . but the first I recall with any fondness. Doctor Bergstrom has theories about that.

"I tore the dhampir down from the cave. I tore it to shreds. I killed it and it was not as hard as that. These creatures . . . they are weak of the flesh and the bone, as compared to we men. They can do nothing for themselves but persuade us. And I would not be persuaded.

"The girls—the women—did return, with men from the church. They were weak too . . . not of flesh and bone, not like the dhampir—the Juke—but of spirit. They carried torches and axes and swords. They were prepared to stop this demon that had violated the sanctuary of the caverns. Of their God. But when they faced him . . . when they faced me . . .

"All they could do was bow down, before their new God.

"I stayed in Vratsa for the remainder of the winter. I was well looked after and might have stayed longer. But I had no wish to be looked after. And the remains of the Juke—which they hung at the mouth of the cave, like the severed head of an enemy . . . I could not abide the smell. I had done what I had come to do. So when the trees began to bud, I left Vratsa. And also, the second Juke that I had killed. Better they be on their own."

Orlok pushed his stool back and sat down on it, and looked around the room, meeting each of their eyes in turn.

"Now, Doctors . . . do you have any questions about my terrible story? My brother Jason tells me that this is how you determine the truth of things."

The gentlemen of the *Société* were finally led to the top floor of the farmhouse—a wide hallway from which branched small bedrooms with barely room to stand, thanks to the slope of the roof. At one end, set against a pair of tall windows, were some chairs and a table. They shared this floor with Johannes Bergstrom, whom Orlok commanded to show them to their own rooms.

"The guest quarters," said Bergstrom as he showed Andrew his room. "Three floors above the front door. Difficult to leave undetected, which I think is the point, after the escape. Secure. Not uncomfortable though." He smiled weakly at Andrew. "Unlike this moment, Doctor Waggoner. You must despise me. Bunking us together is another of Orlok's rather poor jokes."

"I've never met you until today," said Andrew.

"And yet you suffered terribly at the hands of my brother."

"He suffered at his own hand. More, I think, than I did." Andrew looked at Bergstrom. "Maybe you too."

Bergstrom shrugged and turned to go. Andrew grabbed him by his arm. Bergstrom turned and fixed Andrew with an affronted stare.

"You've seen one," said Andrew, and Bergstrom nodded.

"Ja."

"It's still here?"

"Es ist tot."

"Dead. Orlok killed it?"

"So Orlok says. So Jason Thistledown confirms."

"Have you seen it dead?" asked Lewis.

Bergstrom looked around. The men of the *Société* had gathered behind him at the door to Andrew's room. Andrew pointed over their shoulders to the little sitting area by the window.

"Why don't we all go sit," he said, "and talk awhile before we go to bed. That suit, Doctor?"

"I did see the Juke," said Bergstrom, sitting in a hard chair in front of the rain-streaked windows. "Not, I believe, in the form that it finally took when Orlok killed it. That was by all reports much larger. But when it arrived . . . I did help supervise the enclosure."

"How large was it?" asked Lewis. "The Juke. Not the enclosure."

"No bigger than a child," said Bergstrom, and levelled his hand over the floor.

"How did you contain it?"

"It arrived in a glass-walled cage, fed air through a hose from a tank. The cage would not contain it for long but the intention was not to contain for long. We established a compound, in the valley . . . quite elaborate, with infirmaries and laboratories, and including larger cages . . . electricity, from petrol-fuelled generators. All held within concentric rings of fencing on the banks of the stream."

Kurtzweiller leaned forward. "Have you photographs?"

"There are photographs," said Bergstrom. "Of course. But matters are far beyond the Juke. It is dead, and now we are contending with something new."

"Yes," said Lewis. "Orlok. What is he?"

Bergstrom shrugged. "He is a man. And as he told you—he believes that he is a part Juke himself. He may well be. Although his story of his childhood . . . it is fanciful. His great strength and speed . . . it is like a hero from stories."

Lewis shook his head. "Perhaps not. In my field, I have encountered people like this Orlok. They are the product of a mutation, such as a Siamese twin, or a birth defect of the brain . . . but in this case, largely beneficial. Children born with unusual musculature. What baby fat they have, they lose within weeks. They are quick, and very strong from an early age."

"Oh yes," said Bergstrom. "We know of these mutations as well. We had, working here, known about this fellow long before we even knew of, let alone considered, using a Juke. Stories about Orlok—not necessarily by name—had been circulating through Germany since the War. Since before. We had a great interest in locating him. For the same reason we gather the strong and beautiful among our youth here."

"Übermensch," said Kurtzweiller, and Bergstrom nodded, and smiled wryly.

"Or *Nosferatu*. But the *Übermensch*. That is the dream," he said. "Of our partners in this, particularly."

"A superman, somehow strong enough to devour a juvenile Juke . . . in the uterus," said Andrew.

"It is usually the other way around," said Dominic. "The Juke devours the foetus, and latches on to the umbilical itself."

"Or devours a body," said Andrew. "I can see why he calls himself Orlok."

He looked at Bergstrom—and looked away, as he recalled Nils Bergstrom, Johannes's brother, with Jukes writhing under his skin, sucking away his life like . . . well, like vampires. It was a frequent nightmare, that sight.

"He also," said Bergstrom, "grew up believing his mother was raped by a *Nosferatu*."

"This is an interesting theory," said Andrew. "Not sure we can get much further on in without either dissecting Orlok, or psychoanalyzing him. Johannes—Doctor Bergstrom—we came a long way, took a big risk. Now about Jason—"

Bergstrom nodded, and drew a breath.

"What's been done to him?"

"I had done nothing to him," said Bergstrom. "We . . . hired Jason, to help us regain control of the valley."

"And in that you failed."

"It is true. The valley gained control of us."

"And of Jason," said Andrew.

"I do not know," said Bergstrom, "that that is so. I think that Herr Thorn—Herr Thistledown—has found something there. But it has not controlled him. If he were a patient in my care, I would rather say that his time in the valley has had a curative effect on him."

"Curative?"

"Dr. Waggoner," said Bergstrom, "when Jason arrived here . . . granted, against his will . . . I would have diagnosed him with shell shock. Which should not be surprising, given both his war record, and the traumas he endured before the war, alongside yourself, and even prior to your meeting. He was prone to self-harm. He showed signs of malnourishment. He smoked nervously . . . as by compulsion. And associated with the self-harm. And he expressed himself primarily through rage."

"You did kidnap him," said Andrew.

"A fair point." Bergstrom sat up straighter. "Did you come here to rescue him?"

Andrew thought about that for just an instant before he said, "Yes." It was long enough for Bergstrom to pick up on it.

"Ah-hah," he said. "But there would have been other ways to effect that outcome—without travelling here yourself, at great risk. You might have contacted the *Polizei*. You might have hired a private investigator in Munich—there are such fellows, I am told. One or two of them might have assisted, for small compensation.

"But," Bergstrom said, "perhaps you have other interests. Perhaps Herr Thistledown is . . . secondary to those?"

Bergstrom looked to each of the members of the *Société* in turn, and then nodded, and Kurtzweiller finally cleared his throat.

"It is true. We would very much like to see the enclosure," he said, "and also the remains of the Juke Herr Orlok claims to have slain."

The men sat quiet a moment, and Lewis finally broke the silence.

"We have gas masks," he said. "Body suits. Equipment that might protect us from any . . . remaining secretions."

"We have our own photographic equipment," said Kurtzweiller. "Tools for collection . . ."

"This is the culmination," said Lewis, "of many years you understand . . . of inquiry, often fruitless. Most of us—have never seen a full specimen."

"A full living specimen," said Kurtzweiller.

Andrew found himself nodding, as he held his hands together to quiet the trembling that he also that he also thought detected in Dominic—the only other of the four of them who likely had met a living Juke.

For the first time since they had arrived, Bergstrom broke into a broad and delighted grin.

"This is marvellous. Inquiry! Curiosity! Exactly what Doctor Aguillard had hoped to excite when he escaped."

"I beg your pardon?" said Kurtzweiller.

Andrew frowned. "Aguillard?"

"Doctor Aguillard," said Bergstrom. "He is the reason that Orlok has moved me and some others to the top floor of this building . . . so far from the front doors. Aguillard was one of those who had brought the Juke. He managed to sneak off, and his plans were to visit Paris." Bergstrom looked to Andrew. "I half expected, when I heard that you were come to Germany, that you had done so in Aguillard's company. He believed that we needed your expertise, to unravel this mystery—whatever our financiers in Munich might have thought of you."

Andrew shook his head.

"He came to Paris," he said.

"Perhaps not," said Bergstrom. "If you did not meet him . . . he may have been waylaid. Or simply distracted."

"Well," said Andrew, "just as well. Given everything, I'm not sure how well he'd have been received."

"Indeed," said Bergstrom. "Given everything, I think he would not be well-received back here either. If we are to visit the valley—examine the remains of the Juke . . . gather samples, take your photographs . . . which is your wish . . . your own great dream . . . it will be easier as matters stand."

Andrew raised an eyebrow, and Bergstrom clarified:

"There will be less trouble, Doctor Waggoner, if we make the hike alone."

The rain had not lessened when the gentlemen of the *Société de la biologie transcendantale* retired to their rooms. Andrew listened to it for an hour longer, lying sleepless on the thin mattress. It played the shingles like a concerto, rising to crescendo and falling to a gentle lullaby before reasserting itself. Andrew was tempted at a point to hum along with it, but he resisted. A fellow could hum along with anything he wanted, Andrew supposed. It didn't make it music. Andrew rubbed his sore forearm, and not for the first time nor last, wished he had some wine.

Three

It was dawn by the time they made it to the farm—the break of it, and the sky over the mountains was streaked with ribbons of crimson cloud, like blood, Ruth thought, as she looked up at it from the ground where all was still shadowed, and misted, and bloody cold. Getting there had been slower going than Ruth would have thought, but she had never walked by starlight, through the night, on a strange country road. They had stopped to rest twice before Zimmermann declared that they should halt altogether, until there was at least some light by which to navigate.

And so they arrived: in front of a low stone wall—not much higher than the middle of Ruth's chest. There was a gate, a hundred metres to the west, but Albert thought it would be better if they didn't announce themselves there. Who knew if the farm posted guards these days? It was true, there could be eyes anywhere . . . but why make it easy for them?

The wall was made of round river-rock, packed with earth, and would have been easy to climb on a full stomach and a night's sleep—neither of which advantages any of them could boast. Ruth pointed this out.

"I can toss you over if you wish, Fräulein Harper," he said. "It hasn't been long since the rains, and the ground is soft as a sponge. You won't even bruise."

"Well, I can manage it," said Annie, and Ruth said that of course she could too. She shaded her eyes with a hand and peered through the mist. In the far distance, mountains rose—their peaks bristling with pine and haloed with the gold of the rising sun. In the shadows below, she could see smoke rising from rooftops—still distant but not so—and a wide field.

"This is where you landed the plane?" she asked, and Albert pointed some distance away from the house.

"There," he said. "I also took off from there."

She nodded. "Not much of a runway," she said.

"No," he agreed, "it is not."

"Well," said Ruth, as the sun's disk rose over the peak, "let's get a better look." And she put a boot on a sturdy-looking stone, and with just two more steps and a lunge, hefted herself up and over the fence.

They came to the farmhouse without seeming to encounter a soul, but they approached as though they were under close observation: hands held in plain sight, making it clear there were no weapons. The building was clearly inhabited—the smoke from the chimney granted that. And from the size of it, it could be well-inhabited. Ruth's mind went back to her father's house in Eliada, which she recalled as being larger, but not by much. Then she pulled it away again. Her foot didn't hurt very often, but it hurt right now. Enough was enough.

Annie was the one who approached the front door. It was shaded under a long porch awning, itself beneath a wide and poorly executed mural of a dragon or something like it, and she climbed those steps and tried the door. It opened, and she looked back and beckoned—and before Albert and Ruth could so much as wave back, she stepped inside. The doors hung half open for an instant, then swung shut again on their hinges.

"*Who is there?*" asked Albert, and called again a little louder.

Ruth rubbed her elbows at the chill, and checked her surroundings. The mist was clearing in the morning sunlight. There was a truck parked not far, its rear protruding from near the rear corner of the house as they approached. A wheelbarrow leaned against the tailgate. She squinted at the cab. There was no one there. No one anywhere. None that she could see.

Albert touched her hand where it gripped her arm. He leaned close to her.

"We cannot just stand here," he whispered, in English.

Ruth agreed. She took his hand from her elbow and into her hand, and together they climbed the short stairs to the front door. They stood there for another instant, and looked at each other, and Albert took the door handle and pulled it open—and there they were. Inside the farmhouse.

They were in a hall, with a broad, dark oak staircase climbing one side—doors, shut, on either side—and antlers hung like trophies along the walls. A low table along one wall, Ruth saw, was stacked with rifles . . . carbines, hinting rifles, maybe a shotgun. Ruth felt her mouth watering at the smell of frying.

Albert meanwhile held up a hand.

"Do you hear?" he whispered, and pointed down the hall, and Ruth did hear: a low susurration of voices. It was hard to say how many, or who. But they seemed to be coming from along the narrower hallway along the staircase.

They walked forward quietly, and as they passed the table, Albert lifted a carbine. Following his example, Ruth considered taking up a shotgun, but left it and pointed out to Albert that the guns weren't likely loaded.

He shrugged. "Bargaining power," he said, and kept the gun and kept going.

Ruth followed Albert through the door at the end of the hallway, and into a wide kitchen. Ham was frying on an impressive woodstove, next to a pot of what smelled like coffee, the percolator chortling away by the heat of the fire.

Next to that stove: a butcher's block with a loaf of bread half-sliced and a jar of jam with the top off. Beside that, a counter covered in ceramic tile, against which Annie Waggoner leaned, sipping from a mug of what was certainly that coffee.

And beside her . . . Jason.

Ruth could not look away. He wore a dark brown suit, with a high vest, and a pressed white shirt and tie. His light-brown hair was combed neatly to the side, and his face . . . it was smooth as a boy's. As beautiful as she remembered him. He held his own mug of coffee, in two steady hands just over the tie at his neck. He had been in the middle of saying something, but he stopped when Ruth entered the room.

Jason Thistledown could not look away either.

"See who I found?" said Annie.

Jason set the mug down on the counter beside him, and stood up from where he leaned on the counter.

"Jason's all right!" said Annie. "See? It's all fine!"

"Sure I'm all right," said Jason. He raised one hand, looking not at Ruth, but at Albert. "You want to set down that firearm, please, now?"

Albert was holding the gun across his chest, two-handed. He let go of the stock and set it down, barrel leaning against the doorjamb.

"It is empty," said Albert.

"You can never tell," said Jason, "with a rifle."

Albert smiled and shrugged. Jason turned back to Ruth.

"Well, you sure took me by surprise this morning," he said.

"You weren't expecting us?"

"Oh, eventually," said Jason. "But I thought I might surprise you . . . drive into Wallgau, visit you there at that Isar inn you were supposed to be staying at. I got dressed up in my city duds, see?" He spread his arms, to show off that suit.

It fit him well, Ruth thought . . . it wasn't just bought in a shop. Someone had made it for him. "Didn't think you'd walk through the night to come here, but I guess I should have known it. My God, Ruth, it is good to see you."

Ruth's eyes strayed around the kitchen. The counter ran for what might be twelve feet under smoke-stained windows, over to a door that led outside . . . there were two other doors, the same wall as the door that she and Albert had entered. Both those were shut. At the far end was a heavy kitchen table with five chairs around it. Tall pine cupboards. A little door to a pantry, or maybe a cellar.

She couldn't see anyone else but the three of them: Albert Zimmermann, Annie Waggoner, and Jason.

"Where is she?" asked Ruth, and Jason frowned like he was puzzled, so Ruth clarified: "Catherine? Where is Catherine?"

"Ah," said Jason. "Catherine. To be honest, I don't rightly know at the moment. She's not here, if that's what you're asking." His hand strayed to his necktie, and he hooked a finger into his collar and loosened it. "You met her?"

"You sent her," said Ruth sharply, and Jason looked away a moment.

"Not exactly," he said.

Ruth stepped forward, and raised her hands to indicate the whole of that kitchen—the counters and stove and table and doors—and stepped forward again, so that she was face to face with Jason.

"Where are the rest of them?" she demanded.

Jason looked back at her. "We're alone in here Ruth. Just us."

She shook her head, and set her lips. "I can't believe you." She heard her own voice rising. "I can't believe you that we're alone. There were . . . there were scores of people in Wallgau yesterday." She shut her eyes, and swallowed, and opened them again. Jason was looking over her shoulder now, at Albert, pleading. She didn't stop. "Catherine . . . that woman Catherine . . . and others . . . we didn't see them there either. But they were there. We only remembered them."

And then, God help her, she shouted:

"Where are they!"

"Ruth," said Jason, and then he spread his arms, and put them around her shoulders and pulled her into an embrace, and said softly, so only she could hear:

"It's only us."

They set out plates and mugs at the kitchen table, and sat down to fried ham and bread and jam, and coffee. Annie explained that she had already asked Jason about Andrew and the others from the *Société*, and that they were well and looked after.

"That's right," said Jason. "They came through a couple days ago. They've gone off on a bit of an expedition. Good to see Dr. Waggoner. He's looking well. For his age."

"An expedition?" asked Ruth. "Where?"

Jason blinked. "They've gone into yonder mountains," he said, "to take a look at the Juke."

And there it was. Ruth stared at Jason as he folded a piece of ham into his mouth, chewed, and washed it down with a swig of coffee.

"You know about the Juke," said Jason.

"Do you mean Orlok?"

"No." He patted his mouth with a handkerchief. "There's a Juke there. Dead. Old Zimmermann didn't tell you about that?"

"He was unclear on the matter," said Ruth. "But we did learn about Orlok, and what he'd done in the valley, from Dr. Aguillard."

"How'd you come across Aguillard?"

"Annie?" said Ruth.

Annie tucked her chin down and set about sawing at her ham, and Jason raised his eyebrow, and snapped his fingers.

"I got it! He went to see you in Paris!"

"How do you know that?" asked Annie, and Jason explained.

"I got a look at that telegram you sent to Doc Waggoner. You didn't mention him by name. But it sure did sound like him. And you just gave it away now."

Jason tore off a piece of bread and chewed on it, smiling.

"Aguillard ran off from us not long ago," said Jason. "Old Orlok wasn't pleased, but truth be told I was glad to see the last of him."

Annie sipped from her coffee. "You saw the telegram? Did Andrew show it to you?"

"No," said Jason. "We lay hold of it before he got to it."

Annie blinked.

"Andrew replied," she said, then blinked again, and said: "Andrew didn't reply. You did?"

"We did," said Jason. "Catherine did, specifically. We wanted you to come. *I* wanted you to come. At least you, Annie."

"Did you ever show Andrew the telegram?"

"No, Ruth. I didn't." Jason held up his hands, a fork in the right, in a kind of surrender. "I guess I owe you an apology, Annie. But I didn't see fit to." He set the fork down and took up another piece of bread. "I wasn't sure if Herr Zimmermann would have managed to get you, Ruth, over to Paris. But I'm glad he did, and that you came."

"You didn't ask me to bring her there," said Zimmermann, and Jason agreed that he hadn't.

"But I was pretty sure that she'd tell you to take her to Paris," he said. "And that's what happened, right Ruth?"

"Right."

"And then you'd insist on coming back here when the chips were down. I got that right?"

Ruth nodded. Jason crossed his arms, leaned back on his chair and smiled. "Even though you long ago thought it might not be a smart idea, seeing me again."

"I was worried," said Ruth.

"I can see how you might've been," said Jason. "I was worried too for a time there. But now you're here. And it's better. Isn't it?"

Ruth took another swallow of coffee.

"It's better," said Jason.

Then he turned to Annie. He didn't say anything more—just looked at her, like he was waiting. Maybe that's all he was doing; maybe he was doing something more.

Annie finished chewing on her ham, and swallowed. She picked up her coffee mug, looked at it, and set it down. She looked up, and met Jason's eye.

"Hector Aguillard is dead. It was me that did it to him. Poison. In his coffee. Slow way to go, but he had it coming."

She pushed the coffee mug away from her, and looked at each of them—a slow, tentative smile growing on her face.

"So I'm a murderess. There," she said. "I said it."

Annie didn't cry, but by the end of it, Ruth felt as though a crying jag was exactly what she'd witnessed.

Annie Waggoner, formerly Rowe, who'd saved Ruth's life twice—maybe three times—on the banks of the Kootenai River . . . one of the strongest women that Ruth had known, enduring utter and complete collapse.

From that smile, her lips pulled into a pale line, sucked back over the tops of her teeth. Her eyes seemed to withdraw into their sockets too. She drew a breath in by degree, as though pulling her lungs with a winch. Her hands drew into tight fists on the table, either side of her plate, so tight they trembled.

Those were the physical manifestations of Annie's experience. But Ruth apprehended more than that . . . she thought she might have seen more than that. The light seemed to shift where it struck Annie's face, shadows moving dimly across her brow as though the sun were occluded by fast-moving cloud. She seemed at once very old, and a child . . . or a young girl. Young Annie Rowe learning the trade of nursing, among the missionaries aiding the fallen women of Chicago. . . .

All this passed in barely more than an instant and Ruth couldn't really say that it ever had. But when it had passed, Annie seemed exhausted, and drained, and her mouth hung ever so slightly opened. Ruth reached over to touch Annie's hand, which had opened from its fist and was now limp, and damp.

"Did he try to hurt you?" she said, and Annie shook her head.

"He just wanted to talk to Andrew," she said. "About Jukes." She looked at Ruth. "He was no threat at all."

"Then why?"

Annie shook her head again.

"He had it coming," said Jason. He stood up and stepped around the chairs to kneel by Annie's side. "He helped make Eliada. He had a part in all that business. I know he had it coming. I bet he all but told you to do that, didn't he?"

Annie looked at Jason, and for a moment it seemed as though she would fall apart again. But she offered up that same awful, trembling smile—and said: "That's right. That's just what he said."

And that was it for Annie Waggoner for the day, and as far as Jason was concerned it should have been how it went for all of them. There were beds, up on the top floor of the farmhouse, and given as they'd all walked through the night, Jason said they should all at least get a bit of sleep.

Annie was the only one to take Jason up on his advice, and they helped her up the two flights of stairs, to a suite of attic rooms. They would each have a room—small, tidy with a decent mattress, a tiny window low on the wall below the eves . . . But Ruth and Albert both demurred for the moment.

"I never take coffee before bed," said Albert, and Ruth agreed that she wouldn't sleep either. Albert said he would stay outside Annie's door, if it was acceptable for him to smoke.

Jason said sure and suggested they all move to the sitting area by the west windows. Albert shook his head no.

"I will be all right," said Albert. "Why don't you two spend some time together? Without me lurking about. You can talk about your 'wounded souls,' yes?" He laughed at his own joke. "Leave me be," he said. "Madame Waggoner bears watching over . . . given everything. But I will be all right."

Four

"How was Crete?"

They'd found their way to the front porch of the farmhouse, looking out over the meadow, and both leaned on it, peering across it to the hills beyond.

"It's not much changed," said Ruth, "since we were there."

Jason nodded. "Didn't think it would be. Crete's been a quiet place since old King Minos's days."

Ruth laughed.

"Not that quiet," she said. "I couldn't get our villa. Not at first. An English family was finishing their holiday there and the 'blighters' wouldn't budge." Jason laughed at that. Ruth continued: "So I was nearly two weeks in a dreadful little room in Sitia before I could persuade the owner to let it to me."

"Is it still Evangelos?"

"Indeed," said Ruth. "Evangelos and Ariadnh. I am sorry to say they didn't remember me."

"That's fine," said Jason. "We kept to ourselves, as I recall. And it was a very long time ago."

"Not that long," said Ruth. "Just twelve years."

"Thirteen," said Jason.

"That's right. Thirteen."

It was after the Armistice.

Jason had been writing to Ruth, more or less regularly for nearly a year before that, and Ruth had been writing back more regularly than that. At first the letters from Jason had been platonic, jaunty in their tone. He made a joke that the other fellows in the squadron had sweethearts they wrote to, and he didn't want to feel left out. And he hoped that Ruth was well, and he'd been thinking of her, and he thought she ought to know. Ruth had been thinking of Jason too, but she also took care to make her letters back seem just as carefree as his. She told him rather more about business than was interesting——and made jokes about how flying a biplane over No Man's Land was nothing compared to keeping one's fortune intact in No-Ladies-Allowed America.

By the time the war was finished, Jason—improbably to his mind still among the living—found the letters had taken an altogether different tone. Ruth was the one who suggested that they meet in Crete, and Jason wrote back to say he'd be there.

And on the appointed day, he was there. They were both there, thirteen years ago.

"It was lonely this time," said Ruth, "without you. I thought you would come. From your letter. I thought you would come."

"I thought I would too," said Jason. "I'm sorry, Ruth. Things took a turn after I sent that letter."

"It's all right," she said. "You were trying to save me. You did save me. I was nearly captured you know. In Frankfurt!"

"Really?"

"You would have been proud of me. I crashed a car!"

Jason smiled, turned so his right hip leaned on the railing and crossed his arms.

"You don't say."

"It's not that difficult, car-crashing," said Ruth, and Jason laughed and agreed.

"I hope Zimmermann treated you right," he said.

"He did."

They were quiet a moment. "Do you have a cigarette by any chance?" asked Ruth.

Jason shook his head. "All out," he said.

"Wine? Whiskey? Opium?"

He shook his head at each and laughed at the last.

"What," said Ruth levelly, "has happened to you?"

"I guess it's a change, isn't it?"

"It is," said Ruth. "You look younger . . . maybe not than when we first met—" when they first parted, at the other farm, the Thorn farm "—but from Crete. Younger . . . maybe stronger."

Jason smiled at that, but it was a different sort of smile. "That'd be strong," he said. "You were—"

"What's happened to you?"

"What happened? Well. I spent some time here. With Orlok."

"With a Juke."

"No," said Jason. "I told you, it's dead. I'm talking about Orlok. His people."

"Who aren't here either." Ruth reached over and put her hand on his. He turned palm up and curled his fingers with hers.

"I am so much better," he said, and looked right into her eyes. "And you will be too."

They walked together down the steps and out into the meadow. The grass was ankle high, still green from the recent rain but not likely much longer before the winter came. Jason held Ruth's hand tight as they walked.

"You remember when we parted?"

"Which time?"

"I guess I owe you an apology for both times." Jason looked down at their feet. "First time . . . well I was a boy. Lost my ma, not more than two months earlier. And then . . . well, Germaine Frost . . . the Eliada business . . . Mister Juke. After all that . . . I just wasn't strong enough."

They looked down toward the road, and beyond it: the faint line of the Isar River, which would soon enough take to Wallgau and Munich and the rest of the wide world.

"Crete now. That was something different."

"It was."

"Not entirely though." Jason looked at her. "You remember when we met? The very first time?"

"On the riverboat."

"That's right. Heading in to Eliada. You commented on my name."

"Thistledown."

"Thistledown. You knew all about my pa—Jack Thistledown. Infamous gunfighter. Good eye. Strong arm. Could hold his liquor. Well, until he couldn't . . . But you didn't know about that part. As far as you could tell, he was a great hero. Like old Theseus. Or Heracles for that matter. I always thought that was half the reason you took a liking to me. I don't know if I ever told you how bad that offended me."

Ruth started to apologize and Jason stopped her.

"I'm not offended anymore. But we had another talk—years later, in Crete. You remember the one?"

Ruth let go of Jason's hand. "I remember the one where I told you I loved you."

"You did tell me that," said Jason. "I haven't forgotten that. Do you remember the hero talk?"

"Hero talk? Do you mean when I told you you'd been a brave pilot, and how—"

"You told me I was a hero," said Jason. "More than a hero. You called me a superman. Told me I was unkillable."

"I think I called you a god," said Ruth. "A God of the Air."

Jason grinned wryly. "That's right."

"We were making love," said Ruth.

"I remember," said Jason. "And you talked afterward, about the fine, unkillable babies we might make. Your stock and my own."

"It was just talk," said Ruth. Jason reached over to take her hand and when she pulled away, he leaned farther and took hold of it.

"Coming off that war, I didn't see myself as a hero," said Jason. "A God of the Air. I flew a biplane, and I was passing good at it. More than passing, I'll give myself that. And I didn't get killed. But back on the ground—and for many years on the ground, you have to understand—I felt more like my old pa, than I did any hero. Or good breeding stock, even. My pa . . . he wasn't any of those things."

"So I offended you again."

"I took offence," agreed Jason, then appeared to think about it and added: "Not offence. I took a scare. It scared me, that word did. Hero. You know that Germaine Frost used to call me that? Her hero?"

"No," said Ruth.

"Well she did. She had reason, too—she'd opened up a jug of the Cave Germ in the town of Cracked Wheel, and it'd killed everybody there but me. So it made a kind of sense. I was immune. I was a hero. Eugenically speaking, that's what I was."

"So you believed that I was like that awful woman?"

"Your father was," said Jason. "Nils Bergstrom was. You might just have been. To look at it another way, I wasn't what all of you expected me to be. Not in the light I saw myself."

"You didn't say any of that when you left."

"No," said Jason, "I didn't. I just left. And for years, got to work trying to prove myself right."

They stopped and looked back at the farmhouse. From where they stood, they had an excellent view of the mural on the front: the long snake-like dragon, the hero clad in mail, grasping it about the throat. It was still dreadful, Ruth thought.

"But I was wrong," said Jason.

"I beg your pardon?"

Jason turned to Ruth, and took her hand in both hands.

"You were right and I was wrong. That's what Orlok has showed me. You see that painting up there? That's what Orlok did to the Juke. Just took hold of it, and tore off its mouths and limbs until it died. Couldn't stop him."

Ruth looked away—away from Jason and that painting—back at the long drive to the road.

"And Orlok," said Jason, "is my brother."

Ruth deliberately untangled Jason's fingers from her own.

"Where is your brother Orlok now, Jason?" she asked quietly. "Is he here right now?"

"He's not here."

"What about your other brothers and sisters?"

"I got no others," said Jason.

Ruth turned to Jason.

"I know that sometimes they can be hard—impossible—to see. Or to notice . . . Orlok's people. I spent more than a day and a night, failing to notice your Catherine. Is she by any chance here now?"

"No."

"Are any of them here now?"

Jason looked around them.

"None close by."

"But some are around. Within sight."

Jason nodded. "Some."

"Can you show me?"

"Sure." Jason pointed toward the fence. "See?" he said, and Ruth said, "Ah." There were five pale figures, sitting in a row along the fence, looking away from them. "There," said Jason, and pointed across the meadow to a shed. On the rooftop, two others, peering into the distance . . . toward Wallgau, and the Isar.

"Is that all?"

"All in sight."

"So there are others out of sight?"

Jason shrugged.

"Where is Orlok?"

"He's a bit farther off," said Jason.

"Where?"

Jason stepped in front of her so she couldn't look away. "Ruth, I am trying to tell you something important."

Ruth sighed. "Jason," she said, "what you're trying to tell me is that you've let the Juke affect—infect you."

"Ruth—"

"This isn't real, Jason. You were right to begin with, and I was wrong. You're not a hero—"

"Ruth?"

Ruth tilted her head to hear better.

"What's that?" she said.

The sound of truck engines started to rise, and coming from behind a copse of trees, Ruth could see the first of them.

Ruth pointed to the roadway.

"What is that?" she said.

It was . . . five . . . six . . . eight . . . eleven trucks, making their way in a line along the roadway, and the first was turning up the drive. As the others slowed, men poured from the backs of some of them, and then disappeared below the line of the fence.

Jason froze, looking at them, and then tugged at Ruth's arm. "Inside," he said, and then led Ruth back to the house, keeping low until they reached the wall.

"I didn't expect it this soon," said Jason as they made their way to the back of the house. "I wouldn't have let you stay so long if I'd known. I'm sorry. I guess that fellow meant it when he said goodbye."

"What fellow?" asked Ruth, and Jason said: "Joe. Nazi fellow. Come from Berlin, by way of Munich."

"Munich—?" Ruth thought for just an instant, then nodded. "Of course." The battle at *Rottmannstraße* wasn't between communists and brownshirts. It was with Orlok's people. And whatever they'd said publicly, whatever the *Polizei* reported, the brownshirts knew full well who'd killed their comrades.

And they knew where they had come from.

Ruth and Jason hurried around the house and inside, to the kitchen.

He looked straight at the doorway to the front hall. “Where’s the rifle?”

“What?”

“The carbine—Zimmermann set it down there this morning. Remember?”

Albert had done that, after Jason’d asked him to. And sure enough, it was gone. Jason shook his head in frustration, and opened up a drawer under the counter. He pulled out three boxes of ammunition, then hurried into the hall and picked a rifle.

“Go upstairs,” said Jason, “find Zimmermann and Annie, and get them down here.” He pulled back the bolt and began stuffing bullets into the magazine. “I’ll hold them off.”

“With one rifle?”

Jason looked at her. “Don’t worry. I can shoot. It’s in my blood.”

Ruth shook her head in disbelief. “Give me some shotgun shells,” she said, and when he did, she hurried through the front hall, picked up the shotgun there, and loaded it as she hurried up the stairs.

Albert Zimmermann’s rifle was gone. And so was he.

Ruth only determined that after a thorough search of the rooms upstairs. Annie was asleep in her room when Ruth found her, and claimed that she had no idea what had happened to Albert . . . she’d been asleep the entire time, she said. But given Annie’s confession . . . Ruth kept the shotgun with her until they’d checked the last room.

And even then, Ruth asked: “Did you harm Albert?”

“Why would I do that?” Annie asked, and Ruth said: “Why did you kill Aguillard?”

“I didn’t harm Albert,” said Annie. “I don’t know where he is if he’s not up here. Do you think that maybe it something the Juke would do?”

“*Make* him do, you mean?” Ruth ran a hand through her hair. She thought about Jason. “It’s possible.”

“We haven’t taken any precautions against it,” said Annie.

“No,” said Ruth, “we haven’t.”

Albert had run off. The carbine, Ruth recalled, was gone from downstairs. If Annie hadn’t harmed Albert—and she was inclined to think that she hadn’t—then there was a good chance he’d left, and grabbed that weapon on his way. Even if it had no ammunition . . . What was it he’d said?

Bargaining power.

"Is that gunfire?" asked Annie, and Ruth nodded. There were several cracks—they sounded like knots of wood bursting in the fire from the farmhouse.

Ruth stepped over to the big window—close enough to peer out but not enough to make a target of herself. It gave a view of the meadow and the drive from the road.

One of the trucks was stopped, just at the gate. The rest bunched up on the road behind it. That first was askew on the drive, as though it had just run off it, maybe slid halfway into a ditch. Two forms were lying on the ground next to it. At least two, and possibly more. Ruth didn't dare get closer to the glass to find out.

"We need to get downstairs," she said. "We're trapped up here."

The crack of the rifle fire was unmistakable as they mounted the stairs to the ground floor. It was coming from a sitting room off to one side of the stairs. Jason was there, crouched below a windowsill . . . rifle aimed outside . . . firing off shot after shot, pausing to reload. He hadn't noticed Ruth and Annie as they peered through the crack in the door, so Ruth announced them and said they were alone.

"I've killed five," said Jason. "Five shots, five down."

"Well that's something," said Ruth under her breath, and then more loudly: "Albert Zimmermann's gone. I've got Annie here with me. What should we do?"

Jason dug into the box of ammunition for more bullets.

"Huh," he said, and reloaded with a brisk efficiency. Outside, came more rifle fire, and a windowpane shattered above Jason's head. Jason levelled the rifle, chambered a round and pulled the trigger. He repeated three more times, even as another windowpane shattered.

"Ruth," said Annie, and Ruth turned. Annie was pointing at the front door. The handle was turning. And it was opening on a slow sliver of light.

Ruth raised up the shotgun and took aim. She didn't shoot. She had hope, dim hope, that it might be Albert, come to rescue them. But the figure, silhouetted against the light, wore a cap of the sort that Ruth recalled from Munich. He had a pistol, and started to raise it. He wasn't Albert.

The recoil as she fired was nearly enough to knock her off her feet, and the shot went high and to the right. But it was enough. The door swung wide, and he fell to the ground, and his pistol clattered to the floor. Annie stepped forward and scooped it up and raised it in both hands to aim outside, firing again. She stepped back into cover.

"There are a lot of them," said Annie.

Ruth moved against the doorjamb and leaned around to peer out.

There were a lot of them. More than Ruth could count at a glance—spread across the meadow, some crouching, some popping up to shoot. At least a score of them. Probably more.

"Jason," said Ruth, "there are too many."

"There are a lot," said Jason. "Didn't expect them so soon. Orlok . . . I thought we had at least two days for them to gather. Damn, damn. You have to get out of here, Ruth."

"Out where?"

"The back door," said Jason. "Damn. I hoped Zimmermann'd be here. The truck. You remember where the truck is?"

"Yes."

He was finishing loading, and he popped up again and fired three shots quickly out the window. "Take the truck out back. Pile in the two of you. You got to go to the valley," he said, "through the pass. Zimmermann knows the way, it'd be better if he was along. But it's not too hard to find. There's an old road. Out the back of the farm. Bumpy. But you got to drive fast, because they'll be on your tail. You got to get through the pass."

"The pass?"

"Right. You'll meet up with Doc Waggoner," said Jason. "That *Société* of his. You'll get to see how dead that Juke is. And with any luck . . ."

"You know the way, Jason." Ruth stepped forward. "You drive."

Jason shook his head. "I have this to do," he said.

"You'll die," said Annie. "There's too many."

"There's not," he said, and he looked at Ruth. It was likely only for an instant. But his eyes flashed, and the light of the day caught him in a way that seemed to glow. It made a halo about his hair, and he smiled, in a way that Ruth had not seen . . . not since he had stepped into the dark cellar at Eliada . . .

"You know, Ruth," he said. "You've always known."

Ruth stepped close to Annie, and reached for the pistol she'd taken. She handed it over and took the shotgun from Ruth.

"I have," said Ruth, and before Jason could say anything else, she chambered a round and aimed the Luger at his foot.

She wasn't as good at this as Jason, not even as good as he'd been those years ago when he'd done it for her. Ruth had to fire three times, hitting the floor with all three, before the fourth bullet finally hit flesh.

Five

It was a cold morning at the farm, and colder in the mountain pass.

Even once the sun had been up for some time, the road was still in shadow of the steep slopes to either side, and the tall pines blocked out more light still, and more heat. But Andrew Waggoner was bathed in sweat, under his double-filtered gas mask and his body coverings . . . under the weight of the pack.

He was doing better than some of the others for all that. He worried the most about Kurtzweiller, the oldest among them, the least fit. Twice, Kurtzweiller had pulled the gas mask off, let out a visible puff of air and drew it in again. Andrew kept a close eye on him after the first time, which happened at the foot of the pass. He also kept a watch on Dominic, although not for fear he'd expose himself to the mountain air. Dominic was fit—closer to the age of a man that those gas masks had been designed to protect in the trenches of the war. So he was able to get enough wind through the two filters that he could keep a steady pace.

Trouble was, Dominic's pace was too steady. He pulled well ahead of all of them, with a nervous energy that made Andrew think he was trying to escape.

"Bergstrom's the only one," he reminded Dominic when he caught up with him, "who knows this route. Stay close."

Dominic apologized. His eyes behind the goggles weren't all that contrite, though, and Andrew understood the impulse.

"There had been a time that we did not dare go through this pass," said Bergstrom, as he slipped on his own mask—a simpler face mask that did not cover the entire head—and they set out in the pre-dawn after that first night in the farmhouse. "Men were losing themselves.

And even wearing protection . . . the youth who were in the valley would not let one escape. That is why we needed Jason to go in. Now . . . well, now you are here."

At its narrowest, the pass was nearly a gorge, with rocks climbing high and straight—and here, Dominic could not be restrained. Although he was carrying one of the heavier packs, he ran straight ahead. Lewis strode purposefully after him. Andrew stayed alongside Bergstrom, who was keeping an eye on Kurtzweiller bringing up the rear. At least there was no losing them. The gorge was a straight line forward and back.

And when it finally opened up, the sightlines were clear.

And that was the moment that Andrew first thought of it: to rip the mask off himself, dig into his bag for some wasp-sting venom, just so he could see the view more clearly.

The valley was deep and green, falling away before them and rising up again beyond to a row of peaks that this time climbed higher than the treeline—high enough in the distance, that some were capped with snow. Before that, woodland lay patched with brilliant alpine grass—patched further with gold of turning leaves. Directly below, Andrew could make out what he thought were rows of trees—possibly the orchards that were supposedly a part of the estate here. There peeked from this snatches of still blue waters. Dominic and Lewis were not far off, holding their hips and gazing at the place, which if Andrew had succumbed to temptation and removed his mask, he might have thought were some vision of imagined paradise.

Bergstrom touched his arm, and when he had his attention pointed Andrew to the right, along a road a little further up slope.

"There," said Bergstrom, pointing more emphatically and more specifically, toward a break in the trees where at first all Andrew could see was the peaked roofs, the stone walls of the chateau climbing over the trees, and . . . something else . . . "There is your Juke."

An exultation.

That is how the gentlemen of the *Société de la biologie transcendantale* would finally apprehend their first extended encounter with the Juke.

Even Manfred Kurtzweiller, wheezing behind his mask, did not tarry long when Bergstrom pointed out the huge tripod from which the Juke was suspended, poking just above the highest peak of the chateau. They ran like schoolboys along the roadway as it crossed the slope of the valley—as they circled the massive chateau, where Johannes Bergstrom had once practised his psychoanalytic methods amid the firm, smooth Aryan flesh of Hitler's youth.

Bergstrom in fact made a note of precisely this as they circled the building, and came upon the space of ground where the carcass hung.

"This is a cathedral of the mind, of the soul!" he cried, tearing his mask from his face as they stood before the Juke. "And the flesh!"

Thinking back on that moment only a short time later, Andrew would understand that Bergstrom had come upon a mania, not so different from the one his brother Nils had exhibited back at Eliada, suckling juvenile Jukes. Johannes seemed to recognize that himself an instant later, and he shrugged.

As they stood before the great, dangling carcass then, for the first time, Andrew was of a more forgiving frame of mind.

"How long has it been there? Dead, I mean?" asked Andrew.

"Months," said Bergstrom. "Four. Or so."

"There's very little sign of decay," said Lewis.

Andrew and Dominic looked at Lewis. "It's covered in flies," said Dominic.

It was so. The carcass dangled from ties on the tall tripod made of tree trunks, stripped down . . . tied here and there with winding rope, and swarms of fat flies hung around it in clouds . . . crawling on the flesh, or the surfaces of the creature if it weren't precisely flesh . . . such that it seemed to move itself, as a living colony of insects. It was hard to see detail through the goggles of the gas mask—but to Andrew's eye it seemed to writhe like a living thing itself, a great, torn sheet that was as big as a circus tent.

"It's a thing of beauty," Andrew whispered, and Bergstrom, the only one among them so far unmasked, looked at him and nodded reverently.

As the day grew longer, the *Société de la biologie transcendantale* went to work. Dr. Lewis unpacked the Leica, loaded it up and commenced photography . . . circling the creature, drawing in close where parts of it dangled near the ground, waving away flies to photograph an orifice or a torn, hardened membrane. Dominic and Kurtzweiller brought out sample jars, and saws and shears, and collected samples where the creature hung low . . . and later, higher up, as high as Dominic could climb on the tree branches.

Andrew's inquiry was more circumspect. He produced a notebook from his bag, and spent perhaps an hour simply circling the assembly—recording observations about its size—and at times, recollections such as they were of the living thing that he had seen in Eliada, for that instant before he and Annie fled the mill and stepped into the Kootenai.

He spent some time very near—particularly, near to what he determined was one of the thing's mouths. The Juke he had seen in Eliada had many of them . . . how many? No reliable way to tell, even applying the accrued wisdom of the Decameron system. But this one had just three that Andrew could count, and another five appendages that had suffered amputation.

He came near to one, dangling not more than five feet off the ground, and delicately touched its edges. It was circular, like a lamprey eel's, as he remembered . . . perhaps twenty inches in diameter. He wore gloves, but it had, as he could tell, a texture near to rawhide—slightly less flexible than cartilage. He lifted it, so that he could look inside.

The gas mask confounded him in this . . . its lenses fogged with his own exertions. He could see, and touch what seemed like teeth . . . sharp needles, like the claws of a housecat, running in what at first he thought was two rows but then determined might be a single one, spiralled. He reached further in, and encountered what seemed to be a sphincter, barely large enough to admit a finger . . . certainly not a thumb.

He removed the gas mask, but not before taking other precautions: one of the remaining shots of adrenaline, followed for good measure by a drop of wasp venom, administered near the elbow of his half-crippled arm.

He thought he might have screamed. At that point, the gentlemen of the *Société* all stopped in their own inquiries and regarded him quietly, like giant, curious insects in their paraphernalia. But he waved them off—and gathered himself from the ground, to return to the carcass, to that necrotizing maw.

Now Andrew found another familiarity: a perfume that he had not smelled so strongly since . . . the Thorn farm, when he operated on Ruth Harper? No. Sooner than that. He recalled the cabin, where the insensate Lou-Ellen Tavish rested, thick with a Juke . . . still alive before Andrew took a knife to her, and in trying to save her, hastened her death. Then, he hadn't thought of that smell as a perfume, but now—he wondered how he could have thought of it as anything else? Even in death, a floral sweetness issued from the maw. Andrew wondered, were it not for the pain, his racing heart—would this scent draw him to the lie of Heaven again, as it had before?

Andrew made a thin smile. It was a good thing, he thought, that he wasn't a praying man. He gathered his notebook and, from his doctor's bag, calipers, scalpels, and other instruments of dissection—and meticulously, marked down his observations and measurements, drawing diagrams as necessary.

He only slowed when the sun began to set, and Bergstrom suggested they all go inside for a meal, and to meet the others.

Six

"Wer sind diese Männer?"

"They are biologists," said Bergstrom.

They were all standing in the front hall of the chateau . . . Bergstrom in their midst . . . On the stairs, a tall man with a mild, notably triangular face, wavy brown hair combed to the side. Andrew didn't recognize him but Kurtzweiller did. *"Hermann Muckermann."* Kurtzweiller whispered it, his voice muffled further by the filters. *"We meet at last,"* he added.

"Why are they wearing masks?"

"They insist, Mein Herr. They have been examining—"

"I know what they have been doing," said Muckermann. *"We have been watching from the music room. All day. They do not need the masks."* He pointed at Andrew. *"Their Neger wasn't wearing one."*

Andrew was wearing his now—the adrenaline injection had worn off almost immediately, and the wasp venom's effect had long ago devolved from pain to a dull itch—but it wasn't tightly fastened, and he shrugged it off now.

"Pleased to oblige," he said in English.

"Doctor Hermann Muckermann. This is Doctor Andrew Waggoner," said Bergstrom. *"He was in Eliada."*

Muckermann nodded slowly, looking at Andrew as though he wasn't quite prepared to believe it was he. Kurtzweiller took off his mask next, and at that, Muckermann turned immediately to him. He smiled hesitantly, raised a finger as though trying to remember, and Bergstrom obliged: *"Doctor Manfred Kurtzweiller."*

"We have met," said Muckermann. *"A long time ago. And you sought me out in Berlin, not long ago . . . did you not?"*

Kurtzweiller said that he may have.

"Well. Good. Now we are both here. And we can sit down for a meal."

Muckermann led the *Société* through a hall, a set of long, empty rooms and finally into what might have once been a respectably sized ballroom.

But it had been stripped of finery. The windows were high, and bare. The curtains had been ripped down, and rods dangled askew. There were glass doors leading out onto a patio, and past there, a view that contained the entire valley—dark again in the twilight, but the distant peaks were now lit golden with the setting sun. Next to that door, there was a small table with a hand-wound phonograph player atop it. Behind them was another staircase, sweeping to an upper gallery.

And in the middle, there was a long table, with chairs that didn't match one another surrounding it. In the middle of the table were three ceramic jugs, and a covered silver platter. It was set for seven.

"Sit!" commanded Muckermann, opening his arms and raising them high, and looked at Andrew. *"Even you, Neger Waggoner! Even you!"*

Andrew didn't let himself rise to it. He thanked Muckermann for his hospitality, and after setting down his pack with the rest of them, next to the stairs, took a seat next to Bergstrom.

"Did you know about him?" he asked quietly, and Bergstrom said he didn't.

"I only knew about Plaut," he said.

"Plaut?"

"You will see," said Bergstrom mysteriously.

"You are surprised," said Muckermann, as though he had overheard, *"Doctor Bergstrom?"*

"I did not expect you here, it is true," said Bergstrom. *"I thought you had done with this project."*

"Well," said Muckermann, *"in that you were wrong."*

"I did not know you had come," said Bergstrom.

"Perhaps Herr Orlok does not tell you everything." Muckermann took his seat at the head of the table. He lifted one of the pitchers, and poured from it into the goblet set next to his plate, and indicated that the rest of them should also do so. Dominic reached for one nearest him and poured for Lewis, then Kurtzweiller, and then Andrew. When Bergstrom had poured his, Muckermann raised his glass in a toast and Andrew followed, then sipped. It was water.

"Do you enjoy our wine?" asked Muckermann.

"It is water," said Kurtzweiller, and Muckermann shook his head.

"Were you to have come here without those masks . . . were you to have engaged your faith . . . you would taste the grape. You are faithless, Manfred." He narrowed his eyes. *"As you were when we knew each other. In Berlin, before the War."*

Andrew looked at Kurtzweiller, who lowered his eyes sheepishly.

"May as well tell," said Kurtzweiller. "Herr Muckermann and I are acquainted from our youth. We attended certain meetings."

"Certain meetings?"

"The *Germanenorden*," he said. "It was a curiosity in my youth."

Andrew nodded. "We've all had those," he said.

"I did not stay long with them." Kurtzweiller repeated himself in German.

"Nor did I," said Muckermann. *"Of course I had my other faith. My Catholicism. But that was not for you, Manfred."*

"We all take our own paths," said Kurtzweiller. *"I am a scientist. I am moved by the majesty of nature."*

"Biology," said Muckermann. *"Which of course explains your desecration of the Host. Tell me, Manfred. What did you learn, tearing apart its corporeal form?"*

Kurtzweiller looked at Andrew now, and then at Lewis, and finally at Dominic, and then back at Muckermann. *"We found no skeletal structure, beyond teeth,"* he said.

"And they are more like claws," said Andrew. *"Made from something like keratin, not bone."*

Lewis interjected. *"We have collected samples of tissue, which although significantly necrotized should prove useful for analysis at a later date. But—"*

Muckermann interrupted: *"You don't answer my question. I ask you what you learned, and you tell me what you have observed!"*

"Observation precedes learning," said Kurtzweiller.

"And observation is not learning," said Muckermann, *"without reflection. Without perhaps finding the capacity for reflection."* He took a sip from his goblet. *"What might you have learned? I will tell you the answer to save you time. You have learned what it is, to stand before God."*

"It is an animal," said Andrew.

"Spoken," said Muckermann, looking at Andrew at last, *"by an animal."*

Andrew drew a breath, and found his fingers drawing tight on the edge of the table.

"That wine is going to your head," he said in English. He lifted his own goblet, and the nearest jug, and poured the water back, with exaggerated care. "*Vergib mir,*" he said. "*I had forgotten you lacked the capacity for the languages of men. I will try and be clear. In words such as you might understand.*"

Muckermann did not respond, so Andrew continued.

"*Here is what we have learned, Mein Herr . . . after much reflection. We have learned that there may be no God to pray to, no God that will strike us down if we do not pray. But there is a great parasite. We have learned that even wise men might bow down before this thing, and even chaste women might lie down for it.*

"*We have learned that when this happens, when a woman spreads her legs . . . the parasite lays its eggs in her, and steals her uterus, and so propagates itself. We have learned that it will do this in men too, laying its eggs in flesh as a botfly might. We have learned that it then turns to the kin of those men and women . . . and commands them, like the queen to her colony of ants. To look after its worldly needs. The needs of its flesh.*"

Muckermann smiled, hesitantly at first, then laughed and shook his head.

"*Animal,*" he said. "*Do you not know that we have studied this creature? That true men have looked upon it? Of course, there is flesh, and it eats to sustain it. Of course, it borrows our flesh to transmutate. All these matters are points of observation, of the workings of a magnificent biological machine. And I will say that for a time, I thought the same: that it was simply the machine. That it was a blasphemy. How much easier is it to believe that? That the touch of the profound, the spiritual, come from a thing such as that, is merely a mechanism. And must perforce, be a lie.*"

He turned back to Kurtzweiller.

"*Which of course is a fallacy. It may be a lie; it may not. If we rely solely on our senses . . . our observations . . . calling the numinous a lie is easy. For we may then separate ourselves, and deny it, and seek our spiritual engagement elsewhere, or worse, through cynical materialism, forego the spirit entirely. I followed this reasoning also, for a time.*" He emptied his goblet and poured himself more of the water. "*But in the manner of our faith . . . the discipline of my Jesuit order . . . I soon came to understand that this was not enough.*"

Dominic nodded slowly. "*You are employing the Ignatian system of discernment of spirits,*" he said, and Muckermann snapped fingers and pointed at him.

"*Indeed! One of you a good Catholic. Jesuit?*"

"*Taught be one,*" said Dominic and Muckermann smiled broadly.

"Yes. I spent much time in Berlin," he said, *"after we lost our hold on the valley. It seemed to me that we were meddling with a demonic force—a thing that would take us from God. It seemed to me as though it were seducing me, as it might well have seduced the others. And so I left—I fled—and continued my work at the Kaiser Wilhelm Institute, and left the work here to Doctor Bergstrom . . . to old Plaut.*

"But in the absence, I felt . . . a yearning . . . what I thought might be a calling: a seed, that was either of doubt, or of faith in the everlasting." Muckermann took a deep drink. *"And so I meditated upon it and upon the questions that Saint Ignatius had devised. Was this what God would want of me? To deny the Word, without allowing myself to entirely hear it? Was hiding here, reading dispatches from Doctor Bergstrom, a truly courageous act of faith? Or its opposite?*

"Thus it was that I resolved to return here . . . and live, in the manner of the völkisch ideal . . . as Orlok has revealed it." He emptied his goblet once more.

"And so I think I have learned. That outside—" he made an encompassing gesture *"—it is machinery, but it is machinery of divinity. And it is but a part of God's true machine. Now revealed unto us. We men. Perhaps not you, Neger."*

"You worked all of that out by yourself?"

"It was revealed to me."

Andrew sat up a little straighter. *"How?"*

"I do not need to explain myself to you."

Bergstrom put a hand on Andrew's arm. "This doesn't matter," he said in English.

"It matters," said Andrew quietly, and then, in German: *"How can you know? You have only looked inward."*

Muckermann set his elbows on the table on either side of his empty plate. *"I came to a decision,"* he said, *"to draw closer to God. I observed you, Doctor, doing much the same thing, through the entire day—also come here. To what? Beyond communing with the divine?"*

"To understand."

Muckermann smiled.

"It is the same thing," he said.

Bergstrom cleared his throat, in what Andrew took as a naked attempt to change the subject.

"Is there food?" he asked.

"Have you brought any from Herr Orlok?"

"No."

"Then only what you see before you," said Muckermann.

Bergstrom lifted the cover off the platter. It was not precisely bare: there were some apples, rotted brown . . . and there was the remains of a carcass—a rabbit perhaps?—that had long ago dried out, and in any case appeared picked clean. Entirely rotten . . . desiccated . . .

But it was all old enough that it carried scarcely any odour, to mask the sweet perfume of the air in this place.

"Shall we pray?" asked Muckermann. *"Give thanks, for this bountiful feast before us?"*

And with that, the air was filled with a crackling sound—and then music that was, to Andrew's ear, all too familiar.

"Plaut," said Bergstrom under his breath, as the music from Stuttgart filled the ballroom, and the naked creature by the phonograph began to dance.

"Oh, Herr Plaut," he said.

This too: exultation.

The song was the same as the one that had filled *Hauptbahnhof*—unmistakably. But it had a constraint, an orthodoxy to it, not surprisingly, as this was no improvisation, but performed by a proper orchestra, a German vocalist singing the lyric. Andrew took the fork from his place setting into his fist, and pressed the tines of it into his thigh. He knew on a level that he ought to press it in harder . . . to jam it hard enough to break skin . . . but the music, the memory of the thing that had happened in the train station . . . his own inclination, said otherwise: *Wait.*

Andrew wished he had his notebook, and thought about getting up to fetch it from his bag—just across the hall, at the base of the stairs. There were observations to record. He was salivating, at a scent that seemed to suggest a stew, filled with meats and herbs, redolent with garlic and perhaps fruits—maybe apples. He looked to the platter, thinking that he might now see it—that Muckermann's insistence that it contained a bounty might now be borne out. But that was not so . . . it was the same collection of offal . . . dried and rotted . . . that he had seen before. Looking at it did nothing to diminish his appetite.

And there was Plaut—or rather, the creature that Bergstrom had identified as Jurgen Plaut.

The first moment Andrew looked on him, he was struck with the simple oddity of a man, small in height but wide around the middle . . . greying hair, too long, and askew as though he'd slept badly on it . . . and naked. He was bent over the phonograph, having just set the needle on the cylinder, and as Andrew watched, stood straight and looked back at him.

In the swell of the song, Andrew looked away . . . perhaps to confirm the smell of the food against the evidence of his eyes . . . and when he looked back, the thing that was Plaut was grinning at him, a dozen steps nearer, and still staring, with eyes that were all pupil, black chips of obsidian. He swayed, his hands in the air, and Andrew was inclined to do that also, lift his arms in some kind of praise. Instead, he pressed the fork tines harder into his thigh—not quite enough to drive the vision from his mind, but enough to quiet the inclination.

Muckermann showed no such restraint. Plaut had come around the table to find Muckermann and embrace him, as he stood, and clasped his hands over his head. Plaut began to sing along:

"In our small beach basket, in shade from the sun
"We hide in there together, where our love has begun."

Other voices joined in, as the lyric moved to describe two lovers on a sunny beach, snuggling under canvas and perhaps laughing at the others at water's edge—so unfortunate as to be alone with nothing but the emptiness of nature.

Other voices: Johannes Bergstrom, his eyes cast to the ceiling; Lewis, head bobbing in rhythm as he broke key and rhythm; and Kurtzweiller, who had also risen, to reach across to the platter, and take what for an instant seemed a shining plum.

It was not just those voices, though—it seemed like a chorus, of angels perhaps, their voices carrying from the heavens.

And Andrew thought, or rather heard:

Stop waiting.

Choose.

Hermann Muckermann had made a decision. Andrew had to give him that.

The Jesuit had looked upon God—upon a demonstrable lie of God, by a mechanism which he and his cohort had understood well. He had understood it well enough that he was able to cast it away—to remove himself from its influence, and return to himself and his work. He had returned to his other work—curatorial work—and in so doing, turned his eye back toward that transformative moment. And free of influence, he had dug into the matter . . . into his own soul and heart . . . and he had made a choice. To return and to see. See if it were really God, or a revelation from God, or just a demon, a simple animal. Just a lie.

Andrew had to give him that.

And had there been a moment, there in the dining room, he might have confessed that through his own life, he had done much the same thing: fled from Eliada, and the Juke, and America his birthplace. And through those years, Andrew could not look away either. In his own way, he had gone through his own ordeal—not Jesuit, not Catholic, but not wholly secular either. The *Société de la biologie transcendantale* was not only about understanding an organism—was it? Its manner of inquiry . . . perhaps it would have been better to spend the time in meditation, and to have simply looked into themselves rather than the lenses of microscopes.

That might have yielded more useful meaning.

And it might, thought Andrew as Dominic touched his shoulder, and leaned over him to touch his wrist, not be too late to discover that meaning.

Maybe—

Andrew cried out, as Dominic pulled the table fork from Andrew's thigh and stabbed it again, and pulled it out and pressed a wadded napkin onto the fresh wound.

"We have to go, Dr. Waggoner," said Dominic. "Look!"

Andrew pushed down hard on his new injury and pushed his chair back. There was blood—not a lot, he'd missed an artery, which was a blessing—and the pain was extraordinary . . . worse than the wasp venom.

He swore at Dominic, who now had his arms under Andrew's, and was trying to lift him.

"Look!"

Andrew rose to his feet—the motion sending a wave of pain up through his hip now—and looked to where Dominic now pointed.

The room had filled up.

Standing at the stairs were maybe a half-dozen people, naked as Plaut. Perhaps they were the same as they'd seen the night before at the farm—

perhaps they were others. It was difficult to tell, as these ones seemed to be caked in mud and twigs—as though they'd been rutting in the woods outside. They barely seemed human, but for their voices . . . raised up in a chorus.

Streaming in from the front, there were others . . . likewise, singing and swaying. More appeared around Plaut and Muckermann—standing close, moving in an orgiastic harmony. The words of the song had shifted too—no longer German, maybe not a language at all . . . a moaning and hissing sound that still seemed to follow the melody, but drew deeper, and higher.

Kurtzweiller, Lewis . . . they seemed oblivious to all of it, or rather they seemed to be swept up, as a clutch of young people came to lay hold of their arms, and guide them back into what seemed a throng of more.

"Manfred!" Andrew shouted. "John!"

Kurtzweiller looked back at Andrew, and smiling, shook his head. Lewis seemed not to have heard. He raised his hands with the others to the song, and danced.

"Come." Dominic led Andrew away from the table, and this time, Andrew followed. Limping, they made for the wide doors to the patio outside, and stepped through them into the twilight.

"Can you smell it?" asked Dominic. As he said the words, Andrew could: a terrible cloying stench that carried the notes of the stew he thought he'd smelled—but now felt septic, gag-inducing.

"Jukes," said Andrew, and Dominic nodded.

"I remember this smell from Iceland," he said, "from the ruined church building. It is just the same."

Andrew winced and adjusted the napkin on his leg.

"You really got me a good one," he said. "I might slow you down a bit—"

"That is all right," said Dominic. "I'm running on an empty stomach. We'll go as fast as we can."

"Where?"

"Far," said Dominic.

And with that, Andrew Waggoner and Dominic Villart set off from the chateau, as fast as they could, downslope. Although the sky overhead was still bright, the ground was as dark as night, in the shadow of the mountains to either side. The ground was clear for a space . . . then levelled, and they found themselves amid trees, neatly planted. These were the orchards.

They cleared the orchards and loped through taller trees, and along a meadow, and then through a thicker forest . . . and they stopped, finally, when they had no choice. They came against a high fence. Andrew leaned against it, and gingerly removed the cloth, to probe the wound. It still bled, and hurt ferociously, but it wasn't bad.

"This fence," said Dominic. "You know what it is?"

Andrew looked up. The fence was high—he could see the top of it against the sky. Maybe twelve feet? It was steel, and looked fairly new.

"The Juke compound," he said. "The original one. Where they bred these things. They made concentric rings of fencing. This is the outermost."

"We have stumbled into it," said Dominic. He tested the fence, shaking at it with both hands. "Past here, the centre of the mystery." He turned and slid down the fence, to sit beside Andrew. "We should go in."

Andrew regarded him. "We'll need protection," he said, and Dominic shrugged.

"We seem to have gotten this far," he said.

Andrew dabbed his injury. He wished he'd managed to bring his bag.

"It does sting," he said. "What did you do to yourself? For pain? To stop the Juke . . . ?"

Dominic showed him his left hand, and the ring finger.

"See?" he said, and Andrew squinted.

"You tore the nail off," he said, and Dominic nodded.

"I don't want to see any more ghosts," he said.

"Well that's one way—"

And Andrew stopped. They both stopped, as the glare of a bright torch light struck them through the bars of the fence, then vanished, and finally returned, and held.

"Bitten bleiben sie im Licht!"

Dominic helped Andrew up, and gripping the fence with one hand Andrew raised the other in supplication to the order—as he squinted into the encompassing glare.

Seven

Pain is an ordinary thing. And in this aspect, it is extraordinary.

It is the most common experience among us. Perhaps it is common to every living thing. It is one of the few universals—at once a proof of life, and a warning of death.

Pain is the snap of a trap on a leg. It is a cut of a sharp knife into the soft flesh of a palm. It is in the simple kinetic consequence of a bad fall on sharp rocks. It is an elbow, shattered by a tree branch. It is a shattered heart.

Or a bullet, lodged in a foot.

"Why?" said Jason Thistledown.

He saved that question, only asking it after directing Ruth Harper past the old guard shack to where the road climbed into the mountains—after Annie Waggoner had done what, to his mind, was a passable job pulling off his left boot and binding the foot underneath it. There were men on their trail, but they were on foot for now, so Jason reckoned there was a moment of leisure, to get at least the beginning of an explanation from Ruth as to why she'd fired a Luger into his foot as she had.

"You were out of your mind," said Ruth. "I didn't think a slap in the face would be enough." She glanced over, before returning her attention to steering the truck past a particularly tricky drop. "You would have done the same for me."

Jason shifted on his seat, and winced. "I wasn't out of my mind," he said, and looked at Annie, who didn't meet his eye.

The truck slowed as the road narrowed. Ruth looked warily out her window.

"Did people ever drive along here?"

"Horse and wagon was more common," admitted Jason. "But sure they did. Don't worry. It's a clear run." He grimaced as the truck hit a bump. "More or less."

"You having made it so many times," said Ruth. "What are we in for, Jason?"

Jason shut his eyes. "There's a house. Big mansion. Bigger than your pa's, back in Eliada, I'd say. There should be a pretty big crowd of folk."

"Andrew?" asked Annie, and Jason nodded.

"Doc Waggoner and his *Société* friends too. You'll be able to say hello to him before lunch."

The roadway widened and improved somewhat as they approached the pass. The rocks loomed above the trees, the opening in the mountains impossibly dark in the bright Bavarian morning, and Jason found himself grinding his foot against the floor of the cab—just to sharpen the pain. He shut his eyes again, for longer this time, and when they opened, they were in the depths of it . . . the bottom of a gorge, or so it felt, the warmth of the sunlight gone. Jason had to remind himself to breathe—he felt as though he were underwater. He looked to his right, and up. There, somewhere up there, was the old route he'd taken his first time into this place . . . following a pencil-line on a map, to take some photographs, and make some notes for fools who thought they might master a Juke.

He had made this run many times since then. Not up there, in the trees, clambering up and down rock falls. But down here, in the little road that carried into the valley.

It was a fine run, he thought, and gave his ankle an extra twist, hard enough to bring tears and even a sob.

They were met by a procession, or rather joined, as they left the pass and drove along the edge of the valley, toward the great mountain chateau where Orlok had moved. Jason recognized them all, and called out by name, as they flocked around the car: Ari and Gertrude, Victor and Friedrich, and on and on, until he could no longer differentiate, and it was all pale flesh, flitting in and out of shadow from the trees into the sunlight . . . until finally—Catherine.

She wore a gauzy throw—the one that she favoured—and a pair of oversized boots, pulled from one of the S.A. men, when the *Volk* first came from here to the farm. She climbed up on the running board next to Jason and leaned in the open window and squealed a curse in French when she saw Jason's bandaged foot. The truck lurched forward, then stopped, and Catherine stumbled off, and Jason gasped.

"I'm sorry," Ruth said. As Catherine jogged along to catch up, Ruth asked Jason why they were all naked.

"It seems very cold to go without skirt and trousers," she said. "Is it because of the nudist colony?"

"I reckon," said Jason. "Bergstrom used to use that as part of the therapy here before they brought the Juke."

"That therapy for the naked folk, or for Bergstrom?" asked Annie.

"Germans quite like nudism," said Ruth. "It lets them see who's fit and who's not."

Annie shook her head, and Catherine finally caught up.

"Who hurt your foot, *ma chère*? Nazi Germans?" she asked, in her improving English. "Did you kill them for it?"

Jason shook his head.

"I did not kill very many of them," he said.

"I shot him in the foot," said Ruth, but Catherine didn't hear her, or pretended not to.

"Did you fight them off?"

"I killed some of them. The *Volk* on guard at the farm may have killed others. But not many. We didn't have enough there. And they had guns. They came sooner than we thought they might and there were more of them than Orlok figured. We're going to have to face some of them."

Catherine nodded seriously, and as the car slowed for the bend before the main drive, she stepped off and stumbled only a moment before she bolted off to the side into the crowd, who was now drawing back from the road, the truck.

"Charming girl," said Ruth.

"Sure," said Jason, and then they said little else. For the road climbed past a stone wall, through a gate, and to the front of the chateau. Orlok was there on the steps, and it was Jason's experience that he always did kill a conversation, walking into a room or out onto front steps.

"Was ist mit deinem Fuß passiert?"

"My foot got shot," said Jason. He was standing on the steps to the

chateau, his arm around Ruth's shoulder as it was since she'd helped him out of the truck. Orlok nodded.

"You did not drive them off," he said, and Jason agreed that he hadn't. *"I would have fucked them, and driven them off,"* Orlok said. *"I would have broken their spines and stacked them in the corner like a woodpile. Am I not right, Markus?"*

Markus Gottlieb agreed that he was with his usual enthusiasm, then, also as usual, looked off shyly, hands stuffed in his trouser pockets, and withdrew a few steps, in this case toward the doors to the house.

"Who are these?" asked Orlok, looking to Ruth, and then Annie, and Jason told him: *"Annie Waggoner and Ruth Harper."*

Orlok nodded as though he understood and Jason imagined what he might say: *You were distracted by your weakness for your sweetheart.* He didn't say that, and Jason didn't correct him with more details. Orlok summoned them all inside, and started to lead the way.

"Hold up," said Annie.

Orlok stopped, and looked around, and Annie repeated it in German. *"Where is my husband?"* she demanded.

Jason tried to step between them, Annie Waggoner and Orlok, but his shot foot made him slow. And he saw that she had brought the Luger from the truck. It dangled in her right side, half-hidden in her skirts. The way she was holding it, Jason wasn't even sure if she knew she had a gun.

"The Neger Waggoner," said Orlok. *"Not here."*

"He was here though."

"He is not here." Orlok's eye fell on the gun, then went back to meet Annie's. *"He left before I even arrived. Before we arrived. His friends are here somewhere. Ask them."*

Annie looked at the Luger—as though she had indeed first noticed she had it, and considered its implications. Having done so, she knelt down, set the gun on the steps in front of her.

"There are a lot of men coming," she said, *"along that road. I need to find my husband before they get here."*

Orlok laughed. *"They will not get here. We will stop them as they enter the pass. They will all die."*

"Are we ready?"

"We are ready. You told the French girl of your failure. She has told the

rest." Orlok turned back to the house. *"Come inside with your women, to tend your wounds, and let us finish matters."*

Jason made it inside and to the door of an old library room before the pain got to be too much, so Ruth helped him to a chaise longue there, and to lift his feet. Annie set off to find Andrew's "friends" and promised to be back. She wouldn't hear of it when Ruth insisted that she stay. Jason worried about her too, but was happy to not have her in the room with him. He didn't like the look in her eye.

"I'm sorry," Ruth finally said when she sat down herself, on a chair at the head of the longue. "That must hurt."

"It sure does," said Jason. He craned his neck around—it was hard to see her. Most of the room he could see consisted of some bookshelves—a low table with an old Dictaphone recorder on it, next to a metronome whose unclipped arm listed to one side. Finally he rolled on his side, propped himself on an elbow and looked up.

"You should lie still then," said Ruth.

"I will, from here on," Jason promised.

Ruth seemed to approve. She smoothed some hair that had fallen over her forehead, and half-smiled in a way that affected Jason unexpectedly. It might have been the light from the window. But whatever it was, he was put to mind of those early days, before he even knew her name, and he'd walked past her on a train trip, and . . . well, he was young, and so was she, and it'd affected him then too.

"So that," she said, "was your brother."

"My brother?"

"Orlok, wasn't he?"

"Oh. That was him, yes."

"Interesting fellow," she said. "Doesn't speak English?"

"Lots of people don't," said Jason and Ruth nodded agreement.

"He's impressive. Big. Imposing, one might say. Do you think he's the *Übermensch*, really?"

"He—" Jason was going to say that Orlok was exactly that: a superman, the top of the heap. Jason certainly did understand that to be true, on some level at least. Orlok was a kind of a God. Jason . . . well, Jason was too, or so said Orlok some days. But as he thought about it again, he wondered.

"He's a strong man," said Jason. "Strong-willed. But he should have guessed that Goebbels would send men as soon as he did. I should have guessed."

Now Ruth did smile. "I'm not as sorry as that," she said, and when Jason asked her what she meant, she indicated his foot, now stretched out over the edge of the couch.

"You were a little out of your mind," she said. "The pain's done you good."

Jason thought about that. "How come you're not?" he said.

"I beg pardon?"

"How come you're not out of your mind? You're thinking I smelled the Juke smell off him and started thinking crazy stories, and now this jam of pain's pulled me out of it. You might be right. But what about you?"

Ruth frowned and thought about that a moment.

"I think that I am a bit mad, if you want the truth of it," she said. "I can't count the number of people outside . . . not the same, from one minute to the next. I suspect that if we tried to tell each other about the things that we saw during the drive from the farm to this place . . . well, I am going to guess that the Decameron system would tell us two different stories."

"Do you want to—?"

Ruth shook her head. "I've had enough of the Decameron system," she said. "And I daresay I've had enough pain to keep my head clear for a very long time. Clear enough to think things through." She got up and went to the window. The view carried down to the old orchards, the depths of the valley . . . eventually, over to Austria. She put a finger on the metronome arm, pulled it down. It swung back with a pronounced *tick*.

"Although I do wonder," she said, "if my thinking has been at all clear since Eliada. Since the Thorns. Have you ever wondered about that?"

Jason sighed. He rolled over onto his back, sending another wave of pain up his leg.

"You've done all right for yourself, Ruth," he said.

"I have," agreed Ruth. "But most of that has been a result of simply holding the reins. I was given great privilege, in my birth . . . my inheritance." She flicked the metronome again. "But you didn't answer my question."

"Have I wondered whether I'm that smart? Whether I make the best decisions?" Jason winced and propped his bad foot on the toe of his good one. "I don't think I made a bright decision, ever."

"What about your brother Orlok, now," said Ruth. "Do you think that Orlok has a better plan here than he did for you at the farm? I mean for defending us?"

"He's got folk watching the road," said Jason, "through that pass. They'll rain boulders down on anyone who tries to get through. And they got their own guns."

"Do they know how to use them?"

"Some do."

"Reassuring," said Ruth. "What if some get through?"

"It's been awhile," said Jason. "They haven't yet."

There came a knock at the door then, and Ruth got up to see.

It was Annie, and two of the men who'd come with Andrew: the American, Lewis, and the Austrian fellow, Kurtzweiller. Doc Bergstrom was with them too.

Bergstrom came in first, and immediately looked at Jason's foot. He dug around under the table and took out a medical bag.

"This used to be my consulting room, long ago," he said. "It's good to see that it has been kept relatively intact. May I examine your foot, Herr Thistledown?"

Jason nodded sure, and sat up to help remove the bandages, but of course Bergstrom told him to hold still.

"Andrew left two nights ago," said Annie.

"That's correct," said Lewis.

"He left before supper, when we arrived," said Kurtzweiller. "They both did. We thought they might have gone back to the farm."

"You didn't think to look for them?" asked Ruth and Annie said: "Oh no. No they did not."

Ruth rose and took Annie by the arm, guided her to the chair—as though she might want to cry, or scream. He couldn't see whether she was . . . and after a while, he wouldn't be able to tell if she were either. He was doing enough of it himself, as Bergstrom dug into his foot with a pair of forceps, and pulled out the bullet that Ruth had put there. Jason wondered if he might lose the foot, and asked Bergstrom what he thought about it while he sewed up the hole and applied new bandages.

"I do not think so," said Bergstrom. "You have a strong constitution, Herr Thistledown, and infection . . . well."

"We'll just wait and see then," said Jason. He pulled himself onto the couch. He and Bergstrom were alone in the room at this point: during the shouting and cursing, Ruth had suggested the rest of them step out into the hallway. "How long's it been?"

"Since . . . ?"

"Since you started this. Seems like hours."

Bergstrom looked at his pocket watch. "Just over an hour," he said. "I am sorry. It can't have been comfortable."

"I'm used to it," said Jason. He sniffed the air. There was that scent . . . but there was something else. He sat up farther, to try and see out the window. There didn't seem to be much movement. He sniffed again.

"What is that smell?" he asked.

"It is close in here. Would you like me to open the windows?" asked Bergstrom. He stood up and went to the windows, and Jason shouted at him not to.

"Why?"

"It's fresh-cut hay," said Jason.

Bergstrom nodded. "Yes. I smell it too."

"Was taught to sniff that in the war," said Jason sharply. "It's phosgene."

"Phos—" Bergstrom's eyes widened. "Oh!"

"Poison gas," said Jason. "The brownshirts didn't come through the pass. They took that footpath that brought me here the first day. And they're gassing us."

Although it hurt fiercely, Jason sat up the rest of the way and got to his feet . . . or one foot . . . and with Bergstrom's help, hobbled to the door to the main hallway. Ruth and Annie were there, with Andrew's friends. Jason motioned up the stairs, and together, they climbed. Then it was down a hall, through a room, and to another set of stairs—this one spiral—to a fourth floor, and then a fifth floor in a turret. Jason could barely move when he got to the top, last of all. The room was small, not more than nine feet across, and round. Windows on four sides.

Annie spotted the first squad, positioned high on the ridge behind the chateau. There looked to be three of them. They were all wearing hooded gas masks with breathing boxes. They had set up what Jason recognized as a Livens launcher—a tiny portable mortar, that Great Britain had employed in the war. As they watched, there was a *whump!* and a flash, and then very shortly, another.

It was phosgene. Jason had never experienced an attack, but he knew what to do: the smell of fresh-cut hay meant you slung your gas mask on as fast as possible, and if you could, got to high ground.

Looking down at the grounds, Jason knew it would be impossible to see, but it was easy to see its effect. There were three people on the ground, holding their faces. One girl—it looked like she was convulsing, while another person hung close to her. She might well survive, thought Jason, if the gas shelling stopped.

But as he considered that, another *whump!* came from the hillside, and with this one, came the sound of shattering glass. They had sent it downward—likely pierced a window in one of the lower floors . . . filling the chateau with gas, sure as they were slowly filling the valley.

It might not kill them, but when the rest of the brownshirts finally came through, none of Orlok's *Volk* would be in any condition to resist.

And in the best case, the five of them would be trapped here.

"Oh Andrew," said Annie, and Ruth held her close, and Jason thought: *And then there's Andrew.*

Eight

He was nearly a boy—surely, not any older than Dominic. Dark blond hair, combed to one side, with a wave in it. A bit of fat in the cheeks, but otherwise youthfully lean. He introduced himself as Arnold Deutsch. Andrew met him, alone, the morning after he and Dominic were gathered from the valley and brought here. It was still in the valley—and from the number of gates that they passed through, Andrew guessed it was in the very middle of the valley. He and Dominic had been taken finally across close-cut meadow, to a door, sheeted with metal that entered into what seemed like a bunker. It was difficult to apprehend more. Their captors—two of them—kept their torchlights pointed to the ground, so that all Andrew and Dominic could see were the concrete blocks of the wall. Inside, the walls were also concrete, although painted a pale green. They were escorted along a hallway, lit dimly by kerosene, but not far, and finally Andrew was placed in a room with nothing but a cot, a chair, and a little table holding a washbasin, and a chamber pot by the bed.

It was in this room that Deutsch visited him, in the morning after a silent attendant—a dark-haired man with a thin beard—cut away his bloody trouser leg, looked at the punctures in his thigh, cleaned them, and provided him with a bandage. Deutsch brought a folding wooden chair and a tray of breakfast: oatmeal, and a boiled egg. And a pot of coffee, with two mugs. He moved the basin aside and set the tray before Andrew.

"You have been looked after, Doctor Waggoner?" asked Deutsch, once he had introduced himself.

"Yes," said Andrew. "How do you know my name?"

Deutsch smiled. "An educated guess," he said. "We know you were in Munich. We know you came to Wallgau. It was only a matter of time before you entered our sphere." He poured coffee for Andrew, and then for himself. "We have no cream, I am afraid."

"I imagine it's scarce," he said. "This is the compound."

"I am sorry?"

"The compound where the Juke was raised, before it went all to hell here." Andrew sipped his coffee. It was strong, and dark, and it probably could have used some cream. "Another educated guess."

Deutsch laughed and clapped. "Yes, Doctor Waggoner! Very good. We are both excellent guessers today. We are in the compound where the German scientists were trying to contain the Juke, as you call it. I believe you named the Juke didn't you?"

"No," said Andrew. "I didn't."

"Ah. But you were there as it was named. In that little town of Eliada. They called it Mister Juke then, didn't they?"

"That's right," said Andrew. "The first one."

Deutsch nodded. "Named after something that was not it at all: a degenerate criminal family that may have been a figment of another's imagination itself. That's right."

"Mister Deutsch—Herr Deutsch. Who are you? What are doing here? This place is deserted. The Germans fled months ago."

"And my name cannot be more German. But I am not. I am from nearby, though—over the mountains, in Austria. Now who am I? I am like you." He took a drink from his coffee. "Not a physician. A scientist. My speciality is chemistry. I have an interest in psychiatry."

"And who are you working for?"

Deutsch took another drink from his cup, then set it down and poured more.

"This is a Nazi project," said Andrew.

"It was once," said Deutsch. "But as you yourself know, they were incapable of containing it."

"Who, then?"

Deutsch looked into his cup for a moment. "You should eat your breakfast, Doctor Waggoner. Before it goes cold."

Andrew dipped his spoon into his oatmeal and took a mouthful.

"Who are you working for, Mister Deutsch?"

Deutsch pushed his chair back a few inches, and leaned forward with his forearms on the table, as though about to share a confidence.

"We are Communists," he said. "Does this shock you?"

Andrew took a drink. "From Vienna?"

"Amongst other places. It is a worldwide organization."

"It doesn't shock me," said Andrew.

"Good!" Deutsch leaned back, rested his hands on his knees. The pose reminded Andrew of the one that Goebbels had struck, but seated—not standing defiantly. "We have taken up the research here, into the Juke phenomenon. It is a fascinating creature, yes? Such interesting behaviours . . ."

"What behaviours? It's dead."

"That's what you believe?"

"That's what I've been told."

"By who? Orlok?"

"You know about Orlok?"

"We do indeed," said Deutsch. "He killed one, didn't he? That creature they have curing up the hill. It is certainly dead. But this compound is not as empty as you might believe, Dr. Waggoner. It is a prize."

"There are other Jukes here? Living Jukes?"

"Not like that one, which is to say, not mature. But yes. We have been able to capture others."

Andrew pushed his bowl away. His appetite was suddenly gone.

"What is my status here, Mister Deutsch? Am I a prisoner?"

Deutsch started to answer, then stopped himself, and finally shrugged.

"It is best that you don't leave," he said. "But you are not a prisoner. Indeed, I am anxious to confer with you. As a colleague."

"Where's Dominic?"

Deutsch narrowed his eyes and tilted his head.

"Who?"

"Dominic Villart," said Andrew. "My companion. He was with me."

Deutsch's head tilted the other way.

"Why don't you finish up?" he said, and for the second time, seemed to stop himself from saying something else. "Finish your breakfast, and we'll see about that."

Arnold Deutsch left Andrew to himself for a few minutes, and by the time he was finished eating, returned with a change of clothes, tidily folded: grey trousers and a black sweater that both fit well, but had enough of a smell to them that Deutsch felt a need to apologize. They were borrowed from the only other researcher here Andrew's size. "Not a lot of time for laundry here," he said.

Deutsch waited outside while Andrew cleaned up and changed clothes. He had, he said, been thinking about what Andrew had said—about Andrew's question.

"Here is the trouble," said Deutsch. "There is no Dominic Villart. Not here. We found you last night alone. You had hurt yourself, and you were against the fence. But you were entirely alone. Do you understand this?"

Andrew said nothing. He clutched at the doorjamb to the room they'd put him in. Deutsch regarded him measuredly.

"Do you understand this?" he repeated.

"I heard what you said," said Andrew. "I don't believe it."

"Of course," said Deutsch. "Nevertheless. It is so."

"He brought me from . . ." Andrew stopped himself from going on. "I would like to talk to Dominic, please."

Deutsch shrugged. "There is not much I can do for you. There is no Dominic here. You came alone."

Andrew swallowed. "I did not," he said.

"It's all right. We have seen this," said Deutsch.

"This?"

"This delirium," said Deutsch. "Among ourselves . . . Not all of us, but those who were incautious in the beginning." He clapped a hand on Andrew's shoulder.

"You were incautious," he said. "You breathed the perfume of these things. You thought you could withstand a little, and when you failed to withstand a little, you somehow thought you could withstand more. And soon . . . you were lost."

Andrew shook Deutsch's hand from his shoulder, and Deutsch took a polite step back, but he continued.

"Your friend Dominic did not lead you here last night. This delirium did. It took you to the nest of the Juke. Or as close as you could get. Pressed against the fencing . . . If you hadn't hurt yourself so badly, you might have scaled it."

Andrew shook his head no. "I hurt myself—Dominic hurt me—so that I wouldn't be in a delirium as you call it."

"Ah," said Deutsch. "That flagellation remedy." He offered a pitying look. "Why not? It has worked for you before, so far as you knew. Pain. Adrenaline. It didn't matter, really, so long as it was a distraction, am I right?"

Andrew bristled. "It worked," he said.

"It comforted you so," said Deutsch, and his tone sharpened. "Doctor Waggoner," he said, "I swear to you that you came here alone. You believe otherwise: that you came here, accompanied by a young man, a friend yes? But you are addled. You do not know. And you know, I daresay, that this sort of delusion comes upon men who have smelled the flower of the Juke." Deutsch put his hand on Andrew's shoulder again and this time would not let go. "Pain might pull you free for a moment. But it is an escape. A respite. Not a cure. I would guess, based on our own research here, that you have never been cured."

"You would *guess*."

"I'm fairly certain, Doctor. If you were cured from your time in Eliada, truly free of the Juke, that you would never have continued to seek it out." Deutsch smiled thinly. "You would have run, like any clearheaded man, and continued your work as a physician."

"This is absurd," said Andrew. "I am a physician. But I'm also a scientist."

Deutsch released Andrew's shoulder, stepped back and clapped once.

"A scientist. Splendid," he said. "So are we both. I am new to this field. You have studied the Juke within the limits of your capacity for two decades. We both know what it does; you ought to know better than I. You know that it incites delusion. A terrible certainty of delusion, yes? You have fallen into it before yourself. Is it not possible, that you remain in the throes of that delusion now?"

Andrew thought about Molinare—the ghost that Dominic, and finally he himself had seen. Just days past. He nodded yes, it was possible.

"Now tell me: which would you rather do right now? Pursue this likely delusion about Dominic Villart? Which I will continue to deny, and you have no capacity to meaningfully dispute? Or return to the roots of your science, see all that is known about the Juke—things which have now been beyond your reach? Which I am prepared to share, Doctor Waggoner, to the fullest extent."

Andrew had nothing to say. Deutsch's smile broadened.

"Would you care for a tour of our small facility?" he asked, and Andrew finally had to admit that yes—he would.

The facility was not small.

The Germans had marshalled considerable resources to purpose-build the facilities. There were vaults, separately ventilated and otherwise sealed from the main compound, where juveniles were to be kept, and fed in a way that was entirely voluntary. They could be observed through thick glass windows, and Deutsch showed Andrew two of these. The rooms were much like Andrew's bedroom, absent furniture, and there was no way to enter them from within; there was a door that opened to the exterior.

There was an operating theatre—equipped for childbirth, of course. It was sky-lit, and did have a door to the interior as well: heavy and sealed, with an airlock between.

"At the beginning, the Germans here had at least an inkling that the Juke needed to be contained," said Deutsch, "or at the very least kept separate from the researchers. But that protocol was a thin line for them, and by no means permanent. Direct intervention was inevitably a part of the research, and with that, human subjects . . . and so . . ."

Deutsch was leading a new set of researchers—without the same imperative, with entirely different objectives. Interaction now, he said, was less of a risk.

"How many?" asked Andrew.

"Nine in the bunker," said Deutsch. There were more, he said—between fifteen and twenty—stationed on the southern slopes of the valley, guarding a pass that led into Austria.

"That's a lot," said Andrew, and asked how it was that they were able to operate undetected. Deutsch laughed.

"Undetected by who? The Nazis were long ago driven from the valley. Or do you mean Orlok? The children who look to him as their leader? That is not difficult."

"I find that difficult to credit," said Andrew. "It seems as though Orlok has the valley under his control."

"He inhabits it, with his children," said Deutsch. "But it is as difficult to hide from them as it is from a flock of birds. They might fly past you or over your head, but unless they have identified you as prey . . . as food . . . they will miss you. And right now, Orlok's flock is looking elsewhere."

"That's an interesting description," said Andrew. "A flock."

"You don't agree?"

"The Juke's a parasite. A flock of geese doesn't form a triangle because of a worm in their gut."

"Likely not," agreed Deutsch, "although who knows? I recall reading a paper seriously suggesting that geese are telepathic, and that is how they maintain their formations."

"You believe the Jukes are telepaths?"

"I do not believe anything about the Juke one way or another. But of course . . . Orlok is not a Juke."

"No," said Andrew. "Not exactly."

Deutsch smirked. "He devoured one. Isn't that right?"

"That's what he says," said Andrew. "How do you know that? He tell you?"

Deutsch shook his head no. "We've had time. And other resources. The Germans keep such complete records. We have retrieved some of them from that chateau . . . notes, photographs, and a collection of Dictaphone cylinders. Orlok is a much older project than the Juke, did you know that?"

Andrew said he didn't, and Deutsch told him that he doubted that.

They continued down a corridor and a wide set of iron stairs. Here, they finally met some of those researchers. One, a woman with thick Slavic cheekbones and a mouth that rested in a smile, was on her way from a room that Deutsch said had been purposed as an archive. There was another—a small balding man with thick spectacles who wore a fur-lined jacket, despite the heat—who was at work in the room, seated at one of three long tables, poring over one notebook and marking new notes in his own. He said something in a language that Andrew didn't understand, and when Deutsch answered back in the same language, he looked at Andrew and smiled. "Welcome, Doctor Waggoner," he said. "I hope this place meets with your approval."

Andrew started to answer but the man returned to his work, and Deutsch took Andrew's arm and drew him to the shelves, which were filled with journals—and to a glass-topped display case. In here were photographs and artefacts. Deutsch flipped a switch on the side of the case, and electric lights illuminated it. The photographs were in colour—records of a dissection . . . the subject splayed on a board, with pins holding four limbs and a tail. It measured twenty-five centimetres according to the legend at the bottom. Andrew looked at it, then back at the man going over the notes.

"He's Russian, isn't he?" asked Andrew. "The woman we passed too, yes?"

"You are an astute observer," said Deutsch. "Most of the workers here are, indeed."

"Most, but not all," said Andrew. "Albert Zimmermann, for example, is not."

"Oh dear," said Deutsch. "No."

Andrew stepped back from the display case.

"That's what you did," he said. "You sent Albert Zimmermann here . . . or rather, he ended up here, when you had him following Jason Thistledown to Africa. And when he told you about this work here, the Juke and Orlok and the rest, the Nazi Party project . . . you came here, to see for yourselves."

Deutsch cleared his throat and made eye contact with the scholar at the table. He nodded, gathered his notes, and left.

"Albert Zimmermann is in Munich," said Deutsch when they were alone. "With your wife, and Miss Ruth Harper. They arrived there by train from Paris yesterday morning. He is not among the people working here."

"But he is working for you."

"Of course. He told you that he deserted us, didn't he?"

"Yes."

"Did you believe him?"

Andrew sighed and shook his head. "I guess I did."

Deutsch smiled and nodded sadly. "It is understandable. And your instincts were largely correct. He did desert us. He also . . . avoided consequences."

"He saved his family you mean. From you."

Deutsch's smile vanished. "It is not so bad, Doctor Waggoner. He brought you Ruth Harper, and protected her from the others. And in so doing, he has brought you here. To the culmination of your life's work."

Andrew Waggoner and Arnold Deutsch spent the rest of the morning and part of the afternoon in the archive, and not much later, Andrew would lament the time spent there. That was not to say the hours were uninformative. They were very informative.

But they were also a distraction that Andrew found he could not resist . . . the room was like a tide pool where he was shut off from his past, and what might come. He remained there, until it was done with him.

The dissection photos in the display case were just a sample. There were files with dozens of photographs—of the same dissection, but also from microscopic slides—and also, of the living specimen that in its maturity Orlok would slaughter. Here, it was shown through its successive forms. First, a juvenile, just separated from its host—a creature like a lizard, like a cat, like a possum . . . but with slits up and down its torso, vestigial mouths such as Andrew recalled observing on the Juke he extracted from Lou-Ellen Tavish in the hills beyond Eliada. Another one, dated just six weeks later, as it occupied a different form—now vaguely bipedal, with long articulated legs and arms that hung about its side . . . a face that caused Andrew to recall that day in 1911 when he, along with the specimen Mister Juke, was awaiting a lynching on a hillside not far from Eliada. Even though it was only a photograph, Andrew felt he saw a different image each time he regarded it. Another, similarly configured, but larger—the notation at the side indicated a scale that would have put it at nearly four metres tall, even as it sat in a pool of water, three pairs of spindling arms, draped over thick legs with something like musculature, that twisted as tree trunks. Its face bent down, as though searching the shallow water for food.

Although it was in water, it was not outdoors. It seemed to inhabit a cavern, rather, or a large space that was for the most part dark. Light shone on it from above and from the front, casting long shadows across the pool, and against the nearest wall.

All of the photographs until the last were inside—the first two in the chambers that Deutsch had shown Andrew on the way to the archive—the final, in that great cavern that must have been the size of a cathedral.

The last one was outdoors, and at first, it might have been difficult to apprehend the Juke. The photograph appeared as nothing but a landscape, a riverside whose banks were closely encroached by trees under a brilliant blue sky. Not precisely a landscape—the river ran fast and shallow here, and there were two dozen figures standing in it, young men and women. They were naked, and they were beautiful: smooth sunburnt flesh . . . the men, lean and strong, standing straight, and all of them—judging them against the women—very tall. There were fewer women, but they were similar specimens according to the criteria of their genders—wide of hip, of ample of bosom. And all of them yellow-haired. Although by the angle of the photograph it was impossible to tell, Andrew speculated and Deutsch agreed, their eyes would all be blue. *Übermensch*.

It seemed as though they stood in the water, looking at a particularly bent tree on the bank. But that wasn't so.

It was the Juke.

All resemblance to a human form gone: where there had been a face, arms, now there was just a tangle of limbs and throats, something like a thorax that rose from the side of the bank and curved back over the water in a kind of crescent. The branches that extended over the heads of the beautiful German children flowered with mouths such as the one that Andrew had examined in death. This was the Juke living, hungry. A God, and its worshippers. Its *Volk*.

"That is in the innermost circle of fencing," said Deutsch as they looked at it.

"Where we are?"

Deutsch shook his head. "Two fences separate this part of the bunker from that place. The German researchers imagined that might be sufficient."

There was a lengthy account of the day that photo was taken, when the first of the *Hitler-Jugend* were introduced to the mature Juke in its enclosure. It was messily typewritten by someone clearly not used to operating a typewriter, in English. It went into great detail, including medical profiles of each of the youth: fifteen boys, twelve girls, ages ranged between fourteen and nineteen. All the picture of health and fitness.

Andrew read it through.

He read other things, in German, and in French . . . dissection reports, transcripts from the stack of Dictaphone cylinders that were stacked in a corner. Inventories. There was another section, devoted to the mystery of Orlok. This was entirely in German, and much of it contained in those cylinders. Andrew did ask about playing those, but Deutsch suggested that there might be something else that Andrew might be more interested in seeing first.

Andrew's leg ached as he got up from his long time seated at the table, but not enough to bother him. He followed Deutsch out of the archive, down another corridor, and another staircase, through a room that had been set up as a bunkroom. Three men were there, including among them the little one who'd been studying in the archives. He was lying on a lower bunk, reading a paper-bound book by the light of a kerosene lamp that hung from the bedframe. He noted Andrew's passing with a wave.

They continued through the room and down a flight of metal stairs, also lit by kerosene lamps, and through a room where generators chugged and the smell of engine oil hung . . . and then, through a wide set of steel doors, which opened into another room, cement-floored. It was long and narrow, with a high ceiling. One wall was a row of glass windows. Light flickered through these windows, illuminating the four men who sat at benches pressed up against the wall. Two were taking notes—a third, speaking softly into a small microphone, wired to a Dictaphone recorder.

"Have a look," said Deutsch, and motioned to one of the windows, and the chair in front of it.

Andrew approached, and sat as Deutsch moved the chair for him. Andrew leaned forward, and peered through the glass. He blinked and rubbed his eyes and looked again.

"Bonjour, Docteur Waggoner," she said, and he said, *"Bonjour, Madame Pierrepoint."* And behind the glass, she reached into her handbag, and produced a cigarette and a lighter.

"You are the Juke," said Andrew, and Madame Pierrepoint looked to one side, and looked back with a wan smile, and she nodded, because of course she was the Juke. The surviving Juke, that Deutsch and his people were cultivating, and hiding, somehow, from Orlok and his flock. He leaned back and spoke to Deutsch.

"What do you see," he said, "when you're looking through that glass?"

Deutsch asked him what he meant.

"Describe the specimen," he said.

"Ah. Very well. It is bipedal, roughly one hundred and twenty centimetres when standing. It has hair, all over its body, very thin and light—like the hair on the skull of an infant human. Its head, however, resembles to me more that of an elderly man . . . Its eyes are black. All pupil it appears, although dissection reports indicate that . . ."

"I read the report," said Andrew. "This is a Stage Two Juke."

"Indeed it is. But that is not what you are seeing, is it?"

"It's not," said Andrew.

"Fascinating."

"It's a woman. I know her."

"Ah ha. A mistress?"

"A patient. Lucille Pierrepoint." Andrew described Madame Pierrepoint's ailment, and the surgery and its complications. Deutsch gathered another chair and sat down beside Andrew.

"A mistress . . . a patient that you nearly lost . . . that you may indeed have lost, for you left her side and cannot say . . . Either way, the feelings conjured by the memory might be very similar. Guilt. Remorse. Fear. All, aligned to the imperatives of the parasite."

"I am not a parasite."

Madame Pierrepoint drew deep from her cigarette and crossed one leg over the other. She was seated on a wooden stool, high enough that her feet could not touch the ground, so her heel was hitched over the brace. She exhaled a halo of smoke and continued.

"That is a fundamental error you have made throughout your life in my company. I forgive you. But you are wrong, Andrew. I showed you Paris. I elevated your soul. I made you good. That is not what a parasite does."

"What is it?"

"It's speaking," said Andrew. "She's speaking."

"And what is she saying?"

Andrew looked at Deutsch. He was leaning forward, nearer the glass than Andrew, and sweat was beading on his brow.

Andrew considered an instant, then looked back at Madame Pierrepoint.

"I have taken nothing from you," she said. *"I have only ever given."*

"It's not clear," said Andrew. "I don't know what she's saying. I need to listen." He drew a breath.

"I need to go inside," he said.

Madame Pierrepoint waited while Deutsch brought the protective suit for Andrew. It was a sort of gas mask, but with a specific filter that was big enough to require a small suitcase, and it was attached to an oilcloth set of coveralls that fastened to boots and gloves made of rubber. He and two others assisted Andrew in dressing, while a fourth researcher—a small dark-eyed woman who introduced herself as Olga—donned her own suit.

"I need to go in alone," Andrew protested. Deutsch didn't like it. But finally, he agreed, on the condition that Olga would wait near the door and go inside at the first sign of trouble. And so Olga accompanied Andrew through another door that opened outdoors, on a small wooded gully, shaded by the western mountains and a stand of pine trees against the late afternoon sun. Olga pointed down slope, to a bunker wall and a doorway, next to the brook that fed into the wall through a steel grate, and when they stepped down to it, she produced a key and unlocked the door. Andrew stepped through. He tried to close the door behind him, but Olga shook her masked head. There was no discussion on this.

Andrew turned from her and moved deeper into the huge chamber.

It was vast—larger in volume than Andrew could apprehend, because lights were all trained on a single spot: a platform reached by gangways, near the glass through which he had just observed the Juke. The platform, he could tell, was really more of a pier; beyond it was a pool of water, fed by that brook.

Madame Pierrepoint stood on that platform, still smoking but having abandoned the stool. She waved at Andrew, and beckoned him closer.

"I don't think that's right, when you say you took nothing from me," said Andrew.

"Ah, you have been thinking about it."

Andrew raised his bad arm. *"This has never healed."*

"And that injury ruined you for surgery. Evermore." She nodded, then abruptly shook her head. *"I had nothing to do with that."*

"You inspired the men who did it."

"Only in igniting their bestial nature. I frightened them." She looked at him. *"I did not frighten you."*

"You terrified me," said Andrew.

"Not enough that you went off to hang someone." She reached into her handbag and removed a cigarette case. She opened it and offered one to Andrew.

"It wasn't you who terrified me," said Andrew. *"The Juke that did that is dead. And as far as I can tell, it could not speak. Any more than you can."*

"Have a cigarette," she said.

He shook his head. *"It's bad for my wind."*

"You would know." She took a cigarette for herself, and lit it from the tip of the one she was nearly finished. *"If I cannot speak, then why are you answering?"*

"I am hearing a voice."

"And you believe that the voice is not mine. Perhaps your own? An aural hallucination. Madness?" Madame Pierrepoint's face vanished behind a haze of exhaled smoke, and when it cleared it was the face of another. Elongate. An ancient, black-eyed thing that bent above a spindled caricature of human form.

"I elevated you," said the Juke, in perfect English. "And so you have remained." Its mouth widened, into an encompassing grin.

"Elevated. Oracular."

Andrew started to speak, but the creature waved a sinuous appendage and interrupted.

"It is not a lie. You saw Heaven in me, the golden city . . . the Dauphin . . . and it has never left you. You could not drive it away. Pain. Narcotic. A splash of cold river water, or that . . . bestial injury that you coddle."

"That's how I remain myself," said Andrew.

"Yourself." The Juke bent forward, its neck seeming to extend, as though it were engorging. "What would you have done, with only yourself?"

Andrew didn't answer, and the Juke set two arm-like appendages on the platform, so it hunkered on all fours. Now its face shifted, and it appeared as Molinare . . . as Dominic . . . as Jason Thistledown . . .

And finally, as Doctor Hermann Muckermann.

"You pursued the higher path, all your life past the day that we met. Even when those around you failed . . . and fell toward the bestial. Jason. Ruth. Even Annie."

"Annie didn't fail."

The Juke swept nearer Andrew, so near its wide black eyes filled his vision.

"Even Annie," it said, as it embraced him, "but not you, Andrew. You have asked the question, whether you know it or not."

"The question?"

"This: What would God want of you?" it said, as its eyes became as a pit—a familiar and alluring darkness.

"Whether God is me or your own private dream," it said, as Andrew began his tumbling ascent into it, "might the answer not be the same?"

Nine

The chateau had twelve bedrooms: eight on the second floor, another four on the top floor. Dominic Villart was in one of the four, with Hermann Muckermann, who was, he suspected, dying. Dominic thought he himself might be also, but if he was he would be dying more slowly; he had pulled one of the gas masks from the trunk over his head and fastened it properly before the horrors started. His throat burned and his eyes stung and that was that. Muckermann had resorted to a handkerchief over his mouth, and was coughing and weeping and choking before Dominic found him in the ballroom. Dominic took hold of him and moved him up the stairs, to this bedroom that faced away from the hillside . . . where he hoped the air might be clearer. It was a hard climb. Twice, Muckermann fell to his knees, and one of those times he retched bile down his shirt. But finally he was able to stumble to the bedroom, and fasten the door shut. He coughed and spat, and gasped on the bed where he lay. When he could speak, he demanded that Dominic give him his mask.

Dominic refused.

"If I remove this, I may soon be as badly off as you," he said. *"And you are not strong enough to breathe through this filter. See, you can barely draw a breath. This old mask would suffocate you."*

Muckermann glared at Dominic. *"I can't even see if you are joking behind those goggles,"* he said.

"I am not joking," said Dominic and then repeated himself, because it was also hard for Muckermann to hear him through the filters. In some ways, the old Jesuit reminded Dominic of Giorgio Molinare. Not as a lover; his two encounters with Muckermann since arriving were very different from Giorgio, who had been a decade older at least and had used that time to learn a certain languid generosity that Muckermann definitively lacked.

But they both carried with them an alluring air of wisdom, and they both presented, at least in Dominic's presence, a kind of hunger . . . a neediness of flesh and spirit. Perhaps that was what had persuaded Dominic to respond to Muckermann's advances. He was a poor lover and if they spent much more time together, would likely develop to be a bad friend.

But of course they would not spend much more time. They would not make love again, and their friendship now was as good and as bad as it would ever become.

Muckermann fell into a coughing fit, raised his arm to Dominic as though he wanted to say something, then fell to coughing again. Dominic lifted his feet from the floor and lay him down in the bed, and hushed him. When he continued to cough, Dominic thought about leaving him. The attackers would soon be entering the chateau, if they hadn't already. Wheezing old Muckermann would give Dominic away to anyone who stumbled by, whether they were looking for him or not.

He didn't want to turn his back on him though. Two days before, he'd let Andrew Waggoner out of his sight—they all had—and he'd vanished more thoroughly than even Ozzie Hayward and *Le Noir Qui Danse* had from Stuttgart . . . to the tune of the same song, as Dominic thought of it. Dominic had lost himself there too . . . but only himself, climbing the stairs with Muckermann that first moment.

So Dominic stayed, and Muckermann's coughing did give up their hiding spot. Dominic had locked the door with the skeleton key that hung by the wardrobe, and that bought him a moment as the handle rattled—enough time to pick up a chair from the other corner, hold it in front of him as the doorframe shook with one impact, and then another, and then cracked open.

"Herr Orlok!" exclaimed Muckermann.

Orlok stepped through the door. He had taken gas too, but the evidence of it was more difficult to discern. His lids were swollen, and he snuffled loudly, and his shoulders were bent, and he steadied himself on the doorframe as he came in. But he walked, and moved quickly enough when he did. He was entirely in possession, it seemed, of himself.

"Herr Muckermann," said Orlok, stepping past Dominic to the bedside. *"Your friends have betrayed you."*

"What friends?"

"Herr Goebbels. Herr Hitler. Their Nazis. They have come for us, and left you

alone to die a weakling, an old man." Orlok laughed, and then coughed. *"After everything you have done for them. They poison us like we are vermin. You also."*

Now Muckermann coughed. But not just once—again and again and again, so hard that he shook the bedframe. He tried to catch the sputum with a fold of the sheet, and his eyes shut tight, and it seemed to Dominic that he was also sobbing.

Orlok looked to the door, which hung half open onto the hall, and then out the window, which showed a view of the valley. And he seemed to make up his mind. He took Muckermann's head by the ears, and twisted it quickly, as though it might snap. Muckermann whimpered, and reached forward to grasp at Orlok's shirt—push him away. Orlok coughed, and that turned into a low growl, and he tried to twist again, and at that, Dominic understood what Orlok was attempting. He lifted the chair and swung it at Orlok's back. It hit hard in the middle. Orlok half-turned and let go of Muckermann's head, and seemed to see Dominic for the first time. He grabbed the leg of the chair and twisted it from Dominic's grip. He flung it to one side, and pointed.

"Give me that mask."

Dominic made for the door, but the chair was in the way, and Orlok was quick enough. One arm snaked under his arm and took hold of the opposite shoulder, and Dominic's feet left the floor as Orlok lifted him from behind. With his free hand, Orlok grabbed the mask by the filter and tried to yank it off. But it was well fastened, and Dominic felt his own neck twisting as the straps tightened.

Orlok saw it wouldn't work, so flung Dominic to the floor and knelt over him.

"Take the mask off. Give it to me."

Dominic obeyed this time, not just from the order . . . but survival. Orlok had driven the wind from him, and the filter on the mask wouldn't let him breathe . . . He felt as though he were drowning, and gasped when the mask came away. Orlok snatched it for himself, and drew it over his own head as he stood. He kicked Dominic once more in the ribs then turned back to Muckermann.

"Bitte," said Muckermann, and as he pulled a pillow from behind Muckermann's head, Orlok answered: *"Nein."*

At length, Dominic stood. This time, he did not lift the chair, but stepped quietly around it. He looked back at the bed—Orlok's immense form blocking out any view of Muckermann, but his feet, which twitched feebly—then turned, and stepped into the empty hallway. He sniffed, seeing if he might find any hint of the gas that had filled the lower floors. If there was any, it was thin this high. Or it might have simply been overpowered, by that other perfume.

One way or another, Dominic decided, he would have to get to higher ground now that Orlok had robbed him of his mask. Somewhere on this floor, he knew, there was a stair to a turret tower. And so it was that Dominic Villart turned his back on Hermann Muckermann, and set about saving himself by finding it.

The thump-thumping of the Nazi phosgene gas bombardment slowed and then stopped. Jason thought at first they might just have run out—or maybe figured that enough was enough. But it wasn't just that. The *Volk* had found them. It was hard to see that . . . you had to know how to look a certain way to see Orlok's people, and even then, they were easy to miss. The S.A. squads missed most of them as they emerged from trees or simply clambered up the rock face. The one in good view of the tower were simply overwhelmed—as a nude boy, his flesh livid with the effects of the gas, threw the launcher down the slope along with its operator. While the other two occupied themselves with him, two others, who one might have mistaken for birds, came from above. One took a rifle that had been set aside, chambered a round, and shot one of the S.A. men in the neck. Jason did not see what happened to the third squad member, but when he looked, the man was slumped on the rock, his mask torn away, and the *Volk* were gone again.

The end of the gas bombardment did not end the fighting. It merely signalled another phase. Having begun. Ruth drew their attention to the grounds where the Juke carcass still hung. Beneath and around that, more masked stormtroopers were advancing and firing into the chateau. There were bodies around them—more than before, naked and filthy, some coughing but too many still.

Jason cursed to himself. There were no guns in the turret room, and while he wouldn't have used one to shoot the gas squads for fear of giving away their position . . . he might have put one to good use now as the troopers advanced. Or if not now, when the attackers made it up the stairs.

And they would make it up the stairs.

Jason flexed the toes of his injured foot and winced as fresh pain shot from it. More than a gun, he found himself wishing for the oblivion that came living under Orlok's, and the Juke's, spell. Things had seemed a lot better from that perspective.

"Jason," said Ruth, "Annie, get down please."

Annie, peering out a window facing toward the valley, ignored Ruth, but Jason did as he was told. A face in the window wasn't as obvious as a rifleman there, but Ruth was right: it was still a risk. He slid back onto the floor between Bergstrom and Ruth, fast enough that he nearly cried out at the pain in his foot. Kurtzweiller crept over to Annie, and tugged on her skirt.

"Hide yourself," he said, and she shook her head, still looking out over the valley.

"Why would I hide myself from my husband?" she asked. "Here he comes."

"He's not there," said Ruth, and Jason chimed in:

"He's not, Annie. It's the perfume . . . the Juke carcass. It's playing tricks on you. Showing you what you want to see."

Annie smiled and shook her head, and repeated: "Here he comes."

"Here comes someone," said Lewis, who was nearest the stairwell. "Someone's on the stairs."

They all fell silent at that and listened . . . and sure enough, the wooden steps of the spiral staircase were creaking under heavy footfalls. Jason tried to get his good foot in a position that he might be able to move, do something, but he didn't have a sense of things. Ruth held her elbows close—she looked as though she were going to be ill. Lewis, meanwhile, stepped back so he would be out of sight of anyone coming up. . . .

The footfalls stopped.

"Do not shoot," said a voice that Jason thought he recognized, and that Kurtzweiller clearly knew well.

"Dominic!" he said. "No danger of that. Come on up."

The footfalls resumed, and soon young Dominic Villart emerged from the stairwell. Accompanying him was Albert Zimmermann, a gas mask dangling from his neck, and a carbine slung over his shoulder.

"Herr Thistledown," said Zimmermann. "I might have thought you would find the highest ground in a battle."

He held the rifle loosely, barrel pointed downward. Jason thought that might've been the same one as he'd filched from the farmhouse. But there were no bullets in that one. Over his chest, Zimmermann wore a belt of ammunition, and empty spaces indicated that there were likely bullets in the magazine now. This worried Jason more than it did Ruth.

"You abandoned us, Albert," she said. "Where did you go?"

Zimmermann smiled thinly. "Into this valley," he said. "Deep. I am sorry that I didn't say goodbye or explain myself. Matters had become pressing, and I needed to report."

He stepped around Jason and crouched in front of the window, looking out at the Juke, and with a sharp tap of the gun barrel, shattered the glass. He shouldered the carbine, sighted and fired twice, then changed his target and fired once more.

Kurtzweiller turned to Dominic for explanation as Zimmermann reloaded.

"I met him in the hallway on the top floor," said Dominic. "Or rather he found me. He might have shot me. If I had been armed I might have shot him."

"Good thing that you weren't," said Zimmermann as he stuffed the sixth bullet into the carbine. "We were both looking for the highest spot. It is safe from this terrible gas—and a good vantage point for me."

"He is not with the Nazis," said Dominic, and Zimmermann agreed with a sharp laugh. Ruth swatted at a fly that had landed on her cheek. She saw little to be amused about.

"You're working for the Russians," said Ruth. "You have been all along."

"No," said Annie, "I don't think he is."

"You are right, Frau Waggoner. I am working to protect my family," said Zimmermann. "As I have always."

He turned and shouldered the carbine, took aim, fired three more times and then stopped, and raised his head, and peered down, ducking back at the cracking of gunfire.

"What is it?" asked Jason, and Zimmermann said: "Orlok," then looked again and said: "No."

Only it *was* Orlok.

Jason peered down and saw him—striding across the grounds from the house toward the Juke, and he was firing a pistol—a Luger it appeared. Facing him were stormtroopers . . . not so many as before . . . and one or two of them were firing back. Everyone, even Orlok, was wearing gas masks. Everyone who was firing, was missing their marks.

And everyone who was not firing . . . well, they stood transfixed, in the shadow of the living Juke.

The flies peeled away from it like a black veil, swirling into the sky and spreading to the side as if drawn upward by an invisible hand. They filled the turret room too, radiating from the shattered pane where Zimmermann had broken the glass. Zimmermann pulled his gas mask back on, and Jason wished he had one for himself, though not for the flies . . . maybe the air that they were bringing, that was tricking him into seeing what was there underneath those flies, now revealed. He leaned hard on his bad foot, making the pain so bad that it brought tears. It did no good.

This was no illusion.

The sailcloth form of the Juke was writhing, and parts of it were falling away, crumbling like ash. Underneath, strands of wet pink flesh dangled low, and whipped to and fro. As he watched, one of those fleshy strands seemed to flower—and it fell farther until it touched the ground. Jason squinted. That wasn't quite right. It touched the naked buttock of a girl, one of the yellow-haired *Volk* who'd fallen to the phosgene. It quivered, and the flowering thing at the end took hold, and the girl's hip lifted off the ground.

She was not the only one. The ground surrounding the Juke was littered with *Volk* . . . scores of them. Some were dead . . . others merely collapsed and helpless, choking on the gas. More of the flowers . . . the mouths . . . dropped from the great tripod where it had been hung, touching first earth, then as though sniffing their way along, creeping across the dirt to a leg, or a belly, or an upturned face, and then the flower would latch tight, and lift. . . .

Jason swallowed, his mouth dry.

Every time it lifted . . . what it was doing was chewing . . . *digesting* the new offering left in its reach by the unwitting stormtroopers and their phosgene attack. In Eliada, that offering had come from the larders of the workmen and their families, brought into the cathedral of the sawmill. Here, it was simple slaughter. The sacrifice was human.

And the humans—the ones below who still lived—were starting to understand that. The pale forms so far below looked like nothing so much as maggots, as grubs, inching away from the reach of the Juke . . . writhing as one of its flowering maws took hold. Some of those screamed, as best as they could through their damaged throats, and tried to fight. As Jason watched, one of them had some success, tearing away the mouth that had taken hold of his pectoral. But its absence had left him flayed, and he squealed and wept as he tried to right himself—keep the raw flesh away from the dirt.

"Give me the rifle," Jason said to Zimmermann, and when Zimmermann asked him why, he pointed to that one. As Zimmermann stared, Jason took the gun, shouldered it and sighted. He fired three times. Hit twice.

For all the good that it did. The goddamned mouth returned to the corpse and continued feeding. Wordlessly, he handed the rifle back to Zimmermann.

"We can't stay here," said Ruth.

"We can't," agreed Jason. "But the house is full of poison gas. We got one mask in here and old Zimmermann's wearing it. No way out."

"I wouldn't worry," said Zimmermann, still looking outdoors. "We will not be here for very much longer."

"What do you mean?" asked Ruth.

"People are coming for us," said Zimmermann.

"People?"

Zimmermann turned around to face them. His gas mask made him look like nothing so much as a huge insect.

"My masters," he said. "You were right, Fräulein Harper. The Russians, the Communists." Carefully, he set his rifle down against the windowsill overlooking the Juke. "They are nearby. Some are here now. Such as myself. Please, Fräulein, do not be so . . . offended."

"I should be the one offended," said Jason. "I trusted you."

"No," said Zimmermann. "You took a chance with me. You said so yourself at the time. And largely, it has paid off. If you had wished it, I would have helped you escape from here with me when I took the plane. You did not wish it, so I did what you asked of me: kept Ruth Harper safe from the Nazis. I also ensured my own family's safety. By reporting. Will you blame me for that?"

"Scarcely matters," said Jason. "You've got the gun."

"And the mask," agreed Zimmermann. "I am sorry, Jason."

And with that, he lifted the rifle and started toward the stairs.

"I will be back," he said, "very soon."

Jason counted eleven mouths, descended from the middle of that teepee, but Annie spotted three more—not fully distended, but waiting high in the middle like the filaments of a much larger bloom. She had seen such things before—fleeing Eliada with Andrew at her side, in the rafters of the sawmill—and she readily identified these ones, with a cool precision.

"They'd come down and gobble up a pig," she said. "Suck the flesh off the bone."

Of course, that one in Eliada was fresh born, or near to it. This one was . . . what?

"Reborn," said Annie when Jason wondered exactly that.

Kurtzweiller and Lewis set to speculating on this Juke's apparent resurrection. It had, by all their examinations, appeared dead. But there was clearly living tissue in some protected segment of the necrotizing husk that Orlok had boasted of having killed.

It was Ruth who noted that the Juke in Eliada had appeared to be very resilient. "Even when hanged, the creature survived unscathed." Feigning death, she said, may have proven to be a very effective survival strategy in the long run. Particularly when resurrection followed.

The Juke grew still, or nearly so, and the gunfire, sporadic as it was, had ceased altogether. The fighters who still stood stepped back, and watched the Juke's distended throats pulse and quiver as they fed the thing so high above them. Only one approached the carnage, and of course that was Orlok.

Jason pressed his hands and face against the glass, as if that might afford him a better view. Orlok stepped carefully around the bodies on the ground, and finally knelt before one that the Juke had found. It was a boy . . . a fellow that Jason thought he might remember from as early as his first day here in the valley, but not well enough to place a name. Orlok bent close to his face, as though trying to hear. He sat up then, and reached behind his head to loosen the strap on his mask. He pulled it free, let it dangle round his neck, and bent forward again. Did he kiss the boy? Too far for Jason to say. But after that, he reached around and gripped the mouth, which had latched on the boy's thigh. As he pried, the boy screamed, and begged: "*Nein! Nein!*"

Orlok took hold of the Juke's throat next, and tried to tear at it. But he soon gave up at that too, and sat on all fours a moment, gasping. The feeding continued, as if he were not there.

"He murdered Muckermann," said Dominic, watching alongside Jason. "He tried to break his neck, but was too weak from the gas. Finally, it was just a pillow on his face."

Jason looked at him. "When?"

"Just before I came here. To escape that gas. See? That's my mask around his neck. He took it from me."

There was a *crack!* of gunfire again, and another, and then several more. Jason missed the effect at first, but Ruth pointed to the edge of the clearing, where one of the retreating brownshirts had just fallen and two others now knelt and raised their rifles to the side of the house. They fired twice before they too fell.

"Jason," said Ruth, and when he looked he saw that she was crouched down, as were Kurtzweiller and Lewis. Jason followed suit, and so did Dominic.

For the second time, Annie refused.

"Andrew," she said, beaming down at the gunfire. This time, Jason chanced to look himself, and then he looked again, and drew a quick breath, and he said it too.

"Andrew."

Annie made for the stairs, too quickly for any to stop her—let alone Jason with his gunshot foot. Jason was fast enough to stop Ruth. But Dominic went after her.

Ten

The mask was too hot, and close, and Andrew was sorely tempted to pull it off by the time they arrived at the chateau. It was one thing to wear it in the enclosure, at the riverside . . . something else to wear it marching up a hill on a rocky path, on a warm sunny day. He wanted to tear it off. And by some measures, it wouldn't make a difference if he did—any more than it really did when he finally yanked that other mask away, coming through the pass. But it wasn't just the smell of the Juke now. The Germans were using poison gas, that's what Deutsch said. Best case without a mask: Andrew would spend the rest of his life a patient in his own sanatorium.

He held back with Deutsch while the rest of his men, and women, moved forward to take the chateau. They were very skilled, these ones—one or two veterans of the War, but others had been responsible for a more specific sort of work. They were, Deutsch explained as they waited, well-suited to this task. "They are remorseless," he said.

Deutsch was careful never to say that they were professional killers who had come to watch over the bunker and his research. By not using the words he had, Andrew understood that Deutsch meant to help Andrew shield himself from the consequences of their actions. Andrew appreciated that, in the same way, he hoped, that Deutsch would come to appreciate his own omissions.

So they waited.

There was gunfire. Not as much as Andrew would have expected. But he had never attended a gun battle such as this . . . had been spared the war. How could he know one way or another? Deutsch was no help either.

"I am a chemist," he said. "I have learned over time not to guess."

Andrew had been applying that lesson himself, when it came to guessing the fate of Annie, and Ruth, and Jason.

There was nothing but to wait.

They were crouched behind a low ridge, well out of sight of the chateau, when two of Deutsch's comrades returned for them. In their coats and masks, they were hard to discern, but by her height and shape Andrew recognized Olga. She had watched him and pulled him away from his encounter the day before, and he knew her better than some of the others.

"It is clear?" asked Deutsch, and Olga answered in Russian. He turned to Andrew: "It is fine now."

They climbed around the ridge and made their way to the chateau. As they grew nearer, they began to pass bodies: the *Hitler-Jugend*, bare and slender, and others . . . the Nazis, Andrew presumed. They were wearing masks, either on their faces or pulled away. Some of each appeared to have been shot. But not all.

Some still moved. Deutsch urged Andrew not to try to tend to those ones and Andrew moved along. He didn't tell Deutsch that he was not intending to try and help . . . that he knew there was nothing he could do for phosgene gas victims here . . . that truly, he was more interested in arriving at the chateau.

They were met by a group of five Russians, their rifles slung in front of them, on the front steps. They conferred with Deutsch, again in Russian, and Deutsch stepped back, and looked up at the house, and asked again, and nodded.

"We must go to the back of the chateau," he told Andrew, his muffled voice seeming also higher. "Orlok is there. An extraordinary thing has happened."

Andrew asked what that was, and Deutsch was quiet for a moment.

"It lives," he said.

Andrew did try to take his mask off when he saw it, and only Deutsch and Olga's intervention prevented him. The Juke towered over the carnage—undeniably alive—a magnificent echo of the photograph at the riverbank, surrounded by supplicants; now tending to their flesh, drawing from it, haloed by flies. Deutsch pointed to the ground, where pale clouds of the gas clung in divots like puddles, and Andrew resisted. But oh, he wanted to smell it.

"You have work to do here," said Deutsch, and he pointed to the figure crouched beneath the arms, within the forest of throats. It was Orlok. He had a gas mask dangling from his neck—he had made that choice to breathe the air of the Juke here freely. . . .

"You should stop," said Olga to Andrew. "We should retreat. We did not anticipate this."

"Not precisely," said Andrew, and he thought again about Eliada—the true face of the living Juke that he had seen before plunging into the Kootenai—and the photographs, and documents . . . that he had seen before plunging again into another river.

"But I shouldn't be surprised," he said and looked at Olga and the rest. "This doesn't change things."

Olga nodded, in her mask looking like nothing then but an insect—one of the flies, overgrown, that still swirled about this place.

Olga and two others assembled around Andrew. The two held their rifles ready; Olga produced a revolver and held it at her side. And in this way, they stepped into the shadow of the Juke.

Orlok saw them coming and tried to stand. But he slipped and fell back, and coughed long and hard.

"We don't want to fight," said Andrew in German, and introduced himself. Orlok beckoned him closer.

"I had killed it," Orlok said miserably, when Andrew drew near enough. *"You saw it. You looked on it. It was dead."*

"There were no signs it was alive," Andrew agreed.

"I killed it."

Orlok wheezed and coughed and spat, flecks of blood hitting his shirt.

"Put your mask back on," said Andrew, and Orlok grinned at him, with horribly bloody teeth and said: *"Take yours off."*

Andrew regarded Orlok silently a moment. The gas had been at work on him for some time. The skin of his face was blotched red, and his eyes were deeper red and swollen. He was weakened badly. But at the core, like the Juke above him, he had strength.

"Will you put on yours if I do that?" asked Andrew finally, and Orlok nodded, and Andrew thought: *It has come to this. A childish game.*

He drew a breath, and reached behind his head and undid the strap that held it on. He shut his eyes and pulled the mask off. It felt as though he'd had vinegar thrown in his face. After it'd been stung by bees. But he held tight and waited.

Orlok laughed, and coughed, and said: *"Gut!"* Andrew heard him pulling his own mask on, and say again, through the muffling of the filter: *"Good!"*

Andrew reattached his, held the mask away from his face a finger-width, exhaled hard to drive the trace of phosgene away, and tightened it. His eyes still stung as he opened them. Orlok regarded him through the goggles.

"You didn't kill it," said Andrew. *"I don't think you've ever killed one, have you?"*

Olga had stepped around behind Orlok, and another of the Russians stepped to his side. He looked at them both.

"I battled, killed, and ate the first—" said Orlok, and he began to cough, and tried to take off his mask. Olga took one arm, the Russian the other, and bent them behind his back.

"Perhaps," said Andrew, although he knew the correct answer was *no*. Orlok had not fought and devoured a larval Juke *in utero*. He had encountered one. He and the Juke had come to an accommodation.

And in the end, Orlok was still doing God's will.

Andrew nodded to Olga. She draped Orlok's arm over her shoulder, and the other did the same, and together they lifted him and guided him away between the pillars of throats, across the backs of the supplicant dead.

After a moment, Andrew followed.

Albert Zimmermann met Andrew at the doors to the kitchens.

"You removed your gas mask," he said.

"I did. It was the only way to persuade Orlok to put his back on."

Zimmermann shook his head, making the reflected daylight flash in his goggles. "He should be dead."

"He may die yet," said Andrew. "But it won't happen out there." Zimmermann nodded. "How are you?"

Andrew explained that he hadn't drawn breath, and kept his eyes closed, but that he could feel it on his skin.

"It would be good for you to get upstairs," said Zimmermann. "By happy coincidence, there is a tower room with clean air—and that is where Jason took your wife and Ruth."

"And Dominic?"

"He is there, with the rest of your *Société*."

They passed through the main kitchen, and at length into the great hall, where there had been a deadly firefight. Andrew counted seven bodies, clad in gasmasks and coats and stopped. There might have been twice that number, and they were being attended by four of the force from the bunker. Andrew found that he could not look at them—that their number added to the much greater sum of death that he had just left beneath the Juke, and that together, they drew a feeling something like the horror from the banks of the Kootenai, when he'd witnessed the flotsam of the Eliada dead drifting downriver. Them, killed by the Cave Germ. These ones, by gas and bullets.

Zimmermann hurried them up the stairs, and along another hall, and up the stairs again.

"They are all safe," said Zimmermann as they mounted the narrow stairs to the turret room. "Up there, where the air is clear. Just as you had foretold."

Andrew removed his mask.

The air was sweet here in the tower, but it wasn't clear and that was fine with Andrew. He drew deep of it as he climbed the last of the stairs, savouring the scent of the Juke's spoor. When he stepped into the light, he found that all of the despair, the sickness of the things that he had witnessed, nearly all of it, was again receded.

He smiled in the daylight, at his family . . . and they smiled too, all of them, even Johannes Bergstrom, whom neither Zimmermann nor prophecy had warned him of. He stripped off his coat, and before he had, Annie took hold of him and they embraced.

"I knew you were coming," whispered Annie, and Andrew just said: "I knew too."

The risen Juke had ceased its feeding, and the dangling mouths rose up from the backs and bellies of the dead as one, to form a fleshy, quivering mandala that spread outward from its perch atop the tripod. One of those mouths hovered outside the windows of the turret, its spiralling teeth shifting and turning like a hypnotist's coin. The men of the *Société* stared into it as though actually mesmerized—particularly Lewis, who tentatively reached toward the glass again and again, drawing back and gasping when the Juke's appendage twitched in seeming response. The rest of them stayed farther back, in what Andrew supposed was a reasonable fear that that mouth might just start feeding again, on everyone here.

Andrew himself wasn't that worried—not about that.

"What happened to your foot?" Andrew asked Jason. "It doesn't look good."

"Took a bullet," said Jason, and motioned to Ruth. "I guess she figured she owed me one."

"He was out of his mind," said Ruth. "He was going to get himself killed."

"I probably would have," said Jason. He shifted on that foot, and set his jaw as he winced, and he looked around at the window. The Juke. "What is this?" he said. "It was dead."

"Gods don't die," said Andrew, and Jason stomped that bad foot so it was worse, and turned back at him.

"This is not God," he said. "You damn well know that. It's a Juke," said Jason. "A living Juke. Not God. That'd be something other."

Andrew shook his head. "There's nothing other, Jason."

Annie meanwhile was looking close at Andrew's cheek. She ran a fingertip over one of the punctures at the edge of his jaw. Andrew reached up and took her hand, kissed it, and said to them all: "I have a message for you."

Annie stepped away, and Andrew stepped to the middle of the room. His own hand moved to the punctures on his cheek, strayed down to the deeper puncture, in the pit of his bad right arm.

"Not all of you the same. But Annie . . . Ruth, Jason . . . it is especially for you. And Manfred, William, Dominic . . . even you, Johannes . . . it will lay some questions to rest."

Andrew paused again, and drew breath in deep.

"When I was fleeing Eliada, for fear of lynching," he said. "I met the Juke. I understood that when I drew near it, it showed me things that were lies. Heavenly lies."

"They were lies," said Jason.

"They were not true," he said. "And we had always agreed that it therefore followed, that they were not good."

Ruth sidled farther from the Juke's mouth, so she backed on a window that overlooked the chateau's roof.

"That thing is no species of goodness," she said. "What have you done to yourself, Andrew?"

Andrew sighed.

"I've met the Juke," he said. "I've spoken with it."

Bergstrom cleared his throat. "The Juke cannot speak," he said gently. "We know that when a Juke seems to speak, it is really only you. Embellishing its lie."

The Juke's mouth tapped against the glass, and from below, another of those throats swung up. Those who hadn't been looking might have thought a bird had flown into the glass. And then another. And another still.

"I have a message for you all," Andrew repeated.

Albert Zimmermann had heard the message already. And as Andrew spoke, he quietly stepped to the stairs and pulled the gas mask back on. He almost escaped unnoticed. Dominic Villart followed closely, and when they were halfway down stopped him.

"Do you not wish to hear what Doctor Waggoner has to say?" asked Zimmermann.

"What has happened to him?"

"You heard him—he has met the Juke."

"No doubt," said Dominic. "Look at his face. The Juke has infected him."

Zimmermann took a few more steps down the stairs and pulled off his mask. He sniffed; the air was still safe here. It would not be, he thought, as few as five steps lower.

"It may well have. But it has done so most persuasively. He has a message. You should heed it."

"What is the message?" Dominic stepped close to him. "You've heard it already. That is why you are fleeing."

"I have heard the message," said Zimmermann. "And you are correct. It is why I am fleeing."

"What? What is the message?"

"I am not sure that I can do it justice," said Zimmermann. "But it shouldn't be too difficult to guess. Andrew has become . . . oracular, I believe the term is."

"That is correct." Dominic nodded. "And so he preaches that the Juke is God."

"He would not be wrong," said Zimmermann. "But of course the presumption rests on what you might think God is." He leaned on the rail. "Doctor Waggoner persuaded me to bring him here and help him deliver it to his friends . . . his flock, as he called them . . . Herr Thistledown,

Fräulein Harper, Frau Waggoner . . . and I have done that. He's right—it is a message for them first and foremost. But it speaks to us all, Dominic. And I can say that if you hear it . . . it will likely change your life."

"And yet you have heard it, and you flee," said Dominic, and Zimmermann nodded, and pulled his mask to his face.

"Indeed, I flee," he said, and stepped alone into the deathly miasma of the chateau, while above, glass began to shatter.

Jason Thistledown was grinding his heel into the bridge of his injured foot, hard enough that he worried that he might lose that foot after all, when the Juke pierced the turret room. The mouth itself didn't enter all the way, but it sent a spray of glass inside, shattering a pane of glass as it did, and it rested a moment on the shattered sill, opening and expanding, then snapping back, pulling more of the window with it.

"Doc," shouted Jason, "We got to get out of here. Put on that mask of yours. Go get us help. Get us away from this."

"No getting away," said Andrew. "Not from this. This is everywhere."

Jason ground his foot some more, and thought that he would have to thank Ruth properly one day; the pain was nearly crippling, but more importantly, still entirely novel—and as such, it kept the lies, the visions at bay . . . surely better than cuts and cigarette burns and anything else that Jason had tried over the years since Eliada. He slipped, and fell to a knee. Ruth bent down and helped him stand again. As Jason righted himself on the sill, Dominic emerged from the stairs, and announced that Zimmermann had left. Outside, the mouths of the Juke withdrew, and fell again to the ground—and a sweet and familiar smell filled the turret room.

"Breathe deep," said Andrew, and everyone—everyone but Jason—did so. Jason watched each of them as they held it in their lungs: Bergstrom fell to his knees, his eyelids fluttering; Kurtzweiller and Lewis turned to stare out the broken windows, at the giant that now scrabbled at the dirt beneath it. Annie began to laugh, and Dominic joined her. Ruth held onto Jason tightly, and he held onto her back, and finally, took the weight off his foot and allowed himself some relief. . . .

And finally, he did breathe. And the perfume filled him up, and the pain—all the pain, from the moment his ma fell ill to the bullet hole that tore his foot—drifted off like dead leaves in a stream . . . along with all the other troubles and pains and wickedness of the world. And watching that, Jason did laugh.

God help him, he laughed and he laughed.

The Russians had fashioned a special litter, strong enough that it could hold a man as large as Orlok. It was an adaptation of one of the many devices that the Germans had used to wrangle the Juke, when they were in control of the compound. At one point, the casing at its centre had been airtight, but some calamity had ruined that, and in any case, it would not then have fit the man.

It took five men to carry Orlok to the front of the chateau, and from there to a truck that had made its way along crude tracks by the Germans from the compound. It would eventually find its way back to another track made by Austrians, and then on through the mountains. Eventually, the truck would find its way to an airfield, well and safely in Austria, where a fuelled aeroplane waited. Zimmermann emerged from the front doors just as the truck pulled up. He was met by Arnold Deutsch, no longer wearing his gas mask, who waved and clapped him on the shoulder.

"The air is fine out here, Herr Zimmermann," said Deutsch. "The mountain breeze has scrubbed it clean."

Zimmermann pulled off his mask.

"If not, we die together."

Deutsch smiled and shook his head. "I doubt it will come to that. I will miss working with you however."

"I am sorry I cannot say the same."

Now Deutsch laughed. "I understand entirely, Herr Zimmermann. Well, your debt is discharged," he said. "Your family is safe . . . I suspect would be safe, one way or another. And you may live your life as you choose, in Germany if you wish. Of course, if you like, you could come with us. We could use a co-pilot, to fly that one—" he motioned to the truck, and Orlok "—back to Lipetsk. I understand you know the way . . . and of course you are familiar with the passenger and the cargo."

"I think I will leave that to you," said Zimmermann. He looked back at the chateau . . . which from this angle looked just the same as it ever had.

"It is your choice, my friend," said Deutsch. "But I am sure that you will find yourself in the air again, one way or another."

"Where else would I go," said Zimmermann, "at the end of history?"

1940

The Best Of All Possible Worlds

"Was it beautiful?"

"Most definitively."

Ozzie Hayward wasn't going to lie. He was comfortable with himself, and pleased with where he was sitting in life, and everything was good. It *was* beautiful.

"Tell the folks when you first heard it."

Ozzie leaned close to the CBS microphone, a bit too close, and the sound man gave him a look and twisted a dial to reset the level.

"I was in a train station, right here in Germany. Bavaria, I guess. Stuttgart. Nine years ago. You been there?"

"I sure have, but I don't know about the folks at home. Tell us about Stuttgart."

"Great big old train station—fancy as a church cathedral. We were there, on the way to Munich."

"Nine years ago. Those were troubled times here in Germany."

"Especially for Negroes you mean," said Ozzie. His interviewer nodded and because it was for the radio, also said "Yes."

"Well it was, and in a way, that's what we were doing there. We were helping a fellow Negro make it into Germany. He was looking for a friend, you see . . . Remember the Nazi Party?"

A big laugh at that. "Hitler's Nazis. Oh sure. They were all over Munich, now weren't they?"

"That's right. Well, this fellow's friend had fallen in with them. He was going on in to pull his friend back out. Before it was too late. Crazy plan, you think about it.

"So. Me and the boys thought it'd be safer for him if he were travelling with a jazz band. Everybody likes a jazz band. Even then. Don't matter the colour of the skin." Ozzie lit up a cigarette and crossed one leg over the other. "We were coming from Paris, had to switch trains in Stuttgart which is how we ended up there, not Munich. It was the middle of the night. Only a few people around there. I got to tell you something, Eddie . . . mind if I call you Eddie?"

"You go right ahead, Ozzie."

"Well Eddie, that's where I first heard that song. We were catnapping in the station, waiting for our train south to Munich, with all our instruments stacked up around us in a great big pile. And I guess we drew a bit of attention. There were some fellows on their way north, waiting out the night too. And they wanted a show."

"Did they buy a ticket?"

Ozzie laughed. "They did not. They did have something else though. One of those fellows, he wanted to hear a song."

"The song?"

"In a way," said Ozzie. "But not quite. It was a fine song, I suppose. He hummed it for us, ya-da-da-da, like that. He wasn't very good at it, but we got the gist. He gave us the beat all right. And my boys . . . we knew even then how to play, riff, on just a little something. So we started up. And we did."

"So that wasn't the song."

Eddie stubbed his own cigarette out in the ashtray on the dressing room table. It was still mostly empty, hours yet before Ozzie and *Le Noir Qui Danse* would take the stage. Eddie was a slender fellow, dark hair slicked back to the side, and heavy eyebrows that would make him look always angry if he weren't always smiling. Eddie didn't know much about jazz, but that was alright. He knew about asking questions.

"Here's something you ought to know about jazz music," said Ozzie. "Folks think a jazz song is just that—just one song. Goes on for three, four minutes and then it's over. That sound about right to you?"

"Sounds right to me. But I got a feeling you're going to tell me I'm all wrong."

Ozzie laughed and drew smoke. "It's all one song," he said. "Started somewhere back in New Orleans, maybe Cuba, maybe all the way over in Africa, before any of us were born. And the rhythm, the beat . . . it just gets passed along, one player to the next. Sometimes we stop, but we stop to rest, not because we're done."

He looked at his cigarette, and deemed that done, and stubbed it out alongside Eddie's.

"That's not to say that every jazz man's got that song, has the line. But we play—at least I play—in search of it. We listen for it. And that night in Stuttgart, helping out that fellow looking for his friend . . . I think we found it." Ozzie leaned back in his chair—drawing another glare from the sound man. "We never did make it to Munich. We came straight here to Berlin. And we never did stop. Playing, I mean. Of course we did stay in Berlin for quite some time."

"A very long time. Nine years."

"Well you know . . . it's a long song, Eddie. And we have a devoted audience."

"I'll say," said Eddie. He looked to his sound man, who was tapping his watch. Eddie nodded. "Well after just a word from our sponsor, the beautiful melodies of *Le Noir Qui Danse* will finally be coming home, straight from the El Dorado Cabaret stage, here in Berlin, Germany. Stay tuned, America. In just a few minutes, Mr. Ozzie Hayward and his boys are going to change your world."

"Just like we changed the rest of it," said Ozzie, even as the sound man made a throat slashing motion that the take was finished and threw up his hands.

"Do you want to do that again, Mr. Murrow?" he said, and Eddie just shook his head.

"I don't think we're going to get any better than that," he said.

THE END

ACKNOWLEDGEMENTS

I'd never written a sequel until this one, and when I started on *Volk*, I thought it would be easy. I was wrong and I'm glad I was wrong; this was as challenging and sometimes vexing a project as any, and to the extent it succeeds, it does so with the love and help of many people.

First and ever foremost, my wife Madeline Ashby was a bedrock of support in research, writing, and of course life itself. Members of the Cecil Street Writers' Workshop—Natalie Zina Walschots, Jairus Khan, Michael Skeet, Hugh A.D. Spencer, Madeline Ashby (again), Allan Weiss—let me know when I strayed and encouraged me when the story held true.

In the course of researching the book, I had a lot to learn and got some help in so doing. Michael Skeet guided me through aviation history—particularly World War I, but also early 20th-century commercial air travel, and pointed me to some excellent resources about early 20th-century Europe. Peter Watts helped me on the biology and parasitology in *Eutopia*, and continued to aid me in evolving the abominations of *Volk*. Years ago, Hugh Spencer provided me with a metaphor for improvisational jazz that wormed its way into the fabric of *Volk*. Steve Bevan provided me with the perfect name for a jazz man, and also stood by during a still-unfolding life crisis that intersected with the completion of *Volk*. I could not have done it all without him.

There are snippets of dialogue in languages which I do not speak—French and German, specifically—and Jerome Veith and Claude Lalumière helped me turn those into words that a native, and not Google Translate, might actually speak.

And further to that: thanks to ChiZine's Sandra Kasturi, who edited *Volk* and made many more of those words better than they were; Gemma Files, who dove deep into the prose and brought out a shine that I only flatter myself thinking was there all the time Leigh Teetzel, who added the final polish in the proof-read; Jared Shapiro, who laid the text on the page just so, then made it beautiful; Erik Mohr, who made the astonishing cover that might well have persuaded you to pick this book up. . . .

And of course great thanks to my agent Monica Pacheco at Anne McDermid and Associates, who has represented *Volk* and my other books with such passionate and unwavering support.

ABOUT THE AUTHOR

David Nickle is the author of several novels, including *Eutopia: A Novel of Terrible Optimism* (which precedes *Volk: A Novel of Radiant Abomination*), and numerous short stories, some of which have been collected in *Knife Fight and Other Struggles* and *Monstrous Affections*. He lives and works in Toronto as a journalist, with his wife, the author and futurist Madeline Ashby.

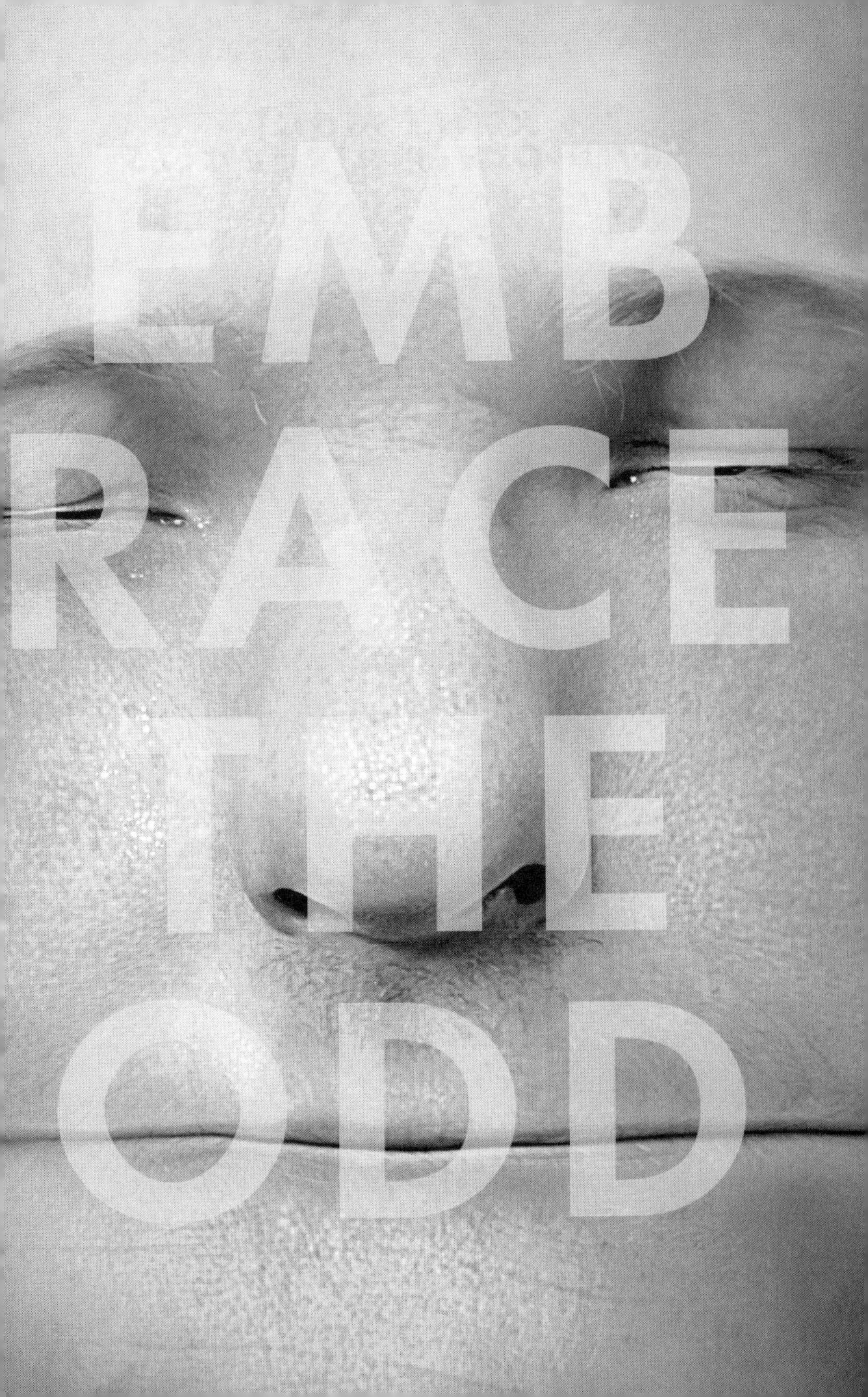

EMB
RACE
THE
ODD

KNIFE FIGHT AND OTHER STRUGGLES

DAVID NICKLE

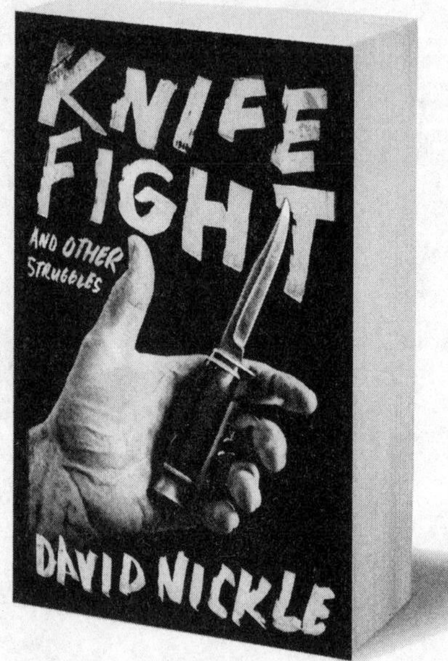

A young man at loose ends finds he cannot look away from his new lover's alien gaze. A young woman out of time seeks her old lover in the cold spaces between the stars. The fleeing worshippers of an ancient and jealous deity seek solace in an unsuspecting New World congregation. In a suburban nursery, a demon with a grudge and a lonely exorcist face off for what could be the last time.

In *Knife Fight and Other Struggles*, David Nickle follows his award-winning debut collection *Monstrous Affections* with a new set of dark tales that span space, time, and genre.

AVAILABLE NOW

ISBN 9781771483049
eISBN 9781771483056